Praise for Sophie Kinsella
and the Shopaholic Novels

"A hilarious tale . . . hijinks worthy of classic *I Love Lucy* episodes . . . too good to pass up." —*USA Today*

"[Sophie Kinsella] gives chick-lit lovers a reason to stay home from the mall." —*Entertainment Weekly*

"Don't wait for a sale to buy this hilarious book."
—*US Weekly*

"Perfect for anyone wishing that bank statements came in more colours than just black and red."
—*Mirror* (London)

"If a crème brûlée could be transmogrified into a book, it would be *Confessions of a Shopaholic*."
—*Newark Star-Ledger*

"Kinsella's heroine is blessed with the resilience of ten women, and her damage-limitation brain waves are always good for a giggle." —*Glamour* (UK)

Also by Sophie Kinsella

Confessions of a Shopaholic
Shopaholic Takes Manhattan
Shopaholic Ties the Knot
Can You Keep a Secret?

SOPHIE KINSELLA

Shopaholic
& Sister

A DELL BOOK

SHOPAHOLIC & SISTER
A Dell Book

PUBLISHING HISTORY
Dial Press hardcover edition published October 2004
Dell mass market international edition published December 2004
Dell mass market domestic edition / December 2006

Published by
Bantam Dell
A Division of Random House, Inc.
New York, New York

This is a work of fiction. Names, characters, places, and incidents
either are the product of the author's imagination or are used
fictitiously. Any resemblance to actual persons, living or dead,
events, or locales is entirely coincidental.

Library of Congress Catalog Card Number: 2004050201

ISBN-13: 978-0-440-24191-1
ISBN-10: 0-440-24191-X

Printed in the United States of America
Published simultaneously in Canada

www.bantamdell.com

OPM 10 9 8 7 6 5

To Gemma and Abigail, in celebration of being sisters.

Shopaholic
& Sister

DICTIONARY OF
INTERNATIONAL TRIBAL DIALECTS
ADDENDUM

(The following terms were mistakenly omitted
from the main dictionary.)

NAMI-NAMI TRIBE OF NEW GUINEA, p. 67

fraa ("frar"): elder tribesman; patriarch

mopi ("mop-i"): a small ladle for serving rice or
   meal

shup ("shop"): to exchange goods for money
   or beads. A concept unknown by the tribe until a
   visit in 2002 by British tourist Rebecca Brandon
   (formerly Bloomwood)

ROYAL CAIRO INSTITUTE OF ARCHAEOLOGY
31 El Cherifeen Street
Cairo

Mrs. Rebecca Brandon
c/o Nile Hilton Hotel
Tahrir Square
Cairo

January 15, 2003

Dear Mrs. Brandon

I am glad you are enjoying your honeymoon in
Cairo. I was pleased to hear that you feel a bond with
the Egyptian people and agree it is quite possible
that you have Egyptian blood in you.

I also welcome your interest in the museum's jewelry
display. However, further to your inquiry, the "sweet
little ring" you refer to is not for sale. It once
belonged to Queen Sobeknefu of the 12th Dynasty
and, I can assure you, would be missed.

I hope you enjoy the rest of your stay.

Yours sincerely,

Khaled Samir
Director

TOWER HOUSE
CANARY WHARF
LONDON E14 5HG

Fax for: Mrs Rebecca Brandon
c/o Four Seasons Hotel
Sydney
Australia

From: Denise O'Connor
Customer Service Coordinator

6 February 2003

Dear Mrs Brandon:

We are sorry to inform you that your Bondi Beach
"carved sand mermaid" has disintegrated during
shipping.

We would remind you that we made no guarantees
as to its safety and advised you against the
shipping process.

Yours sincerely,

Denise O'Connor
Customer Service Coordinator

Alaskan Trails and Adventures, Inc.

PO Box 80034
Chugiak, AK 99567

FAX FOR: Mrs. Rebecca Brandon
c/o White Bear Lodge
Chugiak

FROM: Dave Crockerdale
Alaskan Trails and Adventures

February 16, 2003

Dear Rebecca:

Thank you for your inquiry.

I would strongly advise you against attempting to ship to Britain six husky dogs and a sleigh.

I agree that husky dogs are wonderful animals and am interested in your idea that they could be the answer to pollution in cities. However, I think it unlikely the authorities would allow them on the streets of London, even if you did "customize the sleigh with wheels and add a numberplate."

I hope you are still enjoying your honeymoon.

Kind regards,

Dave Crockerdale
Trail Manager

One

OK. I CAN do this. No problem.

It's simply a matter of letting my higher self take over, achieving enlightenment, and becoming a radiant being of white light.

Easy-peasy.

Surreptitiously I adjust myself on my yoga mat so I'm facing the sun directly, and push down the spaghetti straps of my top. I don't see why you can't reach ultimate-bliss consciousness and get an even tan at the same time.

I'm sitting on a hillside in the middle of Sri Lanka at the Blue Hills Resort and Spiritual Retreat, and the view is spectacular. Hills and tea plantations stretch ahead, then merge into a deep blue sky. I can see the bright colors of tea pickers in the fields, and if I swivel my head a little, I can glimpse a distant elephant padding slowly along between the bushes.

And when I turn my head still further, I can see Luke. My husband. He's the one on the blue yoga mat, in the cutoff linen trousers and tatty old top, sitting cross-legged with his eyes closed.

I know. It's just unbelievable. After ten months of honeymoon, Luke has turned into a totally different person from the man I married. The old corporate Luke has vanished. The suits have disappeared. He's tanned and lean, his hair is long and sun-bleached, and he's still got a few of the little plaits he had put in on Bondi Beach. Round his wrist is a beaded bracelet he got in Tanzania, and in his ear is a tiny silver hoop.

Luke Brandon with an earring! Luke Brandon sitting cross-legged!

As though he can feel my gaze, he opens his eyes and smiles, and I beam back happily. Ten months married. And not a single row.

Well. You know. Only the odd little one.

"*Siddhasana,*" says our yoga teacher, Chandra. He's a tall, thin man in baggy white yoga trousers, and he always speaks in a soft, patient voice. "Clear your minds of all extraneous thought."

Around me I'm aware of the eight or nine others in the group moving into position on their mats. Obediently I place my right foot on my left thigh.

OK. Clear my mind. Concentrate.

I don't want to boast, but I find clearing my mind pretty easy. I don't quite get why anyone would find it difficult! I mean, not thinking has to be a lot easier than thinking, doesn't it?

In fact, the truth is, I'm a bit of a natural at yoga. We've only been on this retreat for five days but already I can do the Lotus and everything! I was even thinking I might set up as a yoga teacher when we go back home.

Maybe I could set up a partnership with Trudie Styler, I think in sudden excitement. God, yes! And we could launch a range of yoga wear, too, all soft grays and whites, with a little logo—

"Focus on your breathing," Chandra is saying.

Oh, right. Yes. Breathing.

Breathe in . . . breathe out. Breathe in . . . breathe out. Breathe—

God, my nails look fab. I had them done at the spa— little pink butterflies on a white background. And the antennae are little diamonds. They are so sweet. Except one seems to have fallen off. I must get that fixed—

"Becky." Chandra's voice makes me jump. He's standing right there, gazing at me with this look he has. Kind of gentle and all-knowing, like he can see right inside your mind.

"You do very well, Becky," he says. "You have a beautiful spirit."

I feel a sparkle of delight all over. I, Rebecca Brandon, née Bloomwood, have a beautiful spirit! I knew it!

"You have an unworldly soul," he adds in his soft voice, and I stare back, totally mesmerized.

"Material possessions aren't important to me," I say breathlessly. "All that matters to me is yoga."

"You have found your path." Chandra smiles.

There's an odd kind of snorting sound coming from Luke's direction, and I look round to see him looking over at us in amusement.

I *knew* Luke wasn't taking this seriously.

"This is a private conversation between me and my guru, thank you very much," I say crossly.

Although, actually, I shouldn't be surprised. We were warned about this on the first day of the yoga course. Apparently, when one partner finds higher spiritual enlightenment, the other partner can react with skepticism and even jealousy.

"Soon you will be walking on the hot coals." Chandra

gestures with a smile to the nearby pit of smoldering ashy coals, and a nervous laugh goes round the group. This evening Chandra and some of his top yoga students are going to demonstrate walking on the coals for the rest of us. This is what we're all supposed to be aiming for. Apparently, you attain a state of bliss so great, you can't actually feel the coals burning your feet. You're totally pain free!

What I'm secretly hoping is that it'll work when I wear six-inch stilettos, too.

Chandra adjusts my arms and moves on, and I close my eyes, letting the sun warm my face. Sitting here on this hillside in the middle of nowhere, I feel so pure and calm. It's not just Luke who's changed over the last ten months. I have too. I've grown up. My priorities have altered. In fact, I'm a different person. I mean, look at me now, doing yoga at a spiritual retreat. My old friends probably wouldn't even recognize me!

At Chandra's instruction, we all move into the *Vajrasana* pose. From where I am, I can just see an elderly Sri Lankan man carrying two old carpetbags, approaching Chandra. They have a brief conversation, during which Chandra keeps shaking his head, then the old man trudges away over the scrubby hillside. When he's out of earshot, Chandra turns to face the group, rolling his eyes.

"This man is a merchant. He asks if any of you are interested in gems. Necklaces, cheap bracelets. I tell him your minds are on higher things."

A few people near me shake their heads as though in disbelief. One woman, with long red hair, looks affronted.

"Couldn't he see we were in the middle of meditation?" she says.

"He has no understanding of your spiritual devotion."

Chandra looks around the group seriously. "It will be the same with many others in the world. They will not understand that meditation is food for your soul. You have no need for . . . sapphire bracelet!"

A few people nod in appreciation.

"Aquamarine pendant with platinum chain," Chandra continues dismissively. "How does this compare to the radiance of inner enlightenment?"

Aquamarine?

Wow. I wonder how much—

I mean, not that I'm interested. Obviously not. It's just that I happened to be looking at aquamarines in a shop window the other day. Just out of an academic interest.

My eye drifts toward the retreating figure of the old man.

"Three-carat setting, five-carat setting, he keeps saying. All half price." Chandra shakes his head. "I tell him, these people are not interested."

Half price? Five-carat aquamarines at half price?

Stop it. Stop it. Chandra's right. Of course I'm not interested in stupid aquamarines. I'm absorbed in spiritual enlightenment.

Anyway, the old man's nearly gone now. He's just a tiny figure on top of the hill. In a minute he'll have disappeared.

"And now." Chandra smiles. "The *Halasana* pose. Becky, will you demonstrate?"

"Absolutely." I smile at Chandra and prepare to get into position on my mat.

But something's wrong. I don't feel contentment. I don't feel tranquillity. The oddest feeling is welling up inside me, driving everything else out. It's getting stronger and stronger . . .

And suddenly I can't contain it anymore. Before I

know what's happening, I'm running in my bare feet as fast as I can up the hill toward the tiny figure. My lungs are burning, my feet are smarting, and the sun's beating down on my bare head, but I don't stop until I've reached the crest of the hill. I come to a halt and look around, panting.

I don't believe it. He's gone. Where did he vanish to?

I stand for a few moments, regaining my breath, peering in all directions. But I can't see him anywhere.

At last, feeling a little dejected, I turn and make my way back down the hillside to the group. As I get near I realize they're all shouting and waving at me. Oh God. Am I in trouble?

"You did it!" the red-haired woman's yelling. "You did it!"

"Did what?"

"You ran over the hot coals! You did it, Becky!"

What?

I look down at my feet . . . and I don't believe it. They're covered in gray ash! In a daze, I look at the pit of coals—and there's a set of clear footprints running through it.

Oh my God. Oh my *God*! I ran over the coals! I ran over the burning hot smoldering coals! I did it!

"But . . . but I didn't even notice!" I say, bewildered. "My feet aren't even burned!"

"How did you do it?" demands the red-haired woman. "What was in your mind?"

"I can answer." Chandra comes forward, smiling. "Becky has achieved the highest form of karmic bliss. She was concentrating on one goal, one pure image, and this has driven her body to achieve a supernatural state."

Everyone is goggling at me like I'm suddenly the Dalai Lama.

"It was nothing, really," I say, with a modest smile. "Just . . . you know. Spiritual enlightenment."

"Can you describe the image?" asks the red-haired woman in excitement.

"Was it white?" someone else chimes in.

"Not really white . . ." I say.

"Was it a kind of shiny blue green?" comes Luke's voice from the back. I look up sharply. He's gazing at me, totally straight-faced.

"I don't remember," I say with dignity. "The color wasn't important."

"Did it feel like . . ." Luke appears to think hard. "Like the links of a chain were pulling you along?"

"That's a very good image, Luke," chimes in Chandra, pleased.

"No," I say shortly. "It didn't. Actually, I think you probably have to have a higher appreciation of spiritual matters to understand."

"I see." Luke nods gravely.

"Luke, you must be very proud." Chandra beams at Luke. "Is this not the most extraordinary thing you have ever seen your wife do?"

There's a beat of silence. Luke looks from me to the smoldering coals to the silent group and back to Chandra's beaming face.

"Chandra," he says. "Take it from me. This is nothing."

After the class is finished everyone heads to the terrace, where cool drinks are waiting on a tray. But I stay on my mat, meditating, to show how dedicated I am to higher things. I'm half concentrating on the white light of my being and half imagining running over hot coals in front of Trudie and Sting while they applaud admiringly, when a shadow falls across my face.

"Greetings, O Spiritual One," says Luke, and I open my eyes to see him standing in front of me, holding out a glass of juice.

"You're just jealous because you don't have a beautiful inner being," I retort, and casually smooth back my hair so the red dot painted on my forehead shows.

"Insanely," agrees Luke. "Have a drink."

He sits down beside me on the ground and hands me the glass. I take a sip of delicious, ice-cold passion-fruit juice and we both look out over the hills toward the distant horizon.

"You know, I could really live in Sri Lanka," I say with a sigh. "It's perfect. The weather . . . the scenery . . . all the people are so friendly . . ."

"You said the same in India," Luke points out. "And Australia," he adds as I open my mouth. "And Amsterdam."

Oh.

God, Amsterdam. I'd completely forgotten we went there. That was after Paris. Or was it before?

Oh, yes. It was where I ate all those weird cakes and nearly fell in the canal.

I take another sip of juice and let my mind range back over the last ten months. We've visited so many countries, it's kind of difficult to remember everything at once. It's almost like a blur of film, with sharp, bright images here and there. Snorkeling with all those blue fish in the Great Barrier Reef . . . the pyramids in Egypt . . . the elephant safari in Tanzania . . . buying all that silk in Hong Kong . . . the gold souk in Morocco . . . finding that amazing Ralph Lauren outlet in Utah . . .

God, we've had some experiences. I sigh happily and take another sip of juice.

"I forgot to tell you." Luke produces a pile of envelopes. "Some post came from England."

I sit up in excitement and start leafing through the envelopes.

"*Vogue!*" I exclaim as I get to my special subscriber edition in its shiny plastic cover. "Ooh, look! They've got an Angel bag on the front cover!"

I wait for a reaction—but Luke looks blank. I feel a tiny flicker of frustration. How can he look blank? I read him out that whole piece about Angel bags last month, and showed him the pictures and everything.

I know this is our honeymoon. But just sometimes, I wish Luke was a girl.

"You know!" I say. "Angel bags! The most amazing, hip bags since . . . since . . ."

Oh, I'm not even going to bother explaining. Instead I gaze lustfully at the photograph of the bag. It's made of soft, creamy tan calfskin, with a transparent resin handle and discreet zipper. But what makes it unique is the beautiful winged angel hand-painted on the front, with the name *Gabriel* underneath in diamanté. There are six different angels: Gabriel, Michael, Dante, Raphael, Uriel, and Ariel. All the celebrities have been fighting over them, and Harrods is permanently sold out. HOLY PHENOMENON says the headline beside the picture.

I'm so engrossed, I barely hear Luke's voice as he holds out another envelope.

"Ooze," he seems to be saying.

"Sorry?" I look up in a daze.

"Here's another letter," he says patiently. "From Suze."

"Suze?" I drop *Vogue* and grab it out of his hand. Suze is my best friend in the world. I have *so* missed her.

The envelope is all thick and creamy white and has a crest on the back with a Latin motto. I always forget how totally grand Suze is. When she sent us a Christmas card it was a picture of her husband Tarquin's castle in Scotland with FROM THE CLEATH-STUART ESTATE printed inside. (Except you could hardly read it because her one-year-old, Ernie, had covered it with red and blue finger-paints.)

I tear it open and a stiff card falls out.

"It's an invitation!" I exclaim. "To the christening of the twins."

I gaze at the formal, swirly engraving, feeling a slight pang. Wilfrid and Clementine Cleath-Stuart. Suze has had two more babies and I haven't even seen them. They must be about two months old by now. I wonder what they look like. I wonder how Suze is doing. So much has been going on without us.

I turn the card over and see that Suze has scrawled a message.

> I know you won't be able to come, but thought you'd like it anyway. . . . Hope you're still having a wonderful time!
>
> All our love, Suzexxx

PS Ernie loves his Chinese outfit, thank you so much!

"It's in two weeks," I say, showing Luke the card. "Shame, really. We won't be able to go."

"No," agrees Luke. "We won't."

There's a short silence. Then Luke meets my eye. "I mean . . . you're not ready to go back yet, are you?" he says casually.

"No!" I say at once. "Of course not!"

We've been traveling for only ten months, and we planned to be away for at least a year. Plus, we've got the spirit of the road in our feet now. Maybe we'll never be able to go back to normal life, like sailors who can't go back and live on the land.

I put the invitation back in its envelope and take a sip

of my drink. I wonder how Mum and Dad are. I haven't heard much from them recently. In fact, the last time I called home, they both seemed a bit distracted. Mum hardly listened to my story about the elephant orphanage, and before I could ask Dad how he did in the golf tournament, he said he had to go.

And little Ernie will be walking by now. I'm his godmother and I've never even seen him walk.

Anyway. Never mind. I'm having amazing world experiences instead.

"We need to decide where to go next," says Luke, leaning back on his elbows. "After we finish the yoga course. We were talking about Malaysia."

"Yes," I say, after a pause. It must be the heat or something, but I can't actually get up much enthusiasm for Malaysia.

"Or back to Indonesia? Up to the northern bits?"

"Mmm," I say noncommittally. "Oh look, a monkey."

I cannot believe I've gotten so blasé about the sight of monkeys. The first time I saw those baboons in Kenya I was so excited I took about six rolls of film. Now it's just, "Oh look, a monkey."

"Or Nepal . . . or back to Thailand . . ."

"Or we could go back," I hear myself saying out of nowhere.

How weird. I didn't intend to say that. I mean, *obviously* we're not going to go back yet. It hasn't even been a year!

Luke sits up straight and looks at me.

"*Back* back?"

"No!" I say with a little laugh. "I'm just joking!" I hesitate. "Although . . ." There's a still silence between us.

"Maybe . . . we don't *have* to travel for a year," I say tentatively. "If we don't want to."

Luke passes a hand through his hair, and the little beads on his plaits all click together.

"Are we ready to go back?" he says.

"I don't know." I feel a little thrill of trepidation. "Are we?"

I can hardly believe we're even talking about going home. I mean, look at us! My hair's all dry and sun-bleached, I've got henna on my feet, and I haven't worn a proper pair of shoes for months.

An image comes to my mind of me walking down a London street in a coat and boots. Shiny high-heeled boots by L.K. Bennett. And a matching handbag.

Suddenly I feel a wave of longing so strong I almost want to cry.

"I think I've had enough of the world." I look at Luke. "I'm ready for real life."

"Me too." Luke takes my hand and weaves his fingers between mine. "I've been ready for a while, actually."

"You never said!" He seemed so into it! I've never had an inkling he's been bored.

"I didn't want to break up the party. But I'm certainly ready."

"You would have kept traveling . . . just for me?" I say, touched.

"Well, it's not exactly hardship." Luke looks at me wryly. "We're hardly roughing it, are we?"

I feel a slight flush come to my cheeks. When we set off on this trip, I told Luke I was determined we were going to be real travelers, like in *The Beach,* and sleep only in little huts.

That was before I'd spent a night in a little hut.

"So when we say 'back' "—Luke pauses—"we *are* talking London?"

He looks at me questioningly.

Oh God. Finally, it's decision time.

We've been talking for ten months about where we should live after the honeymoon. Before we got married, Luke and I were living in New York. And I loved it. But I kind of missed home, too. And now Luke's U.K. business is expanding into more of Europe, and that's where all the excitement is. So he'd like to go back to London, at least for a while.

Which is fine . . . except I won't have a job. My old job was as a personal shopper at Barneys New York. And I adored it.

But never mind. I'm bound to find a new job. An even better one!

"London," I say decisively, and look up. "So . . . can we be back in time for the christening?"

"If you like." Luke smiles, and I feel a sudden leap of exhilaration. We're going to the christening! I'm going to see Suze again! And my mum and dad! After nearly a year! They'll all be so excited to see us. We'll have so many stories to tell them!

I have a sudden vision of myself presiding over candle-lit supper parties with all my friends gathered round, listening avidly to tales of faraway lands and exotic adventures. I'll be just like Marco Polo or someone! Then I'll open my trunk to reveal rare and precious treasures . . . everyone will gasp in admiration—

"We'd better let them know," says Luke, getting up.

"No, wait," I say, grabbing his trousers. "I've had an idea. Let's surprise them! Let's surprise everybody!"

"*Surprise* everybody?" Luke looks doubtful. "Becky, are you sure that's a good idea?"

"It's a brilliant idea! Everyone loves a surprise!"

"But . . ."

"Everyone loves a surprise," I repeat confidently. "Trust me."

We walk back through the gardens to the main hotel—
and I do feel a slight twinge at the thought of leaving.
It's so beautiful here. All teak bungalows and amazing
birds everywhere, and if you follow the stream through
the grounds, there's a real waterfall! We pass the wood-
carving center, where you can watch craftsmen at work,
and I pause for a moment, inhaling the delicious scent
of wood.

"Mrs. Brandon!" The head craftsman, Vijay, has appeared at the entrance.

Damn. I didn't know he'd be around.

"Sorry, Vijay!" I say quickly. "I'm in a bit of a hurry. I'll
see you later. . . . Come on, Luke!"

"No problem!" Vijay beams and wipes his hands on
his apron. "I just wanted to tell you that your table is
ready."

Shit.

Slowly Luke turns to look at me.

"Table?" he says.

"Your dining table," says Vijay in happy tones. "And
ten chairs. I show you! We display the work!" He snaps
his fingers and barks some orders and suddenly, to my
dismay, about eight men troop out, carrying a huge
carved teak table on their shoulders.

Wow. It's a tad bigger than I remembered.

Luke looks absolutely stunned.

"Bring the chairs!" Vijay is bossing the men. "Set it up
properly!"

"Isn't it lovely?" I say in superbright tones.

"You ordered a dining table and ten chairs . . . without telling me?" says Luke, goggling as the chairs arrive.

OK. I don't have many options here.

"It's . . . my wedding present to you!" I say with sudden inspiration. "It's a surprise! Happy wedding, darling!" I plant a kiss on his cheek and smile hopefully up at him.

"Becky, you already gave me a wedding present," says Luke, folding his arms. "And our wedding was a fairly long time ago now."

"I've been . . . saving it up!" I lower my voice so Vijay can't hear. "And honestly, it isn't that expensive . . ."

"Becky, it's not the money. It's the space! This thing's a monstrosity!"

"It's not *that* big. And anyway," I quickly add before he can reply, "we need a good table! Every marriage needs a good table." I spread my arms widely. "After all, what is marriage about if not sitting down at the table at the end of the day and sharing all our problems? What is marriage, if not sitting together at a solid wooden table and . . . and eating a bowl of hearty stew?"

"Hearty stew?" echoes Luke. "Who's going to make hearty stew?"

"We can buy it at Waitrose," I explain.

I come round the table and look up at him earnestly. "Luke, think about it. We'll never again be in Sri Lanka with authentic wood-carvers right in front of us. This is a unique opportunity. And I've had it personalized!"

I point to the panel of wood running down the side of the table. There, beautifully carved in among the flowers, are the words *Luke and Rebecca, Sri Lanka, 2003*.

Luke runs a hand over the table. He feels the weight of one of the chairs. I can see him relenting. Then suddenly he looks up with a slight frown.

"Becky, is there anything else you've bought that you haven't told me about?"

I feel a nervous flip inside, which I disguise by pretending to examine one of the carved flowers.

"Of course not!" I say at last. "Or . . . you know. Maybe just the odd little souvenir along the way. Just here and there."

"Like what?"

"I can't remember!" I exclaim. "It's been ten months, for goodness' sake!" I look at the table again. "Come on, Luke, you *must* love it. We can have fantastic dinner parties . . . and it'll be an heirloom! We can hand it down to our children—"

I break off a bit awkwardly. For a moment I can't quite look at Luke.

A few months ago we had this huge big discussion and decided that we'd like to try for a baby. But so far nothing's happened.

I mean, not that it's a big deal or anything. It will happen. Of course it will.

"All right," says Luke, his voice a little gentler. "You've won me over." He gives the table a pat, then looks at his watch. "I'm going to e-mail the office, tell them about our change of plans." He gives me a wry look. "Presumably you weren't expecting me to burst open the door of the boardroom and yell 'Surprise, I'm back!'?"

"Of course not!" I retort, barely missing a beat.

That is, actually, kind of what I'd pictured. Except I'd be there too, with a bottle of champagne and maybe some party poppers.

"I'm not quite that stupid," I add witheringly.

"Good." Luke grins at me. "Why don't you order us some drinks and I'll be out in a moment."

As I sit down at a table on the shady terrace, I'm just a tad preoccupied. I'm trying to remember all the things I've bought and had shipped home without telling Luke.

I mean, I'm not worried or anything. It can't be *that* much stuff. Can it?

Oh God. I close my eyes, trying to remember.

There were the wooden giraffes in Malawi. The ones Luke said were too big. Which is just ridiculous. They'll look amazing! Everyone will admire them!

And there was all that gorgeous batik art in Bali. Which I *did* intend to tell him about . . . but then kind of never got round to it.

And there were the twenty Chinese silk dressing gowns.

Which . . . OK, I know twenty sounds like quite a lot. But they were such a bargain! Luke just didn't seem to understand my point that if we bought twenty now, they would last us a lifetime and be a real investment. For someone who works in financial PR, he can be a bit slow off the mark sometimes.

So I snuck back to the shop and bought them anyway, and had them shipped home.

The thing is, shipping just makes everything so easy. You don't have to lug anything about—you just point and ship: "I'd like that shipped, please. And that. And that." And you give them your card and off it goes, and Luke never even sees it. . . .

Maybe I should have kept a list.

Anyway, it's fine. I'm sure it's fine.

And, I mean, we want a few souvenirs, don't we? What's the point of going round the world and coming back empty-handed? Exactly.

I see Chandra walking past the terrace and give him a friendly wave.

"You did very well in class today, Becky!" he says, and comes over to the table. "And now I would like to ask you something. In two weeks' time I am leading an advanced meditation retreat. The others are mainly monks and long-term yoga practitioners, but I feel you have the commitment to join us. Would you be interested?"

"I'd love to!" Then I pull a regretful face. "But I can't. Luke and I are going home!"

"Home?" Chandra looks shocked. "But . . . you are doing so well. You are not going to abandon the path of yoga?"

"Oh no," I say reassuringly. "Don't worry. I'll buy a video."

As Chandra walks off, he looks a little shell-shocked. Which actually, isn't surprising. He probably didn't even realize you could *get* yoga videos. He certainly didn't seem to have heard of Geri Halliwell.

A waiter appears and I order a beer for Luke, plus a mango and papaya cocktail, which in the menu is called Happy Juice. Well, that just about suits me. Here I am in the sunshine, on my honeymoon, about to have a surprise reunion with all the people I love. Everything's perfect!

I look up to see Luke approaching the table, holding his handheld computer. Is it my imagination, or is he walking faster and looking more animated than he has for months?

"OK," he says. "I've spoken to the office."

"Is everything all right?"

"It certainly is." He seems full of a suppressed energy. "It's going very well. In fact, I want to set up a couple of meetings for the end of this week."

"That was quick!" I say in astonishment.

Blimey. I'd thought it would take about a week just to get ourselves organized.

"But I know how much you're getting out of this yoga retreat," he adds. "So what I propose is that I go on ahead, and you join me later . . . and then we return to Britain together."

"So, where are your meetings?" I say, confused.

"Italy."

The waiter appears with my Happy Juice and Luke's beer.

"But I don't want to be separated from you!" I say as the waiter retreats. "This is our honeymoon!"

"We have had ten solid months together. . . ." Luke gently points out.

"I know. But still . . ." I take a disconsolate sip of Happy Juice. "Where are you going in Italy?"

"Nowhere exciting," Luke says after a pause. "Just a . . . northern Italian city. Very dull. I recommend you stay here. Enjoy the sunshine."

"Well . . ." I look around, feeling torn. It is pretty nice here. "Which city?"

There's silence.

"Milan," Luke says reluctantly.

"Milan?" I nearly fall off my chair with excitement. "You're going to Milan? I've never been to Milan! I'd love to go to Milan!"

"No," says Luke. "Really?"

"Yes! Definitely! It's the fashion capital of the world! I mean, it's got Prada . . . and Dolce—" I break off as I catch his expression. "And . . . er . . . it's a place of great cultural interest which no modern traveler should miss. Luke, I *have* to come."

"OK." Luke shakes his head ruefully. "I must be mad, but OK."

Elated, I lean back in my chair and take a big slurp of Happy Juice. This honeymoon just gets better and better!

Two

OK, I CANNOT believe Luke was planning to come to Milan without me. How could he come here without me? I was *made* for Milan.

No. Not Milan, *Milano*.

I haven't actually seen much of the city yet except for a taxi and our hotel room—but for a world traveler like me, that doesn't actually matter. You can pick up the vibe of a place in an instant, like bushmen in the wild. And as soon as I looked round the hotel foyer at all those chic women in Prada and D&G, kissing each other while simultaneously downing espressos, lighting cigarettes, and flinging their shiny hair about, I just knew, with a natural instinct: this is my kind of city.

I take a gulp of room-service cappuccino and glance across at my reflection in the wardrobe mirror. Honestly, I look Italian! All I need is some capri pants and dark eyeliner. And maybe a Vespa.

"*Ciao,*" I say casually, and flick my hair back. "*Sì. Ciao.*"

I could so be Italian. Except I might need to learn a few more words.

"*Sì.*" I nod at myself. "*Sì. Milano.*"

Maybe I'll practice by reading the paper. I open the free copy of *Corriere della Sera,* which arrived with our breakfast, and start perusing the lines of text. The first story is all about the president washing his piano. At least I'm pretty sure that's what *presidente* and *lavoro pieno* must mean.

"You know, Luke, I could really live in Italy," I say as he comes out of the bathroom. "I mean, it's the perfect country. It has everything! Cappuccinos . . . yummy food . . . Everyone's so elegant. . . . You can get Gucci cheaper than at home. . . ."

"And the art," says Luke, deadpan. "Da Vinci's *The Last Supper,* for instance."

I was just *about* to mention the art.

"Well, obviously the art," I say, rolling my eyes. "I mean, the art goes without saying."

I flick over a page of *Corriere della Sera* and briskly skim the headlines. Then my brain suddenly clicks.

I put the paper down and stare at Luke again.

What's happened to him?

I'm looking at the Luke Brandon I used to know back when I was a financial journalist. He's completely clean-shaven, and dressed in an immaculate suit, with a pale green shirt and darker green tie. He's wearing proper shoes and proper socks. His earring is gone. His bracelet is gone. The only vestige of our travels is his hair, which is still in tiny plaits.

I can feel a bubble of dismay growing inside. I liked him the way he was, all laid-back and disheveled.

"You've . . . smartened up a bit!" I say. "Where's your bracelet?"

"In my suitcase."

"But the woman in the Masai Mara said we must never take them off!" I say in shock. "She said that special Masai prayer!"

"Becky . . ." Luke sighs. "I can't go into a meeting with an old bit of rope round my wrist."

Old bit of rope? That was a sacred bracelet, and he knows it.

"You've still got your plaits!" I retort. "If you can have plaits, you can have a bracelet!"

"I'm not keeping my plaits!" Luke looks incredulous. "I've got a haircut booked in"—he consults his watch—"ten minutes."

A haircut?

This is all too fast. I can't bear the idea of Luke's sun-bleached hair being snipped off and falling to the floor. Our honeymoon hair, all gone.

"Luke, don't," I say, before I can stop myself. "You can't."

"What's wrong?" Luke turns and looks at me more closely. "Becky, are you OK?"

No. I'm not OK.

"You can't cut off your hair," I say desperately. "Then it will all be over!"

"Sweetheart . . . it is over." Luke comes over and sits down beside me. He takes my hands and looks into my eyes. "You know that, don't you? It's over. We're going home. We're going back to real life."

"I know!" I say, after a pause. "It's just . . . I really love your hair long."

"I can't go into a business meeting like this." Luke shakes his head so the beads in his hair click together. "You know that as well as I do!"

"But you don't have to cut it off!" I say, suddenly inspired. "Plenty of Italian men have long hair. We'll just take the plaits out!"

"Becky . . ."

"I'll do it! I'll take them out! Sit down."

I push Luke down onto the bed and carefully edge out the first few little beads, then gently start to unbraid his hair. As I lean close, I can smell the business-y smell of Luke's expensive Armani aftershave, which he always wears for work. He hasn't used it since before we got married.

I shift round on the bed and carefully start unbraiding the plaits on the other side of his head. We're both silent; the only sound in the room is the soft clicking of beads. As I pull out the very last one, I feel a lump in my throat—which is ridiculous.

I mean, we couldn't stay on our honeymoon forever, could we? And I am looking forward to seeing Mum and Dad again, and Suze, and getting back to real life. . . .

But still. I've spent the last ten months with Luke. We haven't spent more than a few hours out of each other's sight. And now that's all ending.

Anyway, it'll be fine. I'll be busy with a new job . . . and all my friends. . . .

"Done!"

I reach for my Paul Mitchell Gloss Drops, put some on Luke's hair, and carefully brush it out. It's a bit wavy, but that's OK. He just looks European.

"You see?" I say at last. "You look brilliant!"

Luke surveys his reflection doubtfully and for an awful moment I think he's going to say he's still getting a haircut. Then he smiles.

"OK. Reprieved. But it will have to come off sooner or later."

"I know," I say, suddenly feeling light again. "But just not today."

I watch as Luke gathers some papers together and puts them in his briefcase.

"So . . . who exactly are you meeting with today?"

Luke did tell me, on the flight from Colombo—but they were serving free champagne at the time, and I'm not entirely sure I took it all in.

"We're going after a new client. The Arcodas Group."

"That's right. Now I remember. So what are they? Fund managers?"

Luke's company is called Brandon Communications, and it's a PR agency for financial institutions like banks and building societies and investment houses. That's kind of how we met, actually, during my days on *Successful Saving* magazine.

"Nope." Luke snaps his briefcase shut. "We want to broaden out of finance."

"Really?" I look at him in surprise.

"It's something I've been wanting to do for a while. The company's successful as it is, but I want to go bigger. Wider. The Arcodas Group is a very large corporation with lots of different interests. They own property developments . . . sports centers . . . shopping malls . . ."

"Shopping malls?" I say, suddenly alert. "Do you get a discount?"

"If we get the account. Maybe."

"So, does Arcodas have any shopping malls in Milan?" I say, trying to sound helpful. "Because I could go and visit one. For research."

"They haven't got any in Milan. They're only over here for a retail conference." Luke puts his briefcase down and gives me a long look.

"What?" I say.

"Becky . . . I know this is Milan. But please. Don't go crazy today."

"Go crazy?" I say, a little offended. "What do you mean?"

"I know you're going to go shopping. . . ."

How does he know that? Honestly, Luke has such a nerve. How does he know I'm not going to go and see some famous statues or something?

"I'm not going to go shopping!" I say haughtily. "I simply mentioned the shopping malls to show an interest in your work."

"I see." Luke gives me a quizzical look, which bugs me.

"I'm actually here for the culture." I lift my chin. "And because Milan is a city I've never seen."

"Uh-huh." Luke nods. "So you weren't planning to visit any designer shops today?"

"Luke," I say kindly, "I am a professional personal shopper. Do you really think I'm going to get excited by a few designer shops?"

"Frankly, yes," says Luke.

I feel a slight swell of indignation. Didn't we make vows to each other? Didn't he promise to respect me and not ever doubt my word?

"You think I came here just to go shopping? Well, take this!" I reach for my bag, then take out my purse and thrust it at him.

"Becky, don't be silly—"

"Take it! I'll just have a simple walk around the city! I'll go and look at the cathedral."

"OK, then." Luke shrugs and pockets my purse.

Damn. I didn't think he'd actually take it.

Anyway, it doesn't matter, because I have another credit card hidden in my bag, which Luke doesn't know about.

"Fine," I say, folding my arms. "Keep my money. I don't care!"

"I'm sure you'll survive," says Luke. "You can always use the credit card you keep hidden in your bag."

What?

How does he know about that? Has he been *spying* on me?

This has to be grounds for divorce, surely.

"Have it!" I say furiously, reaching into my bag. "Have everything! Take the shirt off my back!" I throw my credit card at him. "You may think you know me, Luke. But you don't. All I want is to soak up a little culture, and maybe invest in the odd souvenir or local artifact."

"Local artifact?" echoes Luke. "By 'local artifact' do you mean 'Versace shoes'?"

"No!" I say, after a short pause.

Which is true.

True-ish.

I was thinking more of Míu Míu. Apparently it's really cheap over here!

"Look, Becky, just don't go overboard, OK?" says Luke. "We're up to our luggage limits as it is." He glances at our open cases. "What with the South American ritual mask and the voodoo stick . . . Oh, and let's not forget the ceremonial dancing swords. . . ."

How many times is Luke going to give me grief about the ceremonial dancing swords? Just because they ripped his stupid shirt.

"For the millionth time, they're presents!" I say. "We couldn't have shipped them. We have to have them with us *as we arrive,* otherwise we won't look like proper travelers!"

"That's fine. All I'm saying is, we don't have room for South American masks *and* six extra pairs of boots."

Oh, he thinks he's so funny.

"Luke, I'm not like that anymore, OK?" I say, a little crushingly. "I've grown up a little. I would have thought you might have noticed."

"If you say so." Luke picks up my credit card, scrutinizes it, then gives it back to me. "You've only got a couple of hundred pounds left on this one, any-way."

What?

"How do you know that?" I say in outrage. "That's my private credit card!"

"Then don't hide the statement under the mattress. The maid in Sri Lanka found it when she was making the bed and gave it to me." He kisses me and picks up his briefcase. "Enjoy the city!"

As the door closes I feel a tad disgruntled. Little does Luke know. Little does Luke know I was actually plan-ning to buy him a *present* today. Years ago, when I first met him, Luke had this belt which he really loved, made of gorgeous Italian leather. But he left it in the bathroom one day and it got hot leg-wax on it.

Which was not entirely my fault. Like I told him, when you're in total agony, you don't think "What would be the most suitable implement to scrape burn-ing wax off my shins?" You just grab the nearest thing.

Anyway. So I was planning to buy him a replacement today. A little "end of honeymoon" gift. But maybe he doesn't deserve it if he's going to spy on me and read my private credit card statements. I mean, what a cheek. Do I read *his* private letters?

Well, actually I do. Some of them are really interest-ing! But the point is—

Oh my God. I freeze, struck by a dreadful thought. Does that mean he saw how much I spent in Hong Kong that day he went off to see the stock exchange?

Fuck.

And he hasn't said anything about it. OK, maybe he does deserve a present, after all.

I take a sip of cappuccino. Anyway, I'm the one laughing, not Luke. He thinks he's so clever, but what he doesn't know is that I've got a secret genius plan.

Half an hour later I arrive downstairs at reception, wearing tight black trousers (not quite capri but close enough), a striped T-shirt, and a scarf knotted round my neck, European-style. I head straight for the foreign exchange desk and beam at the woman behind it.

"*Ciao!*" I say brightly. "*Il . . .*"

I trail off into silence.

What was I thinking? That if I started confidently enough, with hand gestures, Italian would just pour naturally out of my mouth?

"I'd like to change some money into euros, please," I say, switching into English. I reach into my bag and triumphantly pull out a bundle of creased-up notes. "Rupees, dirhams, ringgits . . ." I dump the notes on the counter and reach for some more. "Kenyan dollars . . ." I peer at a strange pink note I don't recognize. "Whatever that one is . . ."

It is incredible how much money I was carrying around with me without even noticing! I had loads of rupees in my bath bag, and a whole bunch of Ethiopian birrs inside a paperback book. Plus there were loads of odd notes and coins floating around at the bottom of my carry-on bag.

And the point is, this is free money! This is money *we already had.*

I watch excitedly as the woman sorts it all into piles. "You have seventeen different currencies here," she says at last, looking a bit dazed.

"We've been to lots of countries," I explain. "So, how much is it all worth?"

As the woman starts tapping on a small computer, I feel quite excited. Maybe the exchange rates on some of these have moved in my favor. Maybe this is all worth loads!

Then I feel a bit guilty. After all, it's Luke's money too. Abruptly I decide that if it's more than a hundred euros, I'll give half back to him. That's only fair. But that'll still leave me with fifty! Not bad, for doing absolutely nothing!

"After commission . . ." The woman looks up. "Seven forty-five."

"Seven hundred and forty-five euros?" I stare at her in joy and amazement. I had no *idea* I was carrying around that kind of money! God, it just shows! All those people who say, "Look after the pennies and the pounds will look after themselves" . . . they're right! Who would have thought it?

I'll be able to buy a present for Luke *and* a pair of Míu Míu shoes, and—

"Not seven hundred and forty-five." The woman scribbles it on a piece of paper and hands it to me. "Seven euros, forty-five cents."

"What?" My happy smile slips off my face. That can't be right.

"Seven euros, forty-five cents," repeats the woman patiently. "How would you like that?"

How can so much genuine money be worth only seven euros? It makes no sense. As I explained to the woman, you could buy absolutely loads in India for those rupees. You could probably buy a whole car . . . or a palace, even. But she wouldn't budge. Oh, well.

I start walking down the street, carefully following the map the hotel concierge gave me. He was such a helpful man. I explained to him how I wanted to take in the cultural sights of Milan, and he started talking about

Da Vinci's *The Last Supper,* which he "knew" I would be desperate to see.

Obviously I *do* want to see it. Very much so. But priorities are priorities. So I politely explained I was actually more interested in *contemporary* Italian culture, and he started going on about some artist who does short films about death.

So then I clarified that by "contemporary Italian culture" I was really referring to cultural icons such as Prada and Gucci—and his eyes lit up in understanding. He marked a street for me which is in an area called the Golden Quadrilateral and is apparently "full of culture" which he was "sure I would appreciate."

It's a sunny day with a light breeze, and the sunlight is glinting off windows and cars, and whizzy Vespas are zipping everywhere. God, Milan is cool. Every single person I pass is wearing designer sunglasses and carrying a designer handbag—even the men!

For a moment I consider buying Luke a continental handbag instead of a belt. I try to imagine him walking into the office with a chic little bag dangling from his wrist. . . .

Hmm. Maybe I'll stick to a belt.

Suddenly I notice a girl in front of me wearing a cream trouser suit, high strappy shoes, and a pink scooter helmet with leopard-print trim.

I stare at her, gripped with desire. God, I want one of those helmets. I mean, I know I haven't got a Vespa—but I could wear the helmet anyway, couldn't I? It could be my signature look. People would call me the Girl in the Vespa Helmet• Plus, it would protect me from muggers, so it would actually be a *safety* feature. . . .

Maybe I'll ask where she got it.

"Excusez-moi, mademoiselle!" I call out, impressed at my own sudden fluency. *"J'adore votre chapeau!"*

The girl gives me a blank look, then disappears round a corner. Which, frankly, I think is a bit unfriendly. I mean, here I am, making an effort to speak her lang—

Oh. Oh, right.

OK, that's a bit embarrassing.

Well, never mind. I'm not here to buy Vespa helmets, anyway. I'm here to buy a present for Luke. That's what marriage is all about, after all. Putting your partner first. Placing his needs before your own.

Plus, what I'm thinking is, I can always fly back here for the day. I mean, it wouldn't take any time from London, would it? And Suze could come too, I think with sudden delight. God, that would be fun. I suddenly have an image of Suze and me, striding down the street, arm in arm, swinging our bags and laughing. A girly trip to Milan! We *have* to do it!

I reach another corner and stop to consult my map. I must be getting closer. He said it wasn't that far away. . . .

Just then a woman walks past me carrying a bag from Versace, and I stiffen with excitement. I have to be getting close to the source! This is just like when we visited that volcano in Peru, and the guide kept pointing out signs that we were nearing the core. If I just keep my eyes peeled for more Versace bags. . . .

I walk forward a little more—and there's another one! That woman in oversize shades having a cappuccino has got one, plus about six zillion bags from Armani. She gesticulates to her friend and reaches inside one of them—and pulls out a pot of jam, with an Armani label.

Armani jam? Armani does *jam*?

Maybe in Milan everything has a fashion label! Maybe Dolce & Gabbana does toothpaste. Maybe Prada does tomato ketchup!

I start walking on again, more and more quickly, prickling with excitement. I can sense the shops in the air. The designer bags are appearing more frequently. The air is becoming heavy with expensive scent. I can practically *hear* the sound of hangers on rails and zips being done up. . . .

And then, suddenly, there it is.

A long, elegant boulevard stretches before me, with the chicest, most designer-clad people on earth milling about. Tanned, model-like girls in Pucci prints and heels are sauntering along with powerful-looking men in immaculate linen suits. A girl in white Versace jeans and red lipstick is pushing along a pram upholstered in Louis Vuitton monogrammed leather. A blond woman in a brown leather miniskirt trimmed with rabbit fur is gabbling into a matching mobile phone while dragging along her little boy, dressed head to foot in Gucci.

And . . . the shops. Shop after shop after shop.

Ferragamo. Valentino. Dior. Versace. Prada.

As I venture down the street, my head swiveling from side to side, I feel giddy. It's complete culture shock. How long has it been since I've seen a shop that wasn't selling ethnic crafts and wooden beads? I mean . . . it's been months! I feel like I've been on some starvation cure, and now I'm gorging on tiramisu with double cream.

Just look at that amazing coat. Look at those *shoes*.

Where do I start? Where do I even—

I can't move. I'm paralyzed in the middle of the street, like the donkey in that Aesop's fable who couldn't choose between the bales of hay. They'll find me in years to come, still frozen to the spot, clutching my credit card.

Suddenly my eyes fall on a display of leather belts and wallets in the window of a nearby boutique.

Leather. Luke's belt. This is what I'm here to buy. Focus.

I totter toward the shop and push open the door, still in a daze. At once I'm hit by the overwhelming smell of expensive leather. In fact, it's so strong it actually seems to clear my head.

The shop is amazing. It's carpeted in pale taupe, with softly lit display cabinets. I can see wallets, belts, bags, jackets. . . . I pause by a mannequin wearing the most amazing chocolate brown coat, all leather and satin. I stroke it fondly, then lift the price tag—and nearly faint.

But, of course, it's in lire. I smile in relief. No wonder it looks so—

Oh no. It's euros now.

Bloody hell.

I gulp, and move away from the mannequin.

Which just proves that Dad was right all along—the single currency *was* a huge mistake. When I was thirteen I went on holiday to Rome with my parents—and the whole point about lire was, the prices looked like a lot *but they weren't really*. You could buy something for about a zillion lire—and in real life it cost about three quid! It was fantastic!

Plus, if you accidentally ended up buying a bottle of really expensive perfume, no one (i.e., your parents) could blame you, because, like Mum said, who on earth can divide numbers like that in their head?

As I start to look through a display of belts, a stocky middle-aged man comes out of a fitting room, chomping on a cigar and wearing an amazing black cashmere coat trimmed with leather. He's about fifty and very tanned, with close-cropped gray hair and piercing blue eyes. The only thing which doesn't look quite so good is his nose, which to be honest is a bit of a mishmash.

"Oy, Roberto," he says in a raspy voice.

He's English! His accent is weird, though. Kind of transatlantic meets cockney.

A shop assistant in a black suit with angular black glasses comes hurrying out from the fitting room, holding a tape measure.

"Yes, Signor Temple?"

"How much cashmere is in this?" The stocky man smooths down the coat critically.

"Signore, this is one hundred percent cashmere."

"The best cashmere?" The stocky man lifts a warning finger. "I don't want you palming me off now. You know my motto. Only the best."

The guy in black glasses gives a little wince of dismay.

"Signore, we would not, er . . . palm you off."

The man gazes at himself in a mirror silently for a few seconds, then nods.

"Fair enough. I'll take three. One to London." He counts off on stubby fingers. "One to Switzerland. One to New York. Got it?"

The assistant in black glasses glances over at me, and I realize it's totally obvious I'm eavesdropping.

"Oh, hi!" I say quickly. "I'd like to buy this, please, and have it gift wrapped." I hold up the belt I've chosen.

"Silvia will help you." He gestures dismissively toward the woman at the till, then turns back to his customer.

I hand the belt over to Silvia and watch idly as she wraps it up in shiny bronze paper. I'm half admiring her deft ability with ribbon and half listening to Mr. Cashmere, who's now looking at a briefcase.

"Don't like the texture," he states. "Feels different. Something's wrong."

"We have changed our supplier recently. . . ." The black glasses guy is wringing his hands. "But it is a very fine leather, signore. . . ."

He trails off as Mr. Cashmere takes his cigar from his mouth and gives him a look.

"You're palming me off, Roberto," he says. "I pay

good money, I want quality. What you'll do is make me up one using leather from the old supplier. Got it?"

He looks over, sees me watching, and winks.

"Best place for leather in the world, this. But don't take any of their crap."

"I won't!" I beam back. "And I love that coat, by the way!"

"Very kind of you." He nods affably. "You an actress? Model?"

"Er . . . no. Neither."

"No matter." He waves his cigar.

"How will you pay, signorina?" Silvia interrupts us.

"Oh! Er . . . here you are."

As I hand over my Visa card I feel a glow of goodness in my heart. Buying presents for other people is so much more satisfying than buying for yourself! And this will take me up to my limit on my Visa card, so that's my shopping all finished for the day.

What shall I do next? Maybe I'll take in some culture. I could go and look at that famous painting the concierge was talking about.

I can hear a buzz of interest coming from the back of the shop and turn idly to see what's happening. A mirrored door to a stockroom is open, and a woman in a black suit is coming out, surrounded by a gaggle of eager assistants. What on earth is she holding? Why is everyone so—

Then suddenly I catch a glimpse of what she's carrying. My heart stops. My skin starts to prickle.

It can't be.

But it is. She's carrying an Angel bag.

Three

IT'S AN ANGEL bag. In the flesh.

I thought they were all sold out everywhere. I thought they were totally impossible to get hold of.

The woman sets it down ceremoniously on a creamy suede pedestal and stands back to admire it. The whole shop has fallen silent. It's like a member of the royal family has arrived. Or a movie star.

I'm transfixed.

It's stunning. It's totally stunning. The calfskin looks as soft as butter. The handpainted angel is all in delicate shades of aquamarine. And underneath is the name *Dante* written in diamanté.

My legs are all wobbly and my hands feel sweaty. This is better than when we saw the white tigers in Bengal. I mean, let's face it. Angel bags are probably *rarer* than white tigers.

And there's one in front of my nose.

I could just buy it flashes through my brain. *I could buy it!*

"Miss? Signorina? Can you hear me?" A voice pierces

my thoughts, and I realize Silvia at the till is trying to get my attention.

"Oh," I say, flustered. "Yes." I pick up the pen and scribble any old signature. "So . . . is that a real Angel bag?"

"Yes, it is," she says in a smug, bored tone, like a bouncer who knows the band personally and is used to dealing with besotted groupies.

"How much . . ." I swallow. "How much is it?"

"Two thousand euros."

"Right." I nod.

Two thousand euros. For a bag.

But if I had an Angel bag I wouldn't need to buy any new clothes. Ever. Who needs a new skirt when you have the hippest bag in town?

I don't care how much it is. I have to have it.

"I'd like to buy it, please," I say in a rush.

There's a stunned silence around the shop—then all the assistants burst into peals of laughter.

"You cannot buy the bag," says Silvia pityingly. "There is a waiting list."

Oh. A waiting list. Of course there would be a waiting list. I'm an idiot.

"Do you want to join the list?" she asks as she hands my Visa card back.

OK, let's be sensible. I'm not really going to go on a waiting list in Milan. I mean, for a start, how would I pick it up? I'd have to get them to FedEx it. Or come over specially, or—

"Yes," I hear my own voice saying. "Yes, please."

After I write down my details, Silvia pops the form in a drawer. "We will call you when one is available."

"And . . . when might that be?" I try not to sound too anxious.

"I cannot say." She shrugs.

"How many people are ahead of me on the list?"

"We do not disclose such details."

"Right."

I feel a tiny dart of frustration. I mean, *there it is*. There's the bag, a few feet away from me . . . and I can't have it.

Never mind. I'm on the list. There's nothing more I can do.

I pick up the carrier bag containing Luke's belt and slowly walk away, pausing by the Angel bag. God, it's heart-stopping. The coolest, most beautiful bag in the world.

I'm suddenly struck by an idea.

"I was just wondering," I say, hurrying back to the till. "Do you know if everyone on the waiting list actually *wants* an Angel bag?"

"They are on the list." Silvia says it as though she's speaking to a total moron.

"Yes, but they might all have changed their minds," I explain, my words tumbling out in excitement. "Or already have bought one! And then it would be my turn! Don't you *see*? I could have *this* bag!"

How can she look so impassive? Doesn't she understand how important this is?

"We will be contacting the customers in turn," says Silvia. "We will be in touch if a bag becomes available for you."

"I'll do it for you, if you like," I say, trying to sound helpful. "If you give me their numbers."

Silvia looks at me silently for a moment.

"No, thank you. We will be in touch."

"All right," I say, deflating. "Well, thanks."

There's nothing more I can do. I'll just stop thinking about it and enjoy the rest of Milan. Exactly. I give a final, longing glance at the Angel bag, then head out of the shop. I'm not going to obsess about this. I'm not even going to *think* about it. I'm going to focus on . . . culture. Yes.

Suddenly I stop dead in the street. I've given her the number of Luke's flat in London. But didn't he say something a while ago about putting in new phone lines?

What if I've left *an obsolete number*?

Quickly I retrace my steps and burst into the shop again.

"Hi!" I say breathlessly. "I just thought I'd give you another set of contact details, in case you can't get through." I rummage about in my bag and pull out one of Luke's cards. "This is my husband's office."

"Very well," Silvia says a little wearily.

"Only . . . come to think of it, if you speak to him, I wouldn't mention the actual *bag*." I lower my voice a little. "Say 'the Angel has landed.' "

"The Angel has landed," echoes Silvia, writing it down as though she makes coded phone calls all the time.

Which, now that I think about it, maybe she does.

"The person to ask for is Luke Brandon," I explain, handing over the card. "At Brandon Communications. He's my husband."

Across the shop, I'm aware of Mr. Cashmere looking up from a selection of leather gloves.

"Luke Brandon," repeats Silvia. "Very well." She puts the card away and gives me a final nod.

"So, have you phoned anyone on the list yet?" I can't resist asking.

"Signora Brandon," snaps Silvia in exasperation. "You will have to wait your turn! I cannot do any better than that!"

"Are you so sure about that?" a raspy voice cuts in and

we both look up to see Mr. Cashmere approaching us from across the shop.

What's he doing?

"Excuse me?" Silvia says haughtily, and he winks at me.

"Don't let them palm you off, girl." He turns to Silvia. "If you wanted to, you could sell her this bag." He jerks his stubby thumb at the Angel bag on the pedestal and puffs on his cigar.

"Signor—"

"I've been listening. If you haven't called anyone on the waiting list, they don't know this has come in. They don't even know it exists." He pauses meaningfully. "And you've got this young lady here, wants to buy it."

"That is not the point, signore." Silvia smiles tightly at him. "There is a strict protocol . . ."

"You have discretion. Don't tell me you don't. Oy, Roberto!" he suddenly calls. The man in the black glasses hurries over from somewhere in the back.

"Signor Temple?" he says smoothly, his eyes darting at me. "Everything is all right?"

"If I wanted this bag for my lady friend, would you sell it to me?" The man blows out a cloud of smoke and raises his eyebrows at me. He looks like he's enjoying this.

Roberto glances at Silvia, who jerks her head at me and rolls her eyes. I can see Roberto taking in the situation, his brain working hard.

"Signor Temple." He turns to the man with a charming smile. "You are a very valued customer. It is a very different matter . . ."

"Would you?"

"Yes," Roberto says, after a pause.

"Well then." The man looks at Roberto expectantly. There's silence. I hold my breath.

"Silvia," Roberto says at last. "Wrap up the bag for the signorina."

Oh my GOD!

"It's my pleasure," says Silvia, shooting me a dirty look.

I can't believe this has happened.

"I—I don't know how to thank you!" I stutter. "That's the most wonderful thing anyone's ever done for me, ever!"

"My pleasure." The man inclines his head and extends his hand. "Nathan Temple."

"Becky Bloomwood," I say, shaking it. "I mean, Brandon."

"You really wanted that bag." He raises his eyebrows appreciatively. "Never seen anything like it."

"I was desperate for it!" I admit with a laugh. "I'm so grateful to you!"

Nathan Temple waves his hand in a "don't mention it" gesture, then takes out a lighter and lights his cigar, which has gone out. When he's puffing away again he looks up.

"Brandon . . . as in Luke Brandon."

"You know Luke?" I'm amazed. "What a coincidence!"

"By reputation." He blows out a cloud of cigar smoke. "He has quite a name, your husband. He's coming back to the company after his year off, I understand?"

"Well . . . yes," I say in surprise. "How did you know that?"

Nathan Temple winks again.

"I've had my eye on him for a while. Talented man. Couple of years ago, all the banks were launching on-line services. But the one that got all the publicity was SBG. Your husband's client."

"Signor Temple." Roberto comes bustling over with

several carrier bags, which he hands to my new friend. "The rest will be shipped according to your orders. . . ."

"Good man, Roberto," says Nathan Temple, clapping him on the back. "See you next year."

"Please let me buy you a drink," I say quickly. "Or lunch! Or . . . anything!"

"Unfortunately, I have to go. Nice offer, though."

"But I want to thank you for what you did. I'm so incredibly grateful!"

Nathan Temple lifts his hands modestly.

"Who knows? Maybe one day you can do a favor for me."

"Anything!" I exclaim eagerly, and he smiles.

"Enjoy the bag. All right, Harvey."

Out of nowhere, a thin blond man in a chalk-striped suit has appeared. He takes the bags from Nathan Temple and the two walk out of the shop.

I lean against the counter, radiant with bliss. I have an Angel bag. *I have an Angel bag!*

"That will be two thousand euros," comes a surly voice from behind me.

Oh, right. I'd kind of forgotten about the two thousand euros part.

I automatically reach for my purse—then stop. Of course. I don't have my purse. And I've maxed out my Visa card on Luke's belt . . . and I have only seven euros in cash.

Silvia's eyes narrow at my hesitation.

"If you have trouble paying . . ." she begins.

"I don't have trouble paying!" I retort at once. "I just . . . need a minute."

Silvia folds her arms skeptically as I reach into my bag again and pull out a Bobbi Brown Sheer Finish compact.

"Do you have a hammer?" I say. "Or anything heavy?"

Silvia is looking at me as though I've gone completely crazy.

"Anything will do. . . ." Suddenly I glimpse a hefty-looking stapler sitting on the counter. I pick it up and start bashing as hard as I can at the compact.

"Oddìo!" Silvia screams.

"It's OK!" I say, panting a little. "I just need to . . . there!"

The whole thing has splintered. Triumphantly I pull out a MasterCard, which was glued to the backing. My Defcon One, code-red-emergency card. Luke *really* doesn't know about this one. Not unless he's got X-ray vision.

I got the idea of hiding a credit card in a powder compact from this brilliant article I read on money management. Not that I have a big problem with money or anything. But in the past, I have had the odd little . . . crisis.

So this idea really appealed to me. What you do is, you keep your credit card somewhere really inaccessible, like frozen in ice or sewn into the lining of your bag, so you'll have time to reconsider before making each purchase. Apparently this simple tactic can cut your unnecessary purchases by 90 percent.

And I have to say, it really does work! The only, tiny, flaw is, I keep having to buy new powder compacts, which is getting a bit expensive.

"I'll pay with this," I say, and hand it to Silvia, who is peering at me as though I'm a dangerous lunatic. She swipes it gingerly through her machine, and a minute later I'm scrawling my signature on the slip. I thrust it back at her, and she files it away in a drawer.

There's a tiny pause. I'm almost exploding with anticipation.

"So . . . can I have it?" I say.

"Here you are," she says sulkily, and hands me the creamy carrier.

My hands close over the cord handles and I feel a surge of pure, unadulterated joy.

It's mine.

As I get back to the hotel that evening I'm floating on air. This has been one of the best days of my life. I spent the whole afternoon walking up and down the via Montenapoleone with my new Angel bag prominently displayed on my shoulder . . . and everyone admired it. In fact, they didn't just admire it . . . they gawped at it. It was like I was a sudden celebrity!

About twenty people came up to me and asked where I got it, and a woman in dark glasses who *had* to be an Italian movie star got her driver to come and offer me three thousand euros for it. And best of all, all I kept hearing was people saying, *"La ragazza con la borsa di Angel"!* Which I worked out means the Girl with the Angel Bag! That's what they were calling me!

I drift blissfully through the revolving doors into the foyer of the hotel to see Luke standing by the reception desk.

"There you are!" he says, sounding relieved. "I was beginning to worry! Our taxi's here." He ushers me out into a waiting taxi and slams the door. "Linate Airport," he says to the driver, who immediately zooms into an oncoming stream of traffic, to a chorus of horns.

"So, how was your day?" I say, trying not to flinch as we're nearly hit by another taxi. "How was the meeting?"

"It went well! If we can get the Arcodas Group as clients it'll be seriously good news. They're expanding hugely at the moment. It's going to be an exciting time."

"So . . . do you think you'll get them?"

"We'll have to woo them. When we get back I'm going to start preparing a pitch. But I'm hopeful. I'm definitely hopeful."

"Well done!" I beam at him. "And was your hair OK?"

"My hair was fine." He gives a wry smile. "In fact . . . it was admired by all."

"You see?" I say with delight. "I knew it would be!"

"And how was your day?" says Luke as we swing round a corner at about a hundred miles an hour.

"It was fantastic!" I'm glowing all over. "Absolutely perfect. I adore Milan!"

"Really?" Luke looks intrigued. "Even without this?" He reaches into his pocket and produces my purse.

God, I'd forgotten all about that.

"Even without my purse!" I say with a little laugh. "Although . . . I did manage to buy you a little something."

I hand over the bronze-wrapped package and watch excitedly as Luke pulls out the belt.

"Becky, that's . . . wonderful!" he says. "Absolutely . . ." He trails off, turning it over in his hands.

"It's to replace the one I ruined," I explain. "With the hot wax, remember?"

"I remember." He sounds utterly touched. "And . . . this is really all you bought in Milan? A present for me?"

"Er . . ."

I give a kind of noncommittal shrug and clear my throat, playing for time.

Marriages are based on honesty and trust. If I don't tell him about the Angel bag, then I'm betraying that trust.

But if I *do* tell him . . . I'll have to explain about my Defcon One, code-red-emergency credit card. Which I'm not sure is such a solid idea.

I don't want to spoil the last precious moments of our honeymoon with some stupid argument.

But we're married, I think in a rush of emotion. *We're husband and wife! We shouldn't have secrets!* OK, I'm going to tell him. Right now.

"Luke—"

"Wait." Luke cuts me off, his voice a little gruff. "Becky, I want to apologize."

Apologize?

"You said you'd changed. You said you'd grown up. And . . . you have." He spreads his hands. "To be honest, I was expecting you to come back to the hotel having made some huge, extravagant purchase."

Oh God.

"Er . . . Luke . . ." I venture.

"I'm ashamed of myself," he says, frowning. "Here you are, your first visit to the fashion capital of the world— and all you've bought is a present for me. Becky . . . I'm really moved." He exhales sharply. "Chandra was right. You do have a beautiful spirit."

There's silence. This is my cue to tell him the truth.

But how can I tell him I don't have a beautiful spirit, I have a crappy old normal one?

"Well . . ." I find myself obsessively refolding the bronze wrapping paper. "Er . . . you know. It's just a belt!"

"It's not just a belt to me," he says quietly. "It's . . . a symbol of our marriage." He clasps my hand for a few moments, then smiles. "I'm sorry . . . what did you want to say?"

I could still come clean.

I could still do it.

"Um . . . well . . . I was just going to tell you . . . the buckle's adjustable." I give him a slightly sickly smile and turn away, pretending to be fascinated by the view out the window.

OK. So I didn't tell the truth.

But in my defense, if he'd just paid attention when I'd read him *Vogue* he would have seen for himself. I mean, I'm not hiding it or anything. Here I am with one of the most coveted status symbols in the world on my arm—and he hasn't even noticed!

And anyway, this is absolutely the last time I lie to him. From now on, no more white lies, no more gray lies, no more fibs. We will have a perfect marriage of honesty and truth. Yes. Everyone will admire our harmonious, loving ways, and people will call us the Couple Who—

"Linate Airport!" The driver's voice interrupts my thoughts. I turn and look at Luke with a sudden apprehensive thrill.

"Here we are," he says, and meets my eyes. "Still want to go home?"

"Absolutely!" I reply firmly, ignoring the nervous flutters in my stomach.

I get out of the taxi and stretch my legs. Passengers are milling about with trolleys, and a plane is taking off with a thunderous roar, almost right above me.

God, we're really doing it. In a few hours we'll be in London. After all these months traveling.

"By the way," says Luke. "There was a message from your mother on my mobile this afternoon. She wanted to know if we were still in Sri Lanka, or had we gone to Malaysia yet?"

He lifts his eyebrows comically at me, and I feel a giggle rise. They are all going to get such a shock! They're all going to be so thrilled to see us!

And suddenly I'm full of excitement. We're on our way home!

Four

OH MY GOD. We've done it. We're back! We're actually back on English soil.

Or, at least, English tarmac. We spent last night in Luke's flat, and now we're driving along the Surrey roads in a hired car, all ready to surprise Mum and Dad. In about two minutes we'll arrive at their house! It's just after eleven, so they'll be having coffee in the garden as usual, with no idea!

I can barely keep still for excitement. In fact, I keep banging my knee on the South American tribal mask. I can just see the looks on Mum and Dad's faces when they see us! Mum's face will light up, and Dad will look astounded, then his face will break into a smile . . . and we'll be running to each other through the clouds of smoke. . . .

Actually, maybe there won't be any clouds of smoke. I'm thinking of *The Railway Children*. But anyway, it'll be fantastic. The most fantastic reunion ever!

To be honest, Mum and Dad have probably found it

quite hard-going without me. I'm their only daughter, and this is the longest they've ever had to go without seeing me. Ten whole months.

I will so make their day, coming back home.

We swing into Mayfield Avenue and for the first time I feel just the tiniest twinge of nerves.

"Luke, should we have called?" I say.

"Too late now," Luke replies calmly, and signals left.

We're nearly at our street. Oh God. I really am starting to feel jittery.

"What if they're so shocked to see us that they have heart attacks?" I say in sudden panic.

"I'm sure they'll be fine!" Luke laughs. "Don't worry!"

And now we're in Elton Road, my parents' road. We're coming up to their house. We're here.

Luke pulls into the drive and turns off the engine. For a moment neither of us moves.

"Ready?" says Luke.

Feeling suddenly self-conscious, I get out of the car and slam the door. It's a bright, sunny day and the street is quiet, apart from a few birds twittering and the distant sound of a lawn mower.

I walk up to the front door, hesitate, and then, with a sudden surge of excitement, lift my hand and firmly press the bell.

Nothing happens.

I wait a few moments, then ring again. But there's silence.

They're not in.

How can they not be in?

I feel indignant. Where on earth are my parents? They're always home! That's where they belong! Don't they realize their only beloved daughter is back from her round-the-world trip?

"We could go for a coffee and come back later," suggests Luke.

"I suppose so," I say, trying to hide my disappointment.

This has ruined my whole plan. I was all ready for our great emotional reunion—not going off for a stupid cup of coffee!

Disconsolate, I walk up the path and lean on the wrought-iron gate. I fiddle with the broken catch, which Dad has said for twenty years he's going to mend, and look at the roses which Mum and Dad had put in last year for our wedding. God, we've been married nearly a year. That's a weird thought.

Suddenly I hear the distant sound of voices traveling along the street. I raise my head and squint. A pair of figures has just rounded the corner.

It's them! It's Mum and Dad! Mum's in a print dress and Dad's in a pink short-sleeve shirt, and they both look tanned and healthy.

"Mum!" I shriek. "Dad!" I open my arms wide. *"We're back!"*

Mum and Dad look up, and both freeze to the spot. Suddenly I notice they've got someone else with them. Some woman. Or girl. I can't see properly in this bright sunlight.

"Mum!" I cry again. "Dad!"

The strange thing is, they aren't moving. They must be too shell-shocked by my appearance or something. Maybe they think I'm a ghost.

"I'm back!" I yell. "It's me, Becky! Surprise!"

Then, to my utter astonishment, Mum and Dad start retreating.

What . . . What are they doing? They were supposed to be running *toward* me.

They disappear round the corner and for a few moments I'm too baffled to speak.

"Luke, was that Mum and Dad?" I say at last.

"I think so." Luke sounds equally puzzled.

"And did they really . . . run away from me?"

I'm stricken. My own parents, running away from me as though I've got the plague.

"No!" Luke says quickly. "Of course not. They probably just didn't see you. Look!" He suddenly points. "There they are again."

Sure enough, Mum and Dad have appeared round the corner again, this time without the girl. They walk along for a few steps, then Dad dramatically grabs Mum and points at me.

"Look!" he says. "It's Becky!"

"Becky!" Mum exclaims in a stilted voice. "It can't be true!"

She sounds just like she did in the amateur dramatics Agatha Christie last year, when she played the lady who discovered the body.

"Becky! Luke!" Dad calls.

And now they really are running toward us, and I feel a huge swell of emotion rising.

"Mum!" I shout. "Dad! We're back!"

I race toward them, throwing my hands out. I land in Dad's arms, and the next moment Mum's there too, and we're all in a great big hug.

"You're home!" Dad exclaims. "Welcome back, darling!"

"Is everything all right?" Mum peers at me anxiously. "Are you OK?"

"We're fine! We just decided to come home early! We wanted to see you all!" I squeeze Mum tightly. "We knew you'd be missing us!"

All three of us walk back to the house, where Dad

shakes Luke's hand and Mum gives him an enormous hug.

"I can't believe it," she says, looking from Luke to me. "I just can't believe it. Luke, your hair! It's so *long*!"

"I know." He grins at me. "It'll be coming off before I go to work."

I open my mouth automatically to protest, then close it again. I'm feeling too joyful to start arguing. Instead I beam happily back at him, my arm still linked inside Dad's. *This* is how I imagined it. Everyone together and happy. Although . . . I'm still wondering what was going on earlier.

Impulsively I hug Mum again with my free arm. "It's so lovely to see you!"

"It's lovely to see *you*, darling!" She hugs me back and I inhale the familiar scent of her Green Irish Tweed perfume, which she's been wearing as long as I can remember.

"That's a relief to hear!" I laugh. "Because it almost looked like you were . . ." I break off, feeling a bit awkward.

"What, love?"

"Well, it kind of *looked* as if you were . . . trying to avoid me!" I give another little laugh, to show what a ridiculous idea this is.

There's a pause—and I'm not totally sure, but I think I see Mum and Dad glance at each other.

"Dad dropped his spectacles!" says Mum brightly. "Didn't you, love?"

"That's right!" Dad chimes in heartily. "I dropped my specs."

"We had to go back for them," Mum explains.

Both she and Dad are watching me with alert expressions.

What's going on? Are they *hiding* something?

"Is that Becky?" A shrill voice pierces the atmosphere, and I look round to see Janice, our next-door neighbor, peering over the fence. She's wearing a pink flowery dress with matching eyeshadow, and her hair has been dyed a very strange shade of auburn. "Becky!" She clasps her hands breathlessly to her chest. "It *is* you!"

"Hi, Janice!" I say, trying to hide my discomfiture. "We're back!"

"You look so well!" she exclaims. "Don't they look well?" she says to my parents. "So *brown*!"

"That's traveling for you," I say nonchalantly.

"And Luke! You look just like Crocodile Dundee!" Janice is goggling at both of us with open admiration, and I can't help feeling gratified.

"Let's go in," says Mum. "And you can tell us all about it!"

This is the moment I've pictured so many times. Sitting down with friends and family and telling all about our foreign adventures. Spreading out a crinkly map . . . describing sunrises over mountains . . . looking at the avid faces . . . listening to the gasps of admiration. . . .

Except that now it's actually happening, it isn't going quite like I imagined.

"Did you go to Tenerife?" Janice keeps interrupting as I try to describe wading through the Amazon. "Or Majorca? You can get some lovely packages. . . ."

"Er . . . no," I say, feeling a twinge of annoyance. "We went to Africa . . . India . . ." I spread my arms. "Everywhere!"

"I can't stand the heat." Janice shakes her head. "Never could. Even in Florida." She suddenly brightens. "Did you go to Disneyland?"

"Er . . . no."

"Oh well." Janice looks sympathetic. "Never mind. Maybe next time!"

Next time? What, next time we spend ten months traveling round the world?

"It certainly sounds like a lovely holiday," she adds encouragingly.

It wasn't a *holiday*! I want to exclaim. It was a *traveling experience*! Honestly. I bet when Christopher Columbus came back from America, people didn't meet him off the boat with "Ooh, Christopher, did you go to Disneyland?"

I glance up at Mum and Dad, but they're not even listening. They're standing by the sink, and Mum's murmuring something to Dad.

I don't like this. There is definitely something going on. I glance at Luke, and he's watching Mum and Dad too.

"We brought you presents!" I exclaim loudly, reaching for my carrier bag. "Mum! Dad! Have a look!"

With some difficulty I pull out the South American mask and present it to Mum. It's in the shape of a dog's face, with big teeth and huge circular eyes, and I have to say, it looks pretty impressive.

"I brought it all the way back from Paraguay!" I add with a glow of pride.

I feel like such an explorer! Here I am, bringing rare artifacts of the indigenous South American culture to Oxshott. I mean, how many people in Britain have even *seen* one of these? Maybe a museum will ask to borrow it for an exhibition or something!

"Goodness!" says Mum, turning it over a little nervously. "What is it?"

"It's a traditional ritual mask made by Chiriguano Indians, isn't it?" Janice says brightly.

"Have you been to Paraguay, Janice?" I say, taken aback.

"Oh no, love." She takes a sip of coffee. "I've seen them in John Lewis."

For a moment I can't quite speak.

"You've seen them in . . . John Lewis?" I say at last.

"In Kingston. The gift department." She beams. "You can buy everything in John Lewis these days!"

"Never knowingly undersold," chimes in Mum.

I do not believe this. I've lugged this mask approximately six thousand miles around the globe. It was supposed to be a rare and exotic treasure. And all the time it's been on sale at bloody John Lewis.

Mum glimpses my face.

"But yours will be the real thing, love!" she says quickly. "We'll put it on the mantelpiece next to Dad's golf trophy!"

"OK," I say a bit gloomily. I glance up at Dad, and he's still staring out the window, not listening to a word. Maybe I'll give him his present later.

"So, what's been happening here?" I say, taking a cup of coffee from Mum. "How's Martin? And Tom?" I ask Janice.

"Both well, thank you!" says Janice. "Tom's living with us for a while."

"Ah." I give an understanding nod.

Tom is Janice and Martin's son, and he's had a bit of a disaster with his marriage. His wife, Lucy, left him, basically because he wouldn't have a tattoo done to match hers.

"They've sold their house," Janice says, looking wistful. "Did very well out of it, actually."

"And is he OK?"

Mum and Janice exchange looks.

"He's been throwing himself into his hobbies," Janice says at last. "Keeping himself busy. His new thing is woodworking. He's made all sorts of things for us!" She looks slightly beleaguered. "Three garden benches . . . two bird tables . . . and now he's working on a two-story summerhouse in the garden!"

"Wow!" I say politely. "That's great!"

An oven timer suddenly starts pinging, and I look up in surprise. Has Mum taken to baking while we've been away?

"Are you cooking something?" I peer at the oven, which appears to be dead.

"No!" Mum gives a trill of laughter. "That's to remind me to check eBay."

"eBay?" I stare at her. "What do you mean, eBay?"

How would Mum know about eBay? She doesn't know anything about computers. Two years ago I suggested she give Luke a new mouse mat for Christmas and she went to a pet shop.

"You know, darling! Internet shopping. I'm bidding on a Ken Hom wok, a pair of candlesticks"—she pulls a flowery notepad out of her pocket and consults it—"oh yes, and a hedge trimmer for Dad. Used only once!"

"eBay is marvelous!" chimes in Janice. "Such fun. Have you used it, Becky?"

"Well . . . no."

"Oh, you'd love it," says Mum at once. "Although I couldn't get through last night to check on my Portmeirion plates." She clicks her tongue. "I don't know *what* was wrong."

"The domain servers were probably down," Janice says knowledgeably. "I've been having trouble with my modem all week. Biscuit, Becky?"

I cannot get my head round this. Mum? On eBay? Next she'll be saying she's up to level six on Tomb Raider.

"But . . . you haven't even got a computer," I say. "You hate modern technology."

"Not anymore, love! Janice and I did a course. We've gone broadband!" She looks at me seriously. "Let me give you a word of advice, Becky. If you're going broadband, I'd install a decent firewall."

OK. This is all wrong. Parents are not supposed to know more about computers than their children. I nod carelessly and take a sip of coffee, trying to hide the fact that I don't have a clue what a firewall is.

"Jane, it's ten to twelve," Janice says cautiously to Mum. "Are you going to . . ."

"I don't think so," Mum says. "You go on."

"What is it?" I look from face to face. "Is something wrong?"

"Of course not!" says Mum, putting down her coffee cup. "It's just we agreed to go to the Marshalls' lunch party today, with Janice and Martin. But don't worry. We'll send our apologies."

"Don't be silly!" I say at once. "You must go. We don't want to mess up your day."

There's a pause.

"Are you sure?" says Mum.

She wasn't supposed to say that. She was supposed to say, "How could my precious daughter mess up my day?"

"Of course!" I say, in overbright tones. "You go to your lunch party and we'll have a proper chat later."

"Well, OK," says Mum. "If you're sure."

"I'll pop over and get ready," says Janice. "Lovely to see you back, Becky!"

As she disappears through the kitchen door I look at Dad, who's still staring out the window, brooding.

"Are you OK, Dad?" I say. "You've been really quiet."

"Sorry," he says, turning round with a quick smile. "I'm just a little distracted at the moment. Thinking about . . . a golf match I've got next week. Very important." He mimes playing a putt.

"Right," I say, trying to sound cheerful.

But inside I feel more and more uneasy. He's not really thinking about golf. Why is he so cagey?

What is going on?

"So . . ." I say lightly. "Who was that I saw you with earlier? That woman you were with."

It's like I've let off a gunshot or something. Mum and Dad are both paralyzed. I can see their eyes darting toward each other, then looking away again. They both look totally panic-stricken.

"Woman?" says Mum at last. "I didn't . . ." She looks at Dad. "Did you see a woman, Graham?"

"Maybe Becky means . . . that passerby," he says in a stilted tone.

"That's right!" exclaims Mum in her theatrical voice again. "There was a woman just passing by on the street. A stranger. That must have been it, love."

"Right. Of course."

I try to smile, but inside I feel a bit sick. Are Mum and Dad *lying* to me?

"Well . . . you go off to your lunch party!" I say. "Have a great time!"

As the front door slams I feel like bursting into tears. I was *so* looking forward to today. But now I almost wish we'd never come back. No one seems particularly excited to see us. My rare, exotic treasure isn't exotic *or* rare. And why are Mum and Dad being so weird?

"Do you want another cup of coffee?" asks Luke.

"No, thanks." I scuff my foot on the kitchen floor.

"Are you OK, Becky?"

"No," I admit in a small voice. "Not really. Coming home isn't like I thought it would be."

"Come here." Luke holds out his arms and I nestle into his chest. "What were you expecting? That they would drop everything and throw a party?"

"No! Of course not!" I look up and meet Luke's eye. "Well . . . maybe. Kind of. We've been away all this time and it's like . . . we just popped out to the shops!"

"It was always going to be a gamble, surprising everyone," he says reasonably. "They weren't expecting us for another two months. It's no wonder they're a bit thrown."

"I know. But it's not just that." I take a deep breath. "Luke—do you think Mum and Dad are . . . hiding something?"

"Yes," says Luke.

"*Yes?*"

I'm gobsmacked. I was expecting him to say, "Becky, you're imagining things," like he usually does.

"There's certainly something going on." Luke pauses. "And I think I know what it might be."

"What?" I stare at him, agog.

"That woman who was with them. The one they wouldn't tell us about? I reckon she's an estate agent. I think they're considering moving."

"Moving?" I echo in dismay. "Why would they do that? This is a lovely house! It's perfect!"

"It is a bit big for them now that you've gone. . . ."

"But why on earth wouldn't they tell me?" My voice rises in distress. "I'm their daughter! I'm their only child! They should confide in me!"

"Maybe they thought you might get upset." Luke suggests.

"I wouldn't get upset!" I exclaim indignantly.

Abruptly I realize I *am* upset.

"Well, OK, maybe I would. But still, I can't believe they'd keep it a secret!"

I break away from Luke's arms and walk over to the window. I can't bear the idea of Mum and Dad selling this place. My eyes sweep over the garden in sudden nostalgia. They *can't* leave this garden. They just *can't*. This is where I learned to walk. This is where Luke and I got *married*.

Suddenly my attention is caught by the sight of Tom Webster in the garden next door. He's dressed in jeans and a T-shirt that says MY WIFE LEFT ME AND ALL I GOT WAS THIS LOUSY T-SHIRT and is struggling to carry the hugest plank of wood I've ever seen.

Blimey. He looks quite ferocious.

"It may not be that," Luke is saying behind me. "I may be wrong."

"You're not wrong." I turn round miserably. "It has to be that. What else could it be?"

"Well . . . don't think about it. Come on. It's the christening tomorrow. You'll see Suze!"

"Yes." I feel my spirits rise. "That's true."

Luke's right. Maybe today hasn't gone quite according to plan—but tomorrow will be fantastic. I'll be reunited with Suze again, my best, most closest friend in the whole entire world. I just can't *wait*.

Five

THE TWINS' CHRISTENING is being held at Suze's parents' house in Hampshire, because they've been living there while the east wing of Tarquin's Scottish castle is being rebuilt. They would have used his house in Pembrokeshire, but at the moment it's being lived in by some distant cousins. And his house in Sussex is being used as a location for a Jane Austen film.

This is what Suze's family is like. Nobody has just one house.

As we drive down the familiar tree-lined avenue I'm jumping with excitement. The stone house looks as huge and grand as ever with its pillared entrance, although some of the ivy has been pruned away from the front. Two stone griffins stand like sentries by the front door, and there are flower garlands around their heads, just like there were on Suze's wedding day.

"Hurry up!" I say as Luke maneuvers the car into a parking space. He hasn't even turned off the engine before I'm leaping out of the car and sprinting over the gravel toward the house. Now that I'm here, I just can't wait to see Suze!

The heavy front door is ajar and I push it open. Inside, the huge flagstone hall is decorated with the most amazing arrangements of lilies. A pair of waiters are striding through with champagne glasses on a tray. And on the ancient chair by the fireplace is a discarded saddle. Nothing's changed here, then.

The waiters disappear down a corridor, and I'm left alone. Walking over the flagstones, I suddenly feel a bit nervous. What if Suze has gone all weird, like my parents?

And then I spot her through an open door, standing in the drawing room. Her blond hair is up in a chignon and she's wearing a gorgeous print wrap dress. And in her arms is a tiny baby dressed in a long christening robe. Wow. That must be one of the twins.

Tarquin is standing nearby holding a second baby, which is also in a christening robe. And although he's wearing the most ancient suit in the world, he's actually looking pretty good! Not quite as . . . stoaty. It occurs to me that maybe Tarquin will get better looking the older he gets. When he's fifty he'll probably be a sex god!

A blond-haired toddler is clutching his leg and, as I watch, Tarquin gently prizes his fingers off.

"Ernie," he says patiently.

Ernie? I feel an almighty shock. My godson, Ernest? But last time I saw him he was a tiny little baby.

"Wilfie looks like a girl!" Suze is saying to Tarquin, her brow crumpled in that familiar way. "And Clementine looks like a boy!"

"My sweet, they both look exactly like babies in christening robes," says Tarquin.

"What if they're both gay?" Suze is looking anxiously

at Tarquin. "What if their hormones got mixed up when they were in the womb?"

"They're fine!"

I feel ridiculously shy, hovering by the door. I don't want to interrupt. They look like a family. They *are* a family.

"What's the time?" Suze tries to consult her watch, but Ernie is now clinging to her arm, trying to jump up. "Ernie, sweetheart, I need to do my lipstick! Leave Mummy's arm alone. . . . Can you take him for a sec, Tarkie?"

"Let me just put Clemmie down somewhere. . . ." Tarquin starts looking around the room as though a cot might magically spring up out of nowhere.

"I'll take her if you like," I say, my voice catching in my throat.

Suze whips round.

"Bex?" Her eyes widen to the size of dinner plates. *"Bex?"*

"We're back!" I try to sound cool. "Surprise!"

"Oh my God! Oh my *God*!"

Suze thrusts the baby at Tarquin, who manfully does a kind of juggling act with the two of them. She races toward me and throws her arms around my neck.

"Bex! Mrs. Brandon!"

"Mrs. Cleath-Stuart!" I return, feeling tears prick at my eyes. I knew Suze wouldn't have changed. I *knew* it.

"I can't believe you're back!" Suze's face is glowing. "Tell me all about your honeymoon! Tell me every single thing you—" She breaks off suddenly, staring at my bag. "Oh my God," she breathes. "Is that a *real* Angel bag?"

Ha! You see? People who know, know.

"Of course it is." I swing it nonchalantly on my arm. "Just a little souvenir from Milan. Er . . . I wouldn't mention it in front of Luke, though," I add, lowering my voice. "He doesn't exactly know about it."

"Bex!" says Suze half reprovingly, half laughing. "He's your husband!"

"Exactly." I meet her eye, and we both start giggling.

God, it's like I never left.

"So, how's married life?" asks Suze.

"It's perfect." I sigh happily. "Totally blissful. Well, you know. Like couples are on their honeymoon!"

"I was pregnant on our honeymoon." Suze looks a bit discomfited. She reaches out and strokes the Angel bag in awe. "I didn't even know you were going to Milan! Where else did you go?"

"We went everywhere! All over the world!"

"Did you go to the ancient shrine of Mahakala?" A booming voice comes from the doorway. I swivel round to see Suze's mother, Caroline, coming into the room. She's dressed in the strangest dress I've ever seen, made out of what looks like pea green canvas, accessorized with maroon tights and clumpy suede boots.

I have never seen Caroline in a normal outfit, ever.

"Yes!" I say in delight. "We did!"

It was Caroline who got me into the idea of traveling in the first place, when she told me her best friend in the world was a Bolivian peasant.

"The ancient Incan city of Ollantaytambo?"

"We stayed there!"

Caroline's eyes gleam as though I've passed the test, and I feel a glow of pride. I am a genuine traveler! I won't add that we were in the five-star spa.

"Now, where's my hat?" She frowns, looking around. "I've mislaid it."

"The African headdress one?" says Suze, flushing. "Er . . . I don't know!"

I give her a piercing look. She's hidden her mum's hat, I know it.

"*Caroline!*" Suze's father's voice comes resounding through the air, and the next moment he's coming into the hall, dressed in a paisley silk dressing gown over a pair of pin-striped trousers. His hair is white and bushy, and his nose has become a lot redder in the year since I last saw him. In fact, it's practically purple.

"Hello, Sir Gilbert," I begin politely. "How are you—"

"Caroline!" he repeats, totally ignoring me. "Fella says we could have a lion in the front paddock. He'll ship it over, do all the paperwork. What about it?" Sir Gilbert's bright blue eyes flash with excitement. "That'd add a bit of spice to life, eh?" He gives a sudden lionlike roar, and I jump.

"A *lion?*" Suze says in horror. "Daddy, you can't have a lion here! It'll eat the babies!"

"Gilbert, the lion belongs in the wild." Caroline looks thunderous. "Free to roam its natural world. Anyone who has crossed the Serengeti Plain and seen a pride feeding at dawn . . ."

"Why does your dad want a lion?" I murmur to Suze as Caroline continues.

"He wants to start a zoo and open it to the public," Suze mutters back. "It's one of his mad schemes. Like the tortoises, remember?"

About four years ago, when Suze and I were sharing a flat in London, her father decided to become a tortoise breeder, and it was *us* who had to take a delivery of twenty baby tortoises and look after them all weekend.

"The noble animal looked at me," Caroline is declaiming momentously, "and a deep understanding seemed to pass between us. . . ."

"You can look at my lion if you like," says Sir Gilbert. "In its cage." He bellows with laughter. "Eh?"

He looks so pleased with himself, and Caroline looks so disapproving, I can't help a giggle. I just love Suze's family. God, it's good to be back.

"Maybe I'll go over to the church," I say, glancing at my watch. "I'll see you later . . ."

"That reminds me!" Caroline breaks off. "I saw the vicar and he was saying some rubbish about warm water for the baptism. I said absolutely not! A bit of cold water'll do these infants the power of good."

"Mummy!" wails Suze. "I especially *asked* for warm water! They're still so tiny!"

"Nonsense!" booms Caroline. "At their age, you were swimming in the lake! At the age of six months you were trekking with me up the Tsodilo Hills of Botswana. No warm water there!"

Suze gives me a despairing look, and I grin back sympathetically.

"I'd better go," she says. "Bex, I'll see you afterwards. You will stay a couple of days, won't you?"

"We'd love to!" I say happily.

"Oh, and you *must* meet Lulu!" she adds, halfway out the door.

"Who's Lulu?" I call back, but she doesn't hear.

Oh, well. I'll soon find out. It's probably her new horse, or something.

I find Luke outside, where a tented walkway has been set up between the house and the church, just like at Suze's wedding. As we start walking along the matting, I can't help feeling a tingle of nostalgia. It was here that we first talked about getting married, in a roundabout sort of way. And then Luke proposed.

And now here we are. Married for nearly a year!

I hear footsteps coming up behind and look round to see Tarquin hurrying along the matting, holding a baby.

"Hi, Tarkie!" I say as he joins us. "So . . . which twin is this?"

"This one is Clementine," says Tarquin, beaming. "Our little Clemmie."

I peer more closely, and try to hide my surprise. Blimey. Suze is right. She does look like a boy.

"She's beautiful!" I say quickly. "Absolutely gorgeous!"

I'm trying to think of something to say which will emphasize her very *feminine* qualities, when there's a faint sound from up above. A kind of *chopper-chopper-chopper*. Now it's getting louder. I look up, and to my astonishment, a huge black helicopter is approaching. In fact . . . it's landing, on the field behind the house.

"Do you have a friend with a helicopter?" I say, amazed.

"Um . . . actually, that's mine," says Tarquin bashfully. "Lent it to a friend for a spin."

Tarquin has a *helicopter*?

"Bought it last year," he explains. "*The Ring* was on at Covent Garden, right in the middle of lambing season. Huge dilemma. I didn't want to miss either."

"Er . . . absolutely!" I nod, as if I really can sympathize.

Which, in a way, I can. If I was given the choice of watching sheep give birth in freezing-cold fields or listening to an endless Wagner opera . . . I'd buy a helicopter too. To escape.

By now we've arrived at the church, which is bustling with guests. Luke and I slip into a pew near the back, and I look around at all Suze's relations. There's Tarquin's dad, wearing an aubergine-colored smoking jacket, and there's Fenella, Tarquin's sister. She's dressed in cream and is shrieking excitedly at some girl with blond hair I don't recognize.

"Who's that, Agnes?" comes a piercing voice behind me. I glance round, and a woman with gray hair and a gigantic ruby brooch is peering at the blond girl too, through a lorgnette.

"That's Fenella, dear!" says the woman in blue sitting next to her.

"I don't mean Fenella! I mean the other girl, talking to her."

"D'you mean Lulu? That's Lulu Hetherington."

I raise my head in surprise. So. Lulu isn't a horse. She's a girl.

Actually, she does look quite like a horse. She's very thin and rangy, like Suze, and wearing a pink tweed suit. She laughs at something Fenella says—and she's got one of those smiles which show all her teeth and gums.

"She's a godmother," Agnes is saying. "*Super* girl. She's Susan's best friend!"

What?

I look up, taken aback. That's ridiculous. *I'm* Suze's best friend. Everyone knows that.

"Lulu moved into the village six months ago and they've become quite inseparable!" Agnes continues. "We see them out riding together every day. She's so like dear Susan. Just look at the two of them together!"

Suze has appeared at the front of the church, holding Wilfrid. I suppose there is a superficial likeness between her and Lulu. They're both tall and blond. They've both got their hair in the same chignon. Suze is talking to Lulu, her face shining with animation, and as I watch, they both burst into peals of laughter.

"And of course they have so much in common!" Agnes's voice cuts through the air behind me. "What with the horses and the children . . . they're *wonderful* support for each other."

"Every girl needs a best friend," says the other woman wisely.

She breaks off as the organ starts playing. The congregation stands up and I reach for my service sheet along with everyone else. But I can't read a word. I'm too jumbled up inside.

After the service is over, we all head back to the house, where a string quartet is playing in the hall and waiters are circulating with drinks. Luke is immediately accosted by some friend of Tarquin's who knows him through business, and I stand for a while on my own, brooding on what I heard in the church.

"Bex!" I wheel round in relief as I hear Suze's voice behind me.

"Suze!" I beam at her. "That was great!"

Just seeing Suze's friendly face sweeps all my worries away. *Of course* we're still best friends!

I have to remember that I've been away for a long time, so Suze had to make friends with people locally or whatever. But the point is, I'm back now!

"Suze, let's go shopping tomorrow!" I say impulsively. "We can go up to London . . . I'll help you with the babies . . ."

"Bex, I can't." Her brow wrinkles. "I promised Lulu I'd go riding tomorrow morning."

For a moment I don't know what to say. Couldn't she cancel riding? She always rides, and I've only just come home.

"Oh, right." I try to smile. "Well . . . no problem. We'll do it another time!"

The baby in Suze's arms has started to wail lustily and she pulls a face.

"I've got to go and feed them now. But then I *must* introduce you to Lulu. You two will love each other!"

"I'm sure we will!" I say, trying to sound enthusiastic. "See you later!"

I watch as Suze disappears into the library.

"Champagne, madam?" says a waiter behind me.

"Oh, right. Thanks."

I take a glass of champagne off the tray. Then, with a sudden thought, I take another. I head for the library door and am about to reach for the handle, when Lulu comes out, closing the door behind her.

"Oh, hello!" she says in a posh, clipped voice. "Suze is feeding in there, actually."

"I know." I smile. "I'm her friend Becky. I've brought her some champagne."

Lulu smiles back—but her hand doesn't move off the door handle.

"I think she'd probably like some privacy," she says pleasantly.

For a moment I'm too astounded to reply.

Privacy? From *me*?

I was with Suze when she gave birth to Ernie! I feel like retorting. I've seen more of her than you *ever* will!

But no. I'm not going to get into scoring points with this person. Come on. Make an effort.

"So you must be Lulu," I say as warmly as I can, and hold out my hand. "I'm Becky."

"You're Becky. Yes, I've heard about you."

Why does she look amused? What has Suze said?

"And you're Clementine's godmother!" I say heartily. "That's . . . lovely!"

I'm trying as hard as I can to make a connection. But there's just something about her that makes me shrink away. Her lips are a bit too thin. Her eyes are a bit too cold.

"Cosmo!" she suddenly barks. I follow her gaze and see a toddler blundering into the string quartet. "Come away, darling!"

"Cosmo! Great name," I say, trying to be friendly. "Like, after the magazine?"

"The *magazine*?" She stares at me as though I'm a total imbecile. "Actually, it comes from the ancient Greek word *kosmos*. Meaning 'perfect order.' "

I feel prickles of embarrassment and resentment. How was I supposed to know that?

Anyway, *she's* the stupid one, because how many people have heard of *Cosmo* magazine? About a million. And how many have heard of some old Greek word? About three. Exactly.

"Do you have children?" she says with polite interest.

"Er . . . no."

"Do you keep horses?"

"Er . . . no."

There's silence. Lulu seems to have run out of questions. I guess it's my turn.

"So . . . how many children do you have?"

"Four," she replies. "Cosmo, Ludo, Ivo, and Clarissa. Two, three, five, and eight."

"Wow. That must keep you busy."

"Oh, it's a different world when you have children," she says smugly. "Everything changes. You can't imagine."

"I probably can," I say with a laugh. "I helped out Suze when Ernie was newborn. So I know what it's like—"

"No." She gives me a patronizing smile. "Until you've actually been a mother you have no idea. None at all."

"Right," I say, feeling squashed.

How can Suze be friendly with this woman? How?

Suddenly there's a rattling at the library door and Suze appears. She's holding a baby in one arm and her mobile in the other and is a picture of consternation.

"Hi, Suze!" I say quickly. "I was just bringing you a glass of champagne!" I hold it out to her, but Suze doesn't seem to notice.

"Lulu, Wilfie's got a rash!" she says anxiously. "Have yours ever had this?"

"Let's have a look," says Lulu, expertly taking the baby out of Suze's grasp. She examines him for a moment. "I think it's heat rash."

"Really?"

"It looks like nettle rash to me," I say, trying to join in. "Has he been near any nettles recently?"

No one seems interested in what I think.

"You want Sudocrem," says Lulu. "I'll get some for you, if you like. I'm popping to the chemist's later on."

"Thanks, Lulu. You're an angel!" Suze takes Wilfie back gratefully, just as her mobile rings.

"Hi!" she says into it. "At last! Where are you?" As she listens, her whole face crumples in dismay. "You're joking!"

"What's wrong?" Lulu and I say simultaneously.

"It's Mr. Happy!" wails Suze, turning to Lulu. "He's got a flat tire! He's by Tiddlington Marsh."

"Who's Mr. Happy?" I say in bewilderment.

"The entertainer!" says Suze desperately. "There's a whole roomful of children in there, just waiting for him!" She gestures to a pair of double doors, beyond which I can see lots of children in party dresses and smart little shirts, racing about and throwing cushions at each other.

"I'll zip along and pick him up," Lulu says, putting down her glass. "At least we know where he is. I'll only be ten minutes. Tell him to stay put and look out for the Range Rover."

"Lulu, you're a total star," says Suze, subsiding in relief. "I don't know what I'd do without you."

Jealousy burns through me. I want to be the one who helps Suze.

"I don't mind picking him up!" I say. "I'll go!"

"You don't know where it is," Lulu says kindly. "Better if I go."

"What about the children?" Suze glances nervously toward the room, where the sound of screaming kids is getting louder.

"They'll just have to wait. If there isn't an entertainer, there isn't an entertainer."

"But—"

"I'll entertain them!" I say, before I can stop myself.

"*You?*" They both turn and gape at me.

"Yes, me," I say confidently.

Ha. I'll show them who's the most supportive friend to Suze.

"Bex . . . are you sure about this?" Suze says, looking anxious.

"No problem!" I say.

"But—"

"Suze . . ." I put a hand on her arm. "Please. I think I can amuse a few children for ten minutes."

Oh my God.

This is utter mayhem.

I can't hear myself think. I can't hear anything except the screaming of twenty excited children running round a room, bashing each other.

"Er . . . excuse me . . ." I begin.

The shrieks increase in volume. I'm sure someone's

being murdered in here, only I can't see who because it's all a blur.

"Sit down!" I bellow over the noise. "Sit down, everyone!"

They're not even stopping for a beat. I climb up onto a chair and put my hands round my mouth.

"Anyone who sits down . . ." I roar. "Will get a *sweetie*!"

Abruptly the screaming stops and there's a crash as twenty children bump down onto the floor.

"Hello, everybody!" I say brightly. "I'm . . . I'm Wacky Becky!" I waggle my head. "Everybody say . . . 'Hello, Wacky Becky!' "

There's silence.

"Where's my sweetie?" pipes up a little girl.

"Er . . ."

I scrabble in my bag, but there's nothing except some herbal sleeping tablets I bought for getting over jet lag. Orange flavored.

Could I—

No. No.

"Later!" I say. "You have to sit still . . . and then you get a sweetie."

"This conjurer is *rubbish*," says a boy in a Ralph Lauren shirt.

"I'm not rubbish!" I say indignantly. "Watch! Er . . ."

I quickly put my hands over my face, then pull them away. "Boo!"

"We're not babies," the boy says scornfully. "We want tricks!"

"Why don't I sing you a nice song," I say in soothing tones. "Row, row, row the boat . . . la la la . . . the moat . . ."

"Do a trick!" squeals a little girl.

"We want a trick!" yells a boy.

"Do-a-trick! Do-a-trick!"

Oh God. They're chanting. And the boys are banging the floor with their fists. Any minute, they're going to get up and start bashing each other again. A trick. A trick. My mind scurries about frantically. Do I *know* any tricks?

"OK!" I say in desperation. "I'll do a trick! Watch this!"

I spread my arms with a flourish, then reach behind my back with swirly, elaborate movements, spinning it all out as long as I can.

Then I unhook my bra through my shirt, trying to remember what color it is.

Oh yes. It's my bright pink gingham one with the bows. Perfect.

The entire room is agog.

"What are you doing?" says a little girl with wide eyes.

"Wait and see!"

Trying to keep the air of mystery, I loop one bra strap discreetly over my arm, then the other. The children are all staring at me avidly.

Now I've got my confidence back, I think I'm doing rather well at this. In fact, I'm a bit of a natural!

"Watch very carefully," I say in a solemn, magician-like voice, "as I am now going to make something . . . *appear!*"

A couple of children gasp.

I really could do with a drumroll here.

"One . . . two . . . three . . ." In a flash of pink I pull my bra out from my sleeve and hold it aloft. "Ta-daah!"

The whole room erupts in ecstatic cheers.

"She did magic!" a red-haired boy shouts.

"Again!" squeals a little girl. "Do it again!"

"Do you want to see me do it again?" I say, beaming in delight.

"Yaaaaay!" they all scream.

"I don't *think* so!" comes a bright, clipped voice from the door. I turn round—and Lulu is standing there, looking at me with undisguised horror.

Oh no.

Oh God. My bra is still whirling round in my hand.

"They wanted me to do a trick," I explain, attempting a nonchalant shrug.

"I hardly think those are the sort of 'tricks' that children are going to appreciate!" she says, raising her eyebrows. She turns to the room with a bright, mummyish smile. "Who wants to see Mr. Happy?"

"We want Wacky Becky!" yells a boy. "She took off her bra!"

Fuck.

"Wacky Becky's got to . . . er . . . go now!" I say brightly. "But see you next time, children!"

Without quite meeting Lulu's eye I squash my bra into a tiny ball, stuff it into my bag, and back out of the room. I head over to the buffet table, where Luke is helping himself to salmon.

"Are you OK?" he says in surprise. "You're very pink."

"I'm . . . fine." I grab his glass and take a deep gulp of champagne. "Everything's fine."

But it's not really fine.

I keep waiting for Lulu to leave, so I can have a good chat with Suze—but she doesn't. She hangs around, helping to make the children's tea and clear up. Every time I try to help, she's there before me with a damp cloth or a beaker or some piece of mummy advice. She and Suze keep up a constant dialogue about the children, and it's impossible for me to get a word in.

It's not until about ten o'clock at night that she leaves,

and I finally find myself alone in the kitchen with Suze. She's sitting by the huge Aga stove, feeding one of the twins and yawning hugely every three minutes.

"So, you had a lovely honeymoon?" she says wistfully.

"It was fantastic. Totally perfect. We went to this amazing place in Australia where you could scuba dive, and—"

I break off as Suze yawns again. Maybe I'll tell her tomorrow.

"How about you? How's life with three kids?"

"Oh, you know." She gives a tired smile. "It's fine. Exhausting. Everything's different."

"And . . . you've been spending loads of time with Lulu," I say casually.

"Isn't she great?" says Suze, her face lighting up.

"Er . . . great." I pause carefully. "She does seem a *teeny* bit bossy. . . ."

"*Bossy?*" Suze looks up in shock. "Bex, how can you say that? She's been my total savior out here! She's helped me so much!"

"Oh, right." I backtrack hastily. "I didn't mean—"

"She knows exactly what I'm going through." Suze sighs. "I mean, she's had four! She really *understands*."

"Right."

And I don't understand. That's what she means.

As I stare into my glass of wine, there's a sudden heaviness about my head. None of my reunions are going quite like I thought they would.

I stand up and wander over to the Aga, where lots of family photos are always pinned up on the cork wall. There's a picture of me and Suze dressed up for a party in feather boas and glittery makeup. And one of Suze and me in hospital with a tiny Ernie.

Then, with a pang, I notice a brand-new picture of

Suze and Lulu, sitting on their horses, in matching riding jackets and hairnets. They're beaming at the camera and look just like identical twins.

And as I gaze at it, I feel a sudden determination growing. I'm not losing my best friend to some bossy, horse-faced riding queen. Whatever Lulu can do, I can do.

"Maybe I'll come riding with you and Lulu tomorrow," I say casually. "If you've got a spare horse."

I'll even wear a hairnet, if that's what it takes.

"You'll come?" Suze looks up, staggered. "But . . . Bex. You don't ride."

"Yes, I do," I say airily. "Luke and I did some riding on our honeymoon, actually."

Which is . . . sort of true. Nearly. We were going to go on a camel ride in Dubai, except in the end we went snorkeling instead.

But anyway, it doesn't matter. I'll just hold on tight . . . and it'll be fine!

Six

By TEN O'CLOCK the next morning I'm ready. And I don't want to boast, but as I survey myself in the mirror, I look utterly fab! I went to the riding shop in the next village first thing in the morning, and totally kitted myself out. I'm wearing snowy white jodhpurs, a tailored black riding jacket, shiny boots, and a beautiful new velvet riding hat.

Proudly I reach for my pièce de résistance—a big red rosette with shiny ribbons. There were loads of them for sale, so I bought one in every color! I carefully pin it onto my collar like a corsage, smooth down my jacket, and look at the effect.

God, I look so cool. I look like I'm going to win at Crufts.

No. I don't mean Crufts, that's the dog show. I mean the other one. The horse one.

I can start riding every day in Hyde Park, I think in a sudden burst of excitement. I'll practice hard and get really good! Then I can come down here every weekend and ride with Suze. While I was in the shop I even filled out a form for a riding competition next month, as a little incentive.

"Tallyho!" says Luke, coming into the bedroom. "You look very dashing. Very sexy." He raises his eyebrows. "Great boots. How long are you going to be?"

"Not that long," I say knowledgeably. "We're just going to go for a hack through the woods."

"Becky . . ." Luke looks at me carefully. "Have you ever been on a horse in your life?"

"Yes! Of course I have!"

Once. When I was ten. And I fell off. But I probably wasn't concentrating or something.

"Just be careful, won't you?" he says. "I'm not quite ready to become a widower."

"I'll be fine!" I say, glancing at my special new "equestrian" watch with compass built in. "I'd better go!"

The horses are all kept some way from the house in a stable block, and as I approach I can hear the sounds of whinnying and hooves clattering in the stable yard.

"Hi!" says Lulu, appearing round the corner in a pair of ancient jodhpurs and a fleece jacket. "All set—" She breaks off as she sees me. "Oh my God." She snorts with laughter. "Suze, come and look at Becky!"

"What is it?" Suze hurries round the corner and stops dead.

"Gosh, Bex," she says. "You're very . . . smart!"

I take in Suze's filthy old jodhpurs, her muddy boots, and her battered riding hat. As I look down at my own shiny gear I suddenly feel mortified. How could I have been so stupid?

But I'm not going to act embarrassed in front of Lulu. Chin up.

"I wanted to make an effort!" I say, trying to sound light and matter-of-fact.

"What's that?" Lulu is looking incredulously at my rosette.

"It's a corsage. They were selling them in the riding shop," I add pointedly.

"For the horses," Suze says gently. "Bex, they go on the horses."

"Oh."

For a moment I'm a bit discomfited. But then . . . why shouldn't people wear them too?

"Here we are!" Albert, who runs the horses at Suze's parents' place, interrupts us. He's leading an enormous brown horse along by the reins. "We're putting you on Ginger today. He's pretty good-natured, aren't you, boy?"

I freeze in horror. This? He's expecting me to get on this monster? I was envisioning some nice little pony.

Albert hands me the reins and I take them automatically, trying not to panic. The horse takes a step forward with an enormous, heavy hoof, and I give a frightened jump out of the way. What if it steps on my foot?

"Aren't you going to mount?" asks Lulu, swinging herself up into the saddle of a horse which is, if anything, bigger than mine.

"Of course!" I say with a nonchalant laugh.

How? How am I supposed to get up there?

"Want a leg up?" says Tarquin, who has been talking to Albert a few yards away. He comes up behind me, and before I know it, he's hefted me right up into the saddle.

Oh my God.

I'm so *high*. When I look down, I feel dizzy. Suddenly Ginger takes a step sideways, and I try not to gasp in fright.

"Shall we go?" calls Suze, who is on her old black horse, Pepper, and with a clip-clop she's off through the gate, into the field. Lulu makes a clicking sound with her tongue, swings her horse round, and follows.

Right. My turn. Go.

Go on, horse. *Move.*

I have no idea what to do next. Do I kick it? Experimentally I pull on one of the reins, but nothing happens.

"Gee-up," I mutter under my breath. "Gee-up, Ginger!"

Suddenly, as though he's noticed that his friends have gone, he starts walking forward. And it's . . . OK. It's fine. It's just a bit more . . . *bumpy* than I'd imagined. I look ahead at Lulu, and she's totally comfortable. In fact, she's got her reins gathered up in one hand.

"Close the gate!" she yells to me.

Close the gate? I think in panic. *How am I supposed to close the gate?*

"I'll do it," Tarquin calls. "Have a good time!"

"OK!" I call back gaily.

Right. As long as we just keep ambling along, I'll be OK. In fact, this could almost be fun. The sun's shining, the breeze is ruffling the grass, and the horses are all lovely and shiny. Some people are walking along the side of the field on a footpath, and as we pass by I give them a nonchalant "Don't I look great on my horse?" nod and twirl my riding crop. And they look really impressed!

Maybe I've found my natural talent. Maybe Luke and I should buy some horses and a few acres of land. We could do field events and show jumping, like Suze—

Shit. What's going on? All of a sudden, Ginger has started jolting up and down.

OK. Don't panic. This must be trotting.

I look at Suze and Lulu, and they're both rising up and falling in time with their horses. I try to copy them, but all that happens is I crash painfully back onto the saddle. Ouch. God, saddles are hard. Why don't they make them padded? If I were a horse saddle designer I'd make them really soft and comfy, with furry cushions and drinks holders, maybe, and—

"Shall we canter?" Suze calls over her shoulder. Before I can reply she's kicked her horse, and it's zooming away like National Velvet, closely followed by Lulu.

"We don't have to canter, Ginger," I say quickly to the horse. "We can just—"

Oh my Goooooood. He's taken off after the others.

Fuck. Oh fuck. I am going to fall off. I know I am. My whole body is rigid. I'm clenching the saddle so hard it's hurting my hands.

"Are you OK, Bex?" shouts Suze.

"Fine!" I call back, but I just want this to stop. The wind is streaming past my face. I feel ill with terror.

I'm going to die. My life is over. The only plus I can think of is it'll sound really cool when they report it in the papers.

A KEEN HORSEWOMAN, REBECCA BRANDON (NÉE BLOOMWOOD) DIED WHILE OUT CANTERING WITH HER FRIENDS.

Oh God. I think he's slowing down. At last. We're trotting . . . we're kind of jogging . . . we're finally coming to a halt.

Somehow I manage to unclench my hands.

"Isn't it lovely?" says Suze, turning round on Pepper. Her blond hair is streaming out from under her hat and her cheeks are flushed pink. "Shall we have a really good gallop?"

Gallop?

You have to be kidding. If Ginger takes one more step, I'll throw up.

"Can you jump yet, Bex?" she asks. "There's just a couple of little ones coming up. But you should be able to manage them," she says encouragingly. "You're really good!"

For a moment I can't speak.

"I just need to . . . er . . . adjust my stirrup," I manage at last. "You two go on."

I wait until the two of them are out of sight before I slither to the ground. My legs are all shaky and I feel nauseous. I am never leaving solid ground again. Never. Why on earth would people do this for fun?

I sink down onto the grass and take off my new riding hat—which, to be honest, has been hurting my ears since I put it on. Suze and Lulu are probably miles away by now. Galloping along and talking about nappies.

"Come on," I say to Ginger. "Let's walk back." I stand up and cautiously pull the reins—and to my astonishment he obediently follows.

This is more like it.

As I walk across the grass, I start to relax a bit. A horse is actually a pretty cool accessory. Who says you need to get on it? I could still go to Hyde Park every day. I could buy a really pretty horse and just lead it around like a dog. And if any passersby asked, "Why aren't you riding?" I'd just give them a knowing smile and say, "We're resting today."

We wander along for a while and at last come to an empty road. I stand for a moment, looking from left to right. In one direction, the road disappears up a hill and round a corner. In the other, I can see what seems to be quite a sweet little village, all beamed houses, and a patch of grass, and . . .

Ooh. Are those . . . shops?

Half an hour later I feel a lot better.

I've bought some gorgeous cheese with walnuts in it,

and some gooseberry preserve, and some huge radishes, which Luke will love. And best of all, I found this amazing little shop that sells hats. Right here in this village! Apparently, the milliner is local and is practically the next Philip Treacy. I mean, not that I wear hats that often . . . but I'm bound to be invited to a wedding soon, or Ascot or something. And the prices were fantastic. So I bought a white one decorated with ostrich feathers and a black velvet one all covered in jewels. They're a bit cumbersome in their hatboxes, but they were *so* worth it.

Ginger whinnies as I approach the lamppost where I tied him up, and stamps his foot on the ground.

"Don't worry!" I say. "I haven't left you out." I bought him a bagful of Chelsea buns and some "extra sheen" shampoo for his mane. I reach in the bag and feed him one of the Chelsea buns, trying not to shudder as he slobbers on my hand.

The only slight problem now is . . . where am I going to put all my shopping? I can't very easily hold all these carrier bags and lead Ginger along the road. Should I try to mount him *carrying* my shopping? What did people do in the olden days?

Then suddenly I notice a big buckle on one of Ginger's saddle straps. I could easily hang a bag off that. I pick up one of the paper carriers and loop it over the buckle—and it hangs there perfectly! And now that I look properly, there are handy buckles all over Ginger's tack. Genius!

Happily I start hanging bags from every available hook, strap, and buckle on Ginger's tack. This is great. I never realized a horse could hold so much shopping. Last of all I tie my two hatboxes onto the side. They are so gorgeous, all pink-and-white candy stripes.

I untie Ginger and start leading him out of the village, trying to stop the hatboxes bobbing up and down too much. A couple of people gawp as we go by, but that's OK. They're probably just not used to strangers in these parts.

We're just approaching the first bend when I hear a clattering sound ahead. The next moment, Suze and Lulu appear on their horses.

"There she is!" says Lulu, shading her eyes against the sun.

"Bex!" cries Suze. "We were worried! Are you OK?"

"I'm fine!" I call back. "We've been having a lovely time!"

As they come nearer I can see Suze and Lulu exchanging stunned glances.

"Bex . . . what have you done to Ginger?" says Suze, her eyes running over all the bags and boxes in disbelief.

"Nothing," I say. "He's fine. I just took him shopping. I got these two great hats!"

I wait for Suze to say "Let's see them!" but she looks totally gobsmacked.

"She took a horse . . . shopping," Lulu says slowly. She glances at me, then leans over and whispers something in Suze's ear.

Suddenly Suze gives a helpless snort and claps her hand to her mouth.

I feel my face flame.

She's laughing at me.

Somehow I never thought Suze would laugh at me.

As soon as we're back at the house, Lulu heads off home, and Suze has to rush in and feed the twins. I'm left in the stable yard with Albert, who is a total sweetie and helps me untie all my bags and packages from Ginger's tack.

I'm walking out when Luke approaches, in his Barbour and Wellingtons.

"So how was it?" he says cheerfully.

"It was . . . all right," I say, staring at the ground. I'm waiting for Luke to ask what's wrong, but he seems distracted.

"Becky, I've just had a call from Gary at the office," he says. "We need to get going on the Arcodas Group pitch. I'm really sorry, but I'm going to have to head back to town. But listen. Why don't you stay on here for a few days?" He smiles. "I know how desperate you were to see Suze."

And suddenly I feel a swell of emotion. He's right. I was desperate to see Suze and I'm bloody well going to. Who cares about stupid Lulu? I'm going to have a proper chat with my best friend, right now.

I hurry into the house to find her in the kitchen, feeding both the twins at once while Ernie fights for a place on her lap.

"Suze, listen," I say eagerly. "It's your birthday coming up. I want to treat you to something really special. Let's go to Milan! Just the two of us!"

"Milan?" She looks up, her face strained. "Ernie, stop it, sweetheart. Bex, I can't go to Milan! What about the babies?"

"They could come with us!"

"No, they *couldn't,*" says Suze, sounding almost sharp. "Bex, you just don't understand!"

I smart at her words. Why does everyone keep telling me I don't understand? How do they know?

"OK, then," I say, trying to stay cheerful. "Let's have a fab birthday lunch right here! I'll bring all the food, you won't have to do a thing. . . ."

"I can't," Suze says, without looking at me. "Actually I've . . . I've already made plans for my birthday. Lulu and I are going to a spa for the day. A special mother and baby day. She's treating me."

I can't hide my shock. Suze and I always spend our birthdays together.

"Right." I focus on the back of the door, where an ancient tweed jacket, about six dog leads, and what seems to be a dead pheasant are hanging. "Well . . . have fun. Enjoy it!"

There's silence in the kitchen. I don't know what to say.

I've never not known what to say to Suze.

"Bex . . . you weren't here," Suze says suddenly, and I can hear the distress in her voice. "You weren't here. What was I supposed to do? Have no friends?"

"Of course not!" I say brightly. "Don't be silly!"

"I couldn't have survived without Lulu. She's been a real support to me out here."

"Of course she has." Tears are suddenly pricking at my eyes and I turn away, fiercely blinking them back. "Well . . . you have fun together. I'm sure you will."

"Bex, don't be like that. Look . . . I'll speak to Lulu about the spa. I'm sure we could find a third place."

She's taking pity on me. I can't bear it.

"No!" With an almighty effort I manage a laugh. "Really, it's no big deal. I probably wouldn't have time anyway. In fact . . . I came in to tell you we have to go back to London. Luke's got work engagements."

"Now?" Suze looks taken aback. "But I thought you were going to stay for a few days."

"We've got loads to do!" I lift my chin. "Everything's different for me, too, you know. I'm a married woman now! I've got to set up the flat . . . look after Luke . . . throw some dinner parties. . . ."

"Right." Suze hesitates. "Well, it's been lovely to see you, anyway."

"You too! It's been fun! We must . . . do it again."

We sound totally false. Both of us.

There's silence. My throat is tight. I'm going to cry.

No, I'm not.

"So . . . I'll just go and pack," I say at last. "Thanks for a lovely time."

I leave the room, pick up my shopping, and walk away. And my bright smile lasts all the way to the stairs.

NETHER PLEATON GYMKHANA

MANOR STABLES
PLEATON
HAMPSHIRE SO20 8 EX

Mrs Rebecca Brandon
37 Maida Vale Mansions
Maida Vale
London NW6 0YF

30 April 2003

Dear Mrs Brandon:

Thank you for your letter concerning the Nether
Pleaton Gymkhana next month. I confirm that I
have withdrawn your name from the following
classes:

     General Horsemanship
     Open Jumping
     Senior Dressage

Perhaps you could let me know if you still wish to
enter for "Best Kept Pony."

With kind regards,

Marjorie Davies
Organiser

Seven

ANYWAY. IT DOESN'T matter. People get married and they move on and their friends change. That's all. It's perfectly normal. Suze has her life . . . and I have my life. It's fine. A week has gone by since the christening—and she's barely crossed my mind.

I take a sip of orange juice, pick up the *Financial Times,* which Luke left on the breakfast counter, and begin flicking briskly through the pages.

Now that I'm married, I expect I'll make loads of new friends, too. It's not like I'm dependent on Suze or anything. I'll start an evening class or a book group or something. And *my* new friends will be really nice ones who don't ride horses and have children with stupid names like Cosmo. . . .

I take a sip of coffee and plaster some more chocolate spread on my toast. I'm sitting in the kitchen of Luke's flat in Maida Vale, having a late breakfast.

I mean . . . *our* flat in Maida Vale. I keep forgetting,

it's half mine now! Luke lived here for ages before we were married, but when we went to live in New York he had it all done up and rented it out. And it is the trendiest place in the world. All minimalist, with this amazing stainless-steel kitchen, pale beige carpets, and just the odd piece of modern art here and there.

I do like it. Of course I do.

Although, I suppose if I'm *totally* honest, it's a tad bare for my taste. Luke has quite a different style from mine when it comes to decorating. His approach is basically "no things anywhere," whereas mine is more "lots of things everywhere."

But it doesn't matter, because I read this article about couples in an interiors magazine, and it said fusing two different styles need not be a problem. Apparently, all we have to do is meld our individual ideas and do some mood boards together and create a signature look.

And today is the perfect day to start. Because any minute now, all our honeymoon purchases are going to be delivered from the storage company! Luke's stayed behind from work especially to help. It'll be quite a project, I expect. Which just shows: I'm so busy, I don't even have *time* for friends.

I'm feeling really excited about seeing all our souvenirs again! Arranging the little mementos of our honeymoon around the apartment. It'll really make a difference to this place, having a few personal objets here and there.

"The post's here," Luke says, coming into the kitchen. He's in his suit, since he'll be going into the office later, and his hair is trimmed all short and businesslike again. He had it cut almost as soon as we got back to London—because, as he said, Italy is one thing, but Britain is another.

I suppose he has a point. But I can't help feeling a bit

wistful every time I see his bare neck. That little un-
tanned patch of skin below his hairline is the only re-
minder of the way he was on our honeymoon.

"There's a letter for you," he adds, handing me an
envelope.

"Oh, right!" I take it from him, feeling nervous.

Ever since we got back to London, I've been approaching all the big department stores for a job as a personal
shopper. I've got a great reference from Barneys and
everyone's been really nice to me—but so far all I'm getting told is that there are no openings right now.

Which, to be honest, has been a bit of a blow. I
thought I'd be fighting off offers. I even had this little
fantasy where all the head personal shoppers at Harrods
and Harvey Nichols and Selfridges took me out to lunch
and gave me free clothes to persuade me to join them.

As calmly as I can, I pull the letter out of the envelope. This one is from a new shop called The Look,
which hasn't even opened yet. It's going to be a huge
new store just up from Oxford Street, full of great
clothes and accessories, and the gimmick is that there
will be loads of personal shoppers available to help you
pull your look together. They want someone to run and
train the team, and had already heard about me from
their contact in New York. I went to see them a couple
of days ago and I *thought* I did OK, but . . .

"Oh my God!" I look up in disbelief. "I got it! They
want me!"

"Fantastic!" Luke's face creases in a smile. "Congratulations!" He puts an arm round me and gives me a
kiss.

"Except . . . I won't be needed for three months," I
say, reading farther down. "That's when the store opens."
I put the letter down and look at him. "Three whole
months. That's quite a long time not to have a job."

Or any money, I'm thinking.

"I'm sure you'll find something to do," says Luke cheerfully. "Some project or other. You'll have plenty to keep you busy."

The buzzer suddenly goes in the hall and we look at each other.

"That must be the delivery people!" I say, feeling my spirits rise. "Let's go down!"

Luke's penthouse has its own lift right to the front door, which is just so cool!

"So, where shall we tell them to put everything?" he says as he presses the ground-floor button.

"I thought we could pile it all up in the corner of the sitting room," I suggest. "Behind the door. Then I can sort it out while you're at work."

Luke nods. "Good idea."

I suddenly remember the twenty Chinese silk dressing gowns. Maybe I'll be able to smuggle them in without Luke's seeing.

"And if there was any overspill," I add casually, "we could always put it in the second bedroom."

"Overspill?" Luke frowns. "Becky, how much stuff are you expecting?"

"Not that much!" I say quickly. "Hardly anything! I just meant if they've packed things in really huge boxes or something. That's all."

Luke looks a bit suspicious, and I turn away, pretending to be adjusting my watch strap. Now the moment's nearly here, I'm feeling just the odd tiny qualm.

I kind of wish I'd told him about the wooden giraffes. Should I quickly confess?

No. It doesn't matter. It'll be fine. Luke's flat is huge. I mean, it's vast! He'll never notice a few extra things.

We push open the double doors of Luke's building and walk out, to see a man in jeans, waiting on the side of the road by a small van.

"Mr. Brandon?" he says, looking up.

I feel a small whoosh of relief. I *knew* we hadn't bought that much stuff. I mean, just look at that van. It's tiny!

"Yes. That's me." Luke holds out his hand, with a pleasant smile.

"Any idea where we can park the lorries?" The man scratches his head. "Only we're in a no-parking zone round the corner."

"Lorries?" echoes Luke. "What do you mean, 'lorries'?"

His smile has kind of frozen on his face.

"We've got two lorries to unload. Can we take them into the parking bay there?" The man gestures at the forecourt of the building.

"Of course!" I say quickly, as Luke doesn't seem able to speak. "Go ahead!"

The man disappears. "So!" I say brightly. "This is fun!"

"Two . . . lorries?" says Luke.

"It must be a shared load!" I say quickly. "With someone else. I mean, *obviously* we haven't bought two lorry-loads of stuff."

Which is true.

I mean, it's ridiculous! In ten months, we couldn't possibly have—

I'm *sure* we couldn't have—

Oh God.

There's a rumbling from round the corner, and a big white lorry appears, closely followed by another. They back into the forecourt of Luke's building, and there are huge grinding noises as the backs are lowered. Luke and I hurry round and peer into the crowded depths.

What an amazing sight. Each whole lorry is crammed with objects and furniture. Some wrapped in plastic, some in paper, and some barely wrapped at all. As I feast my eyes on all the stuff, I start to feel quite emotional. It's like seeing a home video of our entire honeymoon. The kilims from Istanbul. The gourds from Peru. And I'd totally forgotten about buying that papoose carrier!

Some men in overalls start lifting things up and carrying them out. We stand aside to let them pass, but I'm still gazing around the inside of one of the lorries, lost in memories. I suddenly glimpse a bronze statue and turn round with a smile.

"The Buddha! Do you remember when we got that? Luke?"

Luke isn't listening to a word. I follow his gaze, and feel a slight flip of apprehension. He's staring in disbelief at a man carrying a huge paper-wrapped package out of the other lorry. A wooden giraffe's leg is poking out of it.

Shit.

And now here comes another man in overalls with the matching one.

"Becky . . . what are these giraffes doing here?" Luke says evenly. "I thought we agreed *not* to buy them."

"I know," I say hurriedly. "I know we did. But we would have regretted it. So I made an executive decision. Honestly, Luke, they'll look great! They'll be a focal point of the whole apartment!"

"And where did *those* come from?" Now Luke's looking at a pair of huge porcelain urns, which I got in Hong Kong.

"Oh, yes," I say quickly. "I was going to tell you about those. Guess what? They're copies of real Ming! The man said—"

"But what the fuck are they doing here?"

"I . . . bought them. They'll be perfect in the hall. They'll be a focal point! Everyone will admire them!"

"And that rug?" He points to a huge multicolored rolled-up sausage.

"It's called a 'dhurrie,' actually. . . ." My voice trails away at his expression. "I got it in India," I add feebly.

"Without consulting me."

"Er . . ."

I'm not sure I like Luke's expression.

"Ooh, look!" I exclaim, trying to distract him. "It's the spice rack you bought at that Kenyan market."

Luke totally ignores me. He's goggling at a huge, unwieldy contraption being unloaded from the first lorry. It looks like a combination of a xylophone and a set of hanging copper saucepans all in one.

"What the hell is *that*? Is that some kind of musical instrument?"

The gongs all start clanging loudly as the men unload it, and a couple of passersby nudge each other and giggle.

Even I'm having second thoughts about this one.

"Er . . . yes." I clear my throat. "Actually, that's an Indonesian gamelan."

There's a short silence.

"An Indonesian gamelan?" echoes Luke, his voice caught a bit in his throat.

"It's cultural!" I say defensively. "I thought we could learn to play it! And it'll be a great focal point—"

"Exactly how many focal points are we planning to have?" Luke looks beside himself. "Becky, is *all* this stuff ours?"

"Dining table coming out!" calls a guy in overalls. "Mind yourselves."

Thank goodness. OK, quick. Let's redeem the situation.

"Look, darling," I say hurriedly. "It's our dining table from Sri Lanka. Remember? Our personalized table! Our symbol of married love." I give him an affectionate smile, but he's shaking his head.

"Becky—"

"Don't spoil the moment!" I put an arm round him. "It's our special honeymoon table! It's our heirloom of the future! We have to watch it being delivered!"

"OK," Luke says at last. "Whatever."

The men are carefully carrying the table down the ramp, and I have to say, I'm impressed. Bearing in mind how heavy it is, they seem to be managing it quite easily.

"Isn't it exciting?" I clutch Luke's arm as it comes into sight. "Just think! There we were in Sri Lanka—"

I break off, a little confused.

This isn't the wooden table after all. It's a transparent glass table, with curved steel legs. And another guy behind is carrying a pair of trendy red felt-covered chairs.

I stare at it in horror. A cold feeling is creeping over me. Shit. Shit.

The table I bought at the Copenhagen Design Fair. I had *totally* forgotten about that.

How could I forget I bought a whole dining table? How?

"Hold on," Luke's calling, his hand raised. "Guys, that's the wrong table. Ours is wooden. A big carved-wood table from Sri Lanka."

"There's one of them an' all," says the delivery guy. "In the other lorry."

"But we didn't buy this!" says Luke.

He gives me a questioning look and I quickly re-arrange my features as though to say "I'm as baffled as you are!"

Inside, my mind is working frantically: I'll deny I've ever seen it; we'll send it back; it'll all be fine—

" 'Shipped by Mrs. Rebecca Brandon,' " the guy reads aloud from the label. "Table and ten chairs. From Denmark. Here's the signature."

Fuck.

Very slowly, Luke turns toward me.

"Becky, did you buy a table and ten chairs in Denmark?" he says almost pleasantly.

"Er . . ." I lick my lips nervously. "Er . . . I—I might have."

"I see." Luke closes his eyes for a moment as though weighing up a math problem. "And then you bought another table—and ten *more* chairs—in Sri Lanka?"

"I forgot about the first one!" I say desperately. "I totally forgot! Look, it was a very long honeymoon. . . . I lost track of a few things. . . ."

Out of the corner of my eye I can see a guy picking up the bundle of twenty Chinese silk dressing gowns. Shit.

I think I have to get Luke away from these lorries as soon as possible.

"We'll sort it all out," I say quickly. "I promise. But now, why don't you go upstairs and have a nice drink? You just relax! And I'll stay down here and do the supervising."

An hour later it's all finished. The men close up the lorries and I hand them a hefty tip. As they roar away I look over to see Luke coming out the front door of the building.

"Hi!" I say. "Well, that wasn't too bad, was it?"

"Do you want to come upstairs a minute?" Luke says in a strange voice.

As we travel up in the lift I smile at Luke a couple of times, but he doesn't smile back.

"So . . . did you put all the stuff in the sitting room?" I say as we approach the front door. "Or in the—"

My voice dies away as the door swings open.

Oh my God.

Luke's flat is totally unrecognizable.

The beige carpet has disappeared under a sea of parcels, trunks, and pieces of furniture. The hall is crammed with boxes which I recognize from the outlet in Utah, plus the batik paintings from Bali and the two Chinese urns. I edge past them into the sitting room, and gulp as I look around. There are packages everywhere. Rolled-up kilims and dhurries are propped up in one corner. In another, the Indonesian gamelan is jostling for space with a slate coffee table turned on its side and a Native American totem pole.

I'm sensing it's my turn to speak.

"Gosh!" I give a little laugh. "There are quite a lot of . . . rugs, aren't there?"

"Seventeen," says Luke, still in the same strange voice. "I've counted." He steps over a bamboo coffee table which I got in Thailand and looks at the label of a large wooden chest. "This box apparently contains forty mugs." He looks up. "Forty mugs?"

"I know it sounds like a lot," I say quickly. "But they were only about 50p each! It was a bargain! We'll never need to buy mugs ever again!"

Luke regards me for a moment.

"Becky, I never want to buy *anything* ever again."

"Look . . ." I try to step toward him but bump my knee on a painted wooden statue of Ganesh, the god of wisdom and success. "It's . . . it's not that bad! I know it *seems* like a lot. But it's like . . . an optical illusion. Once it's all unpacked, and we put it all away . . . it'll look great!"

"We have five coffee tables," says Luke, ignoring me. "Were you aware of that?"

"Er . . . well." I clear my throat. "Not exactly. So we might have to . . . rationalize a bit."

"Rationalize?" Luke looks around the room incredulously. "Rationalize this lot? It's a mess!"

"Maybe it looks a bit of a mishmash at the moment," I say hurriedly. "But I can pull it all together! I can make it work! It'll be our signature look. If we just do some mood boards—"

"Becky," Luke interrupts. "Would you like to know what mood I'm in right now?"

"Er . . ."

I watch nervously as Luke shifts two packages from Guatemala aside and sinks down on the sofa.

"What I want to know is . . . how did you pay for all this?" he asks, wrinkling his brow. "I had a quick check through our bills, and there's no record of any Chinese urns. Or giraffes. Or tables from Copenhagen . . ." He gives me a hard look. "What's been going on, Becky?"

I'm totally pinned. Even if I did want to run, I'd probably skewer myself on Ganesh's pointy fingers.

"Well." I can't quite meet his eye. "I do have this this credit card."

"The one you keep hidden in your bag?" says Luke without missing a beat. "I checked that too."

Oh God.

There's no way out of this.

"Actually . . . not that one." I swallow hard. "Another one."

"*Another* one?" Luke is staring at me. "You have a *second* secret credit card?"

"It's just for emergencies! Everyone has the odd emergency—"

"What, emergency silk dressing gowns? Emergency Indonesian gamelans?"

There's silence. I can't quite reply. My fingers are all twisted in knots behind my back.

"So . . . you've been paying it off secretly, is that it?" He looks at my agonized face and his expression changes. "You *haven't* been paying it off?"

"The thing is . . ." My fingers twist even tighter. "They gave me quite a big limit."

"For God's sake, Becky—"

"It's OK! I'll pay it off! You don't need to worry about anything. I'll take care of it—"

"With what?" retorts Luke.

My face flames with humiliation. I know I'm not earning right now. But he doesn't have to rub it in.

"When I start my job," I say, trying to sound calm. "I am going to have an income, you know, Luke. I'm not some kind of *freeloader*."

Luke looks at me for a few moments, then sighs.

"I know," he says gently. He holds out his hand. "Come here."

After a moment I pick my way across the crowded floor to the sofa. I find a tiny space to sit down and he puts his arm round me. For a while we both look silently at the ocean of clutter. It's like we're two survivors on a desert island.

"Becky, we can't carry on like this," Luke says at last. "Do you know how much our honeymoon cost us?"

"Er . . . no."

Suddenly it strikes me that I have absolutely no idea what anything has cost. It was me who bought the round-the-world airline tickets, but apart from that, Luke's been doing all the paying, all the way along.

Has our honeymoon *ruined* us?

I glance sideways at Luke—and for the first time see how stressed he looks.

Oh God. We've lost all our money and Luke's been trying to hide it from me.

I suddenly feel like the wife in *It's a Wonderful Life* when James Stewart comes home and snaps at the children. Even though we're on the brink of financial disgrace, it's my role to be brave and serene.

"Luke . . . are we *very* poor?" I ask, as calmly as I can.

Luke turns his head and looks at me.

"No, Becky," he says patiently. "We're not very poor. But we will be if you keep buying mountains of crap."

Mountains of *crap*? I'm about to make an indignant retort when I see his expression. Instead, I close my mouth and nod humbly.

"So I think . . ." Luke pauses. "I think we need to institute a budget."

Eight

A BUDGET.

This is OK. I can handle a budget. Easily. In fact, I'm looking forward to it. It'll be quite liberating, knowing exactly how much I can spend.

Plus everyone knows, the point about budgets is that you make them work *for* you. Exactly.

"So . . . how much is my budget for today?" I say, hovering by the study door. It's about an hour later and Luke is searching for something in his desk. He looks a bit stressed.

"I'm sorry?" he says without looking up.

"I was just wondering what my budget is for today. About twenty pounds?"

"I guess so," Luke says distractedly.

"So . . . can I have it?"

"What?"

"Can I have my twenty pounds?"

Luke stares at me for a moment as though I'm completely mad, then takes his wallet out of his pocket,

gets out a twenty-pound note, and hands it to me.
"OK?"

"Fine. Thanks."

I look at the note. Twenty pounds. That's my challenge. I feel like some wartime housewife being given
her ration book.

It's a very weird feeling, not having my own income.
Or a job. For three months. How am I going to survive
three whole months? Should I get some other job to fill
the space? Maybe this is a great opportunity, it occurs to
me. I could try something completely new!

I have a sudden image of myself as a landscape gar-
dener. I could buy some really cool Wellingtons and
specialize in shrubs.

Or . . . yes! I could start up some company offering
a unique service that no one has ever provided, and
make millions! Everyone would say "Becky's a genius!
Why didn't *we* think of that?" And the unique service
would be—

It would consist of—

OK, I'll come back to that one.

Then, as I watch Luke putting some papers in a
Brandon Communications folder, I'm seized by a brilliant idea. Of course. I can help him in his work!

I mean, that's the whole point of marriage! It should
be a partnership. I can get totally involved in the running of his company, like Hillary Clinton, and everyone
will know it's really me who has all the good ideas. I
have a vision of myself standing by Luke's side in a pas-
tel suit, beaming radiantly while ticker tape rains down
on us.

"Luke, listen," I say. "I want to help."

"Help?" He looks up with an absent frown.

"I want to help you out with the business."

"Becky, I'm not sure—"

"I really want to support you, and I'm free for three months! It's perfect! You wouldn't even have to pay me very much."

Luke looks slightly gobsmacked.

"What exactly would you do?"

"Well . . . I don't know yet," I admit. "But I could inject some new thoughts. Maybe on marketing. Like the time I came up with that slogan for Foreland Investments. You said I was really useful then. And when I came on that press tour to France, and I rewrote that media release for you? Remember that?"

Luke's barely listening.

"Sweetheart, we're really busy with this Arcodas pitch. I haven't got time to take you in. Maybe after the pitch is over—"

"It wouldn't *take* time!" I say in astonishment. "I'd *save* you time! I'd be a help! You once offered me a job, remember?"

"I know I did. But taking on a real, full-time job is a bit different from filling in for three months. If you want to change careers, that's different." He goes back to sorting through his papers.

He is making a big mistake. Everyone knows companies have to cross-pollinate with other industries. My personal shopping experience would probably be invaluable to him. Not to mention my background as a financial journalist.

As I'm watching, Luke tries to put a file away and bumps his shin on a wooden carton full of saris.

"Jesus Christ," he says irritably. "Becky, if you really want to help me . . ."

"Yes?" I say eagerly.

"You can tidy up this apartment."

———

Here I am, prepared to devote myself to Luke's company, and he thinks I should *tidy up*.

I heft a wooden carton onto the slate coffee table and prize the lid off with a knife, and white foam peanuts cascade out everywhere like snowflakes. I dig in through the foam and pull out a bubble-wrapped parcel. For a few seconds I peer at it blankly—then suddenly I remember. These are the hand-painted eggs from Japan. Each one depicts a scene from the legend of the Dragon King. I think I bought five.

I wipe my brow and glance at my watch. I've been at it now for a whole hour, and to be honest, the room doesn't look any better than before. In fact . . . it looks worse. As I survey the clutter, I'm suddenly full of gloom.

What I need is a cup of coffee. Yes.

I head out to the kitchen, already feeling lighter, and turn the kettle on. And maybe I'll have a biscuit, too. I open one of the stainless-steel cupboards, find the tin, select a biscuit, and put the tin away again. Every single movement makes a little clanging sound that echoes through the silence.

God, it's quiet in here, isn't it? We need to get a radio.

I trail my fingers over the granite work-top with a gusty sigh. Maybe I'll give Mum a ring and have a nice chat. Except she's still being all weird. I tried phoning home the other day and she sounded all shifty, and said she had to go because the chimney sweep was there. Like we've ever had a chimney sweep in all my life. She probably had people viewing the house or something.

I could phone Suze. . . .

No. Not Suze.

Or Danny! Danny was my best friend when we lived in New York. He was a struggling fashion designer then, but all of a sudden he's doing really well. I've even seen his name in *Vogue*! But I haven't spoken to him since we got back.

It's not a great time to be calling New York—but that's OK. Danny never keeps regular hours. I dial his number and wait impatiently as it rings.

"Greetings!"

"Hi!" I say. "Danny, it's—"

"Welcome to the ever-expanding Danny Kovitz empire!"

Oh, right. It's a machine.

"For Danny's fashion tips . . . press one. To receive a catalog . . . press two. If you wish to send Danny a gift or invite him to a party, press three. . . ."

I wait till the list comes to an end and a beep sounds.

"Hi!" I say. "Danny, it's Becky! I'm back! So . . . give me a ring sometime!" I give him my number, then put down the receiver.

The kettle comes to a noisy boil and I briskly start spooning grounds into the coffee pot, thinking of who else to call. But . . . there's no one. The truth is, I haven't lived in London for two years. And I've kind of lost touch with most of my old friends.

I'm lonely pops into my head with no warning.

No I'm not. I'm fine.

I wish we'd never come home.

Don't be silly. It's all great. I'm a married woman with my own home and . . . and plenty to be getting on with.

Suddenly the buzzer rings and I look up in surprise. I'm not expecting anyone.

It's probably a package. Or maybe Luke decided to come home early! I walk out into the hall and pick up the entry phone.

"Hello?"

"Becky, love?" crackles a familiar voice. "It's Mum."

I gape at the receiver. Mum? Downstairs?

"Dad and I have come to see you," she continues. "Is it all right if we pop up?"

"Of course!" I exclaim in bemusement, and hit the buzzer. What on earth are Mum and Dad doing here?

I quickly go into the kitchen, pour out the coffee, and arrange some biscuits on a plate, then hurry back out to the lift.

"Hi!" I say as the doors open. "Come on in! I've made you some coffee!"

As I hug Mum and Dad I can see them glancing at each other apprehensively. They're both dressed quite smartly and Mum has even got on the pearl brooch she normally wears to weddings.

What is going on? What?

"I hope we're not disturbing you, love," Mum says as she follows me into the flat.

"No! Of course not!" I say. "I mean, obviously I have my chores . . . things to be getting on with . . ."

"Oh yes." Mum nods. "Well, we don't want to take up your time. It's just . . ." She breaks off. "Shall we go and sit down?"

"Oh. Er . . ." I glance through the door of the sitting room. The sofa is surrounded by boxes spilling their contents, and covered in rugs and foam peanuts. "We haven't *quite* got the sitting room straight yet. Let's go in the kitchen."

Whoever designed our trendy kitchen bar stools obviously never had their parents come over for a cup of coffee. It takes Mum and Dad about five minutes to climb up onto them, while I watch, completely petrified they're going to topple over.

"Spindly legs, aren't they?" puffs Dad as he tries for the

fifth time. Meanwhile Mum's inching slowly onto the
seat, gripping the granite breakfast bar for dear life.

At last, somehow, they're both perched up safely on
the steel seats, looking all self-conscious as though
they're on a TV talk show.

"Are you all right?" I say anxiously. "Because I could
go and get some different chairs . . ."

"Nonsense!" says Dad at once. "This is very comfy!"

He's lying. I can see him clenching his hands round
the edges of the slippery seat and glancing down at the
slate floor below as though he's balanced on a forty-
fourth-floor ledge.

"The seats are a little hard, aren't they, love?" ventures
Mum. "You should get some nice tie-on cushions from
Peter Jones."

"Er . . . maybe."

I hand Mum and Dad their cups, pull out a bar stool
for myself, and nonchalantly swing myself up onto it.

Ow. That hurt.

God, they *are* a bit tricky to get onto. Stupid shiny
seats.

"So . . . are you both well?" I say, reaching for my coffee.

There's a short silence.

"Becky, we came here for a reason," says Dad. "I have
something to tell you."

He looks so grave, I feel worried. Maybe it's not the
house after all. Maybe it's something worse.

"It's to do with me," he continues.

"You're ill," I say before I can stop myself. "Oh God.
Oh God. I knew there was something wrong—"

"I'm not ill. It's not that. It's . . . something else." He
massages his temples, then looks up. "Becky, years
ago—"

"Break it to her gently, Graham!" Mum interrupts.

"I *am* breaking it to her gently!" retorts Dad, swiveling round. "That's exactly what I'm doing!"

"You're not!" says Mum. "You're rushing in!"

Now I'm totally bewildered.

"Break what to me gently?" I say, looking from face to face. "What's going on?"

"Becky, before I met your mother . . ." Dad avoids my gaze. "There was another . . . lady in my life."

"Right," I say, my throat thick.

Mum and Dad are getting divorced and that's why they're selling the house. I'm going to be the product of a broken home.

"We lost touch," Dad continues. "But recently . . . events have occurred."

"You're confusing her, Graham!" exclaims Mum.

"I'm not confusing her! Becky, are you confused?"

"Well . . . a bit," I admit.

Mum leans over and takes my hand.

"Becky, love, the long and the short of it is . . . you have a sister."

A sister?

I stare at her blankly. What's she talking about?

"A half sister, we should say," Dad adds, nodding earnestly. "Two years older than you."

My brain is short-circuiting. This doesn't make any sense. How could I have a sister and not know about it?

"Dad has a daughter, darling," Mum says gently. "A daughter he knew nothing about until very recently. She got in touch with us while you were on honeymoon. We've seen each other a few times, haven't we, Graham?" She glances at Dad, who nods. "She's . . . very nice!"

The kitchen is completely silent. I swallow a few times. I can't quite take this in. Dad had another child?

Dad had another—

"So . . ." I falter. "Who was this other lady in your life?"

I can't believe I'm asking my own father about his love life. Even if it is his love life of thirty years ago.

Dad doesn't flinch at the question.

"Her name was Marguerite," he says with a steadfast gaze. "I was traveling a lot for business then and she was a stewardess on the 7:40 London to Carlisle train."

A stewardess on a train. I have a sudden image of a young Dad sitting in a pale 1970s suit with flappy lapels, smiling up at a uniformed girl as she pours him coffee. She brushes against him as she moves the trolley on. . . .

OK, I'm not sure I want to think about this.

"Daddy was very handsome then," Mum puts in. "When he had his mustache."

I gape at her. Dad had a mustache? God, how many secrets does our family *have*?

Then all of a sudden it hits me.

"That girl! The day we got back." My heart is pounding. "The one you were with. Was that . . . ?"

Mum glances at Dad, who nods.

"That was her. Your half sister. She was visiting us."

"When we saw you, love . . . we didn't know what to do!" says Mum, with an anxious laugh. "We didn't want to give you the shock of your life!"

"We decided we'd tell you when you'd settled in a bit," chimes in Dad. "When you'd got a bit sorted out."

Now I feel totally dazed. That was her. I've *seen* my half sister.

"What's . . . what's her name?" I manage.

"Her name's Jessica," says Dad after a pause. "Jessica Bertram."

Jessica. My sister, Jessica.

Hi. Have you met my sister, Jessica?

I look from Dad's worried face to Mum's bright, hopeful eyes, and suddenly I feel very weird. It's like a bubble is rising up inside me. Like a load of really strong emotions are pushing their way out of my body.

I'm not an only child.

I have my own sister. *I have a sister.*

I have a SISTER!

Nine

FOR THE PAST week I haven't been able to sleep. Or concentrate on anything. All I can think about is the fact that I have a real, blood sister.

At first I felt totally shaken up. It's OK for Mum and Dad; they've had weeks to get used to the idea. But to find out Dad had an affair years ago . . . and got somebody *pregnant*. . . . I never thought Dad was like that, to be honest.

But he's been really sweet about it. The day he and Mum came round to tell me, he could see I was a bit shell-shocked. So he sat down on the sofa with me and told the whole story. He kept reiterating that this all happened before he even met Mum, and that he had no idea he'd fathered a child. Apparently Marguerite the stewardess broke off their relationship with no warning. Dad got on the train one Monday morning, and she just wasn't there. Another stewardess told him she'd had a whirlwind romance and married another passenger, who owned a frozen food business. Dad was so crushed, he started taking another train. And then they moved his work to Birmingham . . . and that was the end of it. He had no idea there was a baby.

But there was. A little girl called Jessica. All my life, without knowing it, I've had a sister, growing up miles away, with no idea I existed either.

And today, at last, I'm going to meet her!

Just the thought makes me feel exhilarated and jumpy all at once. How will we be the same? How will we be different? What will her voice be like? What will her *clothes* be like?

"Do I look OK?" I ask Luke, while anxiously surveying my appearance in the mirror. We're in my old bedroom at my parents' house, and I'm putting the finishing touches to my meeting-my-long-lost-sister outfit. It's taken me several days, but after a lot of thought I've decided on my most flattering Seven jeans, some boots with spiky heels, a gorgeous pale pink Marc Jacobs jacket, and a T-shirt made ages ago for me by Danny.

"You look great," Luke says patiently.

"It's like . . . balancing formal with informal," I explain. "So the jacket says 'This is a special occasion,' whereas the jeans say, 'We're sisters, we can be relaxed with each other!' And the T-shirt says . . ."

I pause. Actually, I'm not sure what the T-shirt says, apart from "I'm friends with Danny Kovitz." And I'm not even sure how true that is anymore. He hasn't called back, even though I've left two messages.

"Becky," says Luke, "I don't honestly think it matters what you wear."

"What?" I wheel round in disbelief. "Of course it matters! This is one of the most important moments of my life! I'll always remember what I was wearing the day I met my sister for the first time. I mean . . . you remember what *you* were wearing when you met me for the first time, don't you?"

Luke looks blank.

He doesn't remember? How can he not remember?

"Well, *I* remember," I say crossly. "You were wearing a gray suit and a white shirt and a dark green Hermès tie. And I was wearing my short black skirt and my suede boots and that awful white top which made my arms look fat."

"If you say so." Luke raises his eyebrows.

I smooth down my T-shirt. "I just want to look right. Like a sister."

"What do sisters look like?" Luke asks, looking amused.

"They look . . . fun!" I think for a moment. "And friendly. And supportive. And like they'll tell you if your bra strap is showing."

"Then you do look exactly like a sister." Luke kisses me. "Becky, relax! It's going to be fine!"

I know I'm a bit wound-up, but I just can't get over the idea of having a sister after being an only child for so long.

Not that I've *minded* being on my own or anything. Mum and Dad and I have always had a great time together. But sometimes I've heard other people talking about their brothers and sisters and wondered what it was like. I never thought I would actually get to find out!

What's really spooky is that all this week, I've suddenly been noticing sisters. They're everywhere! For example, the film of *Little Women* was on telly the other afternoon—and right after was a program about the Beverley Sisters! And every time I've seen two women together in the street, instead of just noticing what they were wearing, I've thought, "Are they sisters?"

It's like there's a whole world of sisters out there and finally I'm part of it.

I feel a smarting in my eyes and blink hard. It's ridiculous, but ever since I heard about Jessica, my emotions have been all over the place. Last night I was reading this brilliant book called *Long-Lost Sisters: The Love They Never Knew They Had* and tears were streaming down my cheeks! The stories were just amazing. One was about these three Russian sisters who were in the same concentration camp during the war but didn't know it. Then there was this woman who was told her sister had been killed but she would never believe it, and then she got cancer and there was no one to look after her three children, but they found the sister alive, just in time for them to say goodbye. . . .

Oh God, I'm going to cry just thinking about it.

I take a deep breath and wander over to the table where I've put my present for Jessica. It's a big basket full of Origins bath stuff, plus some chocolates, plus a little photo album of pictures of me when I was little.

I also got her a silver bean necklace from Tiffany, which exactly matches mine, but Luke said it might be a bit overwhelming, presenting her with jewelry on our first meeting. Which I didn't really understand. I mean, I'd love it if someone gave me a Tiffany necklace! But he was really insistent, so I said I'd keep it for later.

I run my eyes over the basket, slightly dissatisfied. Should I maybe—

"The present is fine," says Luke, just as I open my mouth. "You don't need to add any more."

How did he know what I was going to say?

"OK," I say reluctantly. I look at my watch and feel a swoop of excitement. "Not long now! She'll be here soon!"

The plan is, Jessica's going to phone when her train

gets in to Oxshott Station, then Dad will go and pick her up. It's pure coincidence that she's going to be in London this week. She lives in Cumbria, which is miles away, but apparently she was coming down anyway, for an academic conference. So she's come down a day early, especially to meet me!

"Becky, before all the excitement starts . . . I wanted to have a quick word. On the subject of our honeymoon purchases."

"Oh, right."

I feel a twinge of resentment. Why does Luke have to bring this up *now*? This is a special day! There should be a general reprieve from all arguments, like in the war when they played football on Christmas Day.

Not that we're at war or anything. But we did have a bit of a row yesterday when Luke found the twenty Chinese dressing gowns under the bed. And he keeps asking when I'm going to sort out the apartment.

"I just wanted to let you know that I've spoken to the furniture merchants," says Luke. "They'll be coming by on Monday to take away the Danish table."

"Oh, right," I say sheepishly. "Thanks. So, are they giving us a full refund?"

"Almost."

"Oh, well! So we didn't do too badly in the end!"

"No, we didn't," agrees Luke. "Unless you count the storage costs, the delivery costs, the expense of packaging it all up again . . ."

"Right," I say hurriedly. "Of course. Well, anyway . . . all's well that ends well!"

I try a conciliatory smile, but Luke's not even looking. He's opening up his briefcase and pulling out a wad of—oh God.

Credit card bills. My secret code-red-emergency bills,

to be exact. Luke asked for them the other day and I had no choice but to get them out of their hiding place.

I was kind of hoping he'd be too busy to read them, though.

"Right!" I say, my voice slipping up two notches. "So . . . you've seen those, then!"

"I've paid them all off," Luke says shortly. "Have you cut up the card?"

"Er . . . yes. And thank you for paying them off," I add humbly. Luke gives me a hard look.

"Have you really cut it up?"

"Yes! I threw the pieces in the bin!"

"OK." Luke turns back to the bills. "And there isn't anything else to come? Anything you've paid for recently?"

I feel a tiny clenching in my stomach.

"Er . . . no," I say. "That's all."

I can't tell him about the Angel bag. I just can't. He still thinks all I bought in Milan was a present for him. That's about my only redeeming feature right now.

And, anyway, I can pay it off myself, no problem. I mean, in three months I'll have a job and my own income! It'll be easy!

To my slight relief my mobile phone starts ringing. I scrabble in my bag and pull it out. Suze's number is flashing on the display.

Suze.

At once I feel a gigantic leap of nerves and a familiar hurt starting to rise inside me.

I haven't spoken once to Suze since I left her house. She hasn't called . . . and neither have I. If she's all busy and happy with a fab new life, then so be it. She doesn't even know I've got a sister.

I press the green button and take a deep breath.

"Hi, Suze!" I exclaim in airy tones. "How are you? How's the family?"

"I'm fine," says Suze. "We're all fine. You know . . . same old . . ."

"And how's Lulu?" I say lightly. "I expect you two have been busy doing lots of fun things together?"

"She's . . . fine." Suze sounds awkward. "Listen, Bex . . . about that. I wanted to—"

I cut her off. "Actually, I've got a bit of exciting news of my own. Guess what? It turns out . . . I've got a long-lost sister!"

There's a shocked silence.

"What?" Suze says at last.

"It's true! I've got a half sister that I never knew about. I'm meeting her today for the first time. She's called Jessica."

"I . . . can't believe it." Suze sounds totally poleaxed. "You've got a *sister*? How come . . ."

"My dad. Before he met my mum. It's quite a long story. But isn't it great? I've always wanted a sister!"

"How . . . how old is she?"

"Only two years older than me. Hardly any difference! I expect we'll become really good friends," I add carelessly. "In fact . . . we'll be much *closer* than friends. I mean, we've got the same blood and everything. We'll have a lifelong bond."

"Yes," Suze says after a pause. "I . . . suppose you will."

"Anyway, I must go! She'll be here any moment! I can't wait!"

"Well . . . good luck. Have fun."

"We certainly will!" I say brightly. "Oh . . . and do give my love to Lulu. Have a lovely birthday with her, won't you?"

"I . . . will," says Suze, sounding defeated. "Bye, Bex. And . . . congratulations."

As I switch off the phone I'm a bit hot about the face. Suze and I have never been like this with each other before.

But she's the one who went out and got a new best friend. Not me.

I thrust my mobile phone back into my bag and look up to see Luke regarding me with a raised eyebrow.

"Suze all right?"

"She's fine," I say a little defiantly, shaking my hair back. "Come on."

As I come down the stairs, Suze's hurt voice lingers in my mind, but I try to ignore it. I can't spend time dwelling on her. I've got important things to focus on. Jessica will be arriving here soon! This is one of the biggest days of my life . . . ever!

"All set?" says Mum, as we go into the kitchen. She's wearing a smart blue dress and is wearing her "special occasion" makeup—she uses lots of shiny highlighter under her eyebrows to "open up the eyes." I've seen it in the makeup book Janice gave her for Christmas.

"Did I hear you say you're selling some furniture?" she adds as she turns on the kettle.

"We're returning a table," Luke says easily. "We seem to have ordered two by mistake. But it's been taken care of."

"Only I was going to say, you should sell it on eBay!" says Mum. "You'd get a good price!"

eBay.

"So . . . you can sell anything on eBay, can you?" I ask casually.

"Oh yes!" says Mum. "Anything at all."

Like, say, hand-painted eggs depicting the legend of the Dragon King. Yes! This is the answer. It'll solve everything!

I have to stop myself from punching the air with glee.

"It's exciting, isn't it, love?" says Mum, watching me fondly. "Let's all have some nice coffee while we're waiting."

We all involuntarily glance at the clock. Jessica's train should arrive at Oxshott in five minutes. Five minutes!

"Toodle-oo!" There's a knocking at the back door and we all look round, to see Janice peering through the glass.

Oh my goodness. Where did she get that sparkly blue eyeshadow?

Please don't let her give any to Mum, I find myself praying.

"Come on in, Janice!" says Mum, opening the door. "And Tom! What a nice surprise!"

Blimey, Tom's looking rough. His hair is rumpled and unwashed, his hands are all blistered and cut, and there's a deep furrow in his brow.

"We just came to wish you luck," says Janice. "Not that you need it!" She pops her box of Canderel sugar substitute down on the counter, then turns to look at me. "So, Becky. A sister!"

"Congratulations," says Tom. "Or whatever you say."

"I know!" I say. "Isn't it amazing?"

Janice shakes her head and looks at Mum a bit reproachfully.

"I can't believe you've been keeping this a secret from us, Jane!"

"We wanted Becky to be the first to know," says Mum, patting me on the shoulder. "Hazelnut whirl, Janice?"

"Lovely!" says Janice, taking a biscuit from the plate and sitting down. She nibbles it thoughtfully for a few moments, then looks up. "What I don't understand is . . . why did this girl get in touch? After all this time?"

"There was a very good reason," I say with an air of solemn drama. "It's because we've got a hereditary disease."

Janice gives a little scream.

"A disease! Jane! You never told me that!"

"It's not a *disease*," says Mum. "Becky, you know it's not a disease! It's a 'factor.' "

"A . . . 'factor'?" echoes Janice, looking even more horrified than before. "What kind of factor?" I can see her eyeing her hazelnut whirl as though she's afraid it might contaminate her.

"It's not life-threatening!" laughs Mum. "It's just a blood disorder, which can be a risk in certain situations. In surgery, for example. The blood clots too thickly. . . ."

"Don't!" Janice winces. "I can't bear talking about blood!"

"The doctors told Jess she should warn other members of her family to get tested, and that was the spur. She'd always known she had a father somewhere but didn't know his name."

"So she asked her mother who her long-lost father was. . . ." Janice chimes in avidly, as though she's following a Ruth Rendell miniseries on the telly.

"Her mother is dead," explains Mum.

"Dead!" exclaims Janice, looking appalled. "From the blood factor?"

"No," Mum responds patiently. "From a car crash. But her aunt had the name of Jessica's father written down in an old diary. So she got it out and gave it to Jessica."

"And what was the name?" breathes Janice.

There's a pause.

"Mum, it was Graham!" says Tom, rolling his eyes. "Graham Bloomwood. Obviously."

"Oh yes," says Janice, looking almost let down. "Of course it was. Well, goodness me." She exhales sharply. "What a dreadful shock. For all of you."

"We were in quite a state when we got the news," Mum admits. "You know, that's why we didn't come to the Hawaiian quiz evening at the church. Graham didn't really have a migraine."

"I knew it!" says Janice. "I said to Martin at the time, 'Something's not right with the Bloomwoods.' But I had no idea it was a long-lost family member!"

"Well," says Mum comfortingly, "how could you?"

Janice is silent for a moment, taking it all in. Then suddenly she stiffens and lays a hand on Mum's arm.

"Jane. Just be careful. Has this girl laid any claim to Graham's fortune? Has he altered his will in her favor?"

OK. Janice has definitely been watching too many TV murder mysteries.

"Janice!" says Mum with a laugh. "No! It's nothing like that. As it happens, Jess's family is"—she lowers her voice discreetly—"rather *well-off*."

"Ah!" breathes Janice.

Mum lowers her voice still further. "They're rather big in *frozen food*."

"Oh, I *see*," says Janice. "So she's not all alone in the world, then."

"Oh no," says Mum, back to normal. "She's got a step-father and two brothers. Or is it three?"

"But no sisters," I chime in. "We've both had that gap in our life. That . . . unfulfilled longing."

Everyone turns to look at me.

"Have you had an unfulfilled longing, Becky?" asks Janice.

"Oh yes. Definitely." I take a pensive sip of coffee. "Looking back, I think I always somehow *knew* I had a sister."

"Really, love?" Mum says in surprise. "You never mentioned it."

"I never said anything." I give Janice a brave smile. "But deep down I knew."

"Goodness!" says Janice. "How did you know?"

"I felt it in here," I say, clasping my hands to my chest. "It was as if . . . a part of me was missing."

I make a sweeping gesture with my hand—and make the mistake of catching Luke's eye.

"Which particular part of you was missing?" he says with apparent interest. "Not a vital organ, I hope."

God, he has no heart. None. Last night, he kept reading out bits from my *Long-Lost Sisters* book, then looking up and saying, "You cannot be serious."

"The soul mate part, actually," I shoot back.

"Thanks." He raises his eyebrows.

"Not *that* kind of soul mate! A sisterly soul mate!"

"What about Suzie?" says Mum, looking over in surprise. "She's been like a sister to you, surely. She's such a dear girl."

"Friends come and go," I say, looking away. "She's not like family. She doesn't understand me like a true sister would."

Janice looks at Mum sympathetically. "You're being very brave, dear. But you must have suffered when you found out."

"It was difficult," says Mum, sitting down at the table. "I can't pretend it wasn't. Although, of course, the affair happened *long* before Graham met me."

"Of course!" Janice says hastily. "Of course it did! I wasn't for a moment *suggesting* that . . . that he . . . you . . ."

She breaks off, flustered, and takes a gulp of coffee.

"And in some ways . . ." Mum pauses, stirring her drink, with a rueful smile. "In some ways it was to be expected. Graham was quite the Don Juan when he was younger. It's no wonder he found women throwing themselves at him."

"That's . . . right," Janice says doubtfully.

Dad? Don Juan?

I try to picture him standing at some glamorous bar, with his seventies mustache and a wide, patterned tie, surrounded by gorgeous women drinking martinis. Then my gaze drifts out the window to see him coming over the lawn, toward the back door. His graying hair is all tousled, his face is red, and even though I've told him a million times not to, he's wearing socks inside his sandals.

"Women could never resist him," says Mum. "That's the truth of it." She brightens a little. "But we're having therapy to help us through the crisis. At the new holistic health center in Wood Street."

"Therapy?" I echo in astonishment. "Are you serious?"

"Absolutely!" says Dad, coming in at the back door. "We've had three sessions already."

"She's a very nice girl, our therapist," says Mum. "Although a bit *nervy*. Like all these young people."

Wow. I had no idea Mum and Dad were having therapy. But it makes sense. I mean, bloody hell. How would I feel if Luke suddenly announced he had a long-lost daughter?

"Therapy!" Janice is saying. "I can hardly believe it!"

"We have to be realistic, Janice," says Mum. "You can't expect this kind of revelation to have no repercussions."

"A discovery of this scale can tear a family apart," agrees Dad, popping a hazelnut whirl into his mouth. "It can rock the very foundations of a marriage."

"Goodness." Janice claps a hand over her mouth, looking from Mum to Dad and back with wide eyes. "What . . . what sort of repercussions are you expecting?"

"There'll be anger, I expect," Mum says knowledge-ably. "Recriminations. Coffee, Graham?"

"Yes, thanks, love." He beams at her.

"Therapy is a pile of crap," says Tom suddenly. "I tried it with Lucy."

We all turn and look at him. He's holding a cup of coffee in both hands and glowering at us over the top of it.

"The therapist was a woman," he adds, as though that explains everything.

"I think they often are, love," Mum says cautiously.

"She took Lucy's side. She said she could understand her frustrations." Tom's hands clench more tightly round his cup. "What about my frustrations? Lucy was sup-posed to be my wife! But she wasn't interested in *any* of my projects. Not the conservatory, not the en suite bathroom—"

"I love your summerhouse, Tom!" I cut in quickly. "It's very . . . big!"

In fact, it's monstrous. I nearly died when I saw it out the window this morning. It's three stories high, with gables and a deck.

"We're just a bit worried about the planning regula-tions, aren't we?" says Janice, nervously glancing at Tom. "We're worried it might be classed as a residence."

"Well, it's a real achievement!" I say encouragingly. "To build something like that!"

"I enjoy working with wood," Tom says in a gruff voice. "Wood doesn't let you down." He drains his cup. "In fact, I'd better get back to it. Hope it all goes well."

As the back door closes behind him there's an awk-ward silence.

"He wants to make a boat next," says Janice, looking strained. "A boat, on the lawn!"

"Janice, have another coffee," Mum says soothingly. "Shall I put a splash of sherry in it?"

Janice looks torn.

"Better not," she says at last. "Not before twelve."

She rootles in her handbag and produces a little pill, which she pops into her mouth. Then she zips up her bag again and smiles brightly. "So! What does Jessica look like?"

"She's . . . she's nice-looking," begins Mum. "Isn't she, Graham?"

"Very nice-looking!" says Dad. "Tall . . . slim . . ."

"Dark hair," adds Mum. "Quite a *reserved* girl, if you know what I mean."

I'm listening avidly as they describe her. Although I glimpsed her in the street that day we got back, the sunlight was so bright and I was so distracted by Mum and Dad's weird behavior, I only got a vague impression. So all week I've been trying to build on that image. Mum and Dad keep saying how tall and slim she is, so I've kind of pictured her like Courteney Cox. All willowy and elegant, in a white silk trouser suit, maybe.

I keep having visions of our first meeting. We'll fling our arms round each other, and then she'll smile at me, brushing away the tears, and I'll smile back . . . and we'll have an instant connection. Like we already know each other and understand each other better than anyone else in the world.

I mean, who knows? Maybe it'll turn out that we'll have sisterly psychic powers. Or maybe we'll be like the twins I read about in *Long-Lost Sisters,* who were separated at birth but went on to have the same jobs and marry men with the same name.

I'm gripped by this idea. Maybe it'll turn out that Jessica is a personal shopper, too, and is married to a man called Luke! She'll turn up in exactly the same

Marc Jacobs jacket as me, and we can go on breakfast TV and everyone will say—

Oh, except she's not a personal shopper, I suddenly remember. She's training to be a doctor. Doctor of geography.

No. Geology.

But then . . . didn't *I* once think about training to be a doctor? I mean, that *can't* be just coincidence.

"And where does she live?" Janice is asking.

"In the North," says Mum. "A village called Scully. In Cumbria."

"The North!" says Janice, with as much trepidation as though Mum's said the North Pole. "That's a long way to travel! What time does she arrive?"

"Well." Mum looks at the clock and frowns. "That's a point. She should have arrived by now. Graham, love, what time does Jess's train get in?"

"I thought it was about now. . . ." Dad's brow wrinkles. "Maybe I should phone the station. See if there's been a problem."

"I'll do it if you like," says Luke, looking up from the newspaper.

"She did say she'd phone . . ." Mum begins, as Dad goes out to the hall telephone.

Suddenly the doorbell rings.

We all stare at each other, frozen. A few moments later, Dad's voice comes from the hall. "I think it's her!"

Oh my God.

She's here. My new sister. My new soul mate!

"I'll slip away," says Janice. "Let you have your precious family moment." She squeezes my hand, then disappears out the back door.

"Let me just tidy my hair," says Mum, hurrying out to the hall mirror.

"Quick!" I say. "Where's the present?"

"Here it is," says Luke, handing me the cellophane-wrapped gift basket. "And Becky . . ." He puts a hand on my arm.

"What?" I say impatiently. "What is it?"

"I know you're excited to meet Jessica," he says. "And so am I. But remember. You are strangers. I'd just . . . take it easy."

"We're not strangers!" I say in astonishment. "She's my *sister*! We've got the same blood in us!"

Honestly. Doesn't Luke know anything?

I hurry out to the hall, clutching the basket. Through the frosted glass pane of the front door I can see an indistinct, blurry figure.

"By the way," says Mum as we advance toward the door, "she likes to be called Jess."

"Ready?" says Dad with a twinkle.

This is the moment! I quickly adjust my jacket, smooth down my hair, and put on my widest, most welcoming and loving smile.

Dad reaches for the handle and pulls back the front door with a flourish.

And there, standing on the doorstep, is my sister.

Ten

MY FIRST THOUGHT is that she's not *exactly* like Courteney Cox. Nor is she wearing a white silk trouser suit.

Her dark hair is cropped short, and she's wearing a plain, workmanlike brown shirt over jeans. I guess it's a kind of . . . utility chic.

And she's pretty! Prettyish. Even though I'd say her makeup is maybe a bit *too* natural.

"Hi," she says in a flat, matter-of-fact voice.

"Hi!" I say tremulously. "I'm Becky! Your long-lost sister!"

I'm about to rush forward and fling my arms around her neck when I realize that I'm holding the basket. So instead, I thrust it at her. "This is from me!"

"It's a present, love!" Mum adds helpfully.

"Thanks," says Jess, looking down at it. "That's great."

There's a short silence. I'm waiting for Jess to tear off the wrappings impatiently, or say "Can I open it right now?" or even just exclaim "Ooh, Origins! My favorite!" But she just puts it down on the hall table.

She's probably being polite, it occurs to me. I mean, she's never met me before. Maybe she thinks I'm all formal and correct, and she has to be too. What I must do is put her at her ease.

"I just can't believe you're here," I say momentously. "The sister I never knew I had." I put a hand on her arm and look right into her eyes, which are hazel with little specks.

Oh my God. We're bonding. This is just like one of the scenes in my *Long-Lost Sisters* book!

"You knew, didn't you?" I say, smiling to conceal my rising emotion. "Didn't you somehow know you had a sister all along?"

"No," says Jess, looking blank. "I had no idea."

"Oh, right," I say, feeling a bit discomfited.

She wasn't supposed to say that. She was supposed to say "I always felt you in my heart!" and burst into tears.

I'm not quite sure what to say next.

"Anyway!" Mum says cheerfully. "Come on in, Jess! You must need some coffee after your journey!"

As Mum ushers Jess in, I look in surprise at the brown rucksack she's carrying. It's not very big at all. And she's staying a whole week at the conference!

"Is that all your luggage?" I say.

"That's all I need." She shrugs. "I'm a light packer."

"Did you FedEx the rest?" I say in an undertone, and give her a friendly "I understand" look.

"No." She glances at Mum. "This is all I've brought."

"It's OK." I smile conspiratorially. "I won't say anything."

I knew we'd be kindred spirits. I *knew* it.

"Welcome, my dear girl!" says Dad.

As he gives Jess a hug, I suddenly feel a bit weird. It's

as though it's hitting me for the first time. Dad has another daughter. Not just me.

But then . . . that's what families are about, isn't it? Getting bigger. Adding new members.

"This is Luke, my husband," I say quickly.

"How do you do?" he says pleasantly, coming forward. As he shakes her hand I feel a little glow of pride in each of them. I look at Mum, and she gives me an encouraging smile.

"Let's go through!" She leads the way into the living room, where there are flowers on the table, and plates of biscuits laid out invitingly. We all sit down, Jess looking a little uncomfortable on the soft, squashy sofa.

This is unreal.

I'm sitting opposite my half sister. As Mum pours out the coffee I peer at Jess, mapping her face onto mine, trying to see the similarities between us. And there are loads! Or at least . . . some.

She's got pretty much the same eyes as mine, except a different color and a slightly different shape. Plus her nose would be just like mine if it didn't have that pointy end. And her hair would be *exactly* the same—if she just grew it a bit and dyed it and maybe put on a deep-conditioning treatment.

She's probably scrutinizing me in exactly the same way, I suddenly realize.

"I've hardly been able to sleep!" I say, and give her a slightly bashful smile. "It's so exciting to meet you at last!"

Jess nods but doesn't say anything. Gosh, she *is* very reserved. I'll have to draw her out a bit.

"Am I anything like you imagined?" I give a self-conscious little laugh and smooth my hair back.

Jess surveys me for a moment, moving her eyes around my face.

"I didn't really imagine what you'd be like," she says at last.

"Oh, right."

"I don't imagine things much," she adds. "I just take them as they come."

"Have a biscuit, Jess," Mum says pleasantly. "These are pecan and maple."

"Thanks," says Jess, taking one. "I love pecans."

"Me too!" I look up in astonishment. "I love them too!"

God, it just shows. Genes will out. We were brought up miles away from each other in different families . . . but we still have the same tastes!

"Jess, why didn't you call from the station?" Dad says, taking a cup of coffee from Mum. "I would have picked you up. You didn't need to take a cab!"

"I didn't get a cab," says Jess. "I walked."

"You walked?" says Dad in surprise. "From Oxshott Station?"

"From Kingston. I took the coach down." She gulps her coffee. "It was far cheaper. I saved twenty-five pounds."

"You walked all the way from Kingston?" Mum looks appalled.

"It was no distance," says Jess. "And the bus would have been three pounds fifty."

"Jess is a very keen walker, Becky," explains Mum. She smiles at Jess. "It's your main hobby, isn't it, love?"

This is too much. We should be on a documentary or something!

"Me too!" I exclaim. "It's my hobby too! Isn't that amazing?"

There's silence. I look around at the bewildered faces of my family. Honestly! What's wrong with them?

"Is walking your hobby, love?" Mum says uncertainly.

"Of course it is! I walk round London all the time! Don't I, Luke?"

Luke gives me a quizzical look.

"Certain streets of London have been pounded down by your feet, yes," he agrees.

"Do you do power walking, then?" Jess asks, looking interested.

"Well . . ." I think for a few moments. "It's more like . . . I combine it with other activities. For variety."

"Like cross-training?"

"Er . . . kind of." I nod, and take a bite of biscuit.

There's another little silence, as if everyone's waiting for everyone else to speak. Why are we all so awkward? We should be *natural*.

"Do you like . . . films?" I ask at last.

"Some," replies Jess, frowning thoughtfully. "I like films that say something. That have some sort of message."

"Me too," I agree fervently. "Every film should definitely have a message."

Which is true. I mean . . . take the *Lord of the Rings* movies—they've got loads of messages. Like "Don't lose your ring."

"More coffee, anyone?" says Mum, looking round. "There's another coffeepot ready in the kitchen—"

"I'll go," I chime in, leaping up from the sofa. "And, Luke, why don't you come and . . . er . . . help me? In case I . . . can't find it."

I know I don't sound very convincing, but I don't care. I'm just dying to talk to Luke.

As soon as we're in the kitchen I shut the door and look at him eagerly. "So? What do you think of my sister?"

"She seems very nice."

"Isn't she great? And there are so many similarities between us! Don't you think?"

"I'm sorry?" Luke stares at me.

"Jess and me! We're so alike!"

"Alike?" Luke looks flabbergasted.

"Yes!" I say, a tad impatiently. "Weren't you listening? She likes pecans, I like pecans . . . she likes walking, I like walking . . . we both like films. . . ." I make a whirling motion with my hands. "It's like there's already this amazing understanding between us!"

"If you say so," he says dubiously.

"Don't you like her?" I say, crestfallen.

"Of course I like her! But I've hardly spoken two words to her. And nor have you."

"Well . . . I know," I admit. "But that's because we're all so *stilted* in there. We can't chat properly. So I thought I'd suggest the two of us go out together somewhere. Really have a chance to bond."

"Like where?"

"I don't know. For a walk. Or . . . a little shopping trip, maybe!"

"Aha." He nods. "A little shopping trip. Good idea. I'm assuming this would be on your daily budget of twenty pounds."

What? I cannot *believe* he's bringing up the budget at a time like this. I mean, how many times do you go shopping with your long-lost sister for the very first time?

"This is a one-off, extraordinary event." I'm trying to control my impatience. "Clearly I need an extra budget."

"I thought we agreed, no one-offs," says Luke. "No 'unique opportunities.' Don't you remember?"

I feel a surge of outrage.

"Fine!" I say, folding my arms. "I won't bond with my sister."

The only sound in the kitchen is the ticking of the

wall clock. I give a huge sigh and glance surreptitiously at Luke, but he seems unmoved.

"Becky!" Mum's voice interrupts us. "Where's the coffee? We're all waiting!" She comes into the kitchen and looks from Luke to me in alarm. "There isn't a problem, is there? You're not arguing?"

I turn to Mum.

"I want to take Jess out shopping, but Luke says I've got to stick to my budget!"

"Luke!" exclaims Mum reproachfully. "I think that's a lovely idea, Becky! You two girls should spend some time together. Why not pop to Kingston? You could have lunch, too."

"Exactly!" I'm shooting resentful vibes at Luke. "But I haven't got any money except twenty quid."

"And as I say, we're on a budget," says Luke in implacable tones. "I'm sure you'd agree that successful budgeting is the first rule of a happy marriage, Jane?"

"Yes, yes, of course . . ." says Mum, looking distracted. Suddenly her face brightens. "The Greenlows!"

The who?

"Your cousins in Australia! They sent a check for your wedding present! I've been meaning to give it to you. It's in Australian dollars . . . but even so, it's quite a lot. . . ." She roots around in a drawer and pulls it out. "Here we are! Five hundred Australian dollars!"

"Fantastic!" I take the check from her and examine it.

"So now you can treat yourself and Jess to something nice!" Mum squeezes my arm with a smile.

"You see?" I say in triumph.

"OK. You win. This time." Luke rolls his eyes.

Suddenly excited, I hurry into the living room.

"Hi, Jess!" I say. "D'you want to go out somewhere? Like to the shops?"

"Oh." Jess looks taken aback. "Well . . ."

"Go on, love!" says Mum, coming in behind me. "Have a little spree!"

"We can go and have lunch somewhere . . . really get to know each other. . . . What do you think?"

"Well . . . OK," she says at last.

"Excellent!"

I feel a zing of anticipation. My first-ever shopping trip with my sister! This is so thrilling!

"I'll go and get ready."

"Wait," says Jess. "Just before you go. I brought you something too. It's not much, but . . ."

She goes over to her rucksack, opens it, and takes out a parcel wrapped up in paper printed all over with the words HAPPY NEW YEAR 1999.

That is so cool!

"I *love* kitsch wrapping paper!" I say, admiring it. "Where did you find it?"

"It was free from the bank," says Jess.

"Oh," I say in surprise. "Er . . . excellent!"

I rip off the wrapping and find a plastic box, divided into three compartments.

"Wow!" I exclaim at once. "That's fantastic! Thank you so much! It's just what I wanted!" I fling an arm round Jess's neck and give her a kiss.

"What is it, love?" Mum asks, looking at it with interest.

To be honest, I'm not actually quite sure.

"It's a food saver," explains Jess. "You can keep leftovers in it, and they all stay separate. Rice . . . casserole . . . whatever. I couldn't live without mine."

"That's brilliant! It'll be *so* useful." I look at the three compartments thoughtfully. "I think I'll keep all my lip balms in it."

"Lip balms?" says Jess, clearly taken aback.

"I'm *always* losing them! Aren't you?" I put the lid

back on and admire it for a few more moments. Then I pick up the wrapping paper and crumple it into a ball.

Jess winces as though someone just trod on her foot.

"You could have folded that up," she says, and I look at her, puzzled.

Why on earth would I *fold* used wrapping paper?

But then, maybe this is one of her pet habits that I'll have to get used to. We all have little quirks.

"Oh, right!" I say. "Of course. Silly me!"

I uncrease the crumpled paper, smooth it out, and fold it carefully into quarters.

"There we are." With a cheerful smile I drop it in the wastepaper bin. "Let's go!"

Eleven

IT ONLY TAKES fifteen minutes by car to get to Kingston, which is the nearest big shopping center to Mum and Dad. I find a meter, and after about twenty attempts manage to park the car vaguely in a straight line. Jess sits stoically beside me in the passenger seat, saying nothing. Not even when the lorry driver starts hooting at me.

Anyway, never mind. The point is, we're here! It's a fantastic day, sunny but not too warm, with tiny clouds scudding across the blue sky. As I get out, I look around the sunlit street, feeling all buzzy with anticipation. My first shopping trip with my sister! What shall we do first?

As I start to feed the parking meter, I go through all the options in my head. We should definitely get a free makeover, and check out that new underwear shop Mum was talking about. . . .

"How long exactly are we planning to stay here?" Jess asks as I shove in my sixth pound coin.

"This should take us up to six o'clock . . . and after that, parking's free!"

"Six o'clock?" She looks a bit stunned.

"Don't worry!" I say reassuringly. "The shops don't close at six. They'll be open till at least eight."

And we *have* to go into a department store, and try on lots of evening dresses. One of my best times ever was when I spent a whole afternoon trying on posh dresses in Harrods with Suze. We kept putting on more and more outrageous million-pound frocks, and swooshing around, and all the snooty assistants got really annoyed and kept asking had we made our choice yet?

At last Suze said she *thought* she had . . . but she wanted to see it with a Cartier diamond tiara just to make sure, and could Jewelry possibly send one up?

I think that's when they asked us to leave.

God, Suze and I used to have fun together. She is just the best person in the world for saying "Go on! Buy it!" Even when I was stone broke, she'd say "Buy it! I'll pay! You can always pay me back." And then she'd buy one too, and we'd go and have a cappuccino.

But anyway. There's no point getting all nostalgic.

"So!" I turn to Jess. "What do you feel like doing first? There are loads of shops here: two department stores . . ."

"I hate department stores," says Jess. "They make me feel ill."

"Oh, right." That's fair enough. Loads of people hate department stores.

"Well, there are lots of boutiques too. In fact, I've just thought of the perfect place!"

I lead her off the main high street, away from the pedestrianized shopping precinct, and turn left down a cobbled side road. As we walk, I hitch my Angel bag higher on my shoulder, admiring its reflection in a shop window across the street. That bag was worth every single penny.

I'm slightly surprised Jess hasn't said anything about it, actually. If my sister had an Angel bag, it would be the *first* thing I'd mention. But then, maybe she's trying to be all cool and blasé.

"So . . . where do you normally shop?" I ask.

"Wherever's cheapest," replies Jess.

"Me too! I got the most fab Ralph Lauren top at this designer outlet in Utah. Ninety percent off!"

"I tend to do a lot of bulk buying," says Jess with a little frown. "If you buy large enough quantities, you can get pretty good savings."

Oh my God. We are totally on the same wavelength. I *knew* we would be!

"You are so right!" I exclaim in delight. "That's what I keep trying to explain to Luke! But he just can't see the logic."

"So, do you belong to a warehouse club?" Jess looks at me with interest. "Or a food co-op?"

A food co-op?

"Er . . . no. But on my honeymoon, I did loads of excellent bulk buying! I bought forty mugs and twenty silk dressing gowns!"

"Silk dressing gowns?" echoes Jess, looking taken aback.

"They were such an investment! I *told* Luke it made financial sense, but he just wouldn't listen. . . . OK! Here we are! This is it."

We've arrived at the glass doors of Georgina's. It's a big, light boutique selling clothes, jewelry, and the most gorgeous bags. I've been coming here since I was twelve, and it's one of my favorite shops in the world.

"You are going to *love* this shop," I say to Jess happily, and push the door open. Sandra, one of the assistants, is arranging a collection of beaded purses on a pedestal, and she looks up as the door pings. Her face lights up immediately.

"Becky! Long time no see! How was the honeymoon?"

"Great, thanks!"

"And how's married life treating you?" She grins. "Had your first big bust-up yet?"

"Ha-ha," I say, grinning back. I'm about to introduce Jess, when Sandra shrieks.

"Oh my God! Is that an Angel bag? Is it *real*?"

"Yes," I glow. Owning an Angel bag is just total bliss.

"I don't believe it. She's got an Angel bag!" Sandra calls out to the other two assistants. They rush to the front of the shop, gasping, "Can I touch it? Where did you *get* it?"

"Milan."

"Only Becky Bloomwood." Sandra's shaking her head. "Only Becky Bloomwood would walk in here with an Angel bag. So how much did that cost you?"

"Er . . . enough!"

"Wow." She strokes it gingerly. "It's absolutely . . . *amazing*."

"What's so special?" Jess asks blankly. "I mean . . . it's just a bag."

There's a stunned pause, then we all burst out laughing. God, Jess is quite witty!

"Sandra, I want to introduce you to someone." I pull Jess forward. "This is my sister!"

"Your *sister*?" Sandra looks at Jess in shock. "I didn't know you had a sister."

"Neither did I! We're long-lost sisters, aren't we, Jess?" I put an arm round her.

"Half sisters," corrects Jess, a little stiffly.

"Georgina!" Sandra is calling to the back of the shop.

"Georgina, you have to come out here! You won't believe it! Becky Bloomwood's here—and she's got a sister! There are *two* of them!"

A curtain swishes back and Georgina, the owner of the shop, comes out. She's in her fifties, with slate-gray hair and the most amazing turquoise eyes. She's wearing a velvet tunic top with pencil-thin black trousers and she's holding a fountain pen. Her eyes sparkle when she sees me and Jess.

"Two Bloomwood sisters," she says softly. "Well. What a wonderful thing."

She exchanges looks with the assistants.

"We'll reserve two fitting rooms," says Sandra promptly.

"If there aren't enough, we can always share a fitting room, can't we, Jess!" I say.

"I'm sorry?" Jess looks startled.

"We're sisters!" I give her an affectionate squeeze. "We shouldn't be shy with each other!"

"It's OK," says Sandra, glancing at Jess's face. "There are plenty of fitting rooms. Take your time walking round . . . and enjoy!"

"I told you this was a nice place!" I say happily to Jess. "So . . . let's start here!"

I head over to a rack full of delicious-looking tops and start leafing through the hangers. "Isn't this gorgeous?" I pull out a pink T-shirt with a little butterfly motif. "And this one with the daisy would really suit you!"

"Do you want to try them?" says Sandra. "I can pop them in the fitting rooms for you."

"Yes, please!" I hand them over and smile at Jess.

But she doesn't smile back. In fact, she hasn't moved from the spot.

I suppose it can be a bit weird, shopping for the first time with someone new. Sometimes it just clicks straightaway, like when I went shopping for the first time with

Suze and we both reached for the same Lulu Guinness makeup bag *simultaneously*. But sometimes it can be a bit awkward, not knowing what each other's tastes are yet . . . and you keep trying different things and asking "Do you like this? Or this?"

I think Jess might need a bit of encouragement.

"These skirts are fabulous!" I say, going over to another rack, which is filled with evening wear. "This black one with the netting would look amazing on you!" I take it down and hold it up against Jess. She reaches for the price tag, looks at it, and goes pale.

"I can't believe these prices," she murmurs.

"They're pretty reasonable, aren't they?" I murmur back.

"And the skirt?" says Sandra, popping up behind us.

"Yes, please! And I'll try it in the gray . . . ooh, and the pink!" I add, suddenly noticing a rose-colored skirt hiding at the back.

Twenty minutes later we've been round the whole shop and two piles of clothes are waiting for us in the fitting rooms at the back. Jess hasn't spoken much. In fact, she hasn't spoken at all. But I've made up for it, picking out all the clothes I think would look great on her, and adding them to the pile.

"OK!" I say, exhilarated. "Let's go and try them on! I bet you look fantastic in that pink skirt! You should put it with the off-the-shoulder top, and maybe—"

"I'm not going to try anything on," says Jess. She shoves her hands in her pockets and leans against a patch of empty wall.

I can't have heard her correctly.

"What did you say?"

"I'm not going to try anything on." She nods toward the fitting rooms. "But you go ahead. I'll wait here."

Did I miss something?

"But . . . why?"

"I don't need any new clothes," replies Jess.

Now I'm utterly baffled. Across the shop, I'm aware of the assistants exchanging bewildered glances.

"You must need *something*!" I say. "A T-shirt . . . a pair of trousers . . ."

"No. I'm fine."

"Don't you even want to try on one of those gorgeous tops?" I hold up a fabulous little Juicy T-shirt encouragingly. "Just to see what they look like on?"

"I'm not going to buy them." Jess shrugs. "So what's the point?"

"It's on me!" I say, suddenly realizing. "You do know this is all my treat?"

"I don't want to waste your money. Don't let me stop you, though," she adds.

I'm at a complete loss. What should I do?

"Everything's in the fitting room," Sandra puts in.

"Go on." Jess nods.

"Well . . . OK," I say at last. "I won't be long."

I try on most of the clothes, but my excitement's evaporated. It's not the same on my own. I wanted us to try things on together. I wanted it to be *fun*.

I just don't understand it. How can she not try anything on?

She must totally hate my taste, I realize with a plunge of despair. And she hasn't said anything because she wants to be polite.

"Any good?" says Georgina as I finally emerge.

"Er . . . yes!" I say, trying to sound upbeat. "I'll take two of the tops and the pink skirt. It's really gorgeous on!"

I glance at Jess, but she's staring into space. Suddenly she comes to, as if she's just noticed me.

"Ready?" she says.

"Er . . . yes. I'll just go and pay."

We head over to the front desk, where Sandra starts scanning in my purchases. Meanwhile Georgina is surveying Jess.

"If you're not in the mood for clothes," Georgina says suddenly, "what about jewelry?" She pulls out a tray from under the cash desk. "We've got some lovely bracelets in. Only ten pounds. This might suit you." She lifts up a beautiful bracelet made of plain silver ovals linked together. I hold my breath.

"It's nice." Jess nods, and I feel a huge pang of relief.

"For Becky's sister . . ." says Georgina, "three pounds."

"Wow!" I beam at her. "That's fantastic! Thank you so much, Georgina!"

"No, thanks," says Jess. "I don't need a bracelet."

What?

My head swivels in shock. Did she not understand?

"But . . . it's only three pounds," I say. "It's a total bargain!"

"I don't need it." Jess shrugs.

"But . . ."

I'm at a loss for words. How can you not buy a bracelet for three pounds? How?

"There you are, Becky!" says Sandra, handing over the rope cords of my carrier bags. There are two of them—all pale pink and glossy and scrumptious—but as my hands close round the handles I don't feel my customary rush of delight. In fact, I barely feel anything. I'm too confused.

"Well . . . bye, then!" I say. "And thanks! See you soon!"

"Bye, Becky darling!" says Georgina. "And . . . Jess," she adds. "See you again, I hope."

"Becky!" says Sandra. "Before you go, just let me give you the leaflet about our sale."

She hurries over, hands me a glossy leaflet, and leans forward.

"I'm not being funny or anything," she says into my ear. "But . . . are you *sure* she's your sister?"

"So!" I say uncertainly as we emerge into the street. "That was fun!" I glance at Jess, but she's got that composed, matter-of-fact expression and I can't tell what she's thinking. I wish just *once* she'd smile. Or say, "Yes, it was fab!"

"It's a shame you didn't find anything in Georgina's," I venture. "Did you . . . like the clothes?"

Jess shrugs. I knew it. She just hates my taste. All that pretending she doesn't need any clothes was just to be polite.

I mean, who doesn't need a T-shirt?

Well, never mind. We'll just have to find different shops. Shops that Jess likes. As we head down the sunny street, I'm thinking hard. Not skirts . . . not bracelets . . . Jeans! Everyone likes jeans. Perfect.

"I really need a new pair of jeans," I say casually.

"Why?" Jess frowns. "What's wrong with the jeans you're wearing?"

"Well . . . nothing. But I need some more!" I say with a laugh. "I want some a bit longer than these, not *too* low-slung, maybe in a really dark inky blue. . . ."

I look at Jess expectantly, waiting for her to respond. But she just continues walking.

"So . . . do you need any jeans?" I feel like I'm pushing a heavy rock uphill.

"No," says Jess. "But you go ahead."

"Maybe another time." I force a smile. "It doesn't matter."

By now we've reached the corner—and yes! L.K. Bennett is having a sale!

"Look at these!" I exclaim in excitement, hurrying to the big window filled with colorful strappy sandals. "Aren't they gorgeous? What kind of shoes do you like?"

Jess runs her eyes over the display.

"I don't really bother much with shoes," she says. "No one ever notices shoes."

For a moment my legs feel weak with shock.

No one ever notices shoes?

But . . . of course! She's joking! I'm going to have to get used to her dry sense of humor.

"Ohhhh, you!" I say, and give her a friendly push. "Well . . . I might just pop in and try some on, if you don't mind?"

If I try on enough pairs, I'm thinking, Jess is bound to join in too.

Except . . . she doesn't. Not at the next shop, either. Nor does she try any of the perfumes or makeup at Space.NK. I'm laden with bags, but Jess still doesn't have one thing. She can't be enjoying herself. She must think I'm a rubbish sister.

"Do you need any . . . kitchenware?" I suggest in desperation.

We could buy cool aprons, or some chrome gadgety things. . . . But Jess is shaking her head.

"I get all mine from the discount warehouse. It's much cheaper than the high street."

"Well, what about . . . luggage!" I exclaim, suddenly inspired. "Luggage is one of those areas you can really forget about—"

"I don't need any luggage," says Jess. "I've got my rucksack."

"Right."

I'm totally running out of ideas. What else *is* there? Lamps, maybe? Or . . . rugs?

Suddenly Jess's eyes light up.

"Hang on," she says, sounding more animated than she has all day. "Do you mind if I go in here?"

I stop still. We're outside a tiny, quite nondescript stationery shop, which I've never been into.

"Absolutely!" My words come tumbling out in a whoosh of relief. "Go ahead! Fantastic!"

Stationery! Of course! Why on earth didn't I think of that before? She's a student . . . she writes all the time . . . that must be her thing!

The shop is so narrow I'm not sure I'll fit in with all my carrier bags, so I wait outside on the pavement, thrilled she's finally shown an interest in something. I wonder what she's buying. Gorgeous notebooks? Or handmade cards? Or maybe some beautiful fountain pen?

I mean, all kudos to her. I'd never even noticed this shop before!

"So, what did you buy?" I demand in excitement as soon as she comes out holding two bulging carrier bags. "Show! Show!"

Jess looks blank.

"I didn't buy anything," she says.

"But . . . your carrier bags! What's in them?"

"Didn't you see the sign?" She gestures at a hand-written postcard in the window. "They're giving away used padded envelopes."

She opens up her carriers to reveal a selection of battered Jiffy bags and a bundle of squashed-up, graying bubble wrap.

"I must have saved at least ten pounds," she adds with satisfaction. "And they'll always come in handy."

I'm speechless.

"Er . . . fab!" I manage at last. "They're really gorgeous! I love the . . . um . . . labels. So . . . we've both done really well! Let's go and have a cappuccino!"

There's a coffee shop round the corner, and as we approach it my spirits begin to rise again. So maybe the shopping hasn't gone as I imagined, but it doesn't matter. The point is, here we are, two sisters, coming for a cappuccino and a gossip together! We'll sit at a lovely marble table, and sip our coffees, and tell each other all about ourselves. . . .

"I brought a flask," comes Jess's voice behind me.

I turn round to see Jess taking a white plastic flask out of her rucksack.

"What?" I say faintly.

"We don't want that overpriced coffee." She jabs a thumb at the café. "The markup at those places is appalling."

"But . . ."

"We can sit on this bench. I'll just wipe it clean."

I gaze at her in rising dismay. I cannot have my first-ever coffee with my long-lost sister sitting on some grotty old bench, swigging out of a flask.

"But I want to go into a nice coffee shop!" The words rush out before I can stop them. "And sit at a marble table, and have a proper cappuccino!"

Jess is surveying me with pained disapproval, as though she can't believe anyone would be so shallow.

"Please?" I say plaintively.

"Oh," says Jess. "Well, OK." She closes up her flask. "But you should get into the habit of making your own.

You could save hundreds of pounds a year. Just buy a secondhand flask. And you can use coffee grounds at least twice. The flavor's fine. . . ."

"I'll . . . bear that in mind," I say, barely listening. "Come on!"

The coffee shop is all warm and aromatic, with a fabulous smell of coffee. There are spotlights dancing on the marble tables, and music playing, and a happy, cheerful buzz.

"You see?" I beam at Jess. "Isn't this nice? A table for me and my sister, please," I add happily to a waiter standing by the door.

I so love saying that! *My sister.*

We sit down and I put all my shopping bags on the floor—and feel myself start to relax. This is better. In fact, this is what we should have done first of all.

A waitress who looks about twelve and is wearing a badge saying IT'S MY FIRST DAY! approaches our table.

"Hi!" I greet her. "I'd like a cappuccino, please. We should be having champagne, really," I can't resist adding. "We're long-lost sisters!"

"Wow!" says the waitress. "Cool!"

"I'll just have some plain tap water, thanks," says Jess, closing her menu.

"Don't you want a nice frothy coffee?" I say in surprise.

"I don't want to pay vastly inflated prices to a global moneymaking corporation." She gives the waitress a severe look. "Do *you* think a 400 percent profit margin is ethical?"

"Um . . ." The waitress looks stumped. "Did you want ice in your water?" she says at last.

"Have a coffee too," I say quickly. "Go on." I look at the waitress. "She'll have a cappuccino." I turn to Jess. "You get a free chocolate in the saucer!"

SHOPAHOLIC & SISTER 157

As the waitress scuttles away, Jess frowns.

"Do you know the real cost of making a cappuccino? It's a few pence. And we're being charged nearly two pounds."

God, Jess has a bit of a thing about coffee, doesn't she? But never mind. I'll just change the subject.

"So!" I lean back and spread my arms. "Tell me all about yourself."

"What do you want to know?" says Jess.

"Everything!" I say enthusiastically. "Like . . . what are your hobbies, apart from walking?"

She ponders for a few moments.

"I like caving," she says at last, as the waitress puts two cappuccinos down in front of us.

"Caving!" I echo. "Is that where you . . . go into caves?"

Jess gives me a look over her cup.

"That's basically it, yes."

"Wow! That's really . . ."

I'm struggling for words. What can I say about caves? Apart from they're all dark and cold and slimy.

"That's really interesting!" I say at last. "I'd love to go in a cave!"

"And of course rocks," Jess adds. "That's my main interest."

"Me too! Especially great big shiny rocks from Tiffany's!" I laugh, to show I'm joking, but Jess doesn't react. I'm not entirely sure she got it.

"My Ph.D. is on the petrogenesis and geochemistry of fluorite-hematite deposits," she says, showing more animation than she has all day.

I don't think I understood one bit of that.

"Er . . . great!" I say. "So . . . how come you decided to study rocks?"

"My father got me into it," says Jess, and her face relaxes into a smile. "It's his passion too."

"Dad?" I say in amazement. "I never knew he was into rocks!"

"Not your dad." She gives me a scathing look. "*My* dad. My stepfather. The man who brought me up."

Right.

Of course she didn't mean Dad. That was really stupid.

Suddenly my head is full of questions.

"So . . . did your dad . . . did he always know that you . . ." I trail off, not quite knowing how to put it.

"My dad knew I wasn't his, pretty much from the word *go*." Jess is turning a spoon over and over in her fingers. "But he raised me all the same. He never treated me any different from my brothers."

I dart a look at her averted face.

"Did *you* know?" I ask hesitantly. "That he wasn't really your dad?"

"Yes. But we didn't talk about it. He was my real dad, as far as I was concerned. Still is."

"Didn't you ever want to go looking for your . . . biological father?"

"I might have done." She stops rotating the spoon. "Once. But then Mum died and Dad was all I had left. I didn't need another dad. It was only when I found out about this blood disorder. I realized there could be people related to me, not knowing they were at risk. I felt responsible. It would have preyed on my mind." She looks up. "You should get yourself tested, Becky."

"Oh, I'm going to," I say quickly. "Dad already has been, but he's OK. And . . . er . . . thanks."

"No problem."

"So . . . what's your dad like?"

Jess deliberates for a while. "He's great," she says at last.

I wait for more details . . . but there don't seem to be

any. I don't quite dare ask about her mum. Not until I know her better.

Jess sips her water and I fiddle with my chocolate wrapper, wondering what to talk about next. I'm slightly at a loss, which is ridiculous. This is my sister! Come on!

"So, are you going on holiday this year?" I ask at last. God, I must be desperate. I sound like a hairdresser.

"I don't know yet," says Jess. "It all depends."

Suddenly I have the most marvelous idea.

"We could go on holiday together!" I say in excitement. "Wouldn't that be great? We could get a villa in Italy or something . . . really get to know each other—"

"Rebecca, listen," Jess interrupts flatly. "I'm not looking for another family."

My face is suddenly hot.

"I—I know," I stammer. "I didn't mean . . ."

"I don't *need* another family," she presses on. "I said this to Jane and Graham in the summer. That's not why I tracked you down. It was my duty to contact you about the medical situation. That's all."

"What do you mean by 'that's all'?" I falter.

"I mean it's nice to meet you. And your mum and dad are great. But you've got your life"—she pauses—"and I've got mine."

Is she saying she doesn't want to get to know me? Her own *sister*?

"But we've only just found each other!" I say in a rush. "After all these years! Don't you find it amazing?" I lean forward and put my hand next to hers. "Look! We have the same blood!"

"So what?" Jess looks unmoved. "It's just a biological fact."

"But . . . haven't you always wanted a sister? Haven't you always wondered what it would be like?"

"Not particularly." She must see the hurt on my face. "Don't get me wrong. It's been interesting to meet you."

Interesting? It's been *interesting*?

I push the froth around the cappuccino with my spoon. She doesn't want to get to know me. My own sister doesn't want to get to know me. What's wrong with me?

Nothing's going the way I planned. I thought today would be one of the best days of my life. I thought shopping with my sister would be *fun*. I thought we'd be bonded by now. I thought we'd be having coffee, surrounded by all our fab new things, laughing and teasing each other. . . .

"So, shall we go back to your mum's?" says Jess, draining her cup.

"What . . . already?" I say, startled. "But . . . we've got hours left. You haven't even bought anything yet!"

Jess sighs impatiently.

"Look, Becky. I wanted to be polite, so I came along today. But the truth is, I really can't stand shopping."

My heart sinks. I knew she wasn't having a good time. I knew she hated my taste. I have to salvage this.

"I know we haven't found the right shops yet." I lean forward eagerly. "But there are more. We can go into different ones—"

"No," Jess interrupts. "You don't get it. I don't like shopping. Full stop."

"Catalogs!" I say, suddenly inspired. "We could go home, get a load of catalogs . . . it'd be fun!"

"Can't you get this through your head?" Jess exclaims in exasperation. "Read my lips very carefully. I. Hate. Shopping."

When we arrive home, Luke is in the front garden, talking to Dad. As he sees us pulling into the drive he looks stunned.

"What are you doing back so soon?" he says, hurrying over to the car. "Is anything wrong?"

"Everything's fine!" I say. My brain still feels like it's short-circuited. "We were just . . . quicker than I thought we'd be."

"Thanks," says Jess, getting out.

"It was a pleasure."

As Jess heads toward Dad, Luke gets into the car beside me and closes the door.

"Becky, are you OK?"

"I'm . . . fine. I think."

I can't quite get my head round the day. My mind keeps replaying the way I fantasized it would be. The two of us sauntering along, swinging our bags, laughing happily . . . trying on each other's things . . . buying each other friendship bracelets . . . calling each other by little nicknames. . . .

"So? How was it?"

"It was . . ." I force a bright smile. "It was really good fun. We both had a great time."

"What did you buy?"

"A couple of tops . . . a really nice skirt . . . some shoes . . ."

"Mmm-hmm." Luke nods. "And what did Jess buy?"

For a moment I can't speak.

"Nothing," I whisper at last.

"Oh, Becky." Luke sighs and puts his arm round me. "I know you wanted to find a soul mate. I know you wanted Jess to be your new best friend. But maybe you'll have to accept that you're just . . . too different."

"We're *not* too different," I say stubbornly. "We're sisters."

"Sweetheart, it's OK," says Luke. "You can admit it if you don't get along. No one will think you've failed."

Failed?

"We do get along!" I say, stung. "We do! We just need to find a bit more . . . common ground. So she doesn't like shopping. But that doesn't matter! I like things other than shopping!"

Luke is shaking his head.

"Accept it. You're different people and there's no reason why you should get on."

"But we've got the same blood! We can't be that different! We *can't* be!"

"Becky—"

"I'm not going to give up, just like that! This is my long-lost sister we're talking about!"

"Sweetheart—"

I cut him off. "I know we can be friends. I *know* we can."

With sudden determination I wrench open the car door and get out.

"Hey, Jess!" I call, hurrying across the lawn. "After your conference, do you want to come and stay for the weekend? I promise we'll have a good time."

"That's a nice idea, love!" says Dad, his face lighting up.

"I'm not sure," says Jess. "I really have to get back home. . . ."

"Please. Just one weekend. We don't need to go shopping!" The words come tumbling out of me. "It won't be like today. We can do whatever you like. Just have a really low-key, easy time. What do you think?"

My fingers are twisting into knots. Jess glances at Dad's hopeful face.

"OK," she says at last. "That would be nice. Thanks."

PGNI FIRST BANK VISA

7 CAMEL SQUARE

LIVERPOOL L1 5NP

Mrs Rebecca Brandon
37 Maida Vale Mansions
Maida Vale
London NW6 0YF

12 May 2003

Dear Mrs Brandon:

Thank you for your prompt response to my letter of
20 April.

We are glad to inform you that you have been
successful in your application for the High Status
Golden Credit Card.

In answer to your questions, the card will be delivered
to your home address and will resemble a credit card.
It cannot be "disguised as a cake" as you suggest. Nor
can we provide a distraction outside as it arrives.

If you have any further questions please do not
hesitate to contact me, and we hope you enjoy the
benefits of your new card.

Yours sincerely,

Peter Johnson
Customer Accounts Executive

PGNI FIRST BANK VISA

7 CAMEL SQUARE

LIVERPOOL L1 5NP

Ms Jessica Bertram
12 Hill Rise
Scully
Cumbria CA19 1BD

12 May 2003

Dear Ms Bertram:

Thank you for your prompt response to my letter of
20 April.

I apologize for approaching you with the offer of a
High Status Golden Credit Card. I did not mean to
cause any offence.

By saying you had been personally handpicked for a
£20,000 credit limit, I was not intending to imply
that you are "debt-ridden and irresponsible" nor to
defame your character.

As a gesture of goodwill I enclose a gift voucher of
£25, and look forward to being of service should you
change your mind on the issue of credit cards.

Yours sincerely,

Peter Johnson
Customer Accounts Executive

Twelve

I'M NOT GIVING up.

So maybe my first meeting with Jess didn't go quite as I planned. But this weekend will be better, I just know it will. I mean, in hindsight, the first meeting was *bound* to be a bit awkward. But this time we'll have gotten through that first hurdle and will be far more relaxed and easy with each other. Plus, I'm far more prepared than I was last time. After Jess left on Saturday, Mum and Dad could see I was a bit down, so they made a pot of tea and we had a good old chat. And we all agreed it's impossible to get on with someone straightaway if you don't know anything about her. So Mum and Dad racked their brains for all the details they knew about Jess and wrote them all down. And I've been learning them all week.

Like, for instance: she did nine GCSE exams and got As in all of them. She never eats avocados. As well as caving and walking, she does something called pot-holing. She likes poetry. And her favorite dog is a . . .

Fuck.

I grab the crib sheet and scan down.

Oh yes. A border collie.

It's Saturday morning, and I'm in our spare room, making my final preparations for Jess's arrival. I bought a book this week called *The Gracious Hostess,* and it said the guest room should be "well thought-out, with little individual touches to make your guest feel welcome."

So on the dressing table are flowers and a book of poetry, and by the bed I've put a careful selection of magazines: *Rambling News, Caving Enthusiast,* and *Potholing Monthly,* which is a magazine you can order only on the Internet. (I had to take out a two-year subscription, actually, just to get a copy. But that's all right. I can just forward the other twenty-three copies to Jess.)

And on the wall is my pièce de résistance, which I am so proud of. It's an enormous poster of a cave! With stalag . . . things.

I fluff up the pillows, anticipating the weekend. Tonight will be totally different from last time. For a start, we won't go *near* any shops. I've just planned a nice, simple, relaxed evening in. We can watch a movie and eat popcorn, and do each other's nails, and really chill. And then later on I'll come and sit on her bed and we can wear matching pajamas and eat peppermint creams, and talk long into the night.

"This all looks very nice," says Luke, coming in behind me. "You've done a great job. In fact, the whole apartment looks amazing!" He wanders out, and I follow him into the hall. Although there are still a few boxes here and there, the whole place looks so much clearer!

We walk into the sitting room, now utterly transformed. All the piles of rugs and boxes and crates have disappeared. There are just two sofas, two coffee tables, and the Indonesian gamelan.

"Hats off to you, Becky," says Luke, looking around. "In fact, I owe you an apology. You told me you could make it all work—and I doubted you. But I would never have guessed so much clutter could be so well organized." He looks around the room incredulously. "There were so many things in here! Where have they all gone?"

"I've just . . . found homes for them!" I say brightly.

"Well, I'm really impressed," he says, running his hand over the mantelpiece, which is bare except for the five hand-painted eggs. "You should become a storage consultant."

"Maybe I will!"

OK, I think I want to get off this subject now. Any minute Luke's going to start looking a bit more closely and say something like "Where are the Chinese urns?" or "Where are the wooden giraffes?"

"I'll just check my e-mails," I say casually. "Why don't you make us some nice coffee?"

I wait until Luke's safely in the kitchen, then hurry to my computer and type in www.eBay.co.uk.

eBay has totally saved my life. Totally

In fact, what did I ever do before eBay? It is the most brilliant, genius invention since . . . well, since whoever invented shops.

The minute I got back from Mum's last Saturday I joined, and put up for sale the Chinese urns, the wooden giraffes, and three of the rugs. And in three days they'd all been sold! Just like that! So the next day I put up five more rugs and two coffee tables. And since then, I haven't stopped.

I quickly click on "Items I'm Selling," glancing at the door every so often. I mustn't be long or Luke'll come in and see me, but I'm desperate to find out if anyone has bid on the totem pole.

A moment later the page appears . . . and yes! Result! Someone's bid fifty pounds! I feel a hit of adrenaline and punch the air with a whoop (a quiet one, so Luke won't hear). It's such a power kick, selling stuff! I'm totally addicted!

And the best thing of all is, I'm killing two birds with one stone. I'm solving our clutter problems—*and* I'm making money. Quite a lot of money, actually! I don't want to boast—but every single day this week I've made a profit. I'm just like a City bond trader!

For example, I got £200 for the slate coffee table— and we certainly didn't pay more than a hundred for it. I got £100 for the Chinese urns, and £150 each for the five kilims, which only cost about £40 each in Turkey, if that. And best of all, I made a cool £2,000 on ten Tiffany clocks I don't even remember buying! The guy even paid in cash and came to pick them up! Honestly, I'm doing so well, I could make eBay trading my career! I can hear Luke getting mugs out in the kitchen, and I click off "Items I'm Selling."

Then, very quickly, I click on "Items I'm Bidding On."

Obviously I joined eBay very much as a *seller* rather than a bidder. But I just happened to be browsing the other day when I came across this amazing orange vintage coat from the fifties with big black buttons. It's a total one-off, and no one had made a single bid on it. So I made a tiny exception, just for that.

And also for a pair of Prada shoes, which only had one bid on them, for fifty quid. I mean, Prada shoes for fifty quid!

And that fantastic Yves Saint Laurent evening dress,

which some other bidder got in the end. God, that was annoying. I won't make that mistake again.

I click on the vintage coat—and I don't believe it. I bid £80 yesterday, which is the reserve price, and I've been trumped with £100. Well, I'm not losing this one. No way. I quickly type in "£120" and close down, just as Luke comes in with a tray.

"Any e-mails?" he says.

"Er . . . some!" I say brightly, and take a cup of coffee. "Thanks!"

I haven't told Luke about the whole eBay thing because there's no need for him to get involved in every mundane detail of the household finances.

"I found these in the kitchen." Luke nods toward a tin of luxury Fortnum and Mason chocolate biscuits on the tray. "Very nice."

"Just a little treat." I smile at him. "And don't worry. It's all within the budget."

Which is true! My budget is so much bigger now, I can afford a few luxuries!

Luke takes a sip of coffee. Then his eyes fall on a pink folder lying on his desk.

"What's this?"

I wondered when he was going to notice that.

"That's for you," I say casually. "Just a little thing I've put together to help you. My ideas for the future of the company."

It hit me in the bath the other day. If Luke wins this great big pitch, he's going to have to expand the company. And I know all about expansion.

The reason is, when I was a personal shopper at Barneys, I had this client named Sheri, who owned her own business. I heard the whole saga of how she expanded too fast and all the mistakes she made, like renting six thousand square feet of office space in TriBeCa which she never used. I mean, at the time I thought it was really boring. I actually dreaded her appointments. But now I realize it's all totally relevant to Luke!

So I decided to write down everything she used to say, like consolidating your key markets and acquiring competitors. And that's when an even better idea came to me: Luke should buy up another PR firm.

I even know which one he should buy! David Neville, who used to work for Farnham PR, set up his own firm three years ago, when I was still a financial journalist. He's really talented and everyone keeps saying how well he's doing. But I know he's secretly been struggling, because I saw his wife, Judy, at the hairdresser's last week and she told me.

"Becky . . ." Luke's frowning. "I haven't got time for this."

"But it'll be useful to you!" I say quickly. "When I was at Barneys I learned all about—"

"*Barneys*? Becky, I run a PR company. Not a fashion store."

"But I've had these ideas—"

"Becky," Luke interrupts impatiently. "Right now my priority is bringing in new business. Nothing else. I don't have time for your ideas, OK?" He stuffs the folder into his briefcase without opening it. "I'll look at it sometime."

I sit down, feeling a bit crestfallen. The doorbell rings and I look up in surprise.

"Oh! Maybe that's Jess, early!"

"No, it'll be Gary," says Luke. "I'll let him in."

Gary is Luke's second in command. He ran the London office while we were living in New York and on our honeymoon, and he and Luke get on really well. He even ended up being Luke's best man at our wedding. Kind of.

The wedding's a bit of a long story, actually.

"What's Gary doing here?" I ask in surprise.

"I told him to meet me here," replies Luke, heading out to the entry phone and buzzing it. "We have some work to do on the pitch. Then we're planning to go to lunch."

"Oh, right," I say, trying to hide my disappointment. I was really looking forward to spending a bit of time with Luke today, before Jess arrives. He's so busy these days. He hasn't been home once before eight all week, and last night he didn't arrive back until eleven. I know they're working hard at the moment. And I know the Arcodas pitch is important. But still. For months and months, Luke and I were together twenty-four hours a day . . . and now I hardly ever see him.

"Maybe I could help with the pitch," I suggest. "I could join the team!"

"I don't think so," Luke says without even looking up.

"There must be something I could do," I say, leaning forward eagerly. "Luke, I really want to help the company. I'll do anything—"

"It's all pretty much under control," says Luke. "But thanks. Do you want to come out to lunch with us?" he adds kindly. "You're welcome if you don't mind a bit of shop talk."

"No. It's fine." I give a little shrug. "Have fun. Hi, Gary," I add, as he appears at the front door.

"Hi, Becky!" Gary says cheerfully. He's tall and well-built with a broad, amiable face. He's worked for Luke for three years, and I don't think I've ever seen him look angry, or even rattled.

"Come in," Luke says, and ushers him into the study. The door closes—then almost immediately it opens again and Luke looks out. "Becky, if the phone rings, could you answer it? I don't want to be disturbed for a few minutes."

"No problem!" I say brightly.

Answering the phone is *not* what I meant by helping the company.

I wander down the corridor toward the sitting room, feeling deflated. I'm an intelligent, creative person. I could be a help, I know I could. I mean, Luke and I are supposed to be a partnership. We're supposed to do things *together*.

The phone rings and I jump. Maybe it's Jess. Maybe she's here! I hurry to the receiver and pick it up.

"Hello?"

"Mrs. Brandon?" comes a man's raspy voice.

"Yes!"

"It's Nathan Temple here."

My mind is totally blank. Nathan? I don't know any Nathans. . . .

"You may recall, we met in Milan a few weeks ago."

Oh my God. It's the man from the shop! I should have recognized his voice straightaway.

"Hello! Of course I remember! How are you?"

"I'm well, thank you," he says. "And you? Enjoying your new bag?"

"I absolutely love it!" I can't hide my enthusiasm. "It's changed my whole life! Thank you *so* much again for what you did."

"It was my pleasure."

Down the line I hear the click of his lighter. I'm not entirely sure what to say next.

"Maybe I could buy you lunch," I blurt out. "As a proper thank-you. Anywhere you like!"

"That's not necessary." He sounds amused. "Besides which, my doctor has put me on a diet."

"Oh, right. That's a shame—"

"However, since you mention it . . . As you said yourself in Milan, one good turn deserves another."

"Absolutely! I really owe you one! If there's anything I can do, *anything* at all . . ."

"I was thinking of your husband, Luke. I was hoping he might do me a small favor."

"He'd love to!" I exclaim. "I know he would!"

"Is he there? Might I have a quick word?"

If I get Luke to the phone now I'll have to disturb him. And explain who Nathan Temple is . . . and how I met him . . . and about the Angel bag. . . .

"You know what?" I say, turning back to the phone. "He's not in right now, I'm afraid. But can I take a message?"

"The situation is this. I'm opening a five-star hotel on the island of Cyprus. It's going to be a top-of-the-range resort and I'm planning a big launch. Celebrity party, press coverage. I'd very much like your husband to be involved."

A celebrity party in Cyprus? A five-star hotel?

Oh my God. This would be so wonderful for Luke's business! Forget about Arcodas. The Nathan Temple account could be fab!

"I'm sure he'd love to!" I say, regaining my voice. "It sounds fantastic!"

"Your husband's very talented. He has a very classy reputation. Which is what we want."

"Well." I can't help but glow with pride. "He is pretty good at what he does."

"I gather he specializes in financial institutions, though. Would a hotel launch be a problem?"

My heart starts thudding. I can't let this opportunity slip away. I have to sell Brandon Communications.

"Not at all," I say smoothly. "We at Brandon Communications are skilled in all areas of public relations, from finance to big business to hotels. Versatility is our motto."

"Ah." He sounds pleased. "That's what I was hoping to hear. I attended a party run by your husband last year as a guest of a guest. A property investment launch in New York. Very slick affair, and a huge media attendance. I was impressed."

"In that amazing brownstone?" I chime in, delighted. "With the marble staircase and the champagne cocktails? I was there too!"

I nearly add that I was the one in a backless red Donna Karan dress, but stop myself in time.

"You work for the company, then?" He sounds interested.

"I have a . . . small consultancy role," I say, crossing my fingers. "Specializing in strategy. And by sheer chance, one of our current strategies is an expansion into the . . . er . . . five-star travel arena."

"Then it looks like we might be able to help one another out," says Nathan Temple. "Perhaps we could set up a meeting this week? As I say, we're very anxious to have your husband, Luke, on board."

"Please, Mr. Temple," I say in my most charming manner. "You did me a favor. Now this is my chance to repay it. My husband would be delighted to help you. In fact, he'll make it a priority!" I beam at the phone. "Let me take your number, and I'll get Luke to call you later today."

"I look forward to your husband's call. Nice talking to you again, Mrs. Brandon."

"Please! Call me Becky!"

As I replace the receiver I'm grinning from ear to ear.

There's Luke and Gary, slaving away over their pitch—and meanwhile I've snaffled them a fabulous new client without even trying! And not even some dreary old bank. A five-star hotel in Cyprus! A huge, prestigious job!

Just then the study door opens and Luke comes out, holding a folder. As he picks up his briefcase he glances over and gives me a distracted smile.

"All right, Becky? We're off to lunch. Who was that on the phone?"

"Oh . . . just a friend of mine," I say carelessly. "By the way, Luke . . . maybe I will come along to lunch after all."

"OK," he says. "Great!"

When he hears how I've been wheeling and dealing with top business magnates on his behalf, he'll be totally gobsmacked! And *then* maybe he'll see just how much of a help I can be to him.

Just wait till I tell them the news. Just wait!

All the way to the restaurant, I'm hugging my secret. Honestly, Luke should hire me! I should become some kind of ambassador for the company! A chance meeting in Milan—and this is what results. A brand-new client for the company. Luke's going to be so impressed when I tell him the news. He'll probably order a bottle of champagne straightaway.

This could be an amazing new business opportunity for him! He could start a whole division devoted to five-star hotels and spas. Brandon Communications Luxury Travel. And I could be part of it, maybe.

I could be the one who test-markets the spas.

"So . . . still on the dinner we're hosting," Gary is saying to Luke as we sit down. "You've sorted out the gifts?"

"Yup," says Luke. "They're at home. What about transport? Have we organized cars for them?"

"I'll get someone onto it." Gary makes a careful note on a little pocket pad, then looks up at me. "Sorry, Becky. This must be boring. You know this pitch is pretty important to us."

"That's OK," I say with a demure smile. "Luke was just telling me how winning new business is your number-one priority right now."

"Absolutely." Gary nods.

"I expect it's quite hard work, bringing in new clients," I add innocently.

"Yes, it can be." Gary smiles.

I *so* want to blurt out the whole story. But I must time my revelation perfectly.

As the waiter pours mineral water for Luke and Gary, I suddenly notice three girls at a nearby table, nudging each other and pointing at my Angel bag. Trying to hide my delight, I casually adjust the bag on my chair so that the embossed angel and *Dante* are clearly visible.

It's just amazing. Everywhere I go, people notice this bag. It is the best thing I have ever bought, ever, *ever*. And now it's brought Luke new business, too. It's a lucky charm!

"Cheers!" I say, lifting my glass as the waiter retreats. "To new clients!"

"New clients," Luke and Gary echo in unison. Gary takes a sip of water, then turns to Luke. "So, Luke, just regarding the last proposal we're making . . . I spoke to Sam Church the other day—"

I can't wait a moment longer. I *have* to tell them.

"Speaking of churches!" I interrupt in bright tones.

There's a startled pause.

"Becky, we weren't talking about churches," says Luke.

"Yes, you were! Kind of."

Luke looks bemused. OK, I could have managed this a little more smoothly. But never mind.

"So, *speaking* of churches . . ." I press on. "And . . . er . . . religious buildings in general . . . I suppose you've heard of a man called Nathan Temple, haven't you?"

I look from Luke to Gary, unable to hide my elation. Both men look back at me curiously.

"Of course I've heard of Nathan Temple," says Luke.

Ha! I knew it.

"He's a pretty big player, right? Pretty important." I raise my eyebrows in a cryptic manner. "He's probably someone you'd really like to network with. Maybe even get as a new client?"

"Hardly!" Luke wrinkles his nose as though he's found a worm in his apple.

I pause uncertainly. What's "hardly" supposed to mean?

"Of course you would!" I persist. "He'd be a great client!"

"No, Becky. He wouldn't." Luke takes a sip of water. "Sorry, Gary, what were you saying?"

This is not going according to plan. I had the whole conversation mapped out in my head. Luke was going to say, "I'd adore Nathan Temple as a client, of course—but how does one *get* to him?" Then Gary was going to sigh and say, "No one can get to Nathan Temple." And then I was going to lean across the table with a confidential little smile. . . .

"So, I've spoken to Sam Church," resumes Gary, taking some papers out of his briefcase. "And he gave me these. Have a look."

"Wait!" I interrupt, trying to haul the conversation back on track. "So, Luke, why wouldn't you want

Nathan Temple as a client? I mean, he's rich . . . he's famous. . . ."

"Infamous, more like," Gary puts in with a grin.

"You do know who Nathan Temple is," says Luke.

"Of course I do!" I say. "He's a top businessman and . . . er . . . a high-class hotelier—"

"Becky, he runs the seediest chain of motels in the land."

My smile freezes on my face.

"What?" I manage at last.

"Not anymore," says Gary. "Be fair."

"Then he used to," says Luke. "That's how he made his money. Value Motels. Water beds thrown in for free. And whatever other business went on behind closed doors." He pulls a disdainful face and pours out more water.

"You've heard the rumor he's considering buying up the *Daily World*?" asks Gary.

"Yes, I did," Luke says with a grimace. "Spare us. You know he has a conviction for grievous bodily harm?"

My head is spinning. A conviction? But he seemed so nice. He was so sweet! He got me my Angel bag!

"Apparently he's reformed." Gary shrugs. "Become a new person. So he says."

"A new person?" says Luke dismissively. "Gary, he's little better than a gangster."

I nearly drop my glass on the floor. I owe a favor to a *gangster*?

" 'Gangster's' a little harsh," says Gary, amused. "That was years ago."

"These people never change," says Luke firmly.

"You're a hard man, Luke!" Gary says with a laugh. Then he suddenly spots my face. "Becky, are you OK?"

"Fine!" I say shrilly, and take a gulp of water. "Lovely!"

I feel hot and cold all over. This is not going to plan. This is not going remotely to plan.

My first brilliant networking triumph. The first big client I woo for Brandon Communications. And he turns out to be a motel king with a criminal conviction.

But how was I supposed to know? How? He seemed so charming. He was so well dressed!

And now I've said Luke will work for him.

Kind of.

I mean . . . I didn't actually *promise* anything, did I?

Oh God.

I can hear my own voice now, gaily chirping: "My husband would be delighted to do it. In fact, he'll make it a priority!"

I gaze at my menu, trying to stay calm. OK, it's obvious what I have to do. I have to tell Luke. Yes. Just confess the whole thing. Milan . . . the Angel bag . . . the phone call today . . . everything. It's the grown-up option.

I glance at Luke's taut face as he reads through his paperwork and feel a spasm of fear.

I can't. I just can't.

"It's funny you should have mentioned Nathan Temple, Becky," says Gary, sipping his water. "I haven't even told you this yet, Luke, but he's been in touch with us about doing the PR for some new hotel."

I stare at Gary's genial face and feel a huge wave of relief.

Of course they would have made an official approach too. Of course! I've been worrying about nothing! Luke will do the job and I'll be quits with Nathan Temple and everything will be fine. . . .

"I take it we'll decline," Gary adds.

Decline? My head jerks up.

"Can you think what it would do to our reputation?"

Luke says with a short laugh. "Turn down the job. But tactfully," he adds with a frown. "If he's buying the *Daily World*, we don't want to offend him."

"Don't decline!" I blurt out before I can stop myself.

Both men turn to me in surprise, and I force a light-hearted laugh. "I mean . . . shouldn't you look at both sides of the argument? Before you make your decision."

"Becky, as far as I'm concerned there is only *one* argument," says Luke crisply. "Nathan Temple is not the sort of character I want associated with my company." He opens his menu. "We should order."

"Don't you think that's a bit judgmental?" I say desperately. " 'Cast not the first clout' and all that."

"What?" Luke sounds astonished.

"It's in the Bible!"

Luke gives me a look.

"Do you mean *stone*?" he says.

"Er . . ."

Oh. Maybe he's right. But stone . . . clout . . . what's the difference?

"The point is—" I begin.

"The point is," Luke interrupts, "Brandon Communications does not want to be associated with someone who has a criminal record. Let alone the rest of it."

"But that's so . . . narrow-minded! Most people have probably got a criminal record these days!" I gesture widely with my arms. "I mean, who sitting round this table does not have some kind of criminal record?"

There's a short silence.

"Well," says Luke. "I don't. Gary doesn't. You don't."

I look at him, taken aback. I suppose he's right. I don't.

That's quite a surprise, actually. I'd always thought of myself as living on the edge.

"Even so—"

"Becky, what's brought this on, anyway?" Luke frowns. "Why are you so obsessed with Nathan Temple?"

"I'm not *obsessed*!" I say hurriedly. "I'm just . . . interested in your clients. And prospective clients."

"Well, he's not my client. Nor my prospective client," says Luke with finality. "And neither will he ever be."

"Right. Well . . . that's pretty clear."

We all study our menus. At least, the other two are studying their menus. I'm pretending to study mine, while my mind goes skittering round and round.

So I can't persuade Luke. So I'll just have to manage the situation. This is what supportive wives do. They deal with problems discreetly and efficiently. I bet Hillary Clinton's done this kind of thing millions of times.

It'll be fine. I'll simply phone up Nathan Temple, thank him for his kind offer, and say that, unfortunately, Luke's really, really busy—

No. I'll say he *tried* to call but no one answered. . . .

"Becky? Are you OK?"

I look up to see both men looking at me with concern. Abruptly I realize I'm tapping the table harder and harder with one of Gary's pencils.

"I'm great!" I say, and quickly put it down.

OK. I have a plan. What I will do is . . . I will say that Luke is ill.

Yes. No one can argue with that.

So as soon as we get home and Luke is closeted with Gary in the study, I hurry to the phone in our bedroom. I kick the bedroom door shut and quickly dial the number Nathan Temple gave me. To my huge relief, it clicks straight into voice mail.

And now that I'm listening properly, he sounds *exactly* like a motel king with a criminal past. Why on earth didn't I hear it before? I must be deaf or something!

The beep goes, and I jump in fright.

"Hi!" I say, trying to keep my voice light and easy. "This is a message for Mr. Temple. It's Becky Brandon here. Er . . . I told my husband all about your hotel, and he thought it sounded fab! But I'm afraid he's not very well at the moment. So he won't be able to do the launch after all. Which is a real shame! Anyway, I hope you find someone else! Bye!"

I put the phone down and sink onto the bed, my heart thumping. All this stress is going to give me a heart attack. Maybe I should try some of my yoga exercises from Sri Lanka. I cross my legs and close my eyes.

Breathe in. Breathe out. I am a radiant being of white light. My body is a temple.

Temple. Oh God . . .

"Becky?" Luke opens the door, and I nearly fall off the bed in terror.

"What? What is it?"

"What's wrong?" Luke looks alarmed. "Becky, are you hyperventilating?"

"Just doing a bit of relaxing yoga!" I say breathlessly. "I'm fine!"

"Well, I just wanted to tell you"—Luke smiles—"Jess is here."

Thirteen

"SHE'S COMING UP in the lift," says Luke, opening the front door. "Who were you on the phone with, by the way?"

"Nobody," I say quickly. "I was just . . . er . . . checking the time."

Gradually my pulse is slowing down. It's fine, I tell myself firmly. It's done. Everything's sorted.

I can hear the lift moving, down below. Jess is on her way! Quickly I grab my crib sheet and skim it one last time. Border collies . . . hates avocados . . . math teacher was called Mr. Lewis . . .

"Becky, I'd put that away before she arrives," says Luke, looking amused.

"Oh. Right."

I stuff it into my pocket and take a few deep breaths to prepare myself.

"Listen, Becky," says Luke, watching me. "Before she arrives . . . I sincerely hope you two hit it off this time.

But you are keeping a sense of proportion? You don't have all your hopes pinned on this visit, do you?"

"Really, Luke," I say kindly. "Don't you know me better than that?"

Of course I have all my hopes pinned on this visit. Because I know it's going to work out. Things will be different this time. For a start, we won't do anything that Jess doesn't want to do. I'm just going to follow her lead.

And the other thing I must remember is a tip that Luke gave me. He said it was great that I was so friendly toward Jess—but that she's quite reserved, and maybe great big hugs weren't her style. So he suggested I should be a bit more collected, just until we know each other better. Which is a fair point.

From the hall comes the noise of the lift getting closer. Why is this lift so *slow?* And then suddenly the doors are opening to reveal Jess in jeans and a gray T-shirt, holding her rucksack.

"Hi!" I cry, running forward. "Welcome! We can do whatever you want this weekend! Anything! Just name it! You're the boss!"

Jess doesn't move. In fact . . . she seems frozen to the spot.

"Hi, Jess," Luke says more calmly. "Welcome to London."

"Come on in!" I spread my arms. "Make yourself at home! No avocados here!"

Jess stares at me uncertainly, then glances at the buttons of the lift, almost like she wants to go back down again.

"Let me take your bag," says Luke. "How was your conference?"

He ushers Jess into the flat, and she looks around warily.

"It was good, thanks," she says. "Hi, Becky."

"Hi! It's so great you're here! I'll show you your room."

I open the door of the guest room proudly, waiting for her to comment on the cave picture, or *Potholing Monthly*. But she says nothing, just "Thanks," as Luke puts down her bag.

"Look," I point out. "It's a cave!"

"Er . . . yes," says Jess, looking slightly bewildered.

There's a pause—and I feel a tiny spasm of alarm.

"Let's all have a drink!" I exclaim. "Let's open a bottle of champagne!"

"Becky . . . it's only four o'clock," says Luke. "Maybe a cup of tea would be more appropriate?"

"I'd love a cup of tea," says Jess.

"Tea, then!" I say. "Excellent idea!"

I lead the way into the kitchen, and Jess follows, peering all around the flat.

"Nice place," she says.

"Becky's done a great job on it," Luke says pleasantly. "You should have seen it this time last week. We'd had a load of purchases delivered from our honeymoon . . . and you could not *move* for the stuff." He shakes his head. "I still don't know how you did it, Becky."

"Oh, you know," I say modestly. "Just a question of organization."

I'm switching on the kettle as Gary comes into the kitchen.

"This is my associate, Gary," says Luke. "This is Becky's half sister, Jess. She comes from Cumbria."

"Ah!" says Gary as he shakes Jess's hand. "I know Cumbria! Beautiful part of the country. Whereabouts do you live?"

"A village called Scully," replies Jess. "It's pretty rural. Very different from this."

"I've been to Scully!" says Gary. "Years ago. Isn't there a famous walk nearby?"

"You probably mean Scully Pike."

"That's it! We tried to climb it, but the weather took a turn. Nearly fell off the bloody thing."

"It can be dangerous," says Jess. "You have to know what you're doing. Idiots come up from the south and get in all sorts of trouble."

"That's me," Gary says cheerfully. "But it's worth it for the scenery. Those drystone walls are spectacular," he adds to Luke. "Like works of art. Miles and miles of them, strung out across the countryside."

I'm listening to the conversation in total fascination. I'd love to get to know a bit of rural England a bit better. I'd love to see some drystone walls. I mean, all I know is London and Surrey, which is practically London anyway.

"We should buy a cottage in Cumbria!" I say enthusiastically. "In Jess's village! Then we could see you all the time," I add to Jess. "Wouldn't that be great?"

There's quite a long silence.

"Yes," says Jess at last. "Great."

"I don't think we'll be buying any cottages in the near future," says Luke. "We're on a budget, remember?"

"Yes, I know," I retort. "And I'm sticking to it, aren't I?"

"Well, yes," says Luke. "Incredibly, you are." He looks at the tin of Fortnum biscuits on the counter. "Although, quite frankly, I have no idea how you're managing it." He opens the fridge. "Look at all this. Stuffed olives . . . smoked lobster . . . and this is supposed to be on a *budget*?"

I can't help feeling a little glow of pride. All that food is courtesy of selling those Tiffany clocks! I was so delighted,

I went straight out and bought a big hamperful of all Luke's favorite things.

"Just a question of good household management," I say nonchalantly.

"Hmm." Luke gives me a suspicious look, then turns to Gary. "We must get on."

The two men head out of the kitchen, and I'm left alone with Jess. I perch on a bar stool opposite her.

"So!" I say. "What would you like to do?"

"I'm easy," Jess says with a shrug.

"It's up to you! Totally!"

"I don't really mind." Jess sips her tea.

The kitchen is still and quiet, apart from the tap dripping slowly into the sink.

Which is fine. This is just one of those companionable, quiet moments you can have with members of your family. In fact, it *shows* we're easy with each other. It's not remotely awkward or anything—

Oh God, *speak*. Please.

"I'd like to do some weight training," says Jess suddenly. "I normally work out every day. But I haven't had time this week."

"Right!" I say in delight. "That's a brilliant idea! I'll do it too!"

"Really?" Jess looks surprised.

"Of course!" I take a final sip of tea, then put my cup down. "I'll just go and get ready!"

What a marvelous idea. Doing exercise together will be totally bonding! We can go to Taylor's Health Club round the corner, where I'm a gold member, do a bit of a workout, and then head to the juice bar. I know the juice bar will be open, because I've been there loads of times before at about this hour of the day.

And I should think the gym bit will be open too, downstairs.

Or is it upstairs?

Anyway. Wherever it is.

I yank open my wardrobe doors and pull out my drawer full of gym kit. I could wear my Juicy tracksuit, except I might get too hot . . . or that really cool pink top, except I've seen a girl in the juice bar wearing the same exact one. . . .

At last I select some black leggings with retro piping up the sides, plus a white T-shirt and my fab hi-tech trainers that I got in the States. They cost quite a lot, but then, as the leaflet points out, they *are* biomechanically balanced with a dual-density midsole. Plus their advanced engineering means you can take them seamlessly from the marathon track to the outdoor terrain of the trail hike.

I quickly put on the whole outfit, tie my hair up in a ponytail, and add my cool Adidas sports watch. (Which just shows how wrong Luke is. I *knew* I would need a sports watch one day.) I hurry to the guest room and knock on the door.

"Hi!"

"Come in." Jess's voice sounds muffled and kind of weird. Cautiously I push open the door. She's changed into old gray shorts and a cropped T-shirt and to my surprise is lying on the floor.

Doing sit-ups, I suddenly realize as her entire torso rises off the ground. Blimey. She's quite good at them. And I've never *seen* such a muscled stomach, except in a Cindy Crawford video.

Now she's doing those twisty ones that I've never been able to manage more than about three of.

"So . . . shall we go?" I say.

"Go where?" Jess says without missing a beat.

"To the gym! I thought you wanted to . . ." I trail off as she starts raising her legs off the ground too.

OK, now that's just showing off.

"I don't need to go anywhere. I can work out here."

Here? Is she serious? But there aren't any mirrors. There isn't any MTV. There isn't a juice bar.

My gaze falls on a snakelike scar at the top of Jess's shin. I'm about to ask how she did it, when she catches me looking and flushes red.

Maybe she's sensitive. I'd better not mention it.

"Don't you need weights?" I say instead.

"I've got them." She reaches in her rucksack and pulls out two old water bottles filled with sand.

Those are her weights?

"I wouldn't go near a gym," she says, starting to raise the bottles above her head. "Waste of money. Half the people who join gyms never go, anyway. They buy expensive outfits and never even wear them. What's the point in that?"

"Oh, absolutely!" I say quickly. "I totally agree."

Jess stops and adjusts her grip on one of the weights. Then her eye falls on the back of my leggings.

"What's that?" she says.

"Er . . ." I reach round with my hand.

Damn. It's the price tag hanging out.

"Er . . . nothing!" I say, hastily tucking it in. "I'll just go and get some . . . weights of my own."

As I return from the kitchen with two bottles of Evian, I can't help feeling a bit disconcerted. This isn't exactly what I had in mind. I'd pictured the two of us running effortlessly along on adjacent machines, with some upbeat song playing and the spotlights making our hair look all shiny.

Anyway, never mind.

"So . . . I'll follow you, shall I?" I say, joining Jess on the carpet.

"I'm going on to some biceps work," says Jess. "It's pretty straightforward." She starts raising her arms up and down, and I copy what she's doing. God, she exercises quite fast, doesn't she?

"Shall I put on some music?" I say after a few moments.

"I don't need music," says Jess.

"No. Neither do I," I say quickly.

My arms are starting to ache. This can't be good for them, surely. I glance at Jess, but she's steadfastly pumping away. Casually I lean down, pretending to adjust my shoelace. Then suddenly I have a thought.

"I won't be a moment," I say, and hurry out to the kitchen again. A few moments later I'm back, holding two slim silver bottles.

"Here's a health drink," I say, proudly holding one out to Jess. "So you can rebalance."

"So I can what?" Jess puts down her weights with a frown.

"It says it on the bottle, look," I explain. "It has a unique blend of life-enhancing vitamins and herbs."

Jess is scanning the label.

"It's just sugar and water. Look. Water . . . glucose syrup . . ." She puts it down. "No, thanks."

"But it's got special properties!" I say in surprise. "It rebalances, revitalizes, and moisturizes your skin from the inside."

"How does it do that?"

"I . . . don't know."

"How much is it?" Jess picks the bottle up again and looks at the price tag. "It's £2.95!" She seems totally scandalized. "Three pounds for some sugar and water? You could buy a twenty-kilo sack of potatoes for that!"

"But . . . I don't want a twenty-kilo sack of potatoes."

"Then you should!" says Jess. "Potatoes are one of the most nutritious, cost-effective foods available." She eyes me reprovingly. "People underestimate them. But did you know a potato in its skin has more vitamin C than an orange?"

"Er . . . no," I say nervously. "No, I didn't."

"You could live off potatoes and milk." She starts hefting her weights again. "You'd get practically every nutrient the body needs, just from those two."

"Right!" I say. "That's . . . really good! Er . . . I'll just go and have a shower."

As I close the door of the bedroom, I feel totally bewildered. What was all that about potatoes? I'm not even sure how we got onto the subject.

I head down the corridor and see Luke through the door of the study, getting something down from a shelf.

"You look very sportif," he says, glancing up. "Going to the gym?"

"Jess and I have been working out together," I reply, flicking my ponytail.

"Excellent. So you're getting along?"

"We're getting along brilliantly!" I say, and carry on along the corridor.

Which . . . I think is true. Although to be honest, it's a bit hard to tell with Jess. She doesn't exactly *overwhelm* you.

But anyway, so far so good. And now we've done our workout, we can reward ourselves! What we need is a few drinks, and a bit of a party atmosphere and some music. Then we'll really loosen up.

As I shower, I start to feel excited. You cannot beat a good girls' night in. Suze and I had so many great evenings when we were living together. There was the time Suze had been dumped by her awful boyfriend and we spent the whole evening sending off forms in his name to receive impotence cures. There was the time we made mint juleps and both nearly got alcohol poisoning. There was the time we decided to become redheads—and then had to find a twenty-four-hour hairdresser. And then there were lots of evenings when nothing special happened . . . except we watched movies and ate pizza and talked and laughed, and had a good time.

I pause, halfway through toweling my hair. It's weird, not speaking to Suze anymore. She hasn't called once since I told her about having a sister. Nor have I called her. My chin stiffens. But that's what happens in life. People find new friends and new sisters. It's called natural selection.

And Jess and I will have a fab time tonight. *Better* than I ever had with Suze.

I throw on some jeans and a T-shirt with SISTERHOOD emblazoned in silver, then turn on my dressing table lightbulbs and get out every single item of makeup I own. I rummage in a box under the bed and retrieve my three wigs, four hairpieces, false eyelashes, spray glitter, and temporary tattoos. Then I open up my special cupboard, where all my shoes are stored.

I love my shoe cupboard.

I mean, I *love* my shoe cupboard. It is the best thing in the entire world! All my shoes are arranged in gorgeous rows, and there's even a built-in light so you can see them properly. I look with satisfaction along the rows of L.K. Bennetts and Jimmy Choos for a few moments, then choose all the most fun, spangly high-heeled ones and toss them onto the bed.

Ready for the makeovers!

Next the sitting room. I spread all my favorite videos

out in a fan on the floor, and add piles of magazines. Back in the kitchen I empty crisps, popcorn, and sweets into bowls, light some candles, and get out the champagne. As I look around the kitchen the granite is gleaming, and the stainless steel sparkles in the light. It looks so pretty!

It's nearly six o'clock. Jess must have finished working out by now. I head to the guest room and tap on the door.

"Jess?" I say tentatively.

No answer. She must be in the shower or something.

But as I head to the kitchen, I suddenly hear her voice coming from the study. That's weird. I gently push open the door—and there's Jess, sitting at the computer with Luke and Gary on either side of her, peering at the screen, where I can see Luke's head, talking against a green background.

"You can superimpose the graphics like this," she's saying, tapping at the keyboard. "And synchronize with the sound track. I can do it for you, if you like."

"What's going on?" I say in surprise.

"It's our new corporate CD," says Luke. "The guys who did it had no bloody idea. The whole thing needs reediting."

"Your sister is a real whiz at this software!" says Gary.

"I just know it backwards," says Jess, clicking rapidly. "The whole university went over to it a year ago. And I'm a bit of a techie. I like this kind of stuff."

"That's fantastic!" I say. I hover at the door for a few moments as Jess taps at the keyboard some more. "So . . . do you want to come and have a drink? I've got everything ready for our girls' night in."

"I'm sorry," says Luke, looking at me in sudden realization. "I'm keeping you, Jess. We'll be OK from here. But thanks!"

"Thanks!" echoes Gary.

They're both looking at her with such admiration, I can't help but feel a tiny bit jealous.

"Come on!" I say brightly. "There's champagne waiting."

"Thanks again, Jess," says Luke. "You're a star!"

"No problem." Jess gets up and follows me out of the room.

"Men!" I say as soon as I'm out of earshot. "All they think about is computers!"

"I like computers," says Jess.

"Er . . . me too," I backtrack hastily. "Absolutely!"

Which is kind of true.

I mean, I love eBay.

As I lead Jess into the kitchen I feel a rush of excitement. I reach for the CD remote control, and a moment later, Sister Sledge belts through the kitchen speakers at top volume. I bought the album especially for this!

" 'We are family!' " I sing along, while taking the champagne bottle out of its ice bucket. I pop the cork. "Have some champagne!"

"I'd prefer something soft, if you've got it," she says, looking at the bottle without enthusiasm. "Champagne gives me a headache."

"Oh," I say, halted. "Well . . . OK!"

I pour her out a glass of Aqua Libra and quickly put the bottle away before she can see the price and start talking about potatoes again.

"I thought tonight we could just relax," I say over the music. "Just enjoy ourselves . . . talk . . . have fun . . ."

"Sounds good," says Jess, nodding.

"So, my idea was, we could do makeovers!"

"Makeovers?" Jess looks as though she's never even heard the word.

"Come with me!" I pull her along the corridor and into the bedroom. "We can do each other's makeup . . . try on all different clothes . . . I could blow-dry your hair if you like. . . ."

"I don't know." Jess's shoulders are hunched uncomfortably.

"It'll be fun! Look, sit down in front of the mirror. Try on one of my wigs!" I pull the blond Marilyn one onto my own head. "Isn't that fab?"

Jess flinches.

"I hate mirrors," she says. "And I never wear makeup."

I stare at her, a bit nonplussed. How can anyone hate mirrors?

"Besides, I'm happy with the way I look," she adds a bit defensively.

"Of course you are!" I say in astonishment. "That's not the point! It's just supposed to be . . . you know. Fun."

Jess doesn't reply.

"But anyway!" I say, trying to hide my deflation. "It was just an idea. We don't have to do it."

I take off the Marilyn wig and switch off the dressing table lightbulbs. The room is immediately plunged into semi-gloom, which is kind of how I feel. I was really looking forward to doing Jess up. I had all these great ideas for her eyes.

But never mind. We can still have a good time!

"So! Shall we . . . watch a movie?" I suggest.

"Sure." Jess nods.

And anyway, a movie is *better*. Everyone likes movies, plus we can chat during all the boring bits. I lead the way into the sitting room and gesture enthusiastically at the fanned-out videos on the floor. "Take your pick. They're all here!"

"Right." Jess starts looking through the videos.

"Are you a *Four Weddings* girl?" I prompt her. "Or *Sleepless in Seattle* . . . *When Harry Met Sally* . . ."

"I don't mind," says Jess at last, looking up. "You choose."

"You must have a favorite!"

"These aren't really my kind of thing," says Jess, with a little grimace. "I prefer something a bit more heavy-weight."

"Oh," I say. "Oh, right. Well . . . I can go and get a different video from the rental shop if you like! It won't take me five minutes. Tell me what you'd like to watch—"

"It's OK. I don't want to put you out." She shrugs. "Let's just watch one of these."

"Don't be silly!" I say with a laugh. "Not if you don't like any of them! We can do . . . something else! No problem!"

I smile at Jess, but inside I'm a bit disquieted. I don't quite know what else to suggest. My backup plan was the *Dancing Queen* karaoke tape—but something tells me she won't want to do that either. Plus we're not wearing the wigs.

Why is everything so *awkward*? I thought we'd be laughing hysterically together by now. I thought we'd be having fun.

Oh God. We can't just sit here in silence all night. I'm going to come clean.

"Look, Jess," I say, leaning forward. "I want to do whatever *you* want to do. But you'll have to guide me. So . . . be honest. Suppose I hadn't invited you here for the weekend. What would you be doing right now?"

"Well . . ." Jess thinks for a moment. "I was supposed to be at an environmental meeting this evening. I'm an activist for a local group. We raise awareness, organize pickets and protest marches . . . that kind of thing."

"Well, let's do that!" I say eagerly. "Let's organize a picket! It'd be fun! I could make some banners . . ."

Jess looks nonplussed.

"A picket of what?"

"Er . . . I don't mind! Anything. You're the guest—you choose!"

Jess is just staring at me in disbelief.

"You don't just *organize pickets*. You have to start with the issues. With the environmental concerns. They're not supposed to be *fun*."

"OK," I say hastily. "Let's forget the picket. How about if you *hadn't* been at the meeting? What would you be doing now? And whatever it is . . . we'll do it. Together!"

Jess frowns in thought, and I watch her face with hope. And a sudden curiosity. For the first time I feel like I'm actually going to learn something about my sister.

"I'd probably be doing my accounts," she says at last. "In fact, I brought them with me, in case I had time."

Her accounts. On a Friday night. Her accounts.

"Right!" I manage at last. "Fab! Well, then . . . let's do our accounts!"

OK. This is fine. This is good.

We're both sitting in the kitchen, doing our accounts. At least, Jess is doing her accounts. I'm not quite sure what I'm doing.

I've written *Accounts* at the top of a sheet of paper and underlined it twice.

Every so often Jess glances up, and I quickly scribble something down, just to look like I'm into it. So far my page reads:

20 pounds . . . budget . . . 200 million pounds . . . Hello, my name is Becky. . . .

Jess is frowning over a pile of what look like bank statements, leafing backwards and forwards and consulting a small bankbook.

"Is something wrong?" I say sympathetically.

"I'm just tracking down a bit of lost money," she says. "Maybe it's in one of my other cashbooks." She gets up. "I'll be back in a moment."

As she leaves the kitchen I take a sip of champagne and glance toward the pile of bank statements.

Obviously I'm not going to look at them or anything. They're Jess's private property and I respect that. It's none of my business. None at all. The only thing is, my leg is feeling itchy. It genuinely is. I lean over to scratch it . . . then casually lean a bit farther . . . and a bit more . . . until I can glimpse the bottom figure on the top statement.

£30,002.

I hastily sit up again, nearly knocking over my champagne glass. Thirty thousand pounds? *Thirty thousand pounds?*

That's a bigger overdraft than I've ever had. *Ever!*

Now it's all starting to make sense. It's falling into place. No wonder she makes her own weights. No wonder she takes her coffee flask everywhere. She's probably on an economy drive, just like I went on once. She's probably read *Controlling Your Cash* by David E. Barton!

God, who would have thought it?

As Jess comes back into the room, I can't help looking at her with new eyes. She picks up one of her bank statements and sighs heavily—and I feel a sudden wave of affection for her. How many times have *I* picked up a bank statement and sighed? We're kindred spirits!

She's perusing the figures, still looking hassled. Well, no wonder, with a whopping great overdraft like that!

"Hi," I say, with an understanding smile. "Still trying to track down that bit of money?"

"It must be here somewhere." She frowns and turns to another statement.

God, maybe the bank's about to foreclose on her or something. I should give her a few tips.

I lean forward confidingly.

"Banks are a nightmare, aren't they?"

"They're useless," she replies, nodding.

"I sometimes wonder why they give people overdrafts if they're going to be so unsympathetic . . ."

"I don't have an overdraft," she says, looking puzzled.

"But—"

I stop as her words hit my brain. She doesn't have an overdraft. Which means—

I feel a bit faint.

That thirty thousand pounds is actual . . .

It's actual *money*?

"Becky, are you OK?" Jess gives me an odd look.

"I'm . . . fine!" I say in a strangled voice and take several gulps of my champagne, trying to regain my cool. "So . . . you're not overdrawn. That's good! That's great!"

"I've never been overdrawn in my life," Jess says firmly. "I just don't think it's necessary. Anyone can stay within their means if they really want to. People who get into debt just lack self-control. There's no excuse." She begins to straighten her papers, then stops. "But you used to be a financial journalist, didn't you? Your mum showed me some of your articles. So you must know all this."

Her hazel eyes meet mine expectantly and I feel a ridiculous tweak of anxiety. I'm suddenly not sure I want her to know the truth about my finances. Not the *exact* truth.

"I . . . er . . . absolutely!" I say. "Of course I do. It's all a question of . . . of planning ahead and careful management."

"Exactly!" says Jess with approval. "When any money comes in, the first thing I do is put half aside to save."

Half? Even my dad doesn't save that much.

"Excellent!" I manage. "It's the only sensible option."

I'm in total shock. When I was a financial journalist, I used to write articles telling people to save a percentage of their money all the time. But I never thought anyone would actually save *half*.

Jess is looking at me with a fresh interest and maybe even affection.

"So . . . you do the same, do you, Becky?"

For a few seconds I can't quite formulate a response.

"Er . . . well!" I say at last, and clear my throat. "Maybe not exactly half *every* month . . ."

"I'm just the same." Her face relaxes into a smile. "Sometimes I only manage twenty percent."

"Twenty percent!" I echo feebly. "Well . . . never mind. You shouldn't feel bad."

"But I do," says Jess, leaning forward across the table. "You must understand that."

I've never seen her face look so open.

Oh my God. We're bonding.

"Twenty percent of what?" comes Luke's voice as he and Gary enter the kitchen, both looking in good spirits.

Maybe now is the time to move the conversation on.

"Er . . . nothing!" I say.

"We're just talking about finances," says Jess to Luke. "We've both been doing our accounts."

"Your *accounts*?" says Luke, giving a small shout of laughter. "What accounts would those be, Becky?"

"You know!" I say brightly. "My financial affairs and so forth."

"Ah." Luke nods, pulling a bottle of wine from the fridge. "So . . . have you called out the SWAT teams yet? And the Red Cross?"

"What do you mean?" says Jess, puzzled.

"They're traditionally summoned to disaster areas, aren't they?" He grins at me.

"So!" I say quickly, trying to change the subject. "Did anyone . . . er . . . see *EastEnders* last night?"

No one seems to hear me.

"But Becky was a financial journalist!" says Jess, sounding disconcerted.

"Financial journalist?" Luke looks highly amused. "You want to hear a story about your sister's days as a financial journalist?"

"No," I put in. "She doesn't."

"The cashpoint card," says Gary, reminiscing.

"The cashpoint card!" Luke slaps the table in delight. "This was during Becky's illustrious career as a TV finance expert," he says to Jess. "She was filming an item on the perils of cashpoint use. She put in her own cashpoint card to demonstrate . . ." He starts laughing again. "And it got swallowed on camera."

"They showed that the other night on a TV clips show," says Gary to me. "The bit where you start bashing the machine with your shoe is a classic!"

OK, he is off my Christmas card list.

"But why did it get swallowed?" says Jess, looking perplexed. "Were you . . . *overdrawn*?"

"Was Becky overdrawn?" Luke says cheerfully, getting out some glasses. "Is the Pope Catholic?"

Jess looks confused.

"But, Becky, you said you saved half your salary every month."

Shit.

"I'm sorry?" Luke slowly turns round. "Becky said she did *what*?"

"That's . . . that's not exactly what I said," I say, flustered. "I said it's a *good idea* to save half your salary. In principle. And . . . it is! It's a very good idea!"

"How about not running up huge credit card bills which you keep secret from your husband?" says Luke. "Is that a good idea in principle?"

"Credit card bills?" says Jess, looking at me in horror. "So . . . you're in debt?"

God, why does she have to say it like that? *Debt.* Like it's some kind of plague. Like I'm about to go to the workhouse. This is the twenty-first century. *Everyone's* in debt.

"You know how doctors make the worst patients?" I say with a little laugh. "Well, financial journalists make the worst . . . er . . ."

I wait for her to laugh too, or at least give a sympathetic smile. But she just looks appalled.

This whole exchange is beginning to rankle. OK, so I may have had the odd debt in my time. But she doesn't have to look so *disapproving*.

"By the way, Jess," says Gary. "We've run into a tiny glitch with that program."

"Really?" Jess looks up. "I'll come and have a look if you like."

"Are you sure?" Gary glances at me. "We don't want to interrupt your evening. . . ."

"It's fine," I say, waving my hand. "Go ahead!"

When they've all disappeared into the study I wander along the corridor and into the sitting room. I slump down on the sofa and stare miserably at the blank television.

Jess and I haven't bonded one bit.

We don't get on. That's the truth.

Suddenly I'm weary with disappointment. I've been trying so hard ever since she arrived. I've been making every effort. I bought the picture of the cave . . . and I prepared all those yummy snacks . . . and I tried to plan the best evening I could. And she hasn't even *tried* to join in. OK, so maybe she didn't like any of my films. But she could have pretended, couldn't she? If it was me, I would have pretended.

Why does she have to be such a *misery*? Why can't she just have *fun*?

As I gulp my champagne, resentment is growing inside me.

How can she hate shopping? How? She's got thirty thousand pounds, for God's sake! She should *adore* shopping! And another thing—why is she so obsessed with potatoes? What's so great about bloody potatoes?

I just don't understand her. She's my sister, but I don't understand one single thing about her. Luke was right all along. It *is* all nurture. Nature doesn't come into it.

I start dejectedly leafing through the videos. Maybe I'll watch one of them on my own. And have some popcorn. And some of those yummy Thorntons chocolates.

Jess probably doesn't even eat chocolate. Unless it's chocolate she's made herself, out of potatoes.

Well, good for her. *I'm* going to stuff my face and watch a nice movie.

I'm just reaching for *Pretty Woman* when the phone rings.

"Hello?" I say, picking up.

"Hello, Bex?" comes a familiar high-pitched voice. "It's me."

"Suze!" I feel a huge rush of joy. "Oh my God! Hi! How are you?"

"Oh, I'm fine! Are you OK?"

"I'm fine! I'm fine!"

Suddenly with all my heart I wish Suze were here. Like the old days in Fulham. I miss her so much. *So* much.

"So, how was the spa with Lulu?" I ask, trying to sound casual.

"It was . . . fine," she says after a pause. "You know. Kind of . . . a bit different . . . but fun!"

"Good!"

There's an awkward silence.

"And . . . and I was wondering how it's all going with your new sister," Suze says hesitantly. "Are you . . . are you really good friends?"

I can't admit the truth to Suze. I just can't admit the whole thing's been a failure. That she goes on spa trips with her new friend, but I can't even manage one evening with my own sister.

"It's great!" I say. "Couldn't be better! We're getting on so well!"

"Really?" says Suze, sounding a bit crushed.

"Absolutely! In fact, we're having a girls' night in together right now! Watching movies . . . having a laugh . . . just hanging out. You know!"

"What are you watching?" says Suze at once.

"Er . . ." I look at the blank TV screen. "*Pretty Woman.*"

"I love *Pretty Woman,*" Suze says longingly. "The scene in the shop!"

"I know! That is just the best scene ever!"

"And the end, when Richard Gere climbs up!" Her voice is tumbling out with enthusiasm. "Oh God, I want to watch it right now!"

"Me too!" I say without thinking. "I mean . . . I want to watch the . . . er . . . rest of it."

"Oh," Suze says in a different voice. "I must be interrupting you. Sorry."

"No!" I say quickly. "I mean, it doesn't matter—"

"I'll go. You must want to get back to your sister. It sounds like you're having an amazing time." Her voice is wistful. "You two must have so much to talk about."

"Yes," I say, looking round the empty room. "Yes, we . . . we certainly do!"

"Well . . . I'll see you sometime," she says. "Bye, Bex."

"Bye!" I say, my throat suddenly thick.

Wait! I want to cry out. *Don't go!*

But instead I put down the receiver and stare into space. At the other end of the flat I can hear Luke, Gary, and Jess all laughing about something. They've bonded with her great. It's just me who hasn't.

And I had such huge hopes. I was so excited about having a sister. But I've done everything I can think of, and it's all failed. Jess and I are never going to be friends. Not in a million years.

Ms Jessica Bertram
12 Hill Rise
Scully
Cumbria CA19 1BD

16 May 2003

Dear Ms Bertram:

Thank you for your letter.

Having gone through your accounts in great detail I can only concur that there is a discrepancy of 73 pence.

I am deeply sorry for this error by the bank and have credited your savings account by this amount, back-dated three months. I have also, as you request, added the missing interest.

May I take this opportunity to commend you yet again on your meticulous and thoughtful approach to your finances.

On a personal note, I look forward to seeing you at the upcoming Prudent Savers' Group cheese and wine evening, at which our head of personal accounts will be giving the keynote address "Retightening the Purse Strings."

Yours sincerely,

Howard Shawcross
Customer Account Manager

Fourteen

I WAKE UP the next morning with a splitting headache, which could have something to do with the fact
that I polished off an entire bottle of champagne myself last night, plus one and a half trays of chocolates.
Meanwhile, Jess, Luke, and Gary spent hours around
the computer. Even when I took them in some pizza,
they barely looked up. So I just watched the whole of
Pretty Woman and then half of *Four Weddings and a Fu-
neral*, before going to bed on my own.

As I blearily put on a dressing gown, Luke is already
showered and dressed in the "casual weekend" clothes
he wears when he's actually going to spend the whole
time in the office.

"What time did you finish last night?" I ask, my throat
all hoarse and croaky.

"Not till late." Luke shakes his head. "Once we started
discussing it, we couldn't stop. Jess had a lot of ideas."

"Right!" I try to sound enthusiastic.

"You know, I take it back about her," he adds, tying

up his shoelaces. "Your sister's got a lot going for her. She couldn't have been more helpful last night. She certainly knows her way around a computer!"

"Really?"

"Oh yes. She's great!" He stands up and gives me a kiss. "You were right. I'm very glad you invited her for the weekend."

"Me too!" I say, forcing a bright smile. "We're all having so much fun!"

I shuffle into the kitchen, where Jess is sitting at the counter in her jeans and a T-shirt, with a glass of water.

Cleverclogs. I expect she'll split the atom this morning. In between sit-ups.

"Morning," she says.

"Morning!" I say in my most pleasant, good-hostess manner.

I was rereading *The Gracious Hostess* last night, and it says that even if your guest is annoying you, you must behave with charm and decorum.

Well, fine. I can be charming. I can be decorative.

"Did you sleep well? Let me get you some breakfast!"

I open the fridge and get out the freshly squeezed orange, grapefruit, and cranberry juices. I reach into the bread bin and pull out some seeded granary bread, croissants, and muffins. Then I start rooting around in the cupboards for jams. Three kinds of luxury marmalade, strawberry jam with champagne, wild blossom honey . . . and Belgian chocolate spread. Finally I get down a range of luxury coffees and teas to choose from. There. No one's going to say I don't give my guests a good breakfast.

I'm aware of Jess watching my every move, and as I turn round she's got a strange expression on her face.

"What?" I say. "What's wrong?"

"Nothing," she says awkwardly. She folds her napkin into little squares. "Luke told me last night. About your . . . problem."

"My what?"

"Your spending."

I try to hide my dismay. He did, did he?

"I don't have a problem," I say, flashing her a smile. "He was exaggerating."

"He said you're on a budget." Jess looks concerned. "It sounds like money's a bit tight at the moment."

"That's right," I say pleasantly. Not that it's any of your business, I think. I can't *believe* Luke's been blabbing everything to her.

"So . . . how come you can afford luxury coffee and strawberry jam with champagne?" She gestures at all the food laid out on the counter.

"Thrifty management," I say smoothly. "Prioritizing. If you save on some items you can splash out on others. That's the first rule of financial management. As I learned at financial journalism school," I add.

OK, that's a slight lie. I didn't go to financial journalism school.

"So—which items are you saving on?" says Jess, her brow creased. "I can't see anything in this kitchen that doesn't come from Fortnum's or Harrods."

I'm about to make an indignant rejoinder when I realize she might be right. I got into a bit of a Harrods Food Hall habit after I started making all this money off eBay. But then, Harrods is a perfectly legitimate food shop.

"My husband appreciates a good standard of living," I say crisply, opening a fresh jar of marmalade.

"But you could do it on less." Jess leans forward, looking animated. "You could make savings everywhere! I could give you some tips."

Tips? Tips from Jess?

Suddenly the oven timer goes off with a ping. It's time!

"Are you cooking something?" says Jess, looking puzzled.

"Er . . . not exactly. Just help yourself . . . I'll be back in a minute. . . ."

I hurry into the study and switch on the computer. Bidding on the orange vintage coat ends in five minutes, and I am bloody well going to get it. I tap my fingernails impatiently, and as soon as the screen clears I bring up the saved eBay page.

I knew it. Kittybee111 has bid again—£200.

She thinks she's so clever. Well, take *this*, kittybee111.

I get out Luke's stopwatch from the desk and set it for three minutes. As the time gets near I poise my hands over the keyboard like an athlete on the starting blocks.

OK. One minute before the bidding ends. Go.

As quickly as I can, I type in *@00.50.

Shit. What have I typed? Delete. . . . retype . . . £200.50.

I jab SEND and the next screen comes up. User ID . . . password . . . I'm typing as fast as I can.

You are the current high bidder.

Ten seconds to go. My heart is thumping. What if someone else is bidding *right now*?

Frantically I click on REFRESH.

"What are you doing, Becky?" comes Jess's voice at the door. Shit.

"Nothing!" I say. "Why don't you make yourself some nice toast, while I just—"

The page is coming back up again. Did I . . . did I . . .

Congratulations! You won the item!

"Yeeess!" I cry out, unable to stop myself, and punch the air. "Yes! I got it!"

"Got what?" Jess has advanced across the room and is

peering over my shoulder at the screen. "Is that *you*? You're on a tight budget and you're buying a coat for two hundred pounds?"

"It's not like that!" I say, rattled at her disapproving expression. I get up, close the door of the study, and turn to face her.

"Look," I say, keeping my voice lowered. "It's OK. I've got all this money which Luke doesn't know about. I've been selling off all the stuff we bought on our honeymoon—and I've made loads! I sold ten Tiffany clocks the other day and made two thousand quid!" I lift my chin proudly. "So I can *easily* afford this."

Jess's expression doesn't waver.

"You could have put that money into a high-interest savings account," she says. "Or used it to clear an outstanding bill."

I quell a sudden urge to snap.

"Yeah, well, I didn't," I say, forcing a pleasant tone. "I bought a coat."

"And Luke has no idea?" Jess fixes me with an accusing gaze.

"He doesn't *need* to have any idea! Jess, my husband is a very busy man."

"So you lie to him."

"Every marriage needs an air of mystery," I respond coolly. "It's a well-known fact."

Jess shakes her head.

"And is this how you can afford all the Fortnum's jam, too?" She gestures to the computer. "Shouldn't you just be honest?"

Oh, for God's sake. Doesn't she understand anything?

"Jess . . . let me explain," I say kindly. "Our marriage is a complicated, living organism, which only the two of us can really understand. I naturally know what to

tell Luke and what not to bother him with. Call it instinct . . . call it discretion . . . call it emotional intelli-
gence, if you will."

Jess regards me for a few moments.

"Well, I think you need help," she says at last.

"I do not need *help*!" I retort.

I shut down the computer, push back my chair, and
stalk past her into the kitchen, where Luke is making a
pot of coffee.

"Enjoying your breakfast, darling?" I say in loud tones.

"Fantastic!" says Luke. "Where did you get these quails'
eggs?"

"Oh . . . you know . . ." I give him an affectionate
smile. "I know you like them, so I tracked some down."
I shoot a triumphant look at Jess, who rolls her eyes.

"We're out of bacon, though," says Luke. "And a couple of other things. I've written them down."

"OK," I say, suddenly having an idea. "In fact . . . I'll
go out and get them this morning. Jess, you don't mind
if I do some household chores, do you? I don't expect
you to come, of course," I add sweetly. "I know how
much you despise shopping."

Thank goodness. Escape.

"It's OK," says Jess, filling a glass of water at the tap.
"I'd like to come."

My smile freezes on my face.

"To Harr— To the supermarket? But it'll be very boring. Please don't feel that you have to."

"I'd like to." She looks at me. "If you don't mind."

"Mind?" I say, my smile still rigid. "Why would I
mind? I'll just go and get ready."

As I head into the hall I'm hot with indignation. Who
does she think she is, saying I need help?

She needs help, more like it. Help in how to crank her miserable mouth into a smile.

And what a bloody nerve, giving me advice on my marriage. What does she know about it? Luke and I have a brilliant marriage! We've hardly ever even had a row!

The entry phone buzzes, and I pick up the receiver, still distracted.

"Hello?"

"Hello," comes a man's voice. "I have a delivery of flowers for Brandon."

I press the button in delight. Someone's sent me flowers?

I clap my hand over my mouth. Luke must have sent me flowers. He's so romantic! This is probably some really cute anniversary that I'd forgotten all about, like the first time we had dinner together, or slept together, or something.

Actually . . . that would be the same anniversary, now that I think about it.

But anyway, the point is, this just proves it. This just proves what a fantastic relationship we have and how Jess is totally wrong. About everything.

I throw open the apartment door and stand expectantly by the lift. This'll show her! I'll take my flowers straight into the kitchen and give Luke a huge passionate kiss, and she'll say something really humble like "I had no idea what a perfect relationship you two had." And I'll smile kindly and say "You know, Jess—"

My thoughts are interrupted as the lift doors start opening. And oh . . . my God. Luke must have spent an absolute *fortune*!

Two uniformed deliverymen are carrying the most enormous bouquet of roses—plus a huge fruit basket full of oranges, papayas, and pineapples, all wrapped up in trendy raffia.

"Wow!" I say in delight. "Those are absolutely fantastic!" I beam at the man offering me a clipboard and scribble my signature.

"And you'll pass them on to Mr. Brandon," says the man as he gets back into the lift.

"Of course!" I say gaily.

A moment later his words register.

Hang on a minute. These are for *Luke*? Who on earth is sending flowers to Luke?

I spot a card nestled among the flowers and pull it out with a pleasant thrill of curiosity.

Dear Mr Brandon
 I was extremely sorry to hear of your illness. Please let me know if I can be of any help. And be assured, we can delay the hotel launch as long as is necessary to enable your full recovery.

All best wishes,
Nathan Temple

I'm paralyzed with horror. Nathan Temple wasn't supposed to send flowers. He wasn't supposed to delay the hotel launch. He was supposed to *go away*.

"What's that?" comes Luke's voice. I start in panic and look up to see him heading out of the kitchen toward me.

In one seamless movement I crumple Nathan Temple's card and stuff it into the pocket of my dressing gown.

"Hi!" I say, my voice a little high-pitched. "Aren't these great?"

"Are those for me?" Luke says incredulously, spotting the delivery label. "Who are they from?"

"They're . . . um . . . they're . . . from me!" I say brightly.

"From *you*?" Luke stares at me.

"Yes! I thought I'd like to send you some flowers. And . . . er . . . fruit. Here you are, darling! Happy Saturday!"

Somehow I manhandle the enormous bouquet and basket into Luke's arms, then kiss him lightly on the cheek.

"Becky, I'm very touched," he says, looking bewildered. "Really. But . . . why did you send me all this? Why did you send me a fruit basket?"

"Do I have to have a reason to send my husband a fruit basket?" I say at last, managing to sound a little hurt. "I just thought they could be a token of our marriage. You know, we're coming up to our very first anniversary!"

"Right," says Luke after a pause. "Well . . . thank you. That's lovely." He peers more closely at the bouquet. "What's this?"

I follow his gaze only to see a set of gold plastic lettering nestled inside the flowers, spelling out *Get Well Soon*.

Shit.

"*Get well soon*?" Luke looks up, taken aback.

My mind races frantically.

"That . . . that . . . doesn't *mean* get well soon," I say with a laugh. "It's . . . in code!"

"In *code*?"

"Yes! Every marriage needs a secret code between husband and wife! You know, for little loving secret messages. So I thought I'd introduce one!"

Luke has the same expression he had in Egypt when I said I thought we should take a couples' belly-dancing class.

"So, what does 'get well soon' mean?" he inquires. "In our secret code."

"It's actually . . . er . . . very easy." I clear my throat self-consciously. "*Get* means . . . *I*. And *well* means . . . *love*. And *soon* means . . ."

"*You?*" offers Luke.

"Yes!" I say. "You're getting the idea! Isn't it cunning?"

My hands are clenched by my sides. I have no idea what Luke is thinking.

"And the florist wouldn't have sent the wrong package by mistake?" he suggests.

Oh.

Now, that's a *much* better explanation. Why didn't I think of that?

"You've rumbled me!" I exclaim. "Drat! How did you guess? You just know me too well. Now . . . er . . . go and have some nice breakfast and I'll get ready for the supermarket."

As I put on my makeup my mind is going round and round in circles.

What if Nathan Temple phones up to see how Luke is? What if he sends more flowers? What if he wants to come and visit Luke's *sickbed*?

OK, just . . . stay calm. Let's go through all the options.

Option 1. Tell Luke everything.

No. No way. Just the thought of it makes my stomach churn. He's so busy with this Arcodas pitch. It'll just get him all hassled and angry.

Option 2. Tell Luke something.

Like the edited highlights. Maybe tweaked in a way that leaves out the name Nathan Temple.

Oh God. Impossible.

Option 3. Manage situation in discreet Hillary-style manner.

But I tried that already and it didn't work.

Anyway, I bet Hillary had help. What I need is a team, like in *The West Wing*. Then I'd just go up to Allison Janney and whisper, "We have a problem—but don't let the president know." And she'd murmur, "Don't worry, we'll contain it." Then we'd exchange warm but tense smiles and walk into the Oval Office, where Luke would be promising a group of underprivileged kids that their playground would be saved. And his eyes would meet mine . . . and we'd flash back to the two of us waltzing in the White House corridors the night before, watched only by an impassive security guard—

The grinding motor of a dustbin truck outside brings me back to reality. Luke isn't president. I'm not in *The West Wing*. And I still don't know what to do.

Option 4. Do nothing.

This has a lot of obvious advantages. And the point is . . . do I actually *need* to do anything?

I reach for my lip liner and start applying it thoughtfully. I mean, all that has actually happened is that someone has sent Luke some flowers. That's all.

Plus he wants Luke to work for him. And reckons he's owed a favor.

And is a gangster.

No. Stop it. He's not a gangster. He's a . . . a businessman with a former criminal conviction. It's totally different.

And anyway—*anyway*—he was probably just being polite in that note, wasn't he? Like he's really going to hold up an entire hotel launch so Luke can do it. What a ludicrous idea.

The more I think along these lines, the more reassured I feel. Nathan Temple can't seriously be expecting

Luke to work for him. He'll have found some other PR company already. The whole thing will be under way and he'll have forgotten all about Brandon Communications. Exactly. So I don't have to do anything at all.

Even so, I might write a short letter of thanks. And kind of mention that Luke's unfortunately taken a turn for the worse.

So before we head off to the supermarket I scribble a polite card to Nathan Temple and drop it in the pillar-box outside. As I stride away I actually feel rather satisfied. I have this whole situation under control, and Luke doesn't know a thing. I am superwife!

My spirits rise even further as we walk into the supermarket. God, supermarkets are great places. They're all bright and airy and music is playing, and they're always giving away free samples of cheese or something. Plus you can buy loads of CDs and makeup, and it all goes on the credit card bill as Tesco.

The first thing that catches my eye as I walk in is a display of specialty teas, with a free flower-shaped tea infuser if you buy three.

"Bargain!" I say, grabbing three boxes at random.

"It's not really a bargain," Jess intones disapprovingly beside me. Why did she have to come along?

Never mind. I'll just stay polite and courteous.

"It *is* a bargain," I explain. "They're giving away a free gift."

"Do you ever drink jasmine tea?" she retorts, looking at the box in my hand.

"Er . . ."

Jasmine tea. That's the one that tastes like old compost heaps, isn't it?

But so what? The tea infuser is really cute, and I don't have one.

"You can always find a use for jasmine tea," I say airily, and toss it into my trolley. "Right! What next?"

I head toward the vegetable section, pausing to pick up a copy of *InStyle* as I go.

Ooh. And the new *Elle* is out too. With a free T-shirt!

"What are you doing?" comes Jess's sepulchral voice in my ear. Is she going to quiz me all the way round the bloody shop?

"I'm shopping!" I reply, and sling a new paperback book into the trolley.

"You could get that out of the library for nothing!" says Jess, looking horrified.

The *library*? I look at her in equal horror. I don't want some thumbed copy in a horrible plastic jacket, which I have to remember to take back.

"It's a modern classic, actually," I say. "Everyone should have their own copy."

"Why?" she persists. "Why can't you get it out of the library?"

My temperature is beginning to rise.

Because I just want my own nice shiny copy! And piss off and leave me alone!

"Because . . . I might want to make notes in the margin," I say loftily. "I have quite an interest in literary criticism, you know."

I push my trolley on, but she comes hurrying after me.

"Becky, look. I want to help you. You have to gain control of your spending. You have to learn to be more frugal. Luke and I were talking about it—"

"Oh, really?" I say, stung. "How nice for you!"

"I can give you some tips . . . show you how to be thrifty—"

"I don't need your help!" I retort in indignation. "I'm

thrifty! I'm as thrifty as they come." Jess looks incredulous.

"You think it's thrifty to buy expensive magazines you could read for nothing in a public library?"

For a moment I can't quite think of a reply. Then my glance falls on *Elle*. Yes!

"If I didn't *buy* them, I wouldn't get the free gifts, would I?" I retort in triumph, and wheel my trolley round the corner.

So there, Miss Smarty-pants.

I head to the fruit section and start loading bags into my trolley.

How thrifty is this? Nice healthy apples. I look up—and Jess is wincing.

"What?" I say. "What is it now?"

"You should buy those loose." She gestures to the other side of the aisle, where a woman is laboriously picking her way through a mound of apples and filling a bag. "The unit cost is far lower! You'd save . . . twenty pence."

Twenty whole pence!

"Time is money," I reply coolly. "Frankly, Jess, it's not worth my while to be sorting through apples."

"Why not?" she says. "After all, you're unemployed."

I gasp, affronted. *Unemployed?* I am not unemployed! I'm a skilled personal shopper! I have a job lined up! In fact . . . I'm not even going to dignify that with a response. I turn on my heel and stalk over to the salad counter. I fill two huge cartons with luxury marinated olives and take them back to the trolley—and stop in astonishment.

Who put that huge sack of potatoes in my trolley?

Did I say I wanted a big sack of potatoes? Did I say I wanted *any* potatoes?

What if I'm on the Atkins diet?

I look around furiously, but Jess is nowhere to be seen. And the bloody thing's too heavy to lift on my own. Where's she gotten to, anyway?

Suddenly I spot her coming out of a side door, holding a big cardboard box and talking to a store employee. What's she doing now?

"I've been speaking with the produce manager," she says, approaching me. "We can have all these bruised bananas for nothing."

I look in the box and it's full of the most revolting, manky bananas I've ever seen.

"They're perfectly good. If you cut away the black bits," says Jess.

"But I don't want to cut away the black bits!" My voice is shriller than I intended, but I can't help myself. "I want to have nice yellow bananas! And I don't want this stupid great sack of potatoes, either!"

"You can make three weeks' worth of meals from that one sack," says Jess, looking offended. "They're the most economical, nutritious food you can buy. One potato alone—"

Please! Not another potato lecture.

"Where am I supposed to put them?" I interrupt. "I haven't got a cupboard big enough."

"There's a cupboard in the hall," says Jess. "You could use that. If you joined a warehouse club you could use it to store flour and oats, too."

Oats? What do I want oats for? And anyway, clearly she hasn't looked *inside* that cupboard.

"That's my handbag cupboard," I point out. "And it's totally full." Jess shrugs.

"You could get rid of some of your handbags."

Is she seriously suggesting I should get rid of some of my handbags . . . for *potatoes*?

"Let's carry on," I say at last, and push the trolley forward as calmly as I can.

Stay polite. Stay gracious. She'll be gone in twenty-four hours.

But as we progress round the store I am really starting to lose my cool. Jess's voice is constantly droning in my ear like a bumblebee, on and on until I want to turn round and swat her.

You could make your own pizzas for half the price. . . . Have you considered buying a secondhand slow-cooker? . . . Store-brand washing powder is 40p cheaper. . . . You can use vinegar instead of fabric softener. . . .

"I don't want to use vinegar!" I almost snap. "I want to use fabric softener, OK?" I put a bottle of it into the trolley and stalk off toward the juice section, Jess following behind.

"Any comments?" I say as I load two cartons into the trolley. "Anything wrong with lovely, healthy orange juice?"

"No," says Jess, shrugging. "Except you could get the same health benefits from a glass of tap water and a cheap bottle of vitamin C tablets."

OK. Now I seriously want to slap her.

Defiantly I dump another two cartons in my trolley, yank it round, and make for the bread section. There's a delicious smell of baking in the air, and as I get near I see a woman at a counter, demonstrating something to a small crowd of people. She's got a shiny chrome gadget plugged into the wall, and as she opens it up, it's full of heart-shaped waffles, all golden brown and yummy-looking.

"The waffle-maker is quick and easy to use!" she's

saying. "Wake up every morning to the smell of fresh waffles baking."

God, wouldn't that be great? I have a sudden vision of me and Luke in bed, eating heart-shaped waffles and maple syrup, with big frothy cappuccinos.

"The waffle-maker normally costs £49.99," the woman is saying. "But today we are selling it at a special reduced price of . . . £25. That's 50 percent off."

Fifty percent off? OK, I have to have one.

"Yes, please!" I say, and push my trolley forward.

"What are you doing?" says Jess.

"I'm buying a waffle-maker, obviously." I roll my eyes. "Can you get out of my way?"

"No!" says Jess, planting herself firmly in front of the trolley. "I'm not going to let you waste twenty-five pounds on a gadget you don't need."

I'm outraged. How does she know what I do or don't need?

"I *do* need a waffle-maker!" I retort. "It's on my list of things I need. In fact, Luke said only the other day, 'What this house really needs is a waffle-maker.' "

Which, OK, is a bit of a stretch. What he really said was "Is there anything for breakfast except Coco Pops?"

But he might have done. How would she know he didn't?

"Plus I'm *saving* money, in case you hadn't noticed," I push the trolley round her. "It's a bargain!"

"It's not a bargain if you don't need one!" She grabs the trolley and tries to haul it back.

"Get your hands off my trolley!" I say indignantly. "I need a waffle-maker! And I can easily afford it! Easily! I'll take one," I add to the woman, and take a box off the table.

"No, she won't," says Jess, grabbing it out of my arms. What? *What?*

"I'm only doing it for your own good, Becky! You're addicted to spending! You have to learn how to say no!"

"I can say no!" I practically spit in fury. "I can say no whenever I like! I'm just not choosing to say it right now! I *will* take one," I say to the nervous-looking woman. "In fact, I'll take two. I can give one to Mum for Christmas."

I snatch two more boxes and defiantly put them in my trolley.

"So you're just going to waste fifty pounds, are you?" says Jess contemptuously. "Just throw away money you don't have."

"I'm not throwing it away."

"Yes, you are!"

"I'm bloody not!" I retort. "And I *do* have the money. I have plenty of money."

"You're living in a total fantasyland!" Jess suddenly shouts. "You have money until you run out of stuff to sell. But what happens then? And what happens when Luke finds out what you've been doing? You're just storing up trouble!"

"I'm not storing up trouble!" I lash back angrily.

"Yes, you are!"

"No, I'm no—"

"*Will you two sisters just stop fighting for once!*" interrupts an exasperated woman's voice, and we both jump.

I look around in bewilderment. Mum isn't here, is she?

Then suddenly I spot the woman who spoke. She isn't even looking at us. She's addressing a pair of toddlers in a trolley seat.

Oh.

I push the hair back off my hot face, suddenly feeling a bit shamefaced. I glance over at Jess—and she's looking rather shamefaced too.

"Let's go and pay," I say in dignified tones, and push the trolley on.

We drive home without exchanging a word, but underneath my calm exterior I'm seething. Who does she think she is, lecturing me? Who does she think she is, telling me I have a problem?

We get home and unload the shopping with minimal communication. We barely even look each other in the eye.

"Would you like a cup of tea?" I say with exaggerated formality as I put the last packet away.

"No, thanks," she replies with equal formality.

"I'll just busy myself in the kitchen, if you can amuse yourself for a while."

"Fine."

She disappears into her room and the next moment comes out again holding a book called *Petrography of British Igneous Rocks*.

Boy, she really knows how to have fun.

As she sits down on a bar stool I flick on the kettle and get down a couple of mugs. A few moments later Luke wanders in, looking harassed.

"Hi, darling!" I say, injecting even more warmth into my voice than usual. "I got us a lovely waffle-maker! We can have waffles every morning!"

"Excellent!" he says distractedly, and I shoot a glance of vindication at Jess.

"Would you like a cup of tea?"

"Er . . . yes. Thanks." He rubs his brow and peers behind the kitchen door. Then he looks on top of the fridge.

"Are you OK?" I say. "Is anything wrong?"

"I've lost something." He frowns. "It's ridiculous. Things can't just *vanish*."

"What is it?" I say sympathetically. "I'll help you look."

"Don't worry." Luke shakes his head. "It's just a work thing. It'll turn up. It can't have disappeared out of the apartment."

"But I want to help!" I run an affectionate hand along his shoulders. "I've already told you that, darling. Tell me what you're looking for, and we'll search as a team. Is it a file . . . or a book . . . some papers . . ."

"That's kind of you." He kisses me. "Actually, it's nothing like that. It's a box of clocks. From Tiffany. Ten of them."

My breath catches in my throat.

Across the room I'm aware of Jess lifting her head out of her book.

"Did you say . . . Tiffany clocks?" I manage.

"Uh-huh." He nods. "You know we're hosting a big dinner with the Arcodas Group tomorrow night? It's all part of the pitch. We're basically trying to butter them up. So I bought a load of clocks as corporate gifts—and I don't know what the fuck has happened to them. One minute they were here . . . the next, they'd vanished!"

I can feel Jess's eyes on me like laser beams.

"That's a lot of clocks to go missing," she says tonelessly.

I'm swallowing hard. How can I have sold Luke's corporate gifts? How can I have been so stupid? I mean, I *thought* I didn't remember buying them on honeymoon. . . .

"Maybe I put them down in the garage." Luke reaches for his keys. "I'll go and have a look."

Oh God. I have to confess.

"Luke . . ." I say in a tiny voice. "Luke, please don't get angry. . . ."

"What?" He swivels on his heel—and as he sees my face he's suddenly alert. "What is it?"

"Well." I lick my dry lips. "I might possibly have . . ."

"What?" His eyes are narrowing. "What might you have done, Becky?"

"Sold them," I whisper.

"*Sold* them?"

"You wanted me to declutter the place! I didn't know how to do it! We had too much stuff! So I've been selling everything on eBay. And I . . . I sold the clocks too. By mistake."

I'm biting my lip, half hoping Luke might smile, or even laugh, but he just looks deeply fed up.

"Jesus Christ, Becky. We are up to our fucking *eyes*. We really need this kind of hassle." He reaches for his mobile, jabs in a number, and listens for a few seconds. "Hi, Marie? We've got a small problem with the Arcodas Group dinner tomorrow night. Call me back." He snaps his phone shut and the only sound in the kitchen is the kettle coming to the boil.

"I didn't know!" I say desperately. "If you'd *told* me they were corporate gifts. . . . If you'd let me help—"

"*Help?*" Luke cuts me off. "Becky, you have to be kidding."

Shaking his head, he stalks out of the room.

I look over at Jess. I can see "I told you" in a big thought bubble above her head. A moment later, she gets up and follows him into the study.

"If I can do anything," I hear her saying in a low voice, "just let me know."

"It's fine," he replies. "But thanks."

Jess says something else, but now her voice is muffled. She must have closed the door.

Suddenly I *have* to know what she's saying. I tiptoe to

the door of the kitchen, then creep out to the hall, edging as close as I can to the study door, then press my ear against it.

"I don't know how you can live with her," Jess is saying, and I feel a jolt of indignant shock. How can she say that? She's only just met me!

I can't move, I can't breathe, waiting for Luke's response.

"It's difficult," comes Luke's voice at last.

Something cold plunges into my heart.

Luke finds it difficult to live with me.

There's a noise as if someone's coming toward the door, and I leap back in fright. I hurry back to the kitchen and close the door, my eyes hot with tears.

We've only been married eleven months. How can he find it difficult to live with me?

The kettle's come to a boil, but I don't want tea anymore. I open the fridge, get out a half-open bottle of wine, and slosh some into a glass. I drain the entire thing in three gulps, and am refilling the glass as Jess comes back into the kitchen.

"Hi," she says. "It seems like Luke's sorted out the gift problem."

"Great," I say tightly, and take another swig of wine.

So she and Luke sort everything out now, do they? She and Luke have little conversations which I'm not invited to. As I watch her sit down and open her book again, a great tide of anger and hurt starts welling up inside me.

"I would have thought you might take my side." I'm trying to sound calm. "We are supposed to be sisters, after all."

"What do you mean?" Jess frowns.

"You could have defended me!"

"*Defended* you?" Jess looks up. "You think I'm going to defend you when you're that irresponsible?"

"So I'm irresponsible," I say, a little savagely. "And you're perfect, I suppose."

"I'm not perfect! But yes! You're irresponsible!" Jess claps her book shut. "Frankly, Becky, I think you need to get your act together. You seem to have no idea of personal duty. . . . You're obsessed with spending money. . . . you *lie*—"

"Well, you're a misery!" My words come out in a roar. "You're a skinflint miserable cow who doesn't know how to have a good time!"

"*What?*" Jess looks utterly dumbfounded.

"I made every effort this weekend!" I cry. "I did everything I could to make you welcome, and you wouldn't join in with anything! OK, so you don't like *When Harry Met Sally*. But you could have pretended!"

"So you'd rather I was insincere?" says Jess, folding her arms. "You'd rather I lied? That just about sums you up, Becky."

"It's not *lying* to pretend you like something!" I shout in frustration. "I just wanted us to have a good time together! I did research, and I planned your room and everything . . . and you're so cold! It's like you don't have any feelings!"

Suddenly I feel close to tears. I can't believe I'm yelling at my sister. I can't believe things have disintegrated this badly. I break off and take a few deep breaths, trying to regroup. Maybe I can retrieve things. Maybe we can still make it work.

"The thing is, Jess . . . I did it all because I wanted us to be friends," I say. And it's true. I really did. "I just wanted us to be friends."

I expect to see her face softening, but if anything she looks more contemptuous than before.

"And you always have to get what you want," she says. "Don't you, Becky?"

I feel my face flame.

"Wh-What do you mean?"

"I mean you're spoiled!" Her harsh voice cuts like a knife. "What you want, you get! Everything's handed to you on a plate. If you get into trouble your parents bail you out, and if they don't, Luke does! Your whole life makes me sick." She gestures with her book. "It's empty! You're shallow and materialistic . . . and I've never *met* anyone so obsessed with their own appearance and shopping—"

"Talk about obsessed!" I shriek. "Talk about *obsessed*! You're obsessed with saving money! I've never met anyone so bloody miserly! You've got thirty grand in the bank and you go around like you're penniless! Getting free bubble wrap and horrible bruised bananas! Who *cares* if washing powder costs forty pence less?"

"You'd care if you'd been buying your own washing powder since the age of fourteen," Jess snaps back. "Maybe if you took a little more care of the forty pence here and there you wouldn't get into trouble. I heard about how you nearly ruined Luke in New York. I just don't understand you!"

"Well, I don't understand *you*!" I yell, in tears. "I was so excited when I heard I had a sister, I thought we'd bond and be friends. I thought we could go shopping, and have fun . . . and eat peppermint creams on each other's beds. . . ."

"Peppermint creams?" Jess looks at me as though I'm crazy. "Why would we want to eat peppermint creams?"

"Because!" I flail my arms in frustration. "Because it would be *fun*! You know, 'fun'?"

"I know how to have fun," she snaps.

"Reading about *rocks*?" I grab *Petrography of British*

Igneous Rocks. "How can rocks be interesting? They're just . . . rocks! They're the most boring hobby in the world! Which just about suits you!"

Jess gasps. "Rocks are . . . *not* boring!" she lashes back, grabbing her book. "They're a lot more interesting than peppermint creams and mindless shopping and getting yourself into debt!"

"Did you have a fun bypass operation or something?"

"Did you have a responsibility bypass operation?" yells Jess. "Or were you just born a spoiled brat?"

We glare at each other, both trying to collect ourselves. The kitchen is silent apart from the whir of the fridge-freezer.

I'm not entirely sure what the Gracious Hostess is supposed to do in this situation.

Jess's chin tightens. "Well . . . I don't think there's any point in my sticking around. I can catch a coach back to Cumbria if I leave now."

"Fine."

"I'll get my stuff."

"You do that."

She turns on her heel and leaves the kitchen, and I take another swig of wine. My head is pounding.

She can't be my sister. She can't be. She's a miserable, tightwad, sanctimonious cow, and I never want to see her again.

Never.

The Cindy Blaine Show

Cindy Blaine TV Productions
43 Hammersmith Bridge Road
London W6 8TH

Mrs Rebecca Brandon
37 Maida Vale Mansions
Maida Vale
London NW6 0YF

22 May 2003

Dear Mrs Brandon:

Thank you for your message.

We are sorry to hear you will no longer be able to appear on the Cindy Blaine show "I Found a Sister and a Soul Mate."

May we suggest that you appear instead on our upcoming show "My Sister Is a Bitch!!!" Please give me a call if this idea appeals to you.

Very best wishes,

Kayleigh Stuart
Assistant Producer
(mobile: 077878 3456789)

Finerman Wallstein
Attorneys-at-Law
Finerman House
1398 Avenue of the Americas
New York, NY 10105

Mrs. Rebecca Brandon
37 Maida Vale Mansions
Maida Vale
London NW6 0YF

May 27, 2003

Dear Mrs. Brandon:

Thank you for your message. I have altered your
will according to your instructions. Clause 5,
section (f) now reads:

"And nothing at all to Jess, since she's so mean. And
anyway, she's got heaps of money."

With kind regards,

Jane Cardozo

Fifteen

I DON'T CARE. Who needs a sister? Not me.

I never wanted one in the first place. I never *asked* for one. I'm fine on my own.

And anyway, I'm not on my own. I've got a strong and loving marriage. I don't need some crummy sister!

"Stupid sister," I say aloud, wrenching the lid off a pot of jam. It's nearly two weeks since Jess left. Luke's got a late meeting in town, and Mum and Dad are coming over on their way to the airport, so I'm making breakfast for everyone.

"Sorry?" says Luke, coming into the kitchen. He looks pale and tense, as he has for the last few days. The Arcodas Group are making their decision about the pitch and now all he can do is wait. And Luke's not that good at waiting. Plus, he's stressing about this pitch more than usual, because it's the first mainstream account he's gone for. I heard him talking to Gary on the phone last night, saying if they didn't get it, what kind of message would it send out?

The trouble with Luke is, he always has to succeed straightaway. Maybe I should tell him the story about the plucky little spider trying to build its web over and over again.

On second thought, maybe not.

"I was just thinking about Jess," I say. "You were absolutely right about her. We were never going to get on in a million years! I've never met such a misery-guts!"

"Mmm," says Luke absently, pouring himself some orange juice.

He could be a little more supportive.

"Next time I'll take your advice," I say, trying to engage his attention. "I should never even have invited her here. I can't believe we're actually supposed to be related!"

"I thought she was all right in the end," says Luke. "But I can see why you two wouldn't get on."

He wasn't supposed to say "I thought she was all right." He was supposed to say "What a total bitch, I can't believe you put up with her for even a minute!"

"Becky . . . what are you doing?" Luke's gaze lands on the crumbs and plastic packaging littering the granite work-top.

"Making waffles!"

And that just proves another thing. Jess was totally wrong. I've used the waffle-maker practically every day. So there! I almost wish she were here to see it.

The only tiny thing is, I'm not very good at making the mixture. So my method is: buy ready-made waffles, cut them into heart shapes, and put them in the waffle-maker to heat up.

But what's wrong with that? I'm using it, aren't I? We're eating waffles, aren't we?

"Waffles . . . again?" says Luke, with the tiniest of grimaces. "I think I'll pass, thanks."

"Oh," I say, discomfited. "Well, how about some toast? Or eggs? Or . . . muffins?"

"I'm fine on coffee."

"But you have to have something!" I say, regarding him with sudden alarm. He's definitely gotten thinner, worrying about this pitch. I need to feed him up.

"I'll make you some pancakes!" I say eagerly. "Or an omelette!"

"Becky, leave it!" he snaps. "I'm fine." He strides out of the kitchen, snapping open his mobile phone. "Any news?" I hear him say before the study door closes.

I look down at the broken waffle in my hand, trying to keep my spirits up.

I know Luke's really tense about work. And that's probably why he's being a bit short-tempered with me at the moment. It doesn't mean there's any bigger problem or anything.

But deep down inside, I keep remembering what I heard him say to Jess that night. That he finds it difficult to live with me. In fact, I've been thinking about it for the last two weeks, trying to make sense of it.

How can I be difficult to live with? I mean . . . what do I do wrong?

Abruptly I reach for a pencil and paper. OK. I'll look deep down inside myself and be really, really honest.

Becky Bloomwood: Difficulties of Living With
1.

My mind is blank. I cannot think of a single thing.

Come on. Be truthful and unsparing. There must be something. What are the fundamental problems between us? What are the real issues?

Suddenly it hits me. I always mix and match my

shampoos in the shower, and Luke complains I leave all the lids off and he steps on them.

Becky Bloomwood: Difficulties of Living With
1. Leaves shampoo lids off

Yes. And I'm scatty. I'm always forgetting the number for the burglar alarm. There was the time I had to phone the police and ask them, and they sent two squad cars round.

Becky Bloomwood: Difficulties of Living With
1. Leaves shampoo lids off
2. Forgets alarm number

I consider the list uncertainly. There must be more to it. There must be something really significant and profound.

Suddenly I gasp and clap my hand to my mouth.

The CDs. Luke always complains that I take them out and don't put them back in their cases.

Which I know doesn't sound *that* profound—but maybe it was the last straw in the haystack. And besides, I read an article in *Marie Claire* yesterday which said it's the little, niggling things which count in a relationship.

I hurry to the sitting room and head straight for the jumbled pile of CDs by the music system. As I sort them out I feel a kind of lightness. A liberation. This will be the turning point in our marriage.

I stack them neatly and wait till Luke walks past the door on his way to the bedroom.

"Look!" I call out with a note of pride in my voice. "I've organized the CDs! They're all back in their proper boxes!"

Luke glances into the room.

"Great," he says with an absent nod, and carries on walking.

Is that all he can say?

Here I am, mending our troubled marriage, and he hasn't even *noticed*.

Suddenly the buzzer goes in the hall, and I leap to my feet. This must be Mum and Dad. I'll have to get back to our marriage later.

I knew that Mum and Dad had really got into their counseling, but somehow I wasn't expecting them to turn up with slogans on their sweatshirts. Mum's reads I AM WOMAN, I AM GODDESS and Dad's says DON'T LET THE PASSIVE-AGGRESSIVE BASTARDS GET YOU DOWN.

"Wow!" I say, trying to hide my surprise. "Those are great!"

"We got them at the center," says Mum, beaming. "Aren't they fun?"

"So you must be really enjoying your therapy."

"It's marvelous!" exclaims Mum. "*So* much more interesting than bridge. And so sociable! We did a group session the other day and who do you think should have turned up? Marjorie Davis, who used to live across the road!"

"Really?" I say in surprise. "Did she get married, then?"

"Oh no!" Mum lowers her voice tactfully. "She has *boundary issues*, poor thing."

I can't quite get my head round all this. What on earth are boundary issues?

"So . . . er . . . do *you* have issues?" I say as we go into the kitchen. "Has it all been really hard going?"

"Oh, we've been to the abyss and back," says Mum, nodding. "Haven't we, Graham?"

"Right to the edge," says Dad agreeably.

"But the rage and guilt are behind us now. We're both empowered to live and love." She beams at me and roots around in her holdall. "I brought a nice Swiss roll. Shall we put the kettle on?"

"Mum's found her inner goddess," says Dad proudly. "She walked on hot coals, you know!"

I gape at her.

"You walked on hot coals? Oh my God! I did that in Sri Lanka! Did it hurt?"

"Not at all! It was painless!" says Mum. "I kept my gardening shoes on, of course," she adds as an afterthought.

"Wow!" I say. "That's brilliant." I watch as Mum briskly slices the Swiss roll. "So what kind of things do you talk about?"

"Everything!" She starts arranging the slices on a plate. "I had resentment issues, of course . . ."

"You were in denial," Dad chimes in.

"Oh, I found it hard at first." Mum nods. "The fact that Daddy had another woman in his life. And a daughter, no less. But then . . . it was all before he met me. And the truth is, a man as handsome as your father was bound to have a few escapades." Mum looks at Dad with a coquettish smile. "I could never resist him . . . so why should other women?"

Is Mum *fluttering her eyelashes*?

"I could never resist *you*," Dad replies with a flirty lift to his voice.

They're gazing at each other adoringly over the plate of Swiss roll slices. I might as well not be in the room.

"Ahem." I clear my throat and they both come to.

"Yes! Well. We still have a lot to learn," says Mum, offering me the plate. "That's why we're going on this cruise."

"Right," I say after a pause. "Yes. The . . . therapy cruise." The first time Mum told me about this I thought she had to be joking. "So the idea is you sail round the Mediterranean and everyone has therapy sessions."

"It's not *just* therapy!" says Mum. "There are sightseeing expeditions too."

"And entertainment," puts in Dad. "Apparently they have some very good shows. And a black-tie dinner dance."

"All our chums from the center are going," adds Mum. "We've already organized a little cocktail party for the first night! Plus . . ." She hesitates. "One of the guest speakers specializes in reunions with long-lost family members. Which should be particularly interesting for us."

I feel an uncomfortable twinge. I don't want to think about long-lost family members. Mum and Dad are exchanging looks.

"So . . . you didn't really hit it off with Jess," ventures Dad at last.

Oh God. I can tell he's disappointed.

"Not really," I say, looking away. "We're just . . . not very similar people."

"And why should you be?" says Mum, putting a supportive hand on my arm. "You've grown up totally apart. Why should you have anything more in common with Jess than with . . . say . . ." She thinks for a moment. "Kylie Minogue."

"Becky's got far more in common with Jess than with Kylie Minogue!" exclaims Dad at once. "Kylie Minogue's Australian, for a start."

"That doesn't prove anything," says Mum. "We're all in the Commonwealth, aren't we? Becky would probably get on very well with Kylie Minogue. Wouldn't you, darling?"

"Er . . ."

"They'd have nothing to say to each other," says Dad, shaking his head. "I'm telling you."

"Of course they would!" retorts Mum. "They'd have a lovely conversation! I expect they'd become great friends!"

"Now, Cher," says Dad. "*That's* an interesting woman."

"Becky doesn't want to be friends with Cher!" Mum says indignantly. "Madonna, maybe . . ."

"Yes, well, the day I meet Kylie Minogue, Cher, *or* Madonna, I'll let you know, OK?" I say, a little more snappily than I meant to.

Mum and Dad turn to survey me. Then Mum glances at Dad.

"Graham, go and give Luke his coffee." She hands a mug to Dad, and as soon as he's gone, she gives me a searching look.

"Becky, love!" she says. "Are you all right? You seem a bit tense."

Mum's sympathetic face makes my composure crumble. Suddenly all the worries I've been trying so hard to bury start rising to the surface.

"Don't worry about Jess," she says kindly. "It doesn't matter in the least if you two girls don't get on. Nobody will mind!"

I busy myself with the coffeepot, hoping to stem the tears I can feel right behind my eyes.

"It's not Jess," I say. "At least, it's not just Jess. It's . . . Luke."

"Luke?" says Mum in astonishment.

"Things aren't going too well at the moment. In fact . . ." My voice starts to wobble. "In fact . . . I think our marriage is in trouble."

Oh God. Now I've said it aloud it sounds totally true. *Our marriage is in trouble.*

"Are you sure, love?" Mum looks perplexed. "You both seem very happy to me!"

"Well, we're not! We've just had this horrible huge row!"

Mum bursts into laughter.

"Don't laugh!" I say indignantly. "It was awful!"

"Of course it was, love!" she says. "You're coming up to your first anniversary, aren't you?"

"Er . . . yes."

"Well, then. That's the time for your First Big Row! You knew that, didn't you, Becky?"

"What?" I say blankly.

"Your First Big Row!" She tuts at my expression. "Dear me! What do the women's magazines teach you girls nowadays!"

"Er . . . how to put on acrylic nails?"

"Well! They should be teaching you about happy marriages! All couples have a First Big Row at around a year. A big argument, then the air is cleared, and everything's back to normal."

"I never knew that," I say slowly. "So . . . our marriage isn't in trouble after all?"

This makes a lot of sense. A First Big Row—and then everything's calm and happy again. Like a thunderstorm. Clear air and renewal. Or one of those forest fires that seem awful but in fact are *good* because all the little plants can grow again. Exactly. But the real point is . . . Yes! This means none of it was my fault! We were going to have a row anyway, whatever I did! I'm really starting to cheer up again. Everything's going to be lovely again. I beam at Mum and take a huge bite of Swiss roll.

"So . . . Luke and I won't have any more rows," I say, just to be on the safe side.

"Oh no!" says Mum reassuringly. "Not until your Second Big Row, which won't be until—"

She's interrupted by the kitchen door banging open and Luke appearing in the doorway. He's holding the phone and his face is elated.

"We got it. We've got the Arcodas Group!"

I knew everything was going to be all right! I *knew* it. It's all lovely! In fact, it's been like Christmas all day long!

Luke canceled his meeting and went straight into the office to celebrate—and after seeing Mum and Dad off in a taxi I joined him there. God, I love the Brandon Communications office. It's all chic, with blond wood and spotlights everywhere, and it's such a happy place. Everyone just mills around, merrily swigging champagne all day! Or at least, they do when they've just won an enormous pitch. All day long, there's been the sound of laughter and excited voices everywhere, and someone's programmed all the computers to sing "Congratulations" every ten minutes.

Luke and his senior people held a quick celebration/strategy meeting, which I sat in on. At first they were all saying things like "The work starts here" and "We need to recruit" and "There are huge challenges ahead." But then Luke suddenly exclaimed, "Fuck it. Let's party. We'll think about the challenges tomorrow."

So he got his assistant on the phone to some caterers, and at five o'clock loads of guys in black aprons appeared in the offices with more champagne, and canapés arranged on cool Perspex boxes. All the employees piled into the biggest conference room, and there was music on the sound system, and Luke made a little speech in which he said it was a great day for Brandon C, and well done, and everyone cheered.

And now a few of us are going out to dinner for *another* celebration! I'm in Luke's office redoing my makeup, and he's changing into a fresh shirt.

"Congratulations," I say for the millionth time. "It's fantastic."

"It's a good day." Luke grins at me, doing up his cuffs. "This could pave the way for a lot."

"I'm so proud of you."

"Ditto." Luke's face suddenly softens. He comes over and wraps his arms round me. "I know I've been distracted lately. And I'm sorry."

"It's OK," I say, looking down. "And I'm . . . I'm sorry I sold the clocks."

"That doesn't matter!" Luke strokes my hair. "I know things haven't been easy for you. What with coming home . . . your sister . . ."

"Yes, well," I say at once. "Let's not think about her. Let's think about *us*. The future." I pull his head down and kiss him. "It's all going to be great."

For a while we're both quiet. But in a good way. It's just us, in each other's arms, relaxed and content and together, like we used to be on our honeymoon. I feel a great swell of relief. Mum was so right! That First Big Row totally cleared the air! We're closer than ever!

"I love you," I murmur.

"I love *you*." Luke kisses my nose. "We should get going."

"OK. I'll go down and see if the car's here yet."

I head along the corridor, floating on a cloud of joy. Everything's perfect. Everything! As I pass the caterers' trays, I pick up a glass of champagne and take a few sips. Maybe we'll go dancing tonight. After dinner. When everyone else has gone home, Luke and I will go on to a club and celebrate properly, just the two of us.

I trip happily down the stairs, still holding my glass, and open the door into reception. Then I stop, puzzled. A few yards away, a thin-faced guy in a chalk-striped suit is talking to Janet, the receptionist. He seems kind of familiar, somehow, but I can't quite place him. . . .

Yes. I can.

It's that guy from Milan. The one who carried Nathan Temple's bags out of the shop. What's he doing here?

Cautiously I take a few steps forward so I can hear their conversation.

"So, Mr. Brandon's *not* ill?" he's saying.

Oh no.

I retreat behind a door and slam it shut. What do I do now?

I take a gulp of champagne to calm my nerves—and then another. A couple of guys from IT saunter past and give me an odd look, and I smile gaily back.

OK. I can't cower behind this door forever. I inch my head above the glass panel in the door until I can see into reception—and thank God. Chalk-stripe guy has gone. With a whoosh of relief I push the door open and stride nonchalantly into the reception area.

"Hi!" I say casually to Janet, who's typing busily on her computer. "Who was that just now? That man talking to you."

"Oh, him! He works for a man called . . . Nathan Temple?"

"Right. And . . . what did he want?"

"It was weird!" she says, pulling a face. "He kept asking if Luke was 'better.' "

"And what did you tell him?" I say, trying to depress the tone of urgency in my voice.

"Well, I said he's fine, of course! Never better!" She

laughs gaily, then as she sees my face she suddenly stops typing. "Oh my God. He isn't fine, is he?"

"What?"

"That was a doctor, wasn't it?" She leans forward, looking stricken. "You can tell me, Becky. Did Luke catch some tropical disease while you were away?"

"No! Of course not!"

"Is it his heart, then? His kidneys?" Her eyes are watering. "You know . . . I lost my dear aunt this year. It really hasn't been easy for me. . . ."

"I'm sorry," I say, flustered. "But honestly, don't worry! Luke's fine! Everything's fine, it's all fine. . . ."

I glance up—and the words wither on my lips.

Please, no.

This can't be happening.

Nathan Temple himself is walking into the building.

He's bigger and more barrel-chested than I remember, and is wearing the same leather-trimmed coat he was wearing in Milan. He exudes power and money and a smell of cigars. And his sharp blue eyes are looking right at me.

"Well, hello," he says in his Cockney rasp. "Mrs. Brandon. We meet again."

"Hell-Hello!" I say. "Gosh! What a . . . lovely surprise!"

"Still enjoying the bag?" He smiles briefly.

"Er . . . yes! It's fab!"

I have to get him out of here. I have to get him out of here.

"I've come to talk about my hotel with your husband," he says pleasantly. "Will that be possible?"

"Right!" I swallow. "Of course. Great! The only thing is, Luke's a bit tied up, unfortunately. But would you like a drink? We could go to a bar . . . have a really nice chat. . . . You could tell me all about it. . . ."

Yes. Genius. I'll hustle him out . . . buy him a few drinks. . . . Luke will never know. . . .

"I don't mind waiting," he says, easing his huge frame down into a leather chair. "If you'll let him know I'm here." There's a glint in his eyes. "I gather he's recovered from his illness?"

"Yes! He's . . . he's a lot better! Thanks for the flowers!"

I glance at Janet, who's been following this exchange in confusion.

"Shall I ring up and tell Luke?" she says, reaching for the phone.

"No! I mean . . . don't worry! I'll pop up myself," I say, my voice shrill.

I start walking toward the lifts. OK. I can still deal with this. I get Luke out of the building the back way by telling him somebody's spilled water on the foyer floor and it's really slippery. Yes. And we get in the car . . . then I pretend I've forgotten something, and I go *back* to Nathan Temple, and I say—

"Becky?"

I leap about ten feet and look up. Luke is coming down the stairs, two steps at a time. His face is glowing and he's putting on his coat.

"So, is the car here yet?" He peers at my frozen expression in surprise. "Sweetheart . . . are you all right?"

Or I could tell Luke everything.

When this is over, I promise myself, I will never tell him a lie again. I will be honest and straight and truthful. Plus I will learn to make waffles.

"Er . . . Luke?" I manage at last.

"Yes?"

"There's . . . there's something I have to tell you." I swallow hard. "I should have told you ages ago, but . . . I didn't . . . and I was dealing with it, but—"

Suddenly I realize that Luke isn't listening to a word.

His eyes are darkening as they focus beyond me, on Nathan Temple.

"Is that—" He shakes his head in disbelief. "What's *he* doing here? I thought Gary was getting rid of him."

"Luke—"

"Hold on, Becky. This is important." He pulls out his phone and taps in a number. "Gary," he says in low tones. "What's Nathan Temple doing in our foyer? You were supposed to be dealing with it."

"Luke—" I try again.

"Sweetheart, wait a minute." He turns back to the phone. "Well, he's here. Larger than life."

"Luke, please, listen—" I tug his arm urgently.

"Becky, whatever it is, can't it wait till later?" Luke says with a touch of impatience. "I have a problem here that I have to sort out—"

"But that's what I'm trying to tell you!" I say in desperation. "It's about your problem! It's about Nathan Temple!"

"How can it be to do with Nathan Temple? Becky, you don't even *know* Nathan Temple!"

"Er . . . well . . . actually . . . yes, I do." I bite my lip. "Kind of."

Slowly Luke closes up his phone. "You 'kind of' know Nathan Temple?"

"Here's Mr. Brandon!" A voice rings out and we both look up to see that Janet at the reception desk has spotted us. "Luke, you've got a visitor!"

"Just coming, Janet," Luke calls back with a professional smile. He turns to me, still smiling. "Becky, what the fuck has been going on?"

"It's . . . It's a bit of a long story," I say, my face hot.

"Were you planning to share this story with me at any stage?" Luke's smile is fixed in place, but there's a definite edge to his voice.

"Yes! Of course! I was just . . . waiting for the right moment."

"Do you think *this* might possibly be a good moment? Bearing in mind he's a few fucking yards away?"

"Er . . . yes! Absolutely." I cough nervously. "Well. It all began . . . er . . . in a shop, as it happens—"

"Too late," interrupts Luke in an undertone. "He's coming."

I follow Luke's gaze to see that Nathan Temple has got out of his chair and is advancing toward us.

"So, here he is." His hoarse voice greets us. "The elusive Luke Brandon. You've been keeping your husband from me, young lady, haven't you?" He wags a mock-accusing finger at me.

"Of course not!" I laugh shrilly. "Er . . . Luke, do you know Nathan Temple? We met in Milan, um . . . remember, darling?" I give a bright, fake smile as if I'm a dinner party hostess and this is all perfectly normal.

"Good evening, Mr. Temple," says Luke calmly. "How nice to meet you properly."

"It's a pleasure." Nathan Temple claps Luke on the back. "So, you're feeling better, I hope."

Luke's eyes flicker toward me, then immediately back to Nathan Temple.

"I'm feeling quite well," he replies. "May I ask what this . . . unexpected visit is regarding?"

"Well," says Nathan Temple, reaching in his coat pocket for a monogrammed silver cigar case. "Seems you won't take calls from my office."

"I've been very busy this week," Luke replies without flinching. "I do apologize if my secretaries have failed to pass on your messages. Was there something in particular you wanted to discuss?"

"My hotel project," says Nathan, offering Luke a cigar. "*Our* hotel project, I should say."

Luke starts to reply, but Nathan Temple lifts a hand to stop him. He carefully lights his cigar and puffs on it a few times. "Forgive me for turning up here out of the blue," he says at last. "But when I want something . . . I don't hang around. I go and get it. Much like your good wife here." His eyes twinkle. "I'm sure she told you the story."

"I think she was probably saving up the best part," Luke says with a tight smile.

"I like your wife," Nathan Temple says affably. He blows out a cloud of smoke and runs appraising eyes over me. "You want to come to work for me anytime, sweetheart, you just give me a ring."

"Gosh!" I say, a bit thrown. "Er . . . thanks!"

I glance apprehensively at Luke. A vein is throbbing in his forehead.

"Becky," he says in polite, measured tones. "Might we have a little word? Do excuse us for a moment," he adds.

"No problem." Nathan Temple nods at his cigar. "I'll finish this up. Then we can talk."

Luke marches me into a little meeting room and closes the door. Then he turns to me, his face all tight and businesslike.

Suddenly I'm scared.

"OK, Becky, start from the beginning. No—" He interrupts himself. "Cut to the middle. How do you know Nathan Temple?"

"I met him when we were in Milan. I was in this shop and he . . . he did me this favor."

"He did you a *favor*?" Luke looks taken aback. "What kind of favor? Were you taken ill? Did you get lost?"

My mind is scurrying around, trying to think of the best way to put it. I'm not sure there is one.

"There was this . . . handbag," I say at last.

"A handbag?" Luke looks taken aback. "He bought you a handbag?"

"No! I bought it. But he got me to the top of the list. He was really sweet! And I was really grateful. . . ." I'm twisting my hands into knots. "So then when we were back in England he phoned up and said he wanted you to be involved with his hotel. . . ."

"And what did you say?" says Luke, his voice dangerously quiet.

"The thing is"—I swallow—"I thought you'd love to do a hotel launch."

The door suddenly bursts open and Gary comes into the room.

"What's going on?" he says, wide-eyed. "What's Nathan Temple doing here?"

"Ask Becky." Luke gestures toward me. "It seems she's been having quite the correspondence with him."

"I didn't know who he was!" I say defensively. "I had no idea! He was just this lovely cockney man who got me my bag . . ."

"Bag?" says Gary, his eyes swiveling from me to Luke. "What bag?"

"Becky appears to have offered my services to Nathan Temple in return for a handbag," says Luke curtly.

"A *handbag*?" Gary looks stunned.

"It wasn't just any old handbag!" I exclaim, rattled. "It was a limited edition Angel bag! There's only a few of them in the whole world! It was on the cover of *Vogue*! All the movie stars want one and everything!"

Both men look at me as though I'm speaking Martian.

"And anyway," I say, my face burning, "I thought doing

a hotel launch would be fab! It's five-star and every-thing! You'd get to meet celebrities!"

"Celebrities?" echoes Luke, suddenly losing it. "Becky, I don't *need* to meet those kind of celebrities! I don't need to be launching some tacky criminal's hotel! I need to be here, with my team, focusing on my new client's needs."

"I didn't realize!" I say desperately. "I thought it was a brilliant networking coup!"

"Calm down, boss," Gary says to Luke soothingly. "We haven't promised him anything—"

"She has." Luke gestures toward me, and Gary now seems at a total loss.

"I didn't . . . promise exactly." My voice shakes a lit-tle. "I just said . . . you'd be delighted."

"You realize how much harder this makes it for me?" Luke is holding his head in his hands. "Becky, why didn't you *tell* me? Why didn't you tell me about it in Milan?"

The room is very still.

"Because the Angel bag cost two thousand euros," I say at last in a tiny voice. "I thought you'd be cross."

"Jesus Christ . . ." Luke sounds at the end of his tether.

"And then I didn't want to bother you! You were so busy with the Arcodas pitch. . . . I thought I'd deal with it myself. And I *was* dealing with it."

" 'Dealing with it,' " echoes Luke incredulously. "How were you dealing with it?"

"I told Nathan Temple you were ill," I gulp.

Comprehension dawns on Luke's face.

"The bunch of flowers," he says in even tones. "Was that from Nathan Temple?" Oh God.

"Yes," I whisper.

"He sent you flowers?" says Gary in disbelief.

"And a fruit basket," says Luke shortly.

Gary gives a sudden snort of laughter.

"It's not funny," says Luke, his voice like whiplash. "We've just won the biggest pitch of our lives. We should be out celebrating. Not having to deal with bloody Nathan Temple sitting in our foyer." He sinks into a chair.

"We don't want to make an enemy of him, Luke," says Gary, pulling a small face. "Not if he's going to buy the *Daily World*."

Luke's face is tense and motionless. I don't dare say a word.

Then abruptly he stands up. "We can't sit here all day. I'll go and see him. If I have to do the job I have to do the job." He gives me a look. "I just hope the handbag was worth it, Becky. I really hope it was worth it."

I feel a sudden stab of pain.

"Luke, I'm sorry," I say. "I'm really sorry. I never meant . . . I never realized—"

"Yeah, Becky," he interrupts in weary tones. "Whatever."

He leaves the room, followed by Gary. And I just sit there. Suddenly there's a tear rolling down my cheek. Everything was so perfect. And now it's all ruined.

Sixteen

THIS HAS BEEN the worst week of our entire marriage.

I've barely seen Luke, he's been so tied up with work. He's had meetings every day with the Arcodas Group, plus there's been a huge crisis with one of his banking clients, and one of his main account managers was rushed to the hospital with meningitis. It's all been total mayhem.

And today, instead of having a chance to relax and regroup, he's got to fly out to Cyprus to visit Nathan Temple's hotel and start planning the launch. A launch which he doesn't want to do, but has to—because if he pulls out with some excuse, Nathan Temple might get offended. According to all the business press, it's looking likely that Nathan Temple's going to buy the *Daily World* newspaper. So as Luke said, he can't afford to antagonize him.

"Can I do anything?" I say nervously as I watch him put shirts into a suitcase.

"No," he says shortly. "Thanks."

This is how he's been all week. All quiet and scary and barely looking me in the eye. And when he does look me in the eye, he looks so fed up that I feel a bit sick.

I'm trying really hard to keep positive and look on the bright side. I mean, it's probably totally normal for couples to have blips like this. Just like Mum said. This is the Second Big Row of our marriage, and the air will clear again and everything will be fine. . . . Except I'm not sure the Second Big Row should come two days after the First Big Row. And I'm not sure it should last a whole week.

I tried e-mailing Mum on her cruise ship to ask her advice, but I got a message back saying that the Mind Body Spirit cruise was a retreat from the outside world, and no passengers could be contacted until next Friday, when they dock in Athens.

Luke zips up his suit carrier and disappears into the bathroom without even looking at me. He'll be gone in a few minutes. We can't leave each other like this. We just can't.

He comes out again and dumps his shaving kit in his suitcase.

"It's our first anniversary soon, you know." I'd been hoping Luke and I could do something romantic, like a candlelight picnic. "We should . . . plan something."

"I'm not even sure if I'll be back in time," says Luke.

He sounds like he doesn't care, either. Our first anniversary and he's not even interested. Suddenly my head is hot and I can feel tears pushing at my eyes. The whole week has been awful and now Luke's leaving and he won't even smile at me.

"You don't have to be so unfriendly, Luke," I say in a

rush. "I know I've made a mess, but I didn't mean to. I've said I'm sorry about a zillion times."

"I know," says Luke in the same old weary tones.

"What do you expect me to do?"

"What do you expect *me* to do, Becky?" he retorts in sudden exasperation. "Say it doesn't matter? Say I don't mind that just when I should be putting all my efforts into the Arcodas Group, I find myself flying off to some godforsaken island?" He clicks his case shut. "You want me to say I'm *happy* to be associated with some tacky hotel?"

"It won't be tacky!" I exclaim in dismay. "I'm sure it won't! Nathan Temple said it was going to be of the highest quality! You should have seen him in that shop in Milan, Luke. He would only accept the best! The best leather . . . the best cashmere . . ."

"And I'm sure he'll have the best water beds," Luke says with a sarcastic edge to his voice. "Becky, don't you understand? I have a few principles."

"So do I!" I say in shock. "I have principles! But that doesn't make me a *snob*!"

"I am not a snob," retorts Luke tightly. "I simply have standards."

"You are a snob!" My voice rushes out before I can stop it. "Just because he used to run motels! I've been looking up Nathan Temple on the Internet. He does loads for charity, he helps people. . . ."

"He also dislocated a man's jaw," Luke cuts in. "Did you read about that?"

For a few moments I'm halted.

"That was . . . years ago," I say at last. "He's made amends . . . he's reformed. . . ."

"Whatever, Becky." Luke sighs and picks up his briefcase. "Can we just leave it?"

He heads out of the room and I hurry after him.

"No. We can't leave it. We have to talk, Luke. You've barely looked at me all week."

"I've been busy." He reaches into his briefcase, takes out a foil strip of ibuprofen, and pops out a couple of tablets.

"No, you haven't." I bite my lip. "You've been punishing me."

"Can you *blame* me?" Luke thrusts his hands through his hair. "This has been a hell of a week."

"Then . . . let me help!" I say eagerly. I follow him into the kitchen, where he's running water into a glass. "There must be something I could do. I could do research—"

"Please!" Luke interrupts, and swigs down his ibuprofen. "No more help. All your 'help' does is waste my bloody time. OK?"

I stare at him, my face burning. He must have looked at my ideas in the pink folder. He must have thought they were total rubbish.

"Right," I say at last. "Well . . . I won't bother anymore."

"Please don't." He walks off into the study, and I can hear him opening desk drawers.

I want to say something else. Something witty and incisive which will prove him wrong. But I can't think of it.

As I'm standing there, the blood thumping round my head, I hear the sound of the letter box. I go into the hall, where a package is lying on the doormat. It's a slim Jiffy bag for Luke, with a smudged postmark. I pick it up and stare at the handwriting, written in black marker pen. It looks kind of familiar—except it's not.

"You've got a parcel," I say.

Luke comes out of the study, holding a pile of files, and dumps them in his briefcase. He takes the package from me, rips it open, and pulls out a compact disc, together with a letter.

"Ah!" he exclaims, sounding more pleased than he has all week. "Excellent."

"Who's it from?"

"Your sister," says Luke.

I feel like he's hit me in the solar plexus.

My sister? *Jess?* My eyes drop down to the package in disbelief. That's Jess's handwriting?

"Why . . ." I'm trying to keep my voice calm. "Why is Jess writing to you?"

"She's edited that CD for us." He scans to the bottom of the page. "She really is a total star. She's better than our own IT guys. And you know, she wouldn't take any payment. I *must* send her some flowers."

His voice is all warm and appreciative, and his eyes are glowing. Suddenly there's a huge lump in my throat.

He thinks Jess is fab, doesn't he? Jess is fab . . . and I'm crap.

"So Jess has been a help to you, has she?" I say, my voice trembling.

"Yes. To be honest, she has."

"I suppose you'd rather she was here than me. I suppose you'd rather we swapped places."

"Don't be ridiculous." Luke folds up the letter and pops it back in the Jiffy bag.

"If you think Jess is so great, why don't you just go and live with her?" I can't seem to control the words—they escape in an avalanche. "Why don't you just go and . . . and talk about computers together?"

"Becky, calm down," says Luke, clearly amazed.

But I can't calm down.

"It's OK! You can be honest! If you prefer a miserable skinflint with zero dress sense and zero sense of humor to me . . . just say so! Maybe you should marry her if she's so great! I'm *sure* you'd have a wonderful time to-gether. . . ."

"Becky!" Luke cuts me off with a look which chills me to the marrow. "Just stop right there."

I don't dare move a muscle. I feel like we've plunged to some new, scary place in our relationship.

"I know you didn't get along with Jess," he says at last. "But you should know this. Your sister is a good person. She's honest, reliable, and hardworking. She spent hours on this for us." He taps the disc. "She volunteered to do it herself, and she didn't ask for any pay or any thanks. I would say she's a truly selfless person." He takes a few steps toward me, his expression unrelenting. "You could learn a lot from your sister."

I open my mouth to speak, but nothing will come out. I feel quite hollow with fear. Right now there's nothing in Luke's face to say he's my husband and he loves me.

"I have to go." Luke looks at his watch. "I'll get my stuff."

He strides out of the kitchen. But I can't move from the spot.

"I'm off." Luke reappears at the kitchen door holding his case. "I'm not sure when I'll be back."

"Luke . . . I'm sorry." At last I've found my voice, even if it is all shaky. "I'm sorry I've been such a disappointment to you." I raise my head, trying to keep a grip on myself. "But if you really want to know . . . you've been a disappointment to me too. You've changed. You were fun on our honeymoon. You were fun and you were laid-back and you were kind. . . ."

Suddenly I have a memory of Luke as he was. Sitting on his yoga mat with his bleached plaits and his earring. Smiling at me in the Sri Lankan sunshine. Reaching over to take my hand.

I feel an unbearable yearning for that easy, happy man, who bears no resemblance to the stressed corporate animal standing in front of me.

"You're different." The words come out in a sob and I can feel a tear trickling down my cheek. "You've gone back to the way you used to be before. The way you promised you'd never be again." I wipe away the tear roughly. "This isn't what I thought married life would be like, Luke."

"Nor me," says Luke. There's a familiar wryness to his voice, but he isn't smiling. "I have to go. Bye, Becky."

A few moments later I hear the front door slam.

I sink down onto the floor and bury my face in my knees. And he didn't even kiss me goodbye.

For a while I don't move. I just sit there in the hall, hugging my knees. Our marriage is in tatters. And it hasn't even been a year.

At last I rouse myself and get stiffly to my feet. I feel numb and spaced-out. Slowly I walk into the silent, empty dining room, where our carved wooden table from Sri Lanka is standing proudly in the middle of the room.

The sight of it makes me want to cry all over again. I had such dreams for that table. I had such dreams of what our married life was going to be like. All the visions are piling back into my head: the glow of candlelight, me ladling out hearty stew, Luke smiling at me lovingly, all our friends gathered round the table. . . .

Suddenly I feel an overwhelming, almost physical longing. I have to talk to Suze. I have to hear her sympathetic voice. She'll know what to do. She always does.

I hurry, almost running, to the phone and jab in the number.

"Hello?" It's answered by a high-pitched woman's voice—but it's not Suze.

"Hi!" I say, taken aback. "It's Becky here. Is that—"

"It's Lulu speaking! Hi, Becky! How are you?"

Her abrasive voice is like sandpaper on my nerves.

"I'm fine," I say. "Is Suze there, by any chance?"

"She's just putting the twins into their car seats, actually! We're off for a picnic, to Marsham House. Do you know it?"

"Er . . ." I rub my face. "No. I don't."

"Oh, you should definitely visit it! Cosmo! Sweetie! Not on your Petit Bateau overalls! It's a super National Trust house. And wonderful for the children, too. There's a butterfly farm!"

"Right," I manage. "Great."

"I'll get her to call back in two secs, OK?"

"Thanks," I say in relief. "That would be great. Just tell her . . . I really need to talk to her."

I wander over to the window, press my face against the glass, and stare down at the passing traffic below. The traffic light at the corner turns red and all the cars come to a halt. It turns green again and they all zoom off in a tearing hurry. Then they turn red again—and a new set of cars come to a stop.

Suze hasn't called. It's been more than two secs.

She isn't going to call. She lives in a different world now. A world of Petit Bateau overalls and picnics and butterfly farms. There's no room for me and my stupid problems.

My head feels thick and heavy with disappointment. I know Suze and I haven't been getting on that well recently. But I thought . . . I honestly thought . . .

Maybe I could call Danny. Except . . . I've left about six messages for him and he's never returned any of them.

Never mind. It doesn't matter. I'll just have to pull myself together on my own.

What I will do is . . . I will make myself a cup of tea. Yes. And take it from there. With as much determination as I can muster I walk to the kitchen. I flick on the kettle, drop a tea bag in a mug, and open the fridge.

No milk.

For an instant I feel like falling to the floor again and crying till nightfall. But instead I take a deep breath and lift my chin. Fine. I'll go and buy some milk. And stock up generally. It'll be good to get some fresh air and take my mind off things.

I pick up my Angel bag, slick on some lip gloss, and head out of the apartment. I walk briskly out the gates and down the street, past the weird shop with all the gold furniture, and into the delicatessen on the corner.

The moment I get inside I start to feel a bit more steady. It's so warm and soothing in here, with the most delicious smell of coffee and cheese and whichever soup they're cooking that day. All the assistants wear long striped ticking aprons, and look like they're genuine French cheese-makers.

I pick up a wicker basket, head to the milk counter, and load in a couple of pints of organic semi-skimmed. Then my eye falls on a pot of luxury Greek yogurt. Maybe I'll buy myself a few little treats to cheer myself up. I put the yogurt into my basket, along with some individual chocolate mousses. Then I reach for a gorgeous hand-blown glass jar of gourmet brandied cherries.

That's a waste of money, a voice intones in my head. *You don't even like brandied cherries.*

It sounds a bit like Jess's. Weird. And anyway, I *do* like brandied cherries. Kind of.

I shake my head irritably and thrust the jar into my

basket, then move along to the next display and reach for a mini olive-and-anchovy focaccia pizza.

Overpriced rubbish, comes the voice in my head. *You could make it yourself at home for 20p.*

Shut up, I retort mentally. *No, I couldn't. Go away.*

I dump the pizza in my basket, then move along the displays more swiftly, putting in punnets of white peaches, miniature pears, several cheeses, dark chocolate truffles, a French strawberry gâteau. . . .

But Jess's voice is constantly in my head.

You're throwing money away. What happened to the budget? You think indulging yourself like this will bring Luke back?

"Stop it!" I say aloud, feeling rattled. God, I'm going crazy. Defiantly I shove three tins of Russian caviar into my overflowing basket and stagger to the checkout. I drop the basket down on the counter and reach inside my bag for my credit card.

As the girl behind the till starts unloading all my stuff, she smiles at me.

"The gâteau's delicious," she says, carefully packing it into a box. "And so are the white peaches. And caviar!" She looks impressed. "Are you having a dinner party?"

"No!" I say, taken aback. "I'm not having a dinner party. I'm just . . . I'm . . ."

All of a sudden I feel like a fool. I look at my piles of stupid, overpriced food bleeping through the register and feel my face flame. What am I doing? What am I buying all this stuff for? I don't need it. Jess is right.

Jess is right.

The very thought makes me wince. I don't want to think about Jess.

But I can't help it. I can't escape the thoughts wheeling round in my head like big black crows. Out of nowhere I hear Luke's voice. *She's a good person . . . she's honest, reliable, and hardworking. . . . you could learn a lot from your sister. . . .*

You could learn a lot from your sister.

And suddenly it hits me like a bolt of lightning. Oh my God. This is the answer.

"That'll be a hundred and thirty pounds, seventy-three pence," says the girl behind the checkout.

"I—I have to go," I say. "Now."

"But your food!" says the girl.

"I don't need any of it."

I turn and stumble out of the shop, still clutching my credit card in my hand. It's all fallen into place. I must go and learn from Jess.

Like Yoda.

I'll be her apprentice and she'll teach me all her frugal ways. She'll show me how to become a good person, the kind of person that Luke wants. And I'll learn how to save my marriage.

She tried to help me before and I didn't listen. But this time I'll be grateful. I'll pay attention to every word she says.

I start walking along the street more and more quickly, until I'm breaking into a run. I have to go to Cumbria. Right this minute.

I sprint all the way home, and up about three flights of stairs before I realize my lungs are nearly exploding and I'm never going to make it all the way up to the penthouse. Puffing like a steam engine, I sit down for a few minutes, then take the lift up the rest of the way. I burst into the apartment and run to the bedroom, where I pull a bright red leather suitcase out from under the bed and start throwing things randomly into it, like they do on the telly. A T-shirt . . . some underwear . . . a pair of turquoise pumps with diamanté buckles . . . I mean, it doesn't matter what I take, does it? I just have to get up there and build bridges with Jess.

At last I snap the case shut and haul it off the bed. I grab a jacket, wheel the case down the hall and out onto the landing, then turn and double-lock the front door. I take one last look at it, then step into the lift, feeling strong with a new resolve. Everything's going to change from this moment on. My new life starts here. Off I go, to learn what's really important in—

Oh. I forgot my hair straighteners.

Instinctively I jab at the HALT button. The lift, which was about to descend, gives a kind of grumpy little bump but stays put.

I can't possibly go without my hair straighteners. And my Kiehl's lip balm.

OK, I might have to rethink the whole it-doesn't-matter-what-you-take strategy.

I hurry back out of the lift, unlock the front door, and head back into the bedroom. I haul another case out from under the bed, this one bright lime green, and start tossing things into that too.

Finally I pick up my Angel bag. And as I glimpse my reflection in the mirror, with no warning, Luke's voice resounds through my head: *I just hope the handbag was worth it, Becky.*

I stop still. For a few moments I feel a bit sick.

I almost feel like leaving it behind.

Which would be just ridiculous. How can I leave behind my most prized possession?

I heft it over my shoulder, trying to recapture the desire and excitement I felt when I first saw it. It's an *Angel bag*, I remind myself defiantly. I have the most coveted item in existence. People are fighting over these. There are waiting lists all over the world.

I shift uncomfortably. Somehow it feels heavier on my shoulder than before. Which is very weird. A bag can't just get heavier, can it?

Oh, right. I put my mobile phone charger in there. That's why.

OK. Enough of this. I'm going, and I'm taking the bag with me.

I descend to the ground floor and wheel the cases out of the gates. A lit-up taxi comes barreling along, and I stick out my hand. I load in my cases, feeling suddenly rather stirred up by what I'm planning to do.

"Euston Station, please," I say to the driver, my voice catching in my throat. "I'm going to reconcile with my long-lost-found-then-estranged sister."

The driver eyes me, unmoved.

"Is that the back entrance you want, love?"

Honestly. You'd think taxi drivers would have some sense of drama. You'd think they'd learn it at taxi school.

The roads are clear, and we arrive at Euston in about ten minutes. As I totter toward the ticket booth, dragging my cases behind me, I feel as though I'm in some old black-and-white movie. There should be clouds of steam everywhere, and the shriek and whistle of trains, and I should be wearing a well-cut tweed suit and fur stole, with marcelled hair.

"A ticket to Cumbria, please," I say with a throb of emotion, and drop a fifty-pound note on the counter.

This is where a lantern-jawed man should notice me and offer me a cocktail, or get grit out of my eye. Instead, a woman in an orange nylon uniform is regarding me as though I'm a moron.

"Cumbria?" she says. "Where in Cumbria?"

Oh. That's a point. Does Jess's village even have a station?

Suddenly I have a blinding flash of memory. When I first met Jess, she talked about coming down from—

"North Coggenthwaite. A return, please. But I don't know when I'm coming back." I smile bravely. "I'm going to reconcile with my long-lost-found—"

The woman cuts me off unsympathetically.

"That'll be a hundred and seventy-seven pounds."

What? *How* much? I could fly to Paris for that.

"Er . . . here you are," I say, handing over some of my Tiffany clock cash.

"Platform nine. Train leaves in five minutes."

"Right. Thanks."

I turn and start walking briskly over the concourse to platform nine. But as the huge intercity train comes into view, my confidence wanes a little. People are streaming round me, hugging friends, hefting luggage, and banging carriage doors.

I've come to a standstill. My hands feel sweaty round the suitcase handles. This has all felt like a kind of game up until now. But it's not a game. It's real and I can't quite believe I'm really going to go through with it.

Am I really going to travel hundreds of miles to a strange place—to see a sister who hates me?

Seventeen

OH MY GOD. I'm here.

It's five hours later and I'm actually here, in Cumbria, in Jess's village. I'm in the North!

I'm walking along the main road of Scully—and it's so scenic! It's just like Gary described, with the drystone walls and everything. On either side of me are old stone houses with slate roofs. Beyond the houses are steep, craggy hills with rocks jutting out and sheep grazing on the grass, and looming high above all the others is one huge hill which is practically a mountain.

As I pass a gorgeous little stone cottage I notice a curtain twitching and someone peering out at me. I suppose I do look a teeny bit conspicuous with my red and lime green suitcases. My wheels are trundling noisily on the road, plus my hatbox is banging up and down with every step I take. As I walk past a bench, two old ladies in print dresses and cardigans eye me suspiciously and I can see one pointing to my pink suede shoes. I give them a friendly smile and am about to say "I got them at

SHOPAHOLIC & SISTER   269

Barneys!" when they get up and shuffle off together, still glancing back at me. I take a few more strides along the street, then stop, panting slightly.

It's quite hilly, isn't it? Not that there's anything wrong with hills. This isn't a problem for me at all. But even so, I might just take a few moments to admire the country-side and get my breath back. The taxi driver offered to take me to the door, but I told him I'd rather walk the last bit, just to steady my nerves. I'm starting to feel a bit jittery about seeing Jess again, which is ridiculous be-cause I had hours on the train to prepare.

I even ended up getting some expert help! I'd popped into the train bar and ordered a Bloody Mary—just for a bit of Dutch courage—and there was a whole group of Shakespearean actors, swigging wine and smoking, on tour with *Henry V.* We got to chatting and I ended up telling them the whole story and how I was off to try and reconcile with Jess. And they all got quite stirred up. They said it was just like *King Lear,* and ordered Bloody Marys all round, and insisted on coaching me in my speech.

I'm not sure I'll do *every* single thing they suggested. Like calling myself a "wretched wench." But a lot of their tips were really helpful! For example, never up-stage your fellow actor, which means never stand so they have to turn away from the audience. They all agreed this was the worst possible thing I could do to my sister, and if I did, there would be zero chance of a reconciliation and frankly they wouldn't blame her. I pointed out there wouldn't be an audience, but they said nonsense, a crowd would gather.

The wind is blowing my hair all over the place, and I can feel my lips getting chapped by the strong northern air, so I get out my lip salve and put some on. Then, with a twinge, I reach for my mobile phone for the millionth time to see if Luke has called and I've somehow missed it. But there's no signal at all. We must be out of the area. I stare for a minute at the blank little display, my heart beating with stupid hope. If there's no signal, maybe he's tried to call! Maybe he's phoning right this minute and he just can't get through. . . .

But deep down inside I know it's not true. Six hours have gone by since he left. If he wanted to call, he would have called before now.

Our row has been echoing angrily round my brain all day. Luke's harsh voice. The way he looked at me just before he left, so disappointed and weary. All the things he said. To my horror, tears suddenly start pricking at my eyes, and I furiously blink them back. I'm not going to cry. It's all going to be OK. I'm going to make amends and turn into a new person and Luke won't even recognize me.

Determined, I start wheeling my cases up the hill again, until I reach the corner of Hill Rise. I stop and peer along the gray stone terrace of cottages, stiff with apprehension. This is Jess's road. She lives in one of these houses!

I'm reaching in my pocket to check the exact number when suddenly I notice a movement in an upstairs window a few houses along. I look up—and it's Jess! She's standing at the window, gaping down at me in utter astonishment.

Despite everything that's happened between us, I feel a swell of emotion at the sight of her familiar face. This is my sister, after all. I start running up the street, my cases trundling behind me, my hatbox bouncing up and down. I reach the door, breathless, and am about to lift the knocker, when the door opens. Jess is standing in front of me in pale brown cords and a sweatshirt, looking aghast.

"Becky . . . what the hell are you doing here?"

"Jess, I want to learn from you," I say in a wobbly voice, and lift my hands in supplication like the Shakespearean actors told me. "I've come to be your apprentice."

"What?" She takes a step backwards in horror. "Becky, have you been *drinking*?"

"No! I mean, yes. A few Bloody Marys, maybe . . . but I'm not drunk, I promise! Jess, I want to be a good person." The words come tumbling out in a rush. "I want to learn from you. And get to know you. I know I've made mistakes in life . . . but I want to learn from them. I'm sorry I didn't listen before, but now I'm ready. Jess, I want to be like you."

There's an ominous silence.

"You want to be like me?" she says at last. "I thought I was a 'skinflint miserable cow.' "

Damn. I was hoping she might have forgotten about that.

"Er . . . I'm really sorry I said that," I mutter, abashed. "I didn't mean it."

Jess isn't looking convinced. Quickly I cast my mind back to the coaching session on the train. "Time has healed the wounds between us. . . ." I begin, reaching out for her hand.

"No, it hasn't!" says Jess, pulling it away. "And you've got a bloody nerve coming here."

"But I'm asking you to help me, as my sister!" I say desperately. "I want to learn from you! You're Yoda, and I'm—"

"*Yoda?*" Jess's eyes widen in disbelief.

"You don't *look* like Yoda," I add hastily. "Nothing like! I just meant—"

"Yeah, well, I'm not interested," Jess interrupts. "In you, or your latest stupid idea. Just go away."

She slams the front door shut, leaving me standing on the street. Jess has shut the door on me? Me, her own sister?

"But I've come all the way here from London!" I call through the door.

There's no reply.

I refuse to give up. Not just like that.

"Jess!" I start hammering on the door. "You have to let me in! Please! I know we've had our differences—"

"Leave my door alone!" The door is wrenched open and Jess is standing there again. But this time she doesn't just look hostile. She looks positively livid. "Becky, we haven't just had our differences! We *are* different. I have no time for you. Frankly, I wish I'd never met you. And I have no idea what you're doing here."

"You don't understand," I say quickly, before she can slam the door again. "Everything's gone wrong. Luke and I have argued. I . . . I did something stupid."

"Well, there's a surprise." Jess folds her arms.

"I know I've brought it on myself." My voice starts to tremble. "I know it's my own fault. But I think our marriage is in real trouble. I really do."

As I say the words, I can feel tears threatening again. I blink hard, trying to hold them off.

"Jess . . . please help me. You're the only person I can think of. If I could learn from you, maybe Luke would come round. He likes you." I feel a tightening in my throat, but force myself to look right at her. "He likes you better than he likes me."

Jess shakes her head, but I can't tell whether it's because she doesn't believe me or she doesn't care.

"Go home," she says flatly.

"But—"

"Don't you understand English? Go home!" She waves her hand as though she's shooing a dog.

"But . . . I'm your family!" My voice is starting to shake. "Family help each other! Family watch out for one another. Jess, I'm your *sister*—"

"Well, that's not my fault," says Jess curtly. "I never asked to be your sister. Bye, Becky."

She slams the door shut again, so hard that I flinch. I lift my hand to knock again—but there's no point, is there?

I've come all this way for nothing.

What do I do now? Slowly, I turn round and start trundling my suitcases back along the street.

The thought of going straight home again is unbearable. All those hours on the train—to what? An empty flat. An empty flat and no husband.

And at the thought of Luke, suddenly I can't keep control of myself any longer. Tears start pouring down my cheeks and I can't help but begin sobbing. As I reach the corner, a couple of women with prams look at me curiously, but I barely notice. I'm crying too hard. My makeup must have smeared everywhere . . . and I haven't got a free hand to get a hankie, so I'm having to sniff. . . . I need to stop. I need to sort myself out.

There's a kind of village green to my left, with a wooden bench in the middle. I head for it, then drop my cases and sink down, my head in my hands, and give way to a stream of fresh tears.

Here I am, hundreds of miles away from home, all on my own and no one wants to know me. And it's all my own fault. I've ruined everything.

And Luke will never love me again.

I have a sudden vision of me moving out. Packing up my shoes. Luke telling me he wants to keep the Indonesian gamelan. . . .

Dimly I hear a man's voice above my head. "Now, now. What's all this?"

I look up blearily to see a middle-aged man in tan cords and a green jumper looking down at me, half disapproving, half concerned.

"Is it the end of the world?" he says in abrupt tones. "You've old people trying to take naps around here." He gestures at the cottages around the green. "You're making so much noise, you're scaring the sheep."

He gestures up at the hill, where, sure enough, a couple of sheep are looking inquisitively down at me.

"I'm very sorry I'm disturbing the peace," I gulp. "But things aren't going that brilliantly for me at the moment."

"A tiff with the boyfriend," he states as though it's a foregone conclusion.

"No, I'm married, actually." I lift my left hand so he can see my ring. "But my marriage is in trouble. In fact, I think it might be over. And I've come all this way to see my sister but she won't even speak to me. . . ." I can feel tears spilling over onto my cheeks again. "My mum and dad are away on a therapy cruise, and my husband's gone to Cyprus with Nathan Temple, and my best friend likes someone else more than me, and I haven't got anyone to talk to. And I just don't know where to go! I mean, literally, I don't know where to go after I get up from this bench. . . ."

I give an enormous hiccup, reach for a tissue, and wipe my streaming eyes. Then I look up.

The man looks nonplussed.

"Tell you what, love," he says a bit more kindly. "How does a cup of tea sound?"

"A cup of tea sounds wonderful." I falter. "Thank you very much."

He heads across the green, carrying both my suitcases as though they weigh nothing, while I totter behind with my hatbox.

"I'm Jim, by the way," he says over his shoulder.

"I'm Becky." I blow my nose. "This is really kind of you. I was going to have a cup of tea in London, but I'd run out of milk. In fact . . . that's kind of how I ended up here."

"Long way for a cup of tea," he observes dryly.

That was only this morning, I suddenly realize. It seems a million years ago now.

"We're not about to run out of milk, anyway," he adds, turning into a cottage with SCULLY STORES in black lettering above the doorway. A bell starts tinkling as we walk in, and from somewhere at the back I can hear a dog barking.

"Oh." I look around with fresh interest. "This is a shop!"

"This is *the* shop," he corrects me. He puts down my cases and gently moves me off the mat, at which point the bell stops tinkling. "Been in the family for fifty-five years."

"Wow." I look around the cozy store. There are racks of fresh bread, shelves with tins and packets lined up neatly, old-fashioned jars of sweets, and a display of postcards and gift items. "This is lovely! So . . . are you Mr. Scully?"

Jim looks bemused. "Scully is the name of the village we're in, love."

"Oh yes." I blush. "I forgot."

"My name's Smith. And I think you need that cup of tea. Kelly?" He raises his voice, and a few moments later a girl appears through a door at the back. She's about thirteen, skinny, with fine brown hair pulled into a ponytail and carefully made-up eyes. She's wearing jeans and a pink sleeveless T-shirt, and is holding a *Heat* magazine.

"I was minding the shop, honest, Dad," she says at once. "I just went upstairs for a magazine—"

"It's OK, love. I'd like you to make a nice cup of tea for this lady. She's been through a bit of . . . distress."

"Oh, right." Kelly peers at me a bit doubtfully, and it suddenly occurs to me that I must look an absolute fright.

"Would you like to sit down?" Jim pulls out a chair.

"Thanks," I say gratefully. I put down my hatbox and fish in my Angel bag for my makeup case. I snap open my mirror and peer at myself—and oh God. I have never looked worse in my life. My nose is all red, my eyes are bloodshot, my eyeliner is smudged like a panda, and a streak of turquoise "24-hour eye dazzle" has somehow ended up on my cheek.

I quickly take out a cleansing wipe and get rid of the whole lot until my face is bare and pink, staring sadly at me from the mirror. Half of me feels like leaving it at that. Why should I put on any makeup? What's the point, if my marriage is over?

"Here you are." A steaming cup of tea appears in front of me on the counter, and I look up to see Kelly watching me avidly.

"Thank you so much," I say, my voice still a little unsteady. "You're really sweet."

"It's no trouble," says Kelly, as I take the first delicious sip. God, a cup of tea is the answer to everything.

"Is that . . ." I look up, to see Kelly suddenly gawping at my bag with eyes like dinner plates. It must have been hidden behind the hatbox before. "Is that . . . a real Angel bag?"

I feel a huge inward twinge, which I manage to hide with a weak smile. If she only knew.

"Yes. It's a real Angel bag."

"Dad, she's got an Angel bag!" Kelly exclaims to Jim, who's unloading bags of sugar from a box. "I showed you about them in *Glamour* magazine!" Her eyes are shining with excitement. "All the film stars have got them! They've sold out at Harrods! Where did you get yours?"

"In . . . Milan," I say after a pause.

"Milan!" breathes Kelly. "That's so cool!" Now her eyes have fallen on the contents of my makeup bag. "Is that Stila lip gloss?"

"Er . . . yes."

"Emily Masters has got Stila lip gloss," she says wistfully. "She thinks she's all that."

I look at her lit-up eyes and flushed cheeks, and suddenly I want to be thirteen again. Going to the shops on Saturday to spend my allowance. With nothing to worry about except biology homework and whether James Fullerton fancied me.

"Look . . . have this," I say, scrabbling in my makeup bag for a brand-new Stila lip gloss in grapefruit. "I'm never going to use it."

"Really?" Kelly gasps. "Are you sure?"

"And do you want this cream blusher?" I hand over the box. "Not that you need blusher . . ."

"Wow!"

"Now, wait just a moment," comes Jim's voice from across the shop. "Kelly, you can't take this lady's makeup off her." He shakes his head at her. "Give them back, love."

"She offered, Dad!" says Kelly, her translucent skin staining pink. "I didn't ask for them or anything—"

"Honestly, Jim. Kelly can have them. I'm never going

to use them. I only bought them in the first place because you got a free perfume if you spent over eighty
quid. . . ."

Suddenly tears spring up in my eyes again. God, Jess
is right. I'm a total flake.

"Are you OK?" says Kelly in alarm. "Have them
back—"

"No, I'm fine." I force a smile. "I just need to . . .
think about something else."

I dab my eyes with a tissue, get to my feet, and wander over to the gift display. I might as well get some souvenirs while I'm here. I pick up a pipe rack for Dad and
a painted wooden tray which Mum will like. I'm just
looking at a glass model of Lake Windermere and wondering whether to get it for Janice, when I notice two
women standing outside the window. As I watch, they're
joined by a third.

"What are they waiting for?" I say in puzzlement.

"This," says Jim. He looks at his watch, then puts out
a sign reading TODAY'S BREAD HALF PRICE.

Immediately the women come bustling into the shop.

"I'll take two bloomers, please, Jim," says one with
metal-gray hair and a beige mac. "Have you any reduced croissants?"

"Not today," says Jim. "All full price."

"Oh . . ." She thinks for a moment. "No, I won't
bother."

"I'll take three large wholemeal," chimes in the second woman. She's wearing a green head scarf and holding a big brown handbag. "Who's this?" She jerks her
thumb at me. "We saw you crying on the green. Are you
a tourist?"

"They always get themselves lost," says the first woman.
"Which hotel are you at, love? Does she speak English?
Speke Inglese?"

"She looks Danish," says the third woman knowledgeably. "Who speaks Danish?"

"I'm English," I say. "And I'm not lost. I was upset because . . ." I hesitate, trying to sound matter-of-fact.
"Because my marriage is in trouble. And I came up here
to ask my sister for help, but she wouldn't give it to me."

"Your sister?" says the woman in the head scarf suspiciously. "Who's your sister?"

"She lives in this village." I take a sip of tea. "She's
called Jessica Bertram."

The women look like I've hit them over the head with
a hammer. I look around in confusion, to see Jim's jaw
has dropped by about a foot.

"*You're* Jess's sister?" he says.

"Well . . . yes. I am. Her half sister."

I look around the shop, but no one's moved. Everyone is still gaping at me as if I'm an alien.

"I know we're a bit different to look at . . ." I begin.

"She said you were mad," says Kelly bluntly.

"Kelly!" says Jim.

"What?" I look from face to face. "She said *what*?"

"Nothing!" says Jim, darting a warning look at Kelly.

"We all knew she was going to see her long-lost sister," says Kelly, ignoring him. "And when she came back,
she said you were crazy and lived in a fantasy world. I'm
sorry, Dad, but it's true!"

I can feel my cheeks growing bright red.

"I'm not *crazy*!" I say. "I'm normal! I'm just . . . a bit
different from Jess. We like different things. She likes
rocks. I like . . . shops."

"Are you not interested in rocks, then?" says the
woman with the green head scarf.

"Not really," I admit. "In fact . . . that was a bit of an
issue between us."

"What happened?" Kelly asks, clearly rapt.

"Well . . ." I scuff my foot awkwardly on the floor. "I told Jess I'd never heard of a more boring hobby than rocks in my life, and that it suited her."

There's a universal gasp of incredulity.

"You don't want to be rude about rocks to Jess," says the beige-mac woman, shaking her head. "She loves those rocks of hers, bless her."

"Jess is a good girl," chimes in the green–head-scarf woman, giving me a stern look. "Sturdy. Reliable. She'd make a fine sister."

"Couldn't hope for better," agrees the third woman, pulling her cable-knit cardigan around her.

Their looks make me feel defensive.

"It's not my fault! I want to reconcile with her! But she isn't interested in being my sister! I just don't know how it all went wrong. I so wanted to be friends. I arranged this whole weekend for her, but she didn't like any of it. And she was so *disapproving*. We ended up having a huge row . . . and I called her all sorts of things. . . ."

"What things?" Kelly asks avidly.

"Well . . ." I rub my nose. "I said she was a misery. I said she was really boring. . . ."

There's another huge gasp. Kelly raises a hand as though to stop me, but I don't want to stop. This is cathartic. Now I've started, I want to confess everything.

". . . and the most skinflint person I'd ever met in my life." I'm goaded by their appalled faces. It's like I'm on the crest of a roller coaster. "With zero dress sense, who must have had a fun bypass operation—"

I realize there's a tinkling sound in the air. A tinkling sound which, now that I think about it, has been going on for a few seconds. Cold to the core, I turn round.

Jess is standing in the doorway, her face pale.

"Jess!" I stammer. "God, Jess! I wasn't . . . I didn't *mean* any of . . . I was just explaining. . . ."

"I heard you were in here," she says, speaking with an obvious struggle. "I came to see if you were OK. To see if you wanted a bed for the night. But . . . I think I've changed my mind." She looks directly at me. "I knew you were shallow and spoiled, Becky. I didn't realize you were a two-faced bitch as well."

She turns and strides out, closing the door behind her with a bang.

Kelly is bright red; Jim's looking anywhere but me. The whole atmosphere is prickling with awkwardness.

Then the woman in the green head scarf folds her arms.

"Well," she says. "You buggered that one up, didn't you, love?"

I'm in a state of total shock.

I came up here to reconcile with Jess—and all I've done is made things worse.

"Here you are, love," says Jim, placing a fresh mug of tea in front of me. "Three sugars."

The three women are all drinking cups of tea too. Jim's introduced them to me as Edie (green head scarf), Lorna (metal-gray hair), and Bea (cable-knit cardigan) and has even produced a cake. I get the feeling they're all waiting for me to do something else to entertain them.

"I'm not a two-faced bitch," I say in despair. "Honestly! I'm nice! I came here to build bridges! I mean, I know Jess and I don't get along. But I wanted to learn from her. I thought she could help me save my marriage. . . ."

There's a sharp intake of breath around the shop.

"Is her marriage in trouble as well?" Edie says to Jim, and clicks her tongue. "Dear, oh, dear."

"It never rains but it pours," booms Lorna lugubriously. "Run off with a fancy woman, has he?"

Jim glances at me, then leans toward the women, lowering his voice.

"Apparently he's gone to Cyprus with a man called Nathan."

"Oh." Edie's eyes open very wide. "Oh, I *see*."

"What are you going to do, Becky?" says Kelly, biting her lip.

Go home, flashes through my mind. *Give up.*

But I keep seeing Jess's pale face in my mind, and feeling a little stab in my heart. I know just what it's like to be bitched about. I've known enough horrible bitches in my time. An image comes to me of Alicia Bitch Long-legs, the meanest, snidest girl I ever knew.

I can't bear it if my own sister thinks I'm like her.

"I have to apologize to Jess," I say, looking up. "I know we'll never be friends. But I can't go home with her thinking the worst of me." I take a sip of scalding tea, then look up. "Is there anywhere I can stay around here?"

"Edie runs a bed-and-breakfast," says Jim. "Got any rooms free, Edie?"

Edie reaches into her huge brown bag, then brings out a notebook and consults it.

"You're in luck," she says, looking up. "I've one deluxe single left."

"Edie'll take good care of you," Jim says, so kindly that I feel ridiculous tears welling up again.

"Could I take it for tonight, please?" I say, wiping my eyes. "Thank you very much." I take another sip of tea, then notice my mug. It's blue pottery with *Scully* handpainted on it in white. "This is nice," I say with a gulp. "Do you sell them?"

"On the rack at the back," says Jim, looking at me with amusement.

"Could I have two? I mean, four?" I reach for a tissue and blow my nose. "And I just want to say . . . thank you. You're all being so nice."

The bed-and-breakfast is a large white house directly across the green. Jim carries my suitcases and I carry my hatbox and my carrier bag full of souvenirs, and Edie follows behind me, giving me a list of rules I have to keep.

"No gentleman visitors after eleven . . . no parties of more than three people in the room . . . no abuse of solvents or aerosol cans . . . payment in advance, cash or check accepted, much obliged," she concludes as we reach the lit-up door.

"All right from here, Becky?" says Jim, putting my cases down.

"I'll be fine. And thank you so much," I say, feeling so grateful, I half-want to give him a kiss. But I don't quite dare to—so I just watch as he walks off across the grass again.

"Much obliged," repeats Edie meaningfully.

"Oh!" I say, realizing she means she wants to be paid. "Absolutely!"

I scrabble inside my bag for my purse, and my fingers brush against my mobile phone. From force of habit I pull it out and peer at the display. But there's still no signal.

"You can use the pay phone in the hall if there's anyone you want to call," says Edie. "We have a pull-down privacy hood."

Is there anyone I want to call?

With a twinge I think of Luke in Cyprus, still furious with me; Mum and Dad engrossed in a therapy workshop on their cruise; and Suze, picnicking on some picturesque sun-dappled lawn with Lulu and all their children in cute overalls.

"No. It's OK," I say, trying to smile. "I haven't got anyone to call. To be honest . . . no one will have even noticed I've gone."

5 jun 03 16:54
to Becky
from Suze

Bex. Sorry I missed u. Why aren't u answering the phone? Had disastrous day at picnic. We all got stung by wasps. I miss u. Am coming to London to visit. Call me.

Suzexxxx

6 jun 03 10:02
to Becky
from Suze

Hi, Bex, I'm here. Where RU? Please call!!!!
Suzex

6 jun 03 ?:36
to Becky
from Suze

Bex. Where RU????????????????

Suzexxxx

Eighteen

I DON'T SLEEP well.

In fact, I'm not sure I sleep at all. I seem to have spent the whole night staring at the uneven ceiling of Edie's B&B, my mind going round and round in circles. Except I must have slept for a bit, because when I wake up in the morning my head is full of a terrible dream where I turned into Alicia Bitch Long-legs. I was wearing a pink suit and laughing with a horrible sneer and Jess was looking all pale and crushed. In fact, now that I think about it, Jess looked a bit like me.

Just the thought of it makes me queasy. I have to do something about this.

I'm not hungry, but Edie has cooked a full English breakfast and doesn't seem impressed when I say I normally have just a piece of toast. So I nibble at some bacon and eggs and pretend to have a go at the black pudding, all the while avoiding the attempts at conversation by a kindly German couple on holiday. After a final sip of coffee I leave to find Jess.

As I head up the hill to her house, the morning sun is in my eyes, and a cool wind blows through my hair. Across the green I can see Jim outside his store, unloading crates of apples from a delivery truck, and he lifts his hand in greeting. I wave back, my spirits lifted. This *feels* like a day for reconciliations. Fresh starts and clean slates.

I approach the all-too-familiar brown front door, ring the bell, and wait.

There's no reply.

OK, I am really tired of people not being in when I want to have emotional reunions with them. I squint up at the windows, wondering whether she might be hiding. Maybe I should throw some stones up at the windowpanes.

Except what if I broke one? Then she'd *really* hate me.

I ring the bell a few more times, then give up and walk back down the path. I sit on a piece of wall and settle myself comfortably. This is fine. It's a lovely day. I'll just wait, and when she arrives back home I'll spring up with a speech about how sorry I am.

The wall isn't quite as comfortable as I first thought, and I shift a few times, trying to find a good position. I check the time, then watch an old lady and her little dog walk slowly along the pavement on the other side of the road.

Then I check the time again. Five minutes have gone by.

God, how on earth do stalkers do it? They must get bored out of their minds.

I get up to stretch my legs and walk up to Jess's house again. I ring the bell, just to be on the safe side, then meander back to the wall again. As I do so, I see a policeman coming up the street toward me. What's a policeman doing here, out on this little street at ten o'clock in the morning? I thought they were all tied to their desks by paperwork or zooming around inner cities in squad cars.

I feel a bit apprehensive as I see that he's looking directly at me. But I'm not doing anything wrong, am I? I mean, it's not like stalking is against the law.

Oh. Well, OK, maybe stalking *is* against the law. But I've only been doing it for five minutes. Surely that doesn't count. And anyway, how does he know I'm stalking anyone? I might just be sitting here for pleasure.

"All right?" he says as he approaches.

"Fine, thanks!"

He looks at me expectantly.

"Is there a problem?" I ask.

"Could you move along, miss? This isn't a public seat."

"Why should I?" I say boldly. "That's what is wrong with this country! Anyone who doesn't conform is persecuted! Why shouldn't you be able to sit on a wall without being harassed?"

"That's my wall," he says, and gestures to the front door. "This is my house."

"Oh, right." I flush red and leap to my feet. "I was just . . . er . . . going. Thanks! Really nice wall!"

OK. Stalking over. I'll have to come back later.

I trail down the hill to the village green, and find myself turning toward the shop. As I enter, Kelly is sitting behind the till with a copy of *Elle,* and Jim is arranging apples on the display rack.

"I went to see Jess," I say morosely. "But she wasn't there. I'll have to wait till she comes back."

"Shall I read out your horoscope?" says Kelly. "See if it says anything about sisters?"

"Now, young lady," says Jim reprovingly. "You're supposed to be revising for your exams. If you're not working, you can go and wait at the tea shop."

"No!" says Kelly hastily. "I'm revising!" She pulls a face at me, then puts *Elle* down and reaches for a book called *Elementary Algebra*.

God, algebra. I'd totally forgotten that existed. Maybe I'm quite glad I'm not thirteen anymore.

I need a sugar rush, so I head toward the biscuit section and grab some chocolate digestives and Orange Club biscuits. Then I drift over to the stationery shelf. You can never have too much stationery, so I pick up a packet of thumbtacks in the shape of sheep, which will always come in useful. And I might as well get the matching stapler and folders.

"All right there?" says Jim, eyeing my full arms.

"Yes, thanks!"

I take my goodies over to the till, where Kelly rings them up.

"D'you want a cup of tea?" she says.

"Oh, no, thanks." I say politely. "I couldn't intrude. I'd get in the way."

"Get in the way of what?" she retorts. "Nobody'll be in until four, when the bread comes down. And you can test me on my French vocab."

"Oh, well." I brighten. "If I'd be *useful* . . ."

Three hours later I'm still there. I've had three cups of tea, about half a packet of chocolate digestives, and an apple, and I've stocked up on a few more presents for people at home, like a set of Toby jugs and some place mats, which everyone needs. Plus I've been helping Kelly with her work. Except now we've progressed from algebra and French vocab revision to Kelly's outfit for the school disco. We've got every single magazine open, and I've made her up with each eye different, just to show her what the possibilities are. One side is really dramatic, all smoky shadow and a spare false eyelash I found in my makeup bag; the other is all silvery and sixties, with white space-age mascara.

"Don't let your mother see you like that," is all Jim keeps saying as he walks by.

"If only I had my hairpieces," I say, studying Kelly's face critically. "I could give you the most fantastic pony-tail."

"I look amazing!" Kelly's goggling at herself in the mirror.

"You've got wonderful cheekbones," I tell her, and dust shimmery powder onto them.

"This is so much fun!" Kelly looks at me, eyes shining. "God, I wish you lived here, Becky! We could do this every day!"

She looks so excited, I feel ridiculously touched.

"Well . . . you know," I say. "Maybe I'll visit again. If I patch things up with Jess."

But even at the thought of Jess, my insides kind of crumble. The more time goes by, the more nervous I am at seeing her again.

"I wanted to do makeovers like this with Jess," I add, a bit wistfully. "But she wasn't interested."

"Well, then, she's dumb," says Kelly.

"She's not. She's . . . she likes different things."

"She's a prickly character," Jim puts in, walking by with some bottles of cherryade. "It's hard to credit you two are sisters." He dumps the bottles down and wipes his brow. "Maybe it's in the upbringing. Jess had it pretty hard going."

"Do you know her family, then?" I ask.

"Aye." He nods. "Not well, but I know them. I've had dealings with Jess's dad. He owns Bertram Foods. Lives over in Nailbury. Five miles away."

Suddenly I'm burning all over with curiosity. Jess has

barely told me a word about her family, despite my subtle probing.

"So . . . what are they like?" I say, as casually as I can. "Her family."

"Like I say, she's had a pretty hard time. Her mum died when she was fifteen. That's a difficult age for a girl."

"I never knew that!" Kelly's eyes widen.

"And her dad . . ." Jim leans pensively on the counter. "He's a good man. A fair man. Very successful. He built up Bertram Foods from nothing, through hard work. But he's not what you'd call . . . warm. He was always as tough on Jess as he was on her brothers. Expected them to fend for themselves. I remember Jess when she started big school. She got into the high school over in Carlisle. Very academic."

"I tried for that school," says Kelly to me, pulling a face. "But I didn't get in."

"She's a clever girl, that Jess," says Jim admiringly. "But she had to catch three buses every morning to get there. I used to drive past on my way here—and I'll remember the sight till I die. The early-morning mist, no one else about, and Jess standing at the bus stop with her big schoolbag. She wasn't the big, strong lass she is now. She was a skinny little thing."

I can't quite find a reply. I'm thinking about how Mum and Dad used to take me to school by car every day. Even though it was only a mile away.

"They must be rich," says Kelly, rooting around in my makeup bag. "If they own Bertram Foods. We get all our frozen pies from them," she adds to me. "And ice cream. They've a huge catalog!"

"Oh, they're well off," says Jim. "But they've always been close with their money." He rips open a cardboard box of Cup-a-Soups and starts stacking them on a shelf. "Bill Bertram used to boast about it. How all his kids worked for their pocket money." He straightens a bundle of chicken and mushroom sachets on the shelf. "And if they couldn't afford a school trip or whatever . . . they didn't go. Simple as that."

"School trips?" I can't get my head round this. "But everyone knows parents pay for school trips!"

"Not the Bertrams. He wanted to teach them the value of money. There was a story going around one year that one of the Bertram boys was the only kid in school not to go to the pantomime. He didn't have the money and his dad wouldn't bail him out." Jim resumes stacking the soups. "I don't know if that was true. But it wouldn't surprise me." He gives Kelly a mock-severe look. "You don't know you're born, young lady. You've got the easy life!"

"I do chores!" retorts Kelly at once. "Look! I'm helping out here, aren't I?"

She reaches for some chewing gum from the sweets counter and unwraps it, then turns to me. "Now I'll do you, Becky!" She riffles in my makeup bag. "Have you got any bronzer?"

"Er . . . yes," I say, distracted. "Somewhere."

I'm still thinking about Jess standing at the bus stop, all little and skinny.

Jim is squashing the empty Cup-a-Soup box down flat. He turns and gives me an appraising look.

"Don't worry, love. You'll make up with Jess."

"Maybe." I try to smile.

"You're sisters. You're family. Family always pull through for each other." He glances out the window. "Ay-up. They're gathering early today."

I follow his gaze, and see two old ladies hovering outside the shop. One of them squints at the bread display, then turns and shakes her head at the other.

"Does *nobody* buy bread full price?" I say.

"Not in this village," says Jim. "Except the tourists. But we don't get so many of those. It's mostly climbers who want to have a go at Scully Pike—and they don't have much call for bread. Only emergency services."

"How d'you mean?" I say, puzzled.

"When the stupid buggers get stuck." Jim shrugs and reaches for the half-price sign. "No matter. I've got to thinking of bread as a loss leader, like."

"But it's so yummy when it's all fresh and new!" I say, looking along the rows of plump loaves. Suddenly I feel really sorry for them, like they haven't been asked to dance. "*I'll* buy some. Full price," I add firmly.

"I'm about to reduce it," Jim points out.

"I don't care. I'll have two big white ones and a brown one." I march over to the bread display and pluck the loaves off the shelf.

"What are you going to do with all that bread?" says Kelly.

"Dunno. Make toast." I hand Kelly some pound coins and she pops the three loaves into a bag, giggling.

"Jess is right, you are mad," she says. "Shall I do your eyes now? What look do you want?"

"Customers'll be coming in," warns Jim. "I'm about to put the sign up."

"I'll just do one eye," says Kelly, quickly reaching for a palette of eye shadows. "Then when they've all gone, I'll do the other one. Close your eyes, Becky."

She starts to brush eye shadow onto my eyelid, and I close my eyes, enjoying the brushing, tickling sensation. I've always adored having my makeup done.

"OK," she says. "Now I'm doing some eyeliner. Keep still. . . ."

"Sign's going up now," comes Jim's voice. There's a

pause—then I hear the familiar tinkling sound, and the bustle of people coming in.

"Er . . . don't open your eyes yet, Becky." Kelly sounds a bit alarmed. "I'm not sure if this has gone right. . . ."

"Let me see!"

I open them and grab my makeup mirror. One of my eyes is a wash of bright pink eye shadow, with shaky red eyeliner across the top lid. I look like I have some hideous eye disease.

"Kelly!"

"It said in *Elle*!" she says defensively, gesturing to a picture of a catwalk model. "Pink and red is in!"

"I look like a monster!" I can't help bursting into giggles at my lopsided face. I have never looked so terrible in my life. I glance up to see if any of the customers have noticed and my laughter dies away.

Jess is coming into the shop along with the other reduced-price shoppers.

She looks so cold and hostile, a far cry from that skinny eleven-year-old waiting for the bus in the early morning. Her gaze runs dismissively over the magazines, the open makeup case, and all my makeup scattered over the counter. Then she turns away without speaking and begins to root through the basket of reduced cans.

The bustle of the shop has dwindled to nothing. I'm sure everyone knows exactly what's been going on.

I glance at Jim, who gives me an encouraging nod.

"Er . . . Jess," I begin. "I came to see you this morning. I wanted to explain. . . ."

"Nothing to explain." She turns over the cans roughly, not even looking at me. "I don't know what you're still doing here."

"She's doing makeovers with me," Kelly says loyally. "Aren't you, Becky?"

I dart a grateful smile at her, but my attention is still fixed on Jess.

"I stayed because I want to talk to you. To . . . to apologize. Could I take you out to supper tonight?"

"I wouldn't have thought I was well-dressed enough to have supper with you, Becky," Jess says tonelessly. Her face is still and set—but now I can see the hurt underneath.

"Jess—"

"And anyway, I'm busy." Jess dumps three battered cans on the counter, together with one that has lost its paper covering altogether and is marked at 10p. "Do you know what this is, Jim?"

"Fruit cocktail, I think." He frowns. "But it could be carrots . . ."

"OK. I'll take it." She plonks some coins on the counter and fishes a crumpled paper carrier out of her pocket. "I don't need a bag. Thanks."

"Another night, then!" I say desperately. "Or lunch . . ."

"Becky, leave me alone."

She strides out of the shop and I just sit there, my face tingling as though I've been slapped. Gradually the hush turns into whispers, which grow into full-blown chatter. I'm aware of people's prying eyes as they come up to the counter to pay, but I'm too defeated to care.

"Are you OK, Becky?" Kelly says, touching my shoulder tentatively.

"I've blown it." I drop my arms in a hopeless gesture. "You saw her."

"She always was a stubborn little cuss." Jim shakes his head. "Even when she was a kid. She's her own worst enemy, that Jess. Hard on herself and hard on the rest of the world too." He pauses, cleaning some dirt off his Stanley knife. "She could do with a sister like you, Becky."

"Well, too bad," Kelly says robustly. "You don't need her! Just forget she's your sister. Pretend she doesn't exist!"

"Not as simple as that, though, is it?" says Jim. "Not with family. You can't walk away so easy."

"I don't know." I give a dispirited shrug. "Maybe we can. I mean, we've gone twenty-seven years without knowing each other. . . ."

"And you want to make it another twenty-seven?" Jim looks at me, suddenly stern. "Here's the two of you. Neither of you has a sister. You could be good friends to one another."

"It's not my fault. . . ." I begin defensively, then tail off as I remember my little speech last night. "Well, it's not *all* my fault. . . ."

"Didn't say it was," says Jim. He serves another two customers, then turns to me. "I've an idea. I know what Jess is doing tonight. In fact, I'll be there too."

"Really?"

"Aye. Local environmental protest meeting. Everyone'll be there." His eyes twinkle. "Why not come along?"

FAX MESSAGE

TO: LUKE BRANDON
             APHRODITE TEMPLE HOTEL
             CYPRUS

FROM: SUSAN CLEATH–STUART

6 JUNE 2003

URGENT—EMERGENCY

Luke

Becky *isn't* at the flat. No one has seen her anywhere. I still can't get through on her phone.

I'm really getting worried.

Suze

Nineteen

OK. THIS IS my chance to impress Jess. This is my chance to show her I'm not shallow and spoiled. I must *not* fuck this one up.

The first crucial thing is my outfit. With a frown I survey all my clothes, which I've strewn over the bed in the B&B room. What *is* the perfect environmental protest group meeting outfit? Not the leather trousers . . . not the glittery top . . . My eyes suddenly alight on a pair of combat trousers, and I pluck them from the pile.

Excellent. They're pink, but I can't help that. And . . . yes. I'll team them with a T-shirt with a slogan. Genius!

I haul out a T-shirt that has the word HOT on it and goes really well with the combats. It's not very protest-y, though, is it? I think for a minute, then get a red pen out of my bag and carefully add the word BAN. BAN HOT doesn't exactly make sense . . . but it's the thought that counts, surely. Plus I won't wear any makeup, except a bit of eyeliner and some mascara and a translucent lip gloss.

I put it all on, and tie my hair into plaits, then admire myself in the mirror. I actually look pretty militant! I raise my hand experimentally in a power salute, and shake my fist at the mirror.

"Up with the workers," I say in a deep voice. "Brothers unite."

God, yes. I think I could be really good at this!

The protest meeting is being held in the village hall, and as I arrive I see people milling about, and posters up everywhere, with slogans like DON'T SPOIL OUR COUNTRY-SIDE. I head to a table with cups of coffee and biscuits on it.

"Cup of coffee, love?" says an elderly man in a waxed jacket.

"Thanks," I say. "Er, I mean . . . thanks, brother. Right on." I give him the power salute. "Up the strike!"

The man looks a bit confused, and I suddenly re-member they're not striking. I keep getting this mixed up with *Billy Elliot*. But it's the same thing, isn't it? Soli-darity and fighting together for a good cause. I wander into the center of the hall, holding my cup, and catch the eye of a youngish guy with spiky red hair and a denim jacket covered in badges.

"Welcome!" he says, breaking away from the group he's in and extending his hand. "I'm Robin. I haven't seen you at the group before."

"I'm Becky. Actually, I'm just a visitor. But Jim said it would be OK to come. . . ."

"Of course!" says Robin, shaking my hand with en-thusiasm. "Everyone's welcome. It doesn't matter whether you're a resident or a visitor . . . the issues are the same. Awareness is as important as anything else."

"Absolutely!" I take a sip of coffee and notice the bun-dle of leaflets he's holding. "I could take some of those back to London with me and give them out, if you like. Spread the word."

"That would be great!" Robin's face creases into a smile. "That's the kind of proactive attitude we need more of! What kind of environmental issues are you into particularly?"

Think. Environmental issues. "Um . . ." I take a sip of coffee. "All sorts, really! Trees . . . and er . . . hedge-hogs . . ."

"Hedgehogs?" Robin looks puzzled.

Damn. That only came out because I was thinking that his hair looks just like a hedgehog's.

"When they get squashed by cars," I improvise. "It's a real danger in today's society."

"I'm sure you're right." Robin frowns thoughtfully. "So, are you in an action group specifically looking at the plight of hedgehogs?"

Right. Change the subject, Becky.

"Yes," I hear myself saying. "I am. It's called . . . Prickle."

"Prickle!" He smiles. "Great name!"

"Yes," I say confidently. "It stands for Protect . . . Really . . . Innocent . . . er . . ."

OK. Maybe I should have chosen a word with an *H* in it.

"Creatures . . ." I'm floundering. ". . . of all Kinds . . . including hedgehogs . . ."

I break off in relief as I see Jim approaching, together with a thin, wiry woman dressed in jeans and a plaid shirt. This must be Jim's wife!

"Greetings, Jim," says Robin with a friendly smile. "Glad you could make it."

"Hi, Jim!" I say, and turn to the woman with him. "You must be Elizabeth."

"And you must be the famous Becky!" She clasps my hand. "Our Kelly can't talk about anything but you."

"Kelly's really sweet! We had such fun today doing makeovers . . ." I suddenly catch Jim's frown. "And . . . er . . . revisions for her exams," I hastily add. "Lots of algebra and French vocab."

"Is Jess here?" Jim asks, looking around the room.

"I don't know," I say, feeling the usual apprehension at the mention of her name. "I haven't spotted her yet."

"It's a shame." Elizabeth clicks her tongue. "Jim's told me all about it. Two sisters, not speaking to each other. And you're so young! You've got your whole lives ahead to be friends, you know. A sister is a blessing!"

"They'll make up," Jim says easily. "Ah. Here she is!"

I swivel round and sure enough, there's Jess, striding toward us, looking totally gobsmacked to see me.

"What's *she* doing here?" she says to Jim.

"This is a new member of our group, Jess," says Robin, coming forward with a smile. "Meet Becky."

"Hi, Jess!" I say with a nervous smile. "I thought I'd get into the environment!"

"Becky's special interest is hedgehogs," adds Robin.

"*What?*" Jess takes a few seconds to absorb this news, then starts to shake her head. "No. No. She's not a member of the group. And she's not coming to the meeting. She has to go. Now!"

"Do you two know each other?" asks Robin, trying to put all this together. Jess looks away.

"We're sisters," I explain.

"They don't get on," says Jim, in a stage whisper.

"Now, Jess," says Robin earnestly. "You know our group ethos. We put our personal differences aside at the door. Everyone's welcome. Everyone's a friend!" He smiles at me. "Becky's already volunteered for some outreach work!"

"No!" Jess clasps her head. "You don't understand what she's like—"

"Come on, Becky," says Robin, ignoring Jess. "I'll find you a chair."

Gradually the chatter abates and everyone sits down on chairs arranged in the shape of a horseshoe. As I look around the row of faces I spot Edie and Lorna, and several more people I recognize as customers from Jim's shop.

"Welcome, everyone," says Robin, taking up a position in the center of the horseshoe. "Before we start, I have a few announcements. Tomorrow, as you know, is the sponsored endurance hike up Scully Pike. Can we have numbers, please?"

About half the people there put up their hands, including Jess. I'm half tempted to put mine up too, only there's something about the word *endurance* that puts me off, not to mention *hike*.

"Great!" Robin looks around, pleased. "Those of you attempting it, please remember all your gear. I'm afraid the weather forecast is not good. Mist, and possibly rain."

There's a unified rueful groan, mixed with laughs.

"But be assured, a welcoming party will be waiting at the end with hot drinks," he adds. "And good luck to all participants. Now." He smiles around the room. "I'd like to introduce a new member to the group. Becky comes to us with a specialist knowledge of hedgehogs and . . ." He looks over at me. "Is it other small endangered creatures, or just hedgehogs?"

"Er . . ." I clear my throat, aware of Jess's eyes on me like daggers. "Er . . . mainly just the hedgehogs."

"So, a warm welcome to Becky from all of us. OK.

The serious business." He reaches for a leather satchel and pulls out a sheaf of papers. "The proposed Piper's Hill Shopping Center."

He pauses as though for effect, and there are murmurs of hostility around the room.

"The council is still playing ignorant. However"—he flips through the sheaf with a flourish—"by hook or by crook, I have managed to get hold of a copy of the plans." Robin hands the papers to a man on the end of the row, who starts passing them along. "Obviously we have a lot of major objections. If you could all study the material for a few minutes . . ."

I obediently read the plans along with everyone else, and look at all the drawings. As I glance around, people are shaking their heads in anger and disappointment, which, frankly, doesn't surprise me.

"Right." He looks around and his eyes alight on me. "Becky. Maybe we could hear from you first. As an outsider, what's your initial reaction?"

Everyone turns to look at me, and I feel my cheeks grow hot.

"Er . . . well, I can see the problems straightaway," I say tentatively.

"Exactly," Robin says with satisfaction. "This proves our point. The problems are obvious at first glance, to someone who doesn't even know the area. Carry on, Becky."

"Well." I study the plans for a second, then continue. "For a start, the opening hours are quite restricted. I'd have it open till ten every night. I mean, people have to work during the day! They don't want to have to rush their shopping!"

As I look around, everyone seems a bit stunned. They probably weren't expecting me to hit the nail on the head like that. Encouraged, I tap the list of shops. "And these are rubbish shops. You should have Space.NK . . . Joseph . . . and definitely an L.K. Bennett!"

No one has moved a muscle.

Except Jess, who has buried her head in her hands.

Robin appears dumbstruck, but makes a valiant attempt to smile.

"Becky . . . slight confusion here. We're not protesting about any of the features of the shopping center. We're protesting about its very existence."

"I'm sorry?" I peer at him, uncomprehending.

"We don't want them to build it," says Jess in extra-slow, sarcastic tones. "They're planning to ruin an area of natural beauty. That's what the protest is about."

"Oh." My cheeks flame. "Oh. I see. Absolutely. The natural beauty. I was . . . actually . . . er . . . just about to mention that." Flustered, I start riffling through the plans again. "It'll probably be quite a danger to hedgehogs, too," I say at last. "I've noticed several hedgehog hazard points. Or HHPs, as we call them."

I can see Jess rolling her eyes. Maybe I'd better stop now.

"Good point," says Robin, his smile now a little strained. "So . . . Becky has shared some valuable hedgehog safety concerns. Any other views?"

As a white-haired man starts to speak abut the desecration of the countryside, I sink back down into my chair, my heart thumping. I'm kind of glad I didn't mention my other major concern about the shopping center now. Which was that it isn't big enough.

"My worry is the local economy," a smartly dressed woman is declaiming. "Out-of-town shopping centers ruin rural life. If they build this, it'll put the village shop out of business."

"It's a crime," booms Lorna. "Village shops are the hub of the community. They need to be supported."

More and more voices are joining in now. I can see all the customers of Jim's shop nodding at each other.

"How can Jim compete with the big chains?"

"We need to keep these small shops alive!"

"The government's to blame. . . ."

I know I wasn't going to speak again, but I just can't keep quiet.

"Excuse me?" I venture, raising my hand. "If you all want the village shop to stay alive, why don't you buy bread at full price?"

I look around the room, to see Jess glaring at me.

"That is just *typical*," she says. "Everything comes down to spending money, doesn't it?"

"But it's a shop!" I say, bewildered. "That's the whole point! You spend money! If you all spent a bit more money, the shop would start booming!"

"Not everyone in the world is addicted to shopping, OK, Becky?" snaps Jess.

"Wish they were," Jim puts in with a wry smile. "My revenue's trebled since Becky came to town."

Jess stares at him, her mouth tight. Oh God. She looks really pissed off.

"It was just . . . an idea," I say quickly. "It doesn't matter." I shrink down in my seat again, trying to look unobtrusive.

The discussion starts up again, but I keep my head down and leaf through the shopping center plans again. And I have to say, I was right in the first place. The shops *are* rubbish. Not a single good place for handbags . . . not a single place you can get your nails done . . . I mean, I can really see their point. What is the point of ruining some lovely field with a crappy shopping center full of shops no one wants to visit?

"So we on the committee have decided on immediate, preemptive action," Robin is saying as I raise my head again. "We're holding a rally, to be held in a week's time. We need as much support as possible. And obviously as much publicity as possible."

"It's difficult," says one woman with a sigh. "No one's interested."

"Edgar is writing an article for his parish magazine," says Robin, consulting a piece of paper. "And I know some of you have already drafted letters to the council . . ."

I'm itching to speak.

I open my mouth, catch Jess's eyes on me like daggers, and close it again. But—oh God—I can't keep quiet. I just can't.

"We're producing a very informative leaflet—"

"You should do something bigger!" My voice cuts across Robin's, and everyone turns in my direction.

"Becky, shut up," Jess says furiously. "We're trying to discuss this sensibly!"

"So am I!" I'm hot under all these eyes, but I press on. "I think you should have a huge marketing campaign."

"Wouldn't that be expensive?" says the white-haired man, with a frown.

"In business, if you want to make money, you have to spend money. And it's the same here. If you want to have a result, you have to make the investment!"

"Money again!" exclaims Jess in exasperation. "Spending again! You're obsessed!"

"You could get a sponsorship deal!" I retort. "There must be local businesses who don't want the shopping center either. You should get a local radio station involved . . . put together a press pack. . . ."

"Excuse me, love," a guy sitting near to Jess interrupts sarcastically. "You're very good at talking. But what do you actually *know* about this?"

"Well, nothing," I admit. "Except I used to work as a

journalist. So I know about press releases and marketing campaigns." I look around, sensing interest on a few
faces. "And for two years I worked at Barneys, the department store in New York. We used to run loads of
events, like parties, and special sale weekends, and promotional evenings. . . . In fact, that's an idea!" I turn to
Jim in sudden inspiration. "If you want to boost the village shop, you should celebrate it! Do something positive! You should have a shopping festival. Or a party! It
would be such fun! You could have special offers, and
free gifts . . . tie it in to the protest—"

"*Shut up!*" I stop, startled, to see Jess on her feet, white
with anger. "Just shut up for once, Becky! Why does
everything have to be a party? Why do you have to trivi-
alize everything? Shopkeepers like Jim aren't interested
in parties! They're interested in solid, well-thought-out
action."

"I might be interested in a party," Jim says mildly, but
Jess doesn't seem to hear him.

"You don't know anything about the environment!
You don't know about bloody hedgehogs! You're making it up as you go along! Just butt out and leave us
alone."

"Now, that's a little aggressive, Jess," says Robin.
"Becky's only trying to help."

"We don't need her help!"

"Jess," says Jim in soothing tones. "This is your sister.
Come on, love. Be a bit more welcoming."

"Are these two sisters?" says the white-haired man in
surprise. An interested murmuring grows throughout
the room.

"She's not my sister." Jess has folded her arms tight.
She's refusing even to look at me, and suddenly I feel a
swell of angry hurt.

"I know you don't want me to be your sister, Jess," I

say, standing up to face her. "But I am! And there's nothing you can do about that! We have the same blood! We have the same genes! We have the same—"

"Yeah, well, I don't believe we do, OK?" Jess's voice reverberates in the room.

"What?" I'm not sure I've heard her correctly.

"I don't believe we share the same blood," she says in calmer tones.

"But . . . but we know we do!" I say in confusion. "What are you talking about?"

Jess sighs and rubs her face. When she looks up, there's only a trace of animosity left.

"Look at us, Becky," she says, almost kindly. She gestures to me and then to herself. "We have nothing in common. Not one thing. We can't be from the same family."

"But . . . but my dad's your father!"

"Oh God," says Jess, almost to herself. "Look, Becky, I wasn't going to bring this up till later."

"Bring up what?" I feel a dreadful foreboding. "Bring up what?"

"OK. Here's the thing." Jess exhales sharply. "Originally I was given the name of your dad as my father. But . . . it just doesn't seem to be making sense. So last night I had a long talk about it with my aunty Florence. She admitted my mum was a bit . . . wild. There might have been other men." Jess hesitates. "She thought there probably *had* been other men, although she didn't have any names."

"But . . . you had a test!" I say, bewildered. "A DNA test! So that proves . . ." I trail off as Jess shakes her head.

"No. We never did. We were going to. But I had your dad's name, the dates made sense, and . . . we all just assumed." She looks down at the ground. "I think we assumed wrong."

My head is spinning. They never did a DNA test? They just *assumed*?

The entire room is silent. I don't think anyone is breathing. I catch sight of Jim's anxious, kind face, and quickly look away.

"So . . . this has all been a big mistake," I say at last. Suddenly there's a huge lump in my throat.

"I think it was a mistake," agrees Jess. She looks up and sees my stricken face. "Come on, Becky. If you looked at us as an outsider . . . would you say we were sisters?"

"I . . . I suppose not," I manage.

I'm reeling with shock and disappointment, but at the same time, deep down, a tiny voice is telling me that this makes sense. I feel like for the last few weeks I've been trying to force my foot into a wrong-size shoe. I've been ramming and ramming, chafing the skin . . . and at last I'm admitting it doesn't fit.

She's not my sister. She's not my flesh and blood. She's just . . . a girl.

I'm standing here staring at a girl I barely know, who doesn't even like me.

I really don't want to be here anymore.

"Right," I say, trying to compose myself. "Well . . . I think I'll go. Bye, everybody. Good luck with the protest."

Nobody says anything. Everyone looks too thunder-struck. With trembling hands I pick up my bag, then push back my chair. As I make my way past everyone to the door I catch the odd sympathetic look. I pause when I reach Jim, who looks almost as disappointed as I feel.

"Thanks for everything, Jim," I say, trying to smile.

"Goodbye, love." He clasps my hand warmly. "It was good to know you."

"You too. Say goodbye to Kelly for me."

I reach the door and turn to face Jess.

"Bye, then." I swallow hard. "Have a nice life and everything."

"Bye, Becky," she says, and for the first time there's a flicker of something like compassion in her eyes. "I hope you patch it up with Luke."

"Thanks." I nod, not quite sure what else to say. Then I turn and walk out into the night.

Twenty

I FEEL NUMB. I don't have a sister. After all that.

I've been sitting on the bed in my room at the guest-house for about an hour, just gazing out the window at the distant hills. It's all over. My stupid dream of having a sisterly soul mate to chat and giggle with and go shopping with and eat peppermint creams with . . . is over for good. Not that Jess would ever have gone shopping or eaten peppermint creams with me. Or giggled, come to that. But she might have chatted. We might have got to know each other better. We might have told each other secrets and asked each other's advice. I hug my knees tight to my chest. This never happened in *Long-Lost Sisters: The Love They Never Knew They Had.*

Actually, it happened once. With these two sisters who were going to have a kidney transplant and then they did the DNA test and realized they weren't sisters after all. But the point was, they went ahead with the kidney transplant anyway, and afterwards they said they would always be sisters in the heart. The point was, they *liked* each other.

I feel a single tear roll down my cheek and brush it away crossly. There's no point getting upset. I've been an only child all my life . . . and now I am again. I only had a sister for a few weeks. It's not like I got used to it. It's not like we got attached or anything.

In fact . . . in fact, I'm *glad* this has happened. Who would want Jess for a sister? Not me. No way. I mean, she's right. We have absolutely nothing in common. We don't understand one thing about each other. We should have realized it was a mistake right from the word go.

Abruptly I get to my feet, open my suitcases, and start throwing in my clothes. I'll spend the night here, then head back to London first thing in the morning. I can't waste any more time. I've got a life to get back to. I've got a husband.

At least . . . I think I've got a husband.

As my mind flashes back to the last time I saw Luke I feel a hollow dread in my stomach. He's probably still furious with me. He's probably having a terrible time in Cyprus and cursing me every moment. I hesitate halfway through folding up a jumper. Just the thought of going back and facing him makes me feel a bit sick. But then my chin stiffens and I throw the jumper into the case. So what if things with Luke are shaky? I don't need some crummy sister to help me save my marriage. I'll sort it out myself. Maybe I'll buy a book. There must be one called *How to Save Your Year-Old Marriage*.

I cram in all the souvenirs I bought at Jim's shop, sit on the lid of my lime green case, and snap it shut. That's it. The end.

Just then there's a knock. "Hello?"

Edie puts her head round the door. "You've got a visitor," she says. "Downstairs."

I feel an immediate flicker of hope.

"Really?" I scramble to my feet. "I'm just coming!"

"I'd like to take this opportunity to remind you of the rules." Edie's booming voice follows me as I run down the stairs. "No visitors after eleven o'clock. If there's any carousing I'll have to call the authorities."

I jump down the last few steps and hurry into the little sitting room. "Hi!"

I stop dead in my tracks. It's not Jess. It's Robin. And Jim. And a couple of other people from the meeting. I can see a few glances flying about.

"Hi, Becky," says Robin, taking a step toward me. "Are you OK?"

"Er . . . yes. I'm fine, thanks."

Oh God. This is a pity visit. Maybe they're worried I'm going to slash my wrists or something. As Robin takes breath to speak again, I cut in.

"Really. Everybody. You don't need to worry about me. It's very sweet of you to be concerned. But I'll be all right. I'm just going to go to bed, and catch the train home tomorrow, and . . . just take it from there."

"Er . . . that's not why we're here," says Robin, ruffling his hair awkwardly. "We wanted to ask you something."

"Oh," I say, taken aback. "Right."

"We wondered . . . all of us . . . if you'd help us with the protest." He looks about as though for support, and everyone nods.

"*Help* you?" I stare back, bewildered. "But . . . I don't know anything about it. Jess was right." Even the memory is painful. "I was making it all up. I don't even know about hedgehogs."

"Doesn't matter," says Robin. "You've got loads of ideas, and that's what we need. You're right. We *should* think big. And Jim likes the idea of the party. Don't you, Jim?"

"If it gets folk into the shop before four o'clock, it can't be bad," says Jim.

"You've got experience with these kind of events," chimes in the white-haired man who challenged me at the meeting. "You know how to go about it. We don't."

"When you left the meeting we had a quick straw poll," says Robin. "And it was practically unanimous. We'd like to invite you onto the action committee. Everyone's waiting back at the hall, to hear."

All their faces are so warm and friendly, I feel tears pricking at my eyes.

"I can't." I look away. "I'm sorry, but I can't. There's no need for me to be in Scully anymore. I've got to get back to London."

"Why's that, then?" says Jim.

"I have . . . things to do," I say. "Commitments. You know."

"What commitments would they be?" Jim says mildly. "You don't have a job. Your husband's abroad. Your flat's empty."

This is why you shouldn't pour out your entire sob story to people you've just met. I gaze at Edie's pink and purple swirly carpet, trying to get my thoughts straight. Then I raise my head.

"What does Jess think about all this?"

I look around the group, but no one replies. Robin won't quite meet my eyes. The white-haired man is gazing at the ceiling. Jim just has that same sad expression he had at the village hall.

"I bet she's the only one who voted against me, isn't she?" I try to smile, but my voice wobbles.

"Jess has . . . certain opinions," begins Robin. "But she doesn't have to come into it—"

"She *does*! Of course she does! She's the whole reason I'm here! Look, I'm sorry. But I can't come on your committee. I hope your protest goes really well . . . but I can't stay."

I can see Robin drawing breath to speak again.

"I can't." I look directly at Jim. "You have to understand. I can't."

And I can see it in his eyes. He does understand.

"Fair enough," he says at last. "It was worth a try." He nods at the others as though to say "It's over."

They awkwardly murmur goodbyes and good lucks and file out of the little room. The front door bangs shut and I'm left alone, feeling flatter than ever.

When I wake up the next morning the sky is dark and swollen with gray clouds. Edie serves me a full English breakfast complete with black pudding, but I manage only a cup of tea. I pay her with the rest of my cash, then head upstairs to get ready to leave. Out the window I can just see the hills in the distance, stretching into the mist.

I'll probably never see those hills again. Which is fine by me, I think defiantly. I hate the country. I never wanted to be here in the first place.

I put the last of my things in my red case, then decide to change into my turquoise kitten heels with diamanté straps. They always make me feel cheerful. As I step into them I feel something small and nubby under my toes and reach down, puzzled. I pull out a small wrapped object and look at it in sudden realization.

It's the bean. It's the silver Tiffany bean necklace that I was going to give Jess, still in its little blue bag.

God, that seems a lifetime ago.

I shove it into my pocket, then pick up my cases and stripy hatbox and head downstairs, passing the pay phone in the hall.

Maybe I should call Luke. . . . But then, what's the point?

Edie's nowhere to be seen, so I just pull the door of the bed-and-breakfast closed behind me and trundle my cases across the green to the shop. I want to say goodbye to Jim before I leave.

As I push open the door with its familiar tinkle, Jim looks up from pricing cans of beans. He sees my suitcases and gives a resigned nod.

"So you're off."

"Yes. I'm off."

"Don't go!" Kelly says mournfully from behind the counter, where she has *Julius Caesar* propped up behind *100 Hot Hair Styles*.

"I have to." I put my cases down. "But I've got some more Stila stuff for you. A goodbye present."

As I hand her a selection of lip glosses and eye glazes, her face lights up.

"I've got a present for you too, Becky," she says abruptly. She pulls a friendship bracelet off her wrist and hands it to me. "So you won't forget me."

I'm unable to speak. The simple plaited band in my hand is just like the bracelets Luke and I were given in the Masai Mara ceremony. Luke took his off when he went back to corporate life.

I've still got mine on.

"That's . . . fab." I rouse myself and smile. "I'll always wear it." I slip it onto my wrist and give Kelly a tight hug.

"I wish you weren't going." Kelly's bottom lip sticks out. "Will you ever come back to Scully?"

"I don't know," I say after a pause. "I don't think so. But listen, if you ever come to London, give me a call. OK?"

"OK." Kelly brightens. "Can we go to Topshop?"

"Of course!"

"Should I start saving now?" Jim says ruefully, and we both start giggling.

A tinkle at the door interrupts us and we all look up to see Edie walking into the shop in her green head scarf, together with Lorna and the well-dressed lady from the night before. They're all looking exceedingly self-conscious.

"Edie!" says Jim, glancing at his watch in surprise. "What can I do for you?"

"Morning, Jim," says Edie, avoiding his eye. "I'd like some bread, please. A wholemeal and a bloomer."

"Bread?" says Jim, looking dumbfounded. "But Edie . . . it's ten o'clock in the morning."

"I know the time, thank you," she retorts stiffly.

"But . . . it's full price."

"I'd like some bread," she snaps. "Is that too much to ask?"

"Of . . . course not!" says Jim, still looking dazed. He gets down the loaves and wraps them in paper. "That'll be . . . one pound ninety-six."

There's a pause, and I can hear Edie breathe in sharply. Then she rummages in her bag for her purse and unclips it.

"Two pounds," she says, handing over the coins. "Much obliged."

I do not believe it. Kelly and I just sit there, goggling in silence, as the other two women buy three loaves of bread and a bag of sandwich rolls between them. Lorna even throws in a couple of Chelsea buns at the last moment.

As the door closes behind them, Jim sinks down onto his stool.

"Well. Who would have thought it?" He shakes his head in wonder, then points at me. "That's you, Becky."

"It's not *me,*" I say, flushing a little. "They probably just needed bread."

"It was you!" says Kelly. "It was what you said! Mum told me all about the meeting," she adds. "She said you seemed a nice girl, even if you were a bit—"

"Kelly," Jim puts in quickly. "Why don't you make Becky a cup of tea?"

"No, it's OK. I'm going." I hesitate, then reach into my pocket and pull out the little Tiffany bag. "Jim, I wanted to ask you a favor. Could you give this to Jess? It's something I bought for her a while ago. I know everything's different now . . . but still."

"I'm heading up to her house just now, to take a delivery," says Jim. "Why not leave it there yourself?"

"Oh." I shrink back. "No. I . . . I don't want to see her."

"She won't be there. They've all gone off for the endurance hike. I've got a key to her house."

"Oh, right." I hesitate.

"I could do with the company," Jim adds with a shrug, and picks up a sack of potatoes.

"Well . . ." I put the Tiffany bag back in my pocket. "OK. I'll come."

The clouds are growing thicker as we walk along the empty streets, and I can feel spots of rain on my face. I'm aware of Jim shooting me the odd concerned glance.

"You'll be all right, back in London?" he says eventually.

"I guess."

"Have you spoken to your husband?"

"No." I bite my lip. "I haven't."

Jim pauses, and transfers his potatoes to the other shoulder.

"So," he says easily. "How did a nice girl like you end up with a marriage in trouble?"

"It's my own fault. I did some . . . stupid things. And my husband got really angry. He said . . . he said he wished I were more like Jess."

"Did he?" Jim looks a bit taken aback. "I mean, Jess is a fine lass," he hastily amends. "But I wouldn't have . . . anyway, that's not here or there." He coughs and rubs his nose.

"That's why I came up here. To learn from her. But it was a stupid idea."

We've reached the end of Jess's street, and Jim pauses for a rest before climbing the steep incline. The gray stone houses are glistening in the drizzle, stark against the distant misty hills. I can just see a flock of sheep grazing high up, like dots of cotton wool on the green.

"Too bad about you and Jess," says Jim, and he does sound genuinely sorry. "It's a shame, that is."

"It's just one of those things." I try to keep the disappointment out of my voice. "I should have known all along. We're so different."

"You're different, all right." His face crinkles in amusement.

"She just seems so . . . *cold*." I hunch my shoulders, feeling a familiar resentment rising. "You know, I made every effort. I really did. But she never showed any pleasure . . . or feelings, even. She doesn't seem to care about anything! She doesn't seem to have any passions!"

Jim seems surprised.

"Oh . . . Jess has got passions," he says. "She's got passions, all right. When we get to the house, I'll show you something."

He picks up the sack of potatoes and we resume walking up the hill. As we get nearer Jess's house, I start to feel tiny prickles of curiosity. Not that she's anything to do with me anymore, but still.

As we reach the door, Jim roots in his pocket for a large key ring, selects a Yale key, and unlocks it. I walk into the hall and look around. But the place doesn't give much away. It's a bit like Jess herself. Two tidy sofas in the sitting room. A plain white kitchen. A couple of well-tended potted plants.

I head upstairs and cautiously push open the door to her bedroom. It's immaculate. Plain cotton duvet cover, plain cotton curtains, a couple of boring prints.

"Here." Jim is behind me. "You want to see Jess's real passion? Take a look at this."

He heads over to a door set into the wall of the landing, then turns the key and beckons me over.

"Here are the famous rocks," he says, swinging the door open. "She had this cupboard made especially to house them. Designed it herself down to the last detail, lights and all. Makes an impressive sight, don't you think . . ." He trails off in surprise at my face. "Becky? Are you OK, love?"

I can't speak.

It's my shoe cupboard.

It's my shoe cupboard, exactly. The same doors. The same shelves. The same lights. Except instead of shoes displayed on the shelves, there are rocks. Rows and rows of carefully labeled rocks.

And . . . they're beautiful. Some are gray, some crystal, some smooth, some iridescent and sparkling. There are fossils . . . amethysts . . . chunks of jet, all shiny under the lights. . . .

"I had no idea. . . .They're stunning."

"You're talking about passion?" Jim laughs. "This is a true passion. An obsession, you might say." He picks up a speckled gray rock and turns it over in his fingers.

"You know how she got that leg injury of hers? Clamber-ing after some blasted rock on a mountain somewhere. She was that determined to get it, she'd risk her own safety." Jim grins at my expression. "Then there was the time she was arrested at Customs, for smuggling some precious crystal in under her jumper. . . ."

I gape at him.

"Jess? *Arrested?*"

"They let her off." He waves a hand. "But I know she'd do it again. If there's a particular kind of rock that girl wants, she has to have it." He wrinkles his brow in amusement. "She gets a compulsion. It's like a mania! Nothing'll stop her!"

My head is spinning. I'm staring at a row of rocks, all different shades of red. Just like my row of red shoes.

"She keeps all this pretty quiet." Jim puts down the speckled rock. "I guess she thinks people wouldn't un-derstand—"

"I understand." I cut him off in a shaky voice. "Com-pletely."

I'm trembling all over. She's my sister.

Jess is my sister. I know it more certainly than I've ever known anything.

I have to find her. I have to tell her. Now.

"Jim . . ." I take a deep breath. "I need to find Jess. Right away."

"She's doing the sponsored endurance hike," Jim re-minds me. "Starts in half an hour."

"Then I have to go," I say in agitation. "I have to see her. How do I get there? Can I walk?"

"It's a fair way away," Jim says, and cocks his head quizzically. "Do you want a lift?"

Twenty-one

I KNEW WE were sisters. I knew it. I *knew* it.

And we're not just sisters—we're kindred spirits! After all those false starts. After all those misunderstandings. After I thought I would never have one single thing in common with her, ever.

She's the same as me. I understand her.

I understand Jess!

Everything Jim said chimed a chord. Everything! How many times have I smuggled pairs of shoes in from America? How many times have I risked my own safety at the sales? I even got a leg injury, just like her! It was when I saw someone heading for the last reduced Orla Kiely purse in Selfridges, and I leapt off the escalator from about eight steps up.

God, if I'd just seen her rock cupboard earlier. If I'd *known*. Everything would have been different! Why didn't she tell me? Why didn't she explain?

Abruptly I have a memory of Jess talking about rocks on our first-ever meeting . . . and again at the flat. And I feel ashamed. She did try. I just didn't listen, did I? I didn't believe her when she said they were interesting. I said rocks were . . . stupid. And boring. Just like her.

"Can we go any faster?" I say to Jim. We're rattling along in his ancient Land Rover, past grassy slopes and drystone walls, heading higher and higher into the hills.

"Going as fast as we can," he says. "We'll be in time, easy."

Sheep are scattering off the road as we thunder along, and small stones are hitting the windscreen. I glance out the window—and quickly look away. Not that I'm afraid of heights or anything, but we seem to be approximately three inches away from a steep drop.

"All right," says Jim, pulling into a small parking area, with a crunch of gravel. "This is where they're starting. And that's where they're climbing." He points to the steep mountain looming above us. "The famous Scully Pike." His phone rings, and he reaches for it. "Excuse me."

"Don't worry! Thanks!" I say, and wrench open the door. I get out and look around—and just for a moment I'm floored by the scenery.

Craggy rocks and peaks are all around, interspersed with patches of grass and crevasses, and all are overshadowed by the mountain—a stark, jagged outline against the gray sky. As I peer across the valley, I feel a sudden swooping, a bit like vertigo, I suppose. I honestly hadn't realized quite how high up we are. There's a little cluster of houses visible far below, which I guess is Scully, but apart from that, we could be in the middle of nowhere.

Well, come to think of it, we *are* in the middle of nowhere.

I hurry across the gravel to a small level patch where

a table has been set up, with a banner reading SCULLY EN-VIRONMENTAL GROUP ENDURANCE HIKE, REGISTRATION. Be-hind the table two yellow flags mark the foot of a path leading up the mountain. A man I don't recognize is sit-ting at the table in an anorak and flat cap. But apart from that, the place is empty.

Where is everybody? God, no wonder they don't have any money, if no one turns up for the sponsored walks.

"Hi," I say to the man in the anorak. "Do you know where Jess Bertram is? She's one of the walkers. I really need to speak to her."

I'm totally wound up with anticipation. I cannot wait to tell her! I cannot wait to see her face!

"Too late, I'm afraid," the man says, and gestures up the mountain. "She's gone. They've all gone."

"Already? But . . . the hike starts at eleven. It's only five to!"

"It started at half past ten," corrects the man. "We brought it forward because of the poor weather. You'll have to wait. It'll only be a few hours."

"Oh." I subside in disappointment and turn away. "All right. Thanks." It'll be OK. I can wait. I can be pa-tient. It's not that long, really, a few hours.

Yes, it is. A few hours is *ages*. I want to tell her *now*. I gaze up at the mountain in frustration, only to spot a couple in matching red anoraks, a few hundred yards up. They've got bibs with SCULLY ENVIRONMENTAL GROUP on them. They're part of the hike. And look, a little be-yond them, there's a man in blue.

My mind is working quickly. They haven't got that far. Which means Jess hasn't got that far either. Which means . . . I could catch up with her. Yes!

This kind of news can't wait a few hours. I mean, we're sisters. We're real, genuine sisters! I have to tell her immediately.

I hoist my Angel bag firmly on my shoulder, hurry to the start of the steep mountain path, and look up at it. I can climb this. Easy. There are rocks to hold on to and everything. I take a few tentative steps—and it's not hard at all.

"Excuse me?" The man in the anorak stands up in agitation. "What are you doing?"

"I'm joining the hike. Don't worry, I'll sponsor myself."

"You can't join the hike! What about your shoes!" He points at my turquoise kitten heels in horror. "Do you have a cagoule?"

"A *cagoule*?" I pull a face. "Do I look like someone who would have a cagoule?"

"What about a stick?"

"I don't need a stick," I explain. "I'm not *old*."

Honestly. It's only walking up a hill. What's the fuss?

Just to prove it to him, I start clambering up the path in earnest. The ground is a bit slimy with drizzle, but I stick my kitten heels into the mud as hard as I can and grab on to the rocks lining the path—and in about two minutes I'm already past the first bend.

I'm already breathing hard, and my calves are hurting, but apart from that, I'm doing great! God, it just shows, climbing really isn't that hard. I reach another bend, and look back in satisfaction. I'm practically halfway up the mountain already!

This is so easy. I always knew people who went hiking were showing off about nothing.

Down below, I can faintly hear Jim yelling, "Becky! Come back!" But I close my ears and resolutely keep on, one foot after another. I need to hurry if I'm going to catch up with Jess.

———

Except she must be a pretty speedy walker. Because after about an hour of steady climbing, I still haven't caught up with her. In fact, I haven't caught up with any of them. I kept the red couple in sight for a while, but somehow they seem to have disappeared. The man in blue has vanished too. And I haven't even clapped eyes on Jess.

Which is probably because she's *run* the whole way up, I think a bit disconsolately. She's probably doing twenty one-handed press-ups at the top, because climbing a mountain isn't strenuous enough. God, it isn't fair. You'd think I might have got some of the superfit genes too.

I take a few more steps forward and stop for a breather, wincing at the sight of my mud-spattered legs. My face is hot and I'm panting, so I get out my Evian facial spray and spritz myself. It's getting fairly steep up here. Not that it's *hard* or anything. In fact, I'm really enjoying myself. Apart from the blister on my right foot, which is getting a bit painful. Maybe that guy had a point—these aren't the best shoes in the world for climbing. Although, on the plus side, the heels are really good for slippery bits.

I look around the empty, rugged mountainside. About three feet away is a rocky ledge, and beyond that a sheer drop down into a valley. Which I'm not going to look at. Or think about.

I put the Evian spritzer away and look around, a bit uncertainly. I have no idea how much farther there is to go. I'd kind of counted on catching up with the other walkers and finding out from them. I squint ahead, trying to spot a brightly colored anorak, but the air is hazy with mist.

Oh God. Maybe it's going to rain. And I don't even have a cardigan.

Suddenly I feel a bit stupid. Maybe I shouldn't have rushed up here. Maybe I should go down. Cautiously I take a step backwards . . . but the ground is more slippery than I expected.

"Shiiit!" I grab on to a sharp rock to stop myself slithering toward the rocky ledge. There's a blinding pain in my arm— I must have wrenched a muscle—but somehow I haul myself back up.

OK, I'm not going back down now. Anyway, it's probably *farther* to go back down than carry on. I'll keep on following the path. It'll be fine. If I just speed up a bit I'm bound to reach Jess. It'll be worth it just to see her face. She won't believe her eyes. Then I'll tell her—and she won't believe her ears! She'll be totally, utterly gobsmacked! I hug the thought to myself happily for a few moments, then, with a fresh surge of energy, keep on climbing.

I'm knackered. I can't keep going any longer.

My knees ache, my hands are sore, and my feet are covered in blisters. I've been trudging for what seems like hours, but this bloody mountain goes on forever. Every time I think I must have got to the top, I see another peak rising up in front of me.

Where's Jess? Where *is* everybody? They can't *all* be quicker than me.

I stop for a few moments to catch my breath, holding on to a large boulder for balance. The view over the valley is as stunning as ever, with purple and gray clouds rolling across the sky, and a single bird soaring high above me. Maybe it's an eagle or something. To be honest, I don't care. I just want to sit down with a cup of tea. That's all I want in the world.

But I can't. I have to continue. Come on. This is what they mean by *endurance*.

With a huge effort I let go of the boulder and start climbing again. Left, right. Left, right. Maybe I'll try singing, like the Von Trapps. Yes. That'll cheer me on.

" 'High on a hill . . .' "

No. Forget the singing.

Oh God. I can't climb anymore. I just can't do it.

I must have been walking for hours and I feel sick and dizzy. My face is sweaty, my lungs are burning, my hands are numb. My legs are covered in mud, my shoes are unidentifiable, I've gashed my knee and torn my skirt, and I don't know where I'm supposed to go next.

I stumble over a cluster of rocks and grab on to a bush for support, wincing as it pricks me. OK. I've got to stop for a rest. I sit down on a flat stone and fumble for the Evian facial mister.

I'm desperate for a drink. I spray the very last drops of Evian into my mouth, until it's all gone. I wipe my face with a tissue from my bag and look around the empty mountainside. There is no one in sight. *No one*.

What am I going to do?

Deep down I feel a spasm of fear, which I ignore. It'll be fine. The important thing is to think positive. I'll just keep climbing. I can do it!

No, I can't, comes a small voice inside.

Stop it. Think positive. I can do anything I set my mind to.

My legs are all shaky, but somehow I force myself to my feet, wincing in pain as my shoes dig into my blisters again. Right. Just keep going. I'll get to the top— and maybe that's where the welcoming party is. And

those hot drinks they were talking about. Yes. It'll be
fine—

Suddenly there's a distant rumble of thunder. Oh God.
Please, no. I look up, and the sky has darkened to a men-
acing gray.

A raindrop hits me in the eye. Then another.

I swallow, trying to stay calm. But inside I'm a mush
of panic. What do I do now? Do I keep going up? Do I
go down?

"Hi!" I call out. "Is anyone there?" My voice echoes
round the rocks, but there's no reply.

More raindrops land on my head.

I don't have anything waterproof. I look around the
stark landscape, hollow with fear. What if I can't get
down? What if I'm stuck up here in a storm? I was so
desperate to tell Jess we were sisters. Now I just feel like
a fool. I should have waited. Luke's right. Why can't I
wait for anything in life? It's all my own fault.

There's another distant rumble of thunder, and I
flinch in fright. What if I get struck by lightning? I don't
even know what the rules are for being outside in a
storm. It's something like Stand under a tree. Or maybe
Don't stand under a tree. But which? What if I get it
wrong?

Suddenly, through my agitation, I'm aware of a kind
of chirping noise. Is it . . . an animal?

Oh my God.

Oh my God. It's my mobile. There's a signal up here!
There's a bloody signal!

With shaking fingers I unzip my Angel bag and grab
my flashing mobile. Weak with relief, I see the word
LUKE on the little display. I jab frantically at the green
button.

"Luke!" I say. "It's Becky!"

"Becky? Is anyone there?" The line is crackling, and he sounds all fuzzy and distant.

"Yes!" I shout, as raindrops start falling harder on my head. "Luke, it's me! I'm lost! I need help!"

"Hello?" comes his puzzled voice again. "Can anyone hear me?"

"Yes! I can hear you! I'm here!" With no warning, tears start streaming down my face. "I'm stuck on this awful mountain and I don't know what to do. Luke, I'm so sorry—"

"The line's not working," I can hear him saying to someone else. "I can't hear a bloody thing."

"Luke!" I yell. "Luke, I'm here! I'm right here! Don't go!"

I bang the phone frantically, and the words BATTERY LOW flash at me.

"Hello?" comes Luke's voice again. "Becky?"

"Luke, please hear me!" I cry in desperation. "Please hear me! *Please . . .*"

But the light in the little screen is already fading. And a moment later the phone goes dead.

He's gone.

I look around the desolate mountainside. I have never felt more alone in my life.

A gust of wind blows a flurry of rain into my face and I realize I can't just stand here. I have to find some kind of shelter.

About six feet above me is a kind of ledge sticking out, with a cluster of rocks on top. One of them has an overhanging bit which maybe I can crouch under. The mud is all wet and slithery, but I dig in my heels and grab on to anything I can find, and somehow scrabble up there, grazing my other knee as I climb.

God, it's quite high up. I feel a bit precarious. But never mind. If I don't look down I'll be fine. I firmly take hold of the overhanging bit of rock and am trying to edge underneath without slipping over . . . when suddenly I glimpse a flash of yellow.

Bright yellow. Human-waterproof-climbing-gear yellow. I don't believe it. There's someone else on the mountain. There's someone else! I'm saved!

"Hi!" I yell. "Halloo! Over here!" But my voice is carried the wrong way by the wind and the rain.

I can't see whoever it is properly, because the overhanging rock is in the way. Very slowly and cautiously I maneuver myself around the lip of the ledge until I have a better view. And then I see her clearly.

It's Jess.

She's on the slope below, wearing a yellow cagoule and a backpack. Some kind of rope thing is attaching her to the mountainside, and she's digging carefully at a rock with a metal knife.

"Jess!" I shout, but my voice sounds hardly bigger than a squeak above the wind. "Jess! *Jess!*"

At last her head turns—and her whole face contracts in shock.

"Jesus Christ! Becky! What the hell are you doing up here?"

"I came to tell you we're sisters!" I shout back, but I'm not sure if she can hear me through the buffeting rain. *"Sisters!"* I yell again, taking a step forward, cupping my mouth. "We're SISTERS!"

"Stop!" shouts Jess. "That ledge is dangerous!"

"I'm fine!"

"Get back!"

"I'm OK, honestly," I call. But she looks so alarmed, I obediently take a step back, away from the edge.

And that's when my shoe slips on the wet mud.

I can't regain my balance and I scrabble frantically at the rocks, trying to hold on to anything, trying to save myself, but everything's too slippery. My fingers close round the roots of a shrub, but they're wet with the rain. I can't get a proper grip.

"Becky!" I hear Jess's scream as the roots slip out of my desperate fingers. *"Becky!"*

Then I'm falling in a rush of terror, and all I can hear is screaming, and I have a glimpse of sky and then something thwacks my head, hard.

And then everything goes black.

FEARS FOR MISSING GIRL

Fears were growing last night for the safety of Maida Vale resident Rebecca Brandon, 27. Mrs Brandon (née Bloomwood) disappeared on Thursday from the luxury flat she shares with husband Luke Brandon and has not been seen or heard from since. The alarm was raised by Mrs Brandon's friend Susan Cleath-Stuart, who arrived in London for a surprise visit.

SHOPPING

CCTV footage shows Mrs Brandon in local shop Anna's Delicatessen, shortly before her disappearance, apparently agitated. "She just dropped her shopping and left," said shop assistant Marie Fuller. "She didn't buy anything."

A distressed Ms Cleath-Stuart commented, "That proves something's wrong! Bex would never leave her shopping behind! Never!"

CHAOS

There were scenes of chaos aboard the Mind Body Spirit cruise ship currently touring the Mediterranean as Mrs Brandon's parents, Graham and Jane Bloomwood, insisted the boat be turned around. "You can stuff bloody tranquility!" a hysterical Mrs Bloomwood was reported as shouting. "My daughter's missing!"

STORMS

Meanwhile, storms have prevented Mrs Brandon's husband, Luke Brandon, from leaving Cyprus, where he has been working. He was said yesterday to be "desperately worried" and in close contact with police. His business associate, Nathan Temple, has issued a reward for information leading to the recovery of Mrs Brandon. He commented yesterday, "If anyone harms a hair of that young lady's head I will personally break all their bones. Twice." Mr Temple was convicted in 1984 for grievous bodily harm.

Twenty-two

Ow.

Ouuuch.

God, my head is in agony. Oww. And my ankle's throbbing, and I feel like I might be sick any moment, and something sharp is pressing into my shoulder. . . . Where am I, anyway? Why do I feel so weird?

With a huge struggle I manage to open my eyes and get a flash of blue before they close again. Hmm. Blue. Makes no sense. Maybe I'll go to sleep.

"Becky? Beckeee!" A voice is calling me from a huge distance. "Wake up!"

I force my eyes open again and find myself looking at a face. A blurred face against a blue background.

Jess.

Blimey, it's Jess. And she's all anxious-looking. Maybe she lost something. A rock. That must be it.

"Can you see me?" she says urgently. "Can you count my fingers?"

She thrusts her hand in front of me and I peer at it woozily. Boy, that girl needs a manicure.

"How many fingers?" she keeps saying. "Can you see? Can you hear me?"

Oh, right. Yes.

"Er . . . three?"

Jess stares at me for a moment, then sinks back on her knees and buries her head in her hands. "Thank God. Thank God."

She's shaking. Why on earth is she shaking?

And then, like a tidal wave, it all comes back to me. The walk. The storm. Falling. Crashing down the mountainside. Quickly I try to block it out of my mind, but to my astonishment, tears start to seep out the sides of my eyes and drip down into my ears.

OK. Stop it. I'm safe now. I'm on the ground. I . . . think. To be honest, I can't quite work out where I am. I peer at the bright blue background, but it still makes zero sense. I'd say heaven—except Jess didn't fall too, did she?

"Where am I?" I manage, and Jess raises her head. She still looks white and shaken.

"My tent," she says. "I always carry a tent in my backpack. I didn't dare move you, so I put it up around you."

A tent! Now, that is just so clever. Why don't I take a tent everywhere? I'll start tomorrow. Yes. A little tiny tent that I could keep in my handbag.

The only thing is, it's a bit uncomfortable here on the ground. Maybe I'll get up and stretch my legs. I try to rise, and everything goes black and swirly.

"Oh God," I say feebly, and sink back down again.

"Don't try to get up!" Jess says in alarm. "You had a terrible fall. I thought . . ." She breaks off and exhales sharply. "Anyway, don't get up."

Gradually I'm becoming aware of the rest of my body. My hands are all raw and scraped. With a huge effort I raise my head and glimpse my legs, all bloody with cuts. I can feel a bruise on my cheek, and I lift my hand to it.

"Ow! Is my face bleeding?"

"You're a mess," Jess says bluntly. "Does anything hurt really badly?"

"My ankle. The left one. It's agony."

Jess starts prodding it and I bite my lip, trying not to cry out.

"I think it's sprained," she says at last. "I'll strap you up." She switches on a torch and fastens it to a steel pole, then reaches into a tiny tin. She produces a length of bandage-type stuff and starts winding it expertly round my ankle. "Becky, what the hell were you doing up there, anyway?"

"I . . . I came to find you." Bits of the jigsaw are reappearing in my brain. "I was doing the sponsored endurance hike."

Jess looks gobsmacked.

"But this wasn't the hike route! I went off the trail. The hike route was much lower. Didn't you follow the markers?"

"Markers?" I look at her blankly.

"God, you have no bloody idea about hiking, do you?" she says in agitation. "You shouldn't have been up there! It's dangerous!"

"So why were you there?" I retort, wincing as she bandages me more and more tightly. "What you were doing looked pretty dangerous to me."

Jess's face closes up.

Eventually she says, "Last time I climbed the Pike I saw some ammonite specimens. I wanted to collect one.

It's a bit foolhardy, but I don't expect you to understand—"

"No! I *do* understand!" I interrupt, and struggle onto
my elbows. I have to tell her.

"Jess, I understand. I've seen your rocks. They're fantastic. They're beautiful."

"Lie down," she says, looking worried. "Take it easy."

"I don't want to take it easy! Jess, listen. We're sisters.
We're honestly and truly sisters. That's why I came up
the mountain. I had to tell you."

Jess frowns. "Becky, you've had a bump on the head . . .
you've probably got a concussion—"

"It's not that!" The louder my voice rises the more my
head throbs, but I can't stop myself. "I know we have
the same blood. I know it! I went to your house."

"You *what*?" Jess looks appalled. "Who let you in?"

"Jim. I saw your rock cupboard. It's identical to my
shoe cupboard in London. *Identical.* The lights . . . the
shelves . . . everything!"

For the first time ever, I see Jess's composure slip a
little.

"So what?" she says in brusque tones.

"So we're the same!" I sit up eagerly, ignoring the
swirling in front of my eyes. "Jess, you know the way
you feel about a really amazing rock? That's the way I
feel about a great pair of shoes! Or a dress. I *have* to have
it. Nothing else matters. And I know you feel the same
way about your rock collection."

"I don't," she says, turning away.

"You do! I know you do!" I clutch her arm. "You're
just as obsessed as me! You just hide it better! Oh God,
my head. Ow."

I collapse back down, my head pounding.

"I'll get you a painkiller," Jess says distractedly—but

she doesn't move. She's just standing there, lost in her own thoughts.

I can see I've got to her.

"You came up a mountain in a storm just to tell me this?" Jess says at last.

"Yes! Of course!"

She turns her head to look at me. Her face is paler than ever and kind of wary, as though someone's trying to trick her.

"Why? Why would you do that?"

"Because . . . because it's important! It matters to me!"

"No one's ever done anything like that for me before," she says, and immediately looks away, fiddling in the tin again. "Those cuts need antiseptic on them."

She starts dabbing my legs with a cotton-wool pad, and I try not to flinch as the antiseptic stings my raw flesh.

"So . . . do you believe me?" I say. "Do you believe we're sisters?"

For a few moments Jess just focuses on her feet, which are encased in thick socks and brown hiking boots. She raises her head and surveys my turquoise diamanté kitten heels, all scraped and covered in mud. My Marc Jacobs skirt. My ruined glittery T-shirt. Then she lifts her eyes to my bruised, battered face, and we just look at each other.

"Yes," she says at last. "I believe you."

Three extra-strong painkillers later, and I'm really feeling quite a lot better. In fact, I can't stop gabbling.

"I knew we were sisters," I'm saying, as Jess puts a plaster on my gashed knee. "I knew it! I think I'm a bit psychic, actually. I *felt* your presence on the mountain."

"Mmm," says Jess, rolling her eyes.

"And the other thing is, I'm getting quite similar to you. Like I was thinking I might crop my hair short. It would really suit me. And I've started taking a real interest in rocks—"

"Becky," interrupts Jess. "We don't have to be the same."

"What?" I look at her uncertainly. "What do you mean?"

"Maybe we're sisters." She sits back on her heels. "But that doesn't mean we both have to have cropped hair. Or like rocks." She reaches for another plaster and rips it open.

"Or potatoes," I add before I can stop myself.

"Or potatoes," agrees Jess. She pauses. "Or . . . over-priced designer lipsticks that go out of fashion in three weeks."

There's a little glint in her eyes as she looks at me, and I gape in astonishment. Jess is *teasing* me?

"I suppose you're right," I say, trying to stay nonchalant. "Just because we're biologically related, it doesn't mean we both have to like boring workouts with water bottles instead of cool weights."

"Exactly. Or . . . mindless magazines full of ridiculous ads."

"Or drinking coffee out of a horrible old flask."

Jess's mouth is twitching.

"Or stupid rip-off cappuccinos."

There's a clap of thunder, and we both jump in fright. Rain is beating on the tent like drumsticks. Jess puts a final plaster on my legs and shuts the little tin.

"I don't suppose you brought anything to eat?" she says.

"Er . . . no."

"I've got some, but it isn't much." Her brow wrinkles. "Not if we're stuck here for hours. We won't be able to move, even when the storm's died down."

"Can't you forage on the mountainside for roots and berries?" I say hopefully.

Jess gives me a look.

"Becky, I'm not Tarzan." She hunches her shoulders and wraps her arms round her legs. "We'll just have to sit it out."

"So . . . you don't take a mobile when you go climbing?" I venture.

"I don't have one. I don't usually need one."

"I suppose you don't usually have a stupid injured sister with you."

"Not normally, no." She shifts on the groundsheet and reaches behind her. "I picked up some of your stuff, by the way. It got scattered when you fell."

"Thank you," I say, taking the handful of things from her. A mini hairspray. My manicure set. A compact.

"I couldn't find your bag, I'm afraid," adds Jess. "God knows where it went."

My heart stops.

My Angel bag.

My two-thousand-euro movie-star bag. The bag that everyone in the world is clamoring for. After all that, it's gone. Lost on a mountain in the middle of nowhere.

"It—it doesn't matter." Somehow I force myself to smile. "These things happen."

With sore, stiff fingers I open my compact—and amazingly, the mirror's still intact. Cautiously I take a look at myself and recoil. I look like a beaten-up scarecrow. My hair is everywhere, and both my cheeks are grazed, and there's a huge lump on my forehead.

"What are we going to do?" I snap the compact shut.

"We'll have to stay here until the storm dies down," says Jess.

"Yes, but I mean . . . what shall we *do*? While we wait in the tent."

Jess's expression is unreadable.

"I thought we could watch *When Harry Met Sally* and eat popcorn," she says.

I can't help giggling. Jess does actually have a sense of humor. Underneath it all.

"Shall I do your nails?" I suggest. "I've got my stuff here."

"Do my *nails*?" says Jess. "Becky . . . you realize we're on a mountain."

"Yes!" I say eagerly. "That's the whole point! It's extra-tough lacquer that lasts whatever you do. Look at this!" I show her the bottle of nail polish. "The model's actually *climbing a mountain* in the picture."

"Unbelievable," says Jess, taking the bottle from me and peering at it. "And people fall for this?"

"Come on! What else are we going to do?" I pause innocently. "I mean, it's not like we've got anything *fun* to do, like our accounts. . . ."

Jess's eyes flash at me.

"OK," she says. "You win. Do my nails."

While the storm rages around us, we paint each other's nails a bright sparkly pink.

"That's great!" I say in admiration as Jess finishes my left hand. "You could be a manicurist!"

"Thanks," she says dryly. "You've made my day."

I wave my fingers in the torchlight, then get out my compact to admire my reflection.

"You need to learn to put one finger thoughtfully to your mouth," I explain, demonstrating. "It's the same when you get a new ring or bracelet. Just to let people see." I offer her the mirror, but she turns away, her face closing up.

"No, thanks."

I put away the compact, thinking hard. I want to ask her why she hates mirrors. But I have to put it tactfully.

"Jess . . ." I say at last.

"Yes?"

"Why do you hate mirrors?"

The only sound is the whistling of the wind. At last Jess lifts her head.

"I dunno," she says. "I suppose because every time I looked into a mirror when I was young, my dad told me not to be vain."

"*Vain?*" I look at her, wide-eyed. "What, every time?"

"Most of the time." She shrugs, then sees my face. "Why? What did yours say?"

"My parents used to say . . ." Now I'm a bit embarrassed. "They used to say I was the most beautiful little angel who had ever fallen down from heaven."

"Well." Jess hunches her shoulders as though to say "Go figure."

"God, you're right," I say suddenly. "I've been spoiled. My parents have always given me everything. I've never had to stand on my own two feet. Ever. I've always had people there for me. Mum and Dad . . . then Suze . . . then Luke."

"I had to stand on my feet right from the word go," says Jess. Her face is in the torch's shadow, and I can't make out her expression.

"He sounds quite . . . tough, your dad," I say tentatively.

"Dad never really expressed emotion," she says at last. "Never really told you when he was proud. He felt it," she adds vehemently. "But in our family we don't go blabbing about everything, the way you do."

A sudden gust of wind loosens up a corner of the tent, blowing in a flurry of rain. Jess grabs the flap and reaches for a metal pin.

"I'm the same," she says, banging the metal pin into the ground with a rock. "Just because I don't say things doesn't mean I don't feel them." She looks round and meets my eyes with a visible effort. "Becky, when I came to visit your flat, I didn't mean to be unfriendly. Or . . . cold."

"I should never have called you that," I say in a flood of remorse. "I'm really sorry—"

"No," Jess interrupts. "*I'm* sorry. I could have made more effort. I could have joined in." She puts the rock down on the ground and gazes at it for a few seconds. "To be honest, I was a bit . . . unnerved by you."

"Luke said you might find me overwhelming," I say ruefully, and rub my head, which has started to throb again.

"You should sleep," Jess says, watching me. "It's the best healer. And the best painkiller. Here's a blanket." She gives me a sheet of something that looks like tinfoil.

"Well . . . OK," I say doubtfully. "I'll try."

I put my head down in the least uncomfortable place I can find, and close my eyes.

But I can't sleep. Our conversation is going round and round in my mind, with the lashing rain and flapping of the tent as a sound track.

I'm spoiled. I'm a spoiled brat.

No wonder Luke got pissed off. No wonder our marriage is a catastrophe. It's all my fault.

Oh God. Suddenly tears are rising in my eyes, which is making my head throb even more. And my neck's all cricked . . . and there's a stone in my back. . . .

"Becky, are you OK?" says Jess.

"Not really," I admit, my voice all thick and wobbly. "I can't get to sleep."

There's no reply, and I think Jess can't have heard, or doesn't have anything to say. But a moment later I feel something next to me. I turn round, and she's offering me a small white slab.

"It's not peppermint creams," she says flatly.

"Wh-What is it?" I falter.

"Kendal Mint Cake. Traditional climbing food."

"Thank you," I whisper, and take a bite. It has a weird, sweet taste, and I'm not that keen, but I take a second bite, to show willingness. Then, to my horror, I feel tears starting up again.

Jess sighs, and takes a bite of Kendal Mint Cake herself. "What's wrong?"

"Luke will never love me again," I sob.

"I doubt that."

"It's true!" My nose is running and I wipe it with my hand. "Ever since we got back from our trip, it's been a disaster. And it's all my fault, I've ruined everything—"

"It's not all your fault," interrupts Jess.

"What?" I gape at her.

"I wouldn't say it was all your fault," she says calmly. "It takes two." She folds up the Kendal Mint Cake wrapper, then unzips her backpack and slips it in. "I mean, talk about obsessed. Luke's totally obsessed by work!"

"I know he is. But I thought he'd changed. On our honeymoon he was totally laid-back. Everything was perfect. I was so happy."

Into my mind slips a memory of Luke and me, all brown and carefree. Holding hands. Doing yoga together. Sitting on the terrace in Sri Lanka, planning our surprise return. I had such high hopes. And nothing worked out the way I thought it would.

"You can't be on honeymoon forever," points out Jess. "It was bound to be a bit of a crash."

"But I was so looking forward to being married," I say with a gulp. "I had this image: we were all going to be sitting round the big wooden table in candlelight.

Me, Luke, Suze . . . Tarquin . . . everyone happy and laughing. . . ."

"And what happened?" Jess gives me a shrewd look. "What happened to Suze? Your mum told me she was your best friend."

"She was. But while I was away she . . . found someone else." I focus on the flapping blue canvas, feeling a lump in my throat. "Everyone's got new friends and new jobs and they're not interested anymore. I . . . haven't got any friends."

Jess zips up her backpack and pulls the drawstring tight. Then she looks up.

"You've got me."

"You don't even like me," I say dolefully.

"Well, I'm your sister," says Jess. "I've got to put up with you, haven't I?"

I raise my head, and there's a glimmer of humor in her eyes. And warmth. A warmth I don't think I've ever seen before.

After a pause, I say, "You know, Luke wants me to be just like you."

"Yep. Right."

"It's true! He wants me to be thrifty and frugal." I put the rest of my Kendal Mint Cake down behind a rock, hoping Jess won't notice. "Will you teach me?"

"Teach *you*. To be frugal."

"Yes! Please."

Jess rolls her eyes.

"For a start, if you're going to be frugal, you won't throw away a perfectly good piece of Kendal Mint Cake."

"Oh. Right." A bit shamefaced, I pick it up and take a bite. "Er . . . yummy!"

The wind is whistling with even more force, and the tent is flapping faster and faster. I pull Jess's tinfoil blanket around me tighter, wishing for the millionth time I'd brought a cardigan. Or even a cagoule. Then all of a sudden I remember something. I reach into the pocket of my skirt—and I don't believe it. The little lump is still there.

"Jess . . . this is for you," I say, pulling it out. "I came to your house to give it to you."

I hand Jess the little blue bag. Slowly she unties it and tips the silver Tiffany bean with its thin chain out onto her hand.

"It's a necklace," I explain. "I've got the same one—look."

"Becky." Jess looks stunned. "It's . . . it's really . . ."

For an awful moment I think she's going to say *unsuitable* or *inappropriate*.

"Fab," she says at last. "It's fab. I love it. Thank you."

She fastens the chain around her neck and I survey her with delight. It really suits her! What's a bit weird, though, is that something about her face seems different. It's kind of changed shape. Almost as if . . .

"Oh my God!" I exclaim in astonishment. "You're *smiling*!"

"No, I'm not," says Jess at once, and I can see her trying to stop—but she can't. Her smile broadens, and she lifts a hand to finger the bean.

"Yes, you are!" I can't help laughing. "You so are! I've found your weak point. You are a Tiffany girl at heart."

"No, I'm not!"

"You are! I knew it! You know, Jess—"

But whatever I was about to say is drowned out by the howling wind, as, with no warning, the gale whips up one entire side of the tent.

"Oh my God!" I shriek, as drenching rain lands in my face. "Oh my God! The tent! Get it!"

"Shit!" Jess is hauling the flapping canvas down again and desperately trying to anchor it, but with another huge gust it blows right out of her grasp. It billows like a sailing ship, then disappears down the mountainside.

"What are we going to do now?" I have to shout just to be heard above the noise.

"Jesus Christ." She rubs rain off her face. "OK. We have to find shelter. Can you get up?"

She helps me to my feet, and I can't help crying out. My ankle is total agony.

"We'll have to make for those rocks," Jess says, gesturing through the rain. "Lean on me."

The pair of us start half limping, half shuffling up the muddy slope, gradually getting into an odd kind of rhythm. I'm gritting my teeth against the pain, willing myself not to make a fuss.

"Will anyone come to rescue us?" I manage between steps.

"Unlikely. We haven't been out long enough." Jess pauses. "OK. You need to get up this steep bit. Hold on to me."

Somehow I make it up the rocky incline, aware of Jess's strong grip holding me up. God, she's in good condition. She could easily have climbed down out of the rain, it occurs to me. She could be safe and warm at home now.

"Thanks for helping me," I say gruffly, as we start on our shuffle again. "Thanks for staying with me."

" 'S OK," she says, without missing a beat.

The rain is billowing into my face, almost choking me. My head is starting to whirl again, and my ankle is excruciating. But I have to keep going. I can't let Jess down.

Suddenly I hear a noise through the rain. But I must be imagining it. Or it's the wind. It can't be real. . . .

"Hang on." Jess stiffens. "What's that?"

We both listen. It is. It's real.

The real chopper-chopper sound of a helicopter.

I look up—and lights are dimly approaching through the sleeting rain.

"Help!" I scream, and wave my arms frantically. "Here!"

"Here!" Jess yells, and thrusts her torch beam up, moving it about in the gloom. "We're here! Help!"

The helicopter hovers above us for a few moments, then, to my dismay, it moves on.

"Didn't . . . they see us?" I gasp.

"I don't know." Jess looks taut and anxious. "Hard to tell. They wouldn't land here anyway. They'd land on the ridge at the top and come down by foot."

We both stand motionless for a moment, but the helicopter doesn't return.

"OK," says Jess at last. "Let's keep going. At least the rocks will shelter us from the wind."

We start moving again, as before. But this time all my drive seems to have gone. I just feel exhausted. I'm drenched, and cold, and I have absolutely no reserves of energy left. We're inching up the slope with a painful slowness, heads together, arms locked around each other, both panting and gasping as rain hits us in the face.

"Wait." I stop still. "I can hear something." I clutch Jess, craning my neck.

"What?"

"I heard something—"

I break off as a dim light flashes through the rain. It's a distant torch beam. And I can hear the sound of movement down the mountain.

Oh my God. It's people. At last.

"It's the mountain rescue! They've come!" I yell. "Here! We need help!"

"Here!" Jess calls, and flashes her torch in the air. "We're here!"

The other torchlight disappears briefly, then reappears.

"Help!" shouts Jess. "We're here!"

There's no reply. Where have they gone? Have they missed us?

"Heeelp!" I scream desperately. "Please help! Over here! Can you hear us?"

"Bex?"

A familiar high-pitched voice comes thinly over the sound of the storm. I freeze.

What?

Am I . . . hallucinating? That sounded just like—

"Bex?" comes the voice again. "Bex, where are you?"

"Suze?"

As I stare upward, a figure appears at the edge of the ridge, wearing an ancient Barbour. Her hair is plastered down on her head with the rain, and she's flashing a torch about, shielding her eyes and looking around, her brow creased in anxiety.

"Bex?" she screams. "Bex! *Where are you?*"

I have to be hallucinating. It's like a mirage. I'm looking at a tree waving in the wind, and thinking it's Suze.

"Bex?" Her eyes have lighted on us. "Oh my God! Bex!" She shouts over her shoulder, "I've found her! Over here!" She starts scrambling down the ridge toward us, sending rocks flying. "Bex!"

"Do you know her?" says Jess, looking bewildered.

"It's Suze." I swallow. "It's . . . my best friend."

Something hard is blocking my throat. Suze came to find me. She came all this way to find me.

"Bex! Thank God!" Suze arrives in a final flurry of stones and earth, her face all mud-stained, her blue eyes huge with concern. "Oh my God. You're hurt. I knew it. I knew it—"

"I'm OK," I manage. "Except my ankle."

"She's here, but she's injured!" she says into her mobile, and listens for a moment. "Tarkie's coming down with a stretcher."

"*Tarquin?*" My head is too dazed to take this all in. "Tarquin's here?"

"With his friend from the RAF. The stupid mountain rescue team said it was too early. But I knew you were in trouble. I knew we had to come. I was so worried." Suze's face suddenly crumples. "Oh God. I was so *worried*. No one knew where you were. . . . You just disappeared. We all thought . . . We didn't know what to think. . . . We were trying to track your mobile signal, but there wasn't one . . . then suddenly it appeared. . . . And now here you are, all . . . all beaten up." She looks on the verge of tears. "Bex, I'm so sorry I never called back. I'm so sorry."

She flings her arms tightly round me. And for a few moments we just stand there, clinging to each other, the rain lashing down on us.

"I'm fine," I say at last, gulping. "Really. I fell down the mountain. But I was with my sister. She took care of me."

"Your sister." Suze loosens her grip and slowly turns to Jess, who's standing, watching awkwardly, her hands stuffed in her pockets.

"This is Jess," I say. "Jess . . . this is Suze."

The two look at each other through the driving rain. I can't tell what each of them is thinking.

"Hi, Becky's sister," Suze says at last, and holds out her hand.

"Hi, Becky's best friend," Jess replies, and takes it.

There's a crashing sound, and we all look up to see Tarquin making his way toward us down the slope, in some amazingly cool-looking army gear, including a hat with a headlamp on it.

"Tarquin," I say. "Hi."

"Jeremy's coming down with the fold-up stretcher," he says cheerfully. "Nasty fright you gave us all, Becky." Into his mobile phone he says, "Luke? We've found her."

The mountain seems to wobble. Suze quickly sticks out an arm for me to lean on.

Luke?

"How come . . ." My lips are suddenly trembling so much I can hardly form the words. "How come Luke . . ."

"He's stuck in Cyprus because of bad weather," says Suze, "but he's been on the other end of the line the whole time. God, he's been in a state."

"Here you are, Becky," Tarquin says, holding out the phone to me.

I almost can't take it. I'm keyed up with nerves.

"Is he still . . . angry with me?" I falter.

Suze just looks at me for a moment, the rain pounding down on her hair and running down her face.

"Bex, take it from me. He's not angry with you."

I lift the phone up to my ear, wincing slightly as it presses on my bruised face.

"Luke?"

"Oh my God! Becky. Thank Christ."

He's all distant and crackly and I can hardly make him out. But as soon as I hear his familiar voice, it's like the whole of the last few days comes to a head. Something is welling up inside me. My eyes are hot and my throat feels choked.

I want him. I want him, and I want to go home.

"Thank God you're safe." Luke sounds more over-wrought than I've ever heard him. "I was out of my mind. . . ."

"I know," I say with a gulp. "I'm sorry. . . ." Tears are

spilling over onto my cheeks. I can barely speak. "Luke, I'm really sorry for everything—"

"Don't be sorry. *I'm* sorry. Jesus. I thought . . ." He stops, and I can hear him breathing hard. "Just . . . don't ever go missing again, OK?"

"I won't." I wipe my eyes furiously with my hand. "God, I wish you were here."

"I'll be there. I'll be out as soon as the storm passes. Nathan's offered me his private jet. He's been absolutely tremendous. . . ." To my dismay, his voice is descending into a hissing crackle.

"Luke?"

". . . hotel . . ."

He's breaking up. Nothing is making any sense.

"I love you," I call hopelessly as the phone goes dead. I look up to see all the others watching with compassion. Tarquin pats my shoulder kindly with a dripping hand.

"Come on, Becky. We'd better get you into the helicopter."

Twenty-three

THE HOSPITAL IS all a bit of a blur. There's lots of light and noise and being asked questions and wheeled around on a trolley, and eventually it turns out I've broken my ankle in two places and they've got to set my leg—plus give me stitches where I cut my forehead and check I haven't got tetanus or mad cow disease or anything. While they're doing all that, they give me an injection of some stuff that makes me feel a bit dopey, and when everything's done I flop back on my pillows, suddenly exhausted. God, it's nice to be somewhere clean and warm and white.

In the distance I can hear someone reassuring Jess that she didn't do any damage by moving me, and then telling Suze several times that a full body scan won't be needed in this case, and no, they're not being cavalier with my health. And as it happens, he *is* the top man in the county.

"Becky?" I look up in a daze, to see Tarquin advancing

toward my bed, holding out a mobile phone. "Luke again."

"Luke?" I say into the receiver. "Hi! Guess what? I've got a broken leg!" I look admiringly at my plaster cast, which is propped up on a support. I have *always* wanted a plaster cast.

"I heard. My poor darling. Are they looking after you OK? Do you have everything you need?"

"Er . . . I think so. You know . . ." With no warning I give a huge yawn. "Actually . . . I'm pretty tired. I might go to sleep."

"I wish I was there." Luke's voice is gentle and loving. "Becky . . . just tell me one thing. Why did you go running off to the North without telling anyone?"

I blink at the phone. He doesn't know why?

"Because I needed help, of course," I say matter-of-factly. By now, I've almost come to terms with the situation. "Our marriage was in tatters. Jess was the only person I could turn to."

Luke seems to be struck dumb.

"Our marriage was in what?" he says at last.

"Tatters!" My voice wobbles. "You know it was! It was awful! You didn't even kiss me goodbye!"

"Darling, I was pissed off. We had a row! That doesn't mean our marriage is in tatters."

"Oh. Well, I thought it was. I thought it was all over. I thought you wouldn't care where I was."

"Oh, Becky." Luke's voice has gone all strange, like he's trying not to laugh. Or possibly cry. "Do you have any idea what I've been going through?"

"No." I bite my lip, hot with shame. "Luke, I'm really sorry. I . . . I didn't think . . . I never realized—"

He cuts me off. "Anyway, you're safe. That's all that matters now. You're safe."

I'm feeling totally guilty. He's being so nice about it.

But what kind of hell have I put him through? And there he is, stuck on Cyprus . . . In a rush of emotion I clutch the phone more tightly to my ear.

"Luke . . . come home. I know you're hating it out there. I know you're miserable. And it's all my fault. Just leave stupid Nathan Temple and his horrible hotel. Find some excuse. You can blame me."

There's a bit of a pause.

"Yesss," says Luke. "There's something I need to say about that. I think that quite possibly—" He breaks off again. "You were right. And I was . . . wrong."

What? Did I hear that properly?

"I was prejudiced," Luke says. "Now that I've gotten to know Nathan, he's a very bright guy. Great commercial mind. We're getting on well."

"You're getting on *well*? But . . . what about him having a conviction?"

"Ah," says Luke, sounding sheepish. "Nathan explained about that. He was defending one of his motel staff from a drunken guest when it happened. He 'went a little far,' as he put it. He says it was a mistake. And I believe him."

My head is throbbing. I can't quite take all this in.

"In a lot of ways he's a guy after my own heart," Luke continues. "He told me the other night why he set up his motel chain. It was after he was refused entry to a smart hotel because he wasn't wearing a tie. He went straight to a pub and sketched out a business plan for Value Motels. Had twenty up and running in a year. You have to admire that drive."

"I don't believe it," I say, rubbing my forehead in a daze. "You *like* him."

"I do like him." Luke pauses. "And . . . he's been tremendous over this whole affair. Couldn't have been kinder. He stayed up all night with me, listening for news."

I wince in guilt as I imagine the two of them in dressing gowns, waiting by the phone.

God, I am never, ever going to disappear again.

I mean, not that I was planning to. But, you know.

"What about the hotel?" I ask. "Is it tacky?"

"The hotel is supremely tacky," Luke says, sounding cheerful. "But you were right. It's top-quality tack."

I can't help a little giggle, which turns into an enormous yawn. I can really feel the drugs kicking in now.

"So . . . I was right all along," I say, my voice bleary. "It was a brilliant networking coup."

"It was a brilliant networking coup," agrees Luke. "Becky . . . I'm sorry." He suddenly sounds more serious. "For that and . . . a lot of things." He hesitates. "I realize you've had it hard these last few weeks. I got too obsessed with the Arcodas deal. I haven't supported you. And I didn't appreciate what a crash it was for you, coming back to Britain."

As his words filter into my brain they sound weirdly familiar.

Has he been talking to Jess?

Has Jess been . . . *sticking up* for me?

Suddenly I realize Luke is still talking.

"And another thing," he's saying. "I finally read through your pink folder on the plane. And I liked your idea. We should approach David Neville and see if he wants to sell."

"You really liked my idea?" Through my stupor I feel a glow of delight.

"I really did. Although I have no idea where you've picked up all this specialist knowledge on business expansion—"

"At Barneys! I told you!" I sink contentedly into my

pillows. "David'll want to sell—I know he will. He's really regretting having gone on his own. And they want another baby. . . ." I can hardly get the words out, I'm so tired. "And Judy says she just wants him to have a normal sara . . . salary . . ."

"Sweetheart, we'll talk about it another time. You should rest."

"All right." My eyelids are getting really heavy now and it's a struggle to keep them open.

"Let's start over," Luke says softly. "When I get back. No more tatters. OK?"

"What's that?" a tart voice interrupts. It's the head nurse, approaching. "Mobile phones are *not* allowed on the wards. And you need some sleep, young lady!"

"OK," I quickly say into the phone. "OK."

The nurse removes the phone from my fingers and my eyes crash shut.

When I open them again, everything is different. The room is dim. The chatter has gone. It must be nighttime.

I'm absolutely parched, and my lips are painfully dry. I remember there was a jug of water on my nightstand, and I'm trying to sit up and get it when I knock something onto the floor with a clatter.

"Bex? Are you OK?" I look over to see Suze in a chair by my bed. She rubs the sleep out of her eyes and leaps up. "D'you want something?"

"Some water," I croak. "If there is any."

"Here you are." Suze pours me out a glassful and I drink it thirstily. "How are you feeling?"

"I'm . . . fine." I put the glass down, feeling a lot better, then look around the dim, curtained cubicle. "Where is everyone? Where's Jess?"

"She's OK. The doctors looked her over and then Tarkie took her home. But they wanted to keep you in for observation."

"Right." I rub my dry face, wishing I had some moisturizer with me. Then suddenly I notice the time on Suze's wristwatch.

"It's two o'clock!" I look up in consternation. "Suze, why are you here? You should be in bed!"

"I didn't want to go." She bites her lip. "I didn't want to leave you."

"Shh!" hisses a voice from the other side of my curtain. "Keep the noise down!"

Suze and I look at each other in surprise—and suddenly I can feel the laughter rising. Suze sticks out her tongue at the curtain, and I give a helpless snuffle.

"Have some more water," says Suze in a lower voice. "It'll keep your skin hydrated." She pours another glassful and perches on the side of my bed. For a while neither of us speaks. I take a few more sips of water, which is lukewarm and tastes of plastic.

"This reminds me of when Ernie was born," says Suze. "Do you remember? You stayed with me all night then."

"God, yes." I have a sudden memory of a teeny, tiny Ernie in Suze's arms, all pink and wrapped in a blanket. "That was some night." I meet her eyes and she smiles.

"You know, when the twins were born . . . it didn't feel quite right, you not being there." Suze is still smiling, but her eyes are sheeny. "I know that sounds really stupid—"

"No. It's not." I look down at the white hospital sheet, pleating it hard between my fingers. "I've really missed you, Suze."

"I've missed you too." Her voice is a little husky. "And

I . . . I need to say something. I'm sorry for the way I be-
haved when you got back."

"No," I say at once. "Don't be silly. I overreacted. You
had to make other friends while I was gone. Of course
you did. I was . . . stupid."

"You weren't stupid." Suze won't meet my eye. "It was
me. I was envious."

"*Envious?*" I'm utterly dumbfounded.

"There you were, all tanned and glamorous, with
your Angel bag." Her voice trembles a little. "And there
I was, stuck in the country with three kids. You came
swanning in with all these stories about your amazing
round-the-world honeymoon, and I felt really . . . drab."

"Suze, you could never be drab!" I say in dismay.
"Never in a million years!"

"So I was thinking." She looks at me, her face determined. "When you're better, let's go to Milan for the
weekend. Just you and me. What do you think?"

"What about the babies?"

"They'll be fine. Tarkie'll look after them. It can be my
late birthday treat."

"What about the spa?" I say cautiously. "Wasn't that
your treat?"

For a moment Suze contemplates the floor.

"The spa was OK," she says at last. "But it wasn't the
same as with you. No one's like you, Bex."

"So do you hate Lulu now?" I ask hopefully.

"Bex!" Suze gives a shocked giggle. "No, I don't *hate*
her. But . . ." She breaks off. "As I said, no one's like you,
Bex."

I can't quite find a reply, so I reach for my water glass
again—and find myself looking at a small packet on the
nightstand.

"Jess left you that," says Suze, looking a bit puzzled.
"She said we might want to eat it."

I can't help smiling. It's Kendal Mint Cake.

"It's kind of . . . a private joke," I say. "I don't think she's expecting me to eat it."

There's quiet for a while, apart from the noise of a trolley being wheeled along in the distance, and the thwump of double doors opening and closing.

"So . . . you really have got a sister," says Suze at last. I can hear the wistfulness in her voice. For a few moments I look through the dimness at her familiar, anxious, lovely face.

"Suze . . . you'll always be my sister," I say at last. And I hug her tight.

Twenty-four

IT'S INCREDIBLE, THE number of things I was convinced I didn't like . . . and now it turns out I love them!

For example:

1. Jess
2. Black pudding (If you put lots of tomato ketchup on it, it's actually quite yummy!)
3. Being a skinflint

Honestly. I'm not joking. Being frugal is totally fantastic. It's so *satisfying*! How come I never realized this before? Like, yesterday I sent Janice and Martin a postcard to thank them for their lovely flowers . . . and instead of buying one, I cut it out of a cereal box! It had *Kellogg's* on the front! How cool is that?

Jess gave me that tip. She is teaching me so much. I've been staying with her ever since I got out of the hospital, and she's been just brilliant. She gave me her bedroom because there are fewer stairs up to it than to the guest room, and she helps me get in and out of the bath with my plaster cast, and she makes vegetable soup every day for lunch. She's even going to teach me how to make it, because if you do it with lentils and . . . and something else, which I can't remember . . . it's a fully balanced meal in itself and it only costs 30p a portion. And then, with the extra money you save, you can buy something really nice like one of Elizabeth's homemade fruit pies! (That was the tip I gave to Jess. You see, we're helping each other!)

Now I hobble over to the sink, carefully empty half the coffee grounds out of the cafetiere into the bin, sprinkle on some new ones, and switch on the kettle. The rule in this house is that you reuse coffee grounds, and, like Jess says, it does make total sense. The coffee only tastes a little bit tinny—and you save loads!

I have so changed. Finally, I am a frugal and sensible person. Luke will not believe it when he sees me again.

Jess is chopping an onion, and I helpfully pick up the mesh bag it came in, to throw away.

Jess looks up. "Don't! We can use that!"

"An onion bag?" Wow. I'm learning new things all the time! "So . . . how can you use an onion bag?"

"You can turn it into a scourer."

"Right." I nod intelligently, even though I'm not *entirely* sure what a scourer is.

"You know." Jess gives me a look. "Scouring. Like exfoliating, but for kitchens."

"Oh *yes!*" I say, and beam at her. "Cool!"

I get out my Thrifty Household Tips notebook and write it down. There's just so much to take in. Like, did you know you can make a garden sprinkler out of an old milk carton?

Not that I need a garden sprinkler . . . but still!

I make my way into the sitting room, one hand resting on my crutch, the other holding the cafetiere.

"Hi." Suze looks up from where she's sitting on the floor. "What do you think?" She lifts up the banner she's been painting. It reads LEAVE OUR LANDSCAPE ALONE in vibrant red and blue with an amazing leafy, grassy border.

"Wow!" I gaze at it in admiration. "Suze, that's fantastic! You're such an amazing artist." I look at the pile of banners, which Suze has been steadily painting over the last few days, draped on the sofa. "God, the campaign's lucky to have you."

It's been so fantastic having Suze here, just like old times. She and Tarquin have been staying in Edie's guesthouse for the last few days and Tarquin has pretty much taken charge of the babies, except when Suze needs to feed them in the mornings and evenings.

And it's been so great. We've spent loads of time together, chilling, and eating, and talking about everything under the sun. Sometimes just me and Suze—and sometimes with Jess too. Like last night, the three of us made margaritas and watched *Footloose* . . . which I *think* Jess enjoyed. Even though she didn't know every song by heart, like we did.

Then one night, when Suze went to visit some relation of hers who lives twenty miles away, Jess and I spent the evening together. She showed me all her rocks and told me all about them—and in return, I told her about my shoes and drew pictures. I think we both learned a lot.

"The campaign's lucky to have *you*," retorts Suze, lifting her eyebrows. "Let's face it, Bex. If it weren't for you, this protest would be three people and a dog."

"Well, you know." I shrug, trying to look modest. But I am secretly pretty pleased with the way things are going. I've been in charge of the protest publicity ever since

I got out of the hospital, and we have gotten so much coverage! The rally is this afternoon, and at least four local radio stations ran news stories this morning. It's been in all the local papers, and a TV crew is even talking about coming out!

It's all due to a brilliant combination of factors. It turns out the head of news at Radio Cumbria is Guy Wroxley, who I used to know in London when I was a financial journalist. He gave me the phone numbers of everyone locally who might be interested, and ran a huge feature piece yesterday afternoon on *Cumbria Watch*. But the best thing is our fabulous human interest story! The first thing I did when I took control was call a meeting of the environmental group. Everyone had to tell me every little thing they knew about the site, even if it didn't seem important. And it turns out that twenty years ago, Jim proposed to Elizabeth in the very field which is going to be wrecked by the shopping center!

So we set up a photo shoot in the field, with Jim kneeling down just like he did then (except, apparently, he didn't kneel—but I told him not to mention that), looking all mournful. The *Scully and Coggenthwaite Herald* printed it on their front page yesterday morning under the headline MASSACRE OF OUR LOVING MEMORIES, and the protest hotline (Robin's mobile) has been ringing with support ever since!

"How long have we got?" asks Suze, sitting back on her heels.

"Three hours. Here you are." I hand her a cup of coffee.

"Oh, right." Suze gives a slight grimace. "Is this your thrifty coffee?"

"Yes!" I eye her defensively. "What's wrong? It's delicious!"

There's a ring at the doorbell and I hear Jess striding down the passage to answer it.

"Maybe that's another bunch of flowers," says Suze with a giggle. "From your admirer."

I have been bombarded with bouquets ever since the accident. About half of them are from Nathan Temple, saying things like *In hugest gratitude* and *In appreciation of your supportive gesture.*

Well. So he should be grateful. There was Luke, all set to fly home, and it was *me* who said he should stay in Cyprus and finish the job and I'd be fine staying with Jess for a few days. So he did, and he's on his way home today. The plane should be landing any minute.

I just know things are going to work out well between me and Luke. We've had the ups and downs . . . we've had the tempests . . . but from now on it's going to be smooth, easy waters. For a start, I'm a different person now. I've become a grown-up, prudent woman. And I'm going to have a grown-up relationship with Luke. I'm going to discuss everything with him. I'm going to tell him everything. No more stupid situations where we end up at loggerheads. We're a team!

"You know, I honestly think Luke won't know me," I say, taking a pensive sip of coffee.

"Oh, I think he will," says Suze, studying me. "You don't look *that* bad. I mean, the stitches are pretty awful, but that huge bruise is looking a bit better. . . ."

"I don't mean in appearance!" I say. "I mean in personality. I've totally changed."

"Have you?" says Suze, looking puzzled.

She's my best friend. Hasn't she noticed *anything*?

"Yes! Look at me! Making thrifty coffee and organizing a protest march and eating soup and . . . everything!"

I haven't even told Luke about organizing the protest.

He'll be so gobsmacked when he sees his wife has become an activist. He'll be so impressed!

"Becky?" Jess's voice interrupts us and we both look up to see her standing at the door, an odd expression on her face. "I've got something for you. Some walkers have just come back from Scully Pike, and . . . they found this." From behind her back she produces a hand-painted calfskin bag adorned with diamanté.

My Angel bag.

I thought I'd never ever see it again.

"Oh my God," I hear Suze breathe.

I'm speechless. It's a bit battered and there's a tiny scratch near the handle—but apart from that it looks just the way it did. The angel is the same. The sparkling *Dante* is the same.

"It seems fine," Jess is saying, turning it over in her hands. "It must have gotten a bit wet and thrown about, but apart from that, no harm done. Here you are." She holds it out.

But I don't move. I can't take it from her.

"Becky?" Jess looks perplexed. "Here!" She thrusts it toward me and I flinch.

"I don't want it." I look away. "This bag nearly ruined my marriage. From the moment I bought it, everything started going wrong. I think it's cursed."

"*Cursed?*" says Jess, exchanging looks with Suze.

"Bex, it's not cursed," Suze says patiently. "It's a totally fab bag! Everyone wants an Angel bag!"

"Not me. Not anymore. It's only brought me trouble." I look from face to face, feeling suddenly rather sage. "You know, the last few days have really taught me a lot. I've got a lot of things in perspective. And if it's a choice between my marriage or a totally fab bag"—I spread my arms—"I'll take the marriage."

"Wow," says Suze. "You *have* changed. Sorry," she adds sheepishly, as she sees my face.

Honestly, what is she like? I would *always* have taken the marriage.

I'm . . . pretty sure I would have.

"So what will you do with it?" asks Jess. "Sell it?"

"You could donate it to a museum!" Suze says excitedly. "It could be 'From the collection of Rebecca Brandon.' "

"I've got a better idea," I say. "It can be star prize of the raffle this afternoon." I grin at them. "And we'll rig it so Kelly wins."

By one o'clock the house is full of people. Everyone has gathered here for a final pep talk, and the atmosphere is just amazing. Jess and I are handing out bowls of vegetable soup, and Suze is showing all her painted banners to Robin, and everywhere there's a buzz of conversation and laughter.

God, why have I never been on a protest before? It's just the best thing ever!

"Isn't it exciting!" says Kelly, coming up with a bowl of soup in her hand. She's wearing camouflage combat pants and a T-shirt with HANDS OFF OUR LAND written on it in marker pen.

"It's great!" I beam at her. "So . . . have you bought a raffle ticket for later?"

"Yes, of course! I've bought ten!"

"Have this one too," I say casually, handing her number 501. "I've got a good feeling about it."

"Oh, right!" She tucks the ticket into her pants pocket. "Thanks, Becky!"

I smile and sip my soup. "How's the shop looking?"

"It's fantastic!" Her eyes shine. "We've got helium balloons everywhere, and ribbons, and sparkling wine, and loads of free gifts all ready. . . ."

"It's going to be a wonderful party. Don't you think, Jess?" I add, as she walks by with a saucepan of soup. "The party in Jim's shop."

"Oh," she says. "I suppose so." She gives a grudging, almost disapproving shrug, and ladles more soup into Kelly's bowl.

Like she's really fooling me with that act.

I mean, come on. I'm her *sister*.

"So . . . it's amazing that we got a donation to fund the party," I remark to Kelly. "Don't you think?"

"It's incredible!" says Kelly. "A thousand pounds out of nowhere! We couldn't believe it!"

"Amazing," says Jess with a small frown.

"Funny that the donor wants to stay anonymous," I add, taking a spoonful of soup. "Robin said they were quite firm about it."

"Yes." The back of Jess's neck is reddening a little. "I heard."

"You'd think they'd want some credit," says Kelly, wide-eyed. "You know, for being so generous!"

"I agree. You'd think they would." I pause, then add innocently, "What do you think, Jess?"

"I suppose," she replies, roughly stacking bowls on a tray. "I wouldn't know."

"I guess not." I hide a smile. "Great soup."

"Everyone!" Jim bangs on a table and the hubbub dies down. "Just to remind you. Our Village Shop party begins at five, right after the protest. Everyone's welcome to come along and spend as much as they can. Hear that, Edie?"

Edie brandishes her purse back at him, and the room erupts in laughter.

"Anyone spends more than twenty pounds gets a free gift," adds Jim. "And everyone gets a free drink."

"Now you're talking!" shouts the gray-haired man, and there's another huge laugh.

"Bex?" comes Suze's voice in my ear. "Phone for you. It's Luke."

I hurry into the kitchen, still elated, and seize the receiver.

"Luke!" I say. "Hi! Where are you? At the airport?"

"Nope, I'm already in the car."

"That's great!" I cannot *wait* to see him. "How soon can you be here? There's loads going on! I'll give you directions to exactly where we'll be—"

His voice cuts me off. "Becky . . . I'm afraid there's a hitch. I don't know how to tell you this . . . but I can't make it to you until much later."

"What? But . . . why? You've been away all week! I haven't seen you!"

"I know. I'm livid. But something's come up." He exhales sharply. "There's a PR crisis with the Arcodas Group. Normally I'd leave it to Gary and the team, but this is a new client. It's the first problem, and I'm going to have to deal with it myself."

"Right." My whole body is drooping in disappointment. "I understand."

"But I've had an idea." He hesitates. "Becky, come and join me."

"What?" I gape at the phone.

"Come now. I'll send a car. I've missed you so much."

"Me too." I feel a pang. "I've so missed you."

"But it's not just that." He hesitates. "I've spoken to Gary . . . and we're both agreed. We'd love your input on this. We could do with a few bright ideas. What do you think?"

I stare at the phone, transfixed with longing. This is exactly what I always wanted! Husband and wife helping each other. Brainstorming together. A real, proper partnership.

But I can't let Jess down. Not now.

"Luke, I can't come." I bite my lip. "I really want to, but I've got something planned for today. I promised Jess. And . . . some others. I can't just abandon them. I'm sorry."

"Fair enough," says Luke, sounding rueful. "My fault for not hiring you when I had the chance. Well . . . I'll see you this evening." He sighs. "I don't know what time I'll be finished, but I'll call when I have an idea."

"You poor thing," I say sympathetically. "I hope it all goes well. I'll be there in spirit. Where will you be?"

"Well, that's about the one positive thing. I'll be up in the North. Fairly near where you are, in fact."

"Oh, right," I say, with interest. "So . . . what's the crisis? Another fat-cat businessman cooking the books?"

"Worse," Luke says grimly. "Some environmental bloody protest group which has sprung up out of nowhere."

"An environmental group?" I say in amazement. "You're kidding! That is such a coincidence, because—"

Abruptly I stop. My face suddenly feels hot and prickly. It couldn't be . . .

No. Don't be ridiculous. There must be millions of protests every day, all over the country—

"Whoever's taken control is clearly pretty media savvy," Luke says. "There's a rally this afternoon; they've had press coverage; TV news is interested. . . ." He laughs. "Get this, Becky. They're protesting against a shopping center."

The room seems to swim. I clutch the phone, trying to stay calm.

It can't be the same thing. It can't. We're not protesting against the Arcodas Group. I know we're not. We're protesting against Maybell Shopping Centers.

Luke interrupts my thoughts. "Sweetheart, I have to go. Gary's on the other line, waiting to brief me. But I'll see you later. Oh, and have fun doing whatever you're doing with Jess."

"I'll . . . try," I manage.

As I walk back into the sitting room, my heart is beating rather fast. Everyone is sitting in an attentive semicircle watching Robin, who's holding up a big diagram of two stick figures, labeled RESISTING POLICE ARREST.

"The groin area is particularly useful in this respect. . . ." he's saying as I walk in. "Everything OK, Becky?"

"Absolutely!" I say, my voice two notches higher than usual. "Just one quick question. We *are* protesting against Maybell Shopping Centers?"

"That's right."

"So this has nothing to do with the Arcodas Group."

"Well . . . yeah." He looks at me in surprise. "Maybell's owned by the Arcodas Group. You knew that, didn't you?"

I open my mouth, but I can't quite produce a reply. In fact, I'm feeling a bit faint. I have just orchestrated a huge media campaign against Luke's newest, most important client. Me. His wife.

"Evil bastards." Robin looks around the room. "Guess what I heard today! They're getting in their PR company to 'deal' with us. Some big-shot firm from London. They're flying the chief guy back from holiday especially, I heard."

Oh God. I cannot cope. What am I going to do? What?

I have to pull out. Yes. I have to tell everyone right now that I'm pulling out and disassociate myself from the whole thing.

"They think we're small fry." Robin's eyes are shining intensely. "They think we have no resources. But we have our passion. We have our beliefs. And most of all"—he turns to me—"we have Becky!"

"What?" I jump in panic as everyone turns toward me and starts clapping. "No! Please. Really. I've . . . nothing to do with it."

"Don't be modest!" exclaims Robin. "You've transformed the protest! If it weren't for you, none of this would be happening!"

"Don't say that!" I say, rattled. "I mean . . . I just want to take a backseat. In fact . . . there's something I need to say. . . ."

Come on. Just tell them.

I catch Jim's warm gaze and look away. This is hard.

"Wait," comes a trembling voice behind me, and I look round in surprise, to see Jess advancing toward me. "Before you speak . . . I'd like to say something."

As she comes and stands beside me, the room falls silent in expectation. Jess lifts her chin and faces the crowd squarely.

"A lot of you heard me the other night, telling Becky that we weren't sisters. A lot of you heard me . . . disown her. Well, it turns out we are sisters." She pauses and the color rises in her cheeks. "But even if we weren't . . . even if we weren't"—she looks round the room, a little fiercely—"I would be honored to know Becky and to count her as a friend."

"Hear, hear!" Jim cries hoarsely.

"And going on this march today . . . with all of you . . .

and my sister . . ." Jess puts an arm through mine. "It's one of the proudest moments of my life."

The room is utterly silent.

"I'm sorry, Becky." Jess turns to me. "What did you want to say?"

"I . . . um . . . well," I say weakly. "I was just going to say . . . let's smash 'em."

Twenty-five

LEAVE OUR LAND alone!" yells Robin through his loudspeaker.

"Out, out, out!" we all yell back, and I give Jess an exhilarated thumbs-up. If ever I had any doubts about whether I was doing the right thing, they've totally vanished. You just have to look around. You just have to see what would be ruined. We're standing on Piper's Hill, and it's the most stunningly beautiful place I've ever been. There's a wood at the top, and wildflowers nestling in the grass, and I've already seen about six butterflies. I don't care if they're Luke's clients or not. *How* could they build a shopping center on this? Especially a rubbish one with no Space.NK!

"Leave our land alone!"

"Out, out, out!" I yell at the top of my voice. Protesting is just the coolest thing I have done, ever! I'm at the top of the hill with Robin, Jim, and Jess, and the sight before us is just amazing. About three hundred people have turned up! They're marching up the lane

oward the proposed site, waving placards, blowing whis-
.les, and banging drums, with two local TV crews and a
bunch of journalists in tow.

I keep peering at the crowd, but there's no sign of
anyone from the Arcodas Group—or Luke. Which I'm
a tad relieved about. I mean, not that I'm ashamed of
being here. Quite the opposite. I am someone who will
stand up for her beliefs and fight for the oppressed, no
matter what others think. But having said that, if Luke
does turn up, I'm thinking I might put on a balaclava
and quickly hide behind someone. He'll never spot me
among all these people. It'll be fine.

"Leave our land alone!"

"Out, out, out!"

Jess is waving her WILDLIFE MURDERERS placard ener-
getically, and blowing on her whistle. Edie and Lorna
are wearing fluorescent pink wigs and holding up a
huge sign which says KILLING OUR LAND, KILLING OUR
COMMUNITY. Suze is in a white T-shirt and army combat
trousers, which she pinched from Tarquin, and holding
up one of her own banners. And I'm wearing one of
Jess's World Wildlife Fund T-shirts over my D&G cropped
jeans. Finally, we've swapped clothes like sisters should!
(I lent her a black Karen Millen vest top, which she's
wearing under that gray STOP THE CONSUMPTION T-shirt.)
The sun is shining, and everyone's in fantastic spirits.

"Leave our land alone!"

"Out, out, out!"

The crowd is thickening now, and at a little nod from
me, Robin puts down his placards and climbs the stepladder we've rigged up. There's a microphone in front of
it, and the view of blue sky and unspoiled countryside
behind him is breathtaking. The photographer I hired
for the occasion kneels down and starts taking photos,

and is soon joined by the TV crews and local newspaper photographers.

The crowd gradually quiets down, and everyone turns expectantly toward Robin.

"Friends, supporters, lovers of the countryside," he begins, his voice echoing in the clear afternoon air. "I ask you all to take a moment and look around at what we have. We have beauty. We have wildlife. We have all we need."

He pauses for effect, just like I coached him, letting the message sink in. The wind is ruffling his hair, and his face is flushed with animation.

"Do we need a shopping center?"

"No! No! No!" we all yell back at the tops of our voices.

"Do we need pollution?"

"No! No! No!"

"Do we need any more pointless consumerist rubbish? Does anyone need any more"—he casts around derisively—"*cushions?*"

"No . . ." I begin with everyone else—then stop myself. I could actually do with some nice cushions for our bed. In fact, I saw some really nice cashmere ones in a magazine only yesterday.

But . . . that's OK. Everyone knows activists sometimes disagree on minor technical points. And I agree with everything else Robin is saying. Just not about the cushions.

"Do we want an eyesore on our land?" shouts Robin, spreading his arms.

"No! No! No!" I yell back happily. Jess blows her whistle, and I look at it a bit enviously. Next time I go on a protest, I'm definitely taking a whistle.

"Now let's hear from another of our activists!" yells Robin, "Becky! Get up here!"

My head jerks up.

What? This wasn't in the plan.

"The girl who's held this campaign together!" he says. "The girl whose ideas and spirit have made this happen! Let's hear it for Becky!"

Everyone is turning toward me with admiring faces. Robin starts applauding, and everyone gradually joins in.

"Go on, Becky," says Jess, over the noise. "They really want you!"

I do a quick scan around. There's no sign of Luke.

Oh, come on. I have to show my support.

It's difficult to walk with my plaster cast, but somehow I hobble through the crowd to the stepladder and carefully climb to the top with Robin's help. Below me is a sea of excited faces, all looking up in the sunshine.

"Hello, Piper's Hill!" I yell into the microphone, and an almighty cheer comes back from the crowd, complete with hoots and whistles and frantically beating drums.

God, this is fantastic! It's like being a pop star!

"This is our country!" I shout, gesturing at the rippling green grass around us. "This is our land! We won't give it up!"

Another delighted cheer erupts.

"And to anyone who *wants* us to give it up . . ." I shout, waving my arms around. "To anyone who thinks they can come and *take it away from us* . . . I say this! I say, *Go home!*"

There's a third uproarious cheer. I'm totally elated. This seems to come naturally! Maybe I should be a politician!

"I say, *give up now*!" I yell. "Because we're going to *fight*! On the *beaches*! And on the—"

There's a slight kerfuffle going on in the crowd, and I break off, trying to see what's happening.

"They're coming!" I can hear people shouting.

"Boo!" The whole crowd is hissing and jeering.

"It's them!" cries Robin, from the grass below. "Bastards! Let 'em have it!"

And suddenly I freeze. Five men in dark suits are making their way swiftly to the front of the crowd.

One of them is Luke.

OK, I think, I need to get down off this ladder. At once.

Except it's not as easy as that, when one leg is in bloody plaster. I can barely move.

"Er . . . Robin, I'd like to get down now!" I call.

"You stay there!" shouts Robin. "Carry on with your speech! It's great!"

I frantically grasp my crutch and am trying to maneuver myself off the top, when Luke looks up and sees me.

I have never seen him so shell-shocked. He stops dead and just stares at me. I can feel my face burning.

Something tells me organizing a protest against your husband's client has got to be even worse than selling his Tiffany clocks.

"Don't let the bastards intimidate you, Becky!" Robin hisses urgently from below. "Ignore them! Keep speaking! Go *on*!"

I'm stuck. There's nothing else I can do. I clear my throat and focus on Kelly's enthusiastic face.

"Um . . . we're going to fight!" I call out, my voice cracking a bit. "I say . . . er . . . *go home!*"

By now the five men are standing in a row, arms folded, looking up at me. Three men who I don't recognize, plus Gary and Luke.

The trick is to not look at them.

"Let us keep our land!" I shout, with more confidence. "We don't want your *concrete jungle!*"

A huge cheer breaks out, and I can't help darting a

triumphant glance at Luke. His brow is furrowed and he looks furious.

But there's a twitch at his mouth, too. Almost like he wants to laugh. Our eyes lock, and I have this awful feeling I'm about to start giggling hysterically.

"Give up!" I yell. "Because you *won't win*!"

"I'll go and speak to the ringleader," Luke says gravely to one of the men I don't recognize. "See what I can do."

Calmly he walks across the grass to the stepladder and climbs up three steps until he's level with me. We're only inches apart. The breeze is carrying the scent of his aftershave. And now he's so close, I'm longing to throw my arms around him. I want to tell him how much I missed him. How scared I was on the mountain. How much I love him.

On the other hand, he may not be in the mood for a hug right now.

"Hello," says Luke at last.

"Oh! Er . . . hi!" I say as nonchalantly as I can manage. "How are you?"

"Quite a party you have here." Luke surveys the scene. "Is this all your doing?"

"Er . . . I had some help." I clear my throat. "You know how it is. . . ." I catch my breath as my gaze lands on Luke's immaculate shirt cuff. Nestling beneath it— only just visible—is a tatty plaited rope bracelet.

I look away quickly, trying to stay cool. We're on opposing sides here.

"You do realize you're protesting *against* a shopping center, Becky?" Luke says.

"With crap shops," I retort, without missing a beat.

"Don't negotiate, Becky!" Robin yells from down below.

"Spit in his face!" chimes in Edie, shaking her fist.

"You realize the Arcodas Group is my biggest client," says Luke. "That has crossed your mind."

"You wanted me to be more like Jess," I reply, a little defiantly. "That's what you said, isn't it? 'Be like your sister.' Well, here you are, then." I lean forward to the microphone and shout into it, "Go back to London with your fancy ways! Leave us in peace!"

The crowd erupts in an approving cheer.

"Go back to London with my fancy ways?" echoes Luke in disbelief. "What about *your* fancy ways?"

"I don't have any fancy ways," I say haughtily. "I've changed, if you want to know. I'm really frugal. And I care about the countryside. And evil developers coming and ruining beauty spots like this."

Luke leans forward and whispers in my ear, "Actually . . . they're not planning to build a shopping center on this site."

"What?" I look up with a frown. "Yes, they are."

"No, they're not. They changed their plans weeks ago. They're using another site. In fact, they're redeveloping an existing office complex."

I search his face suspiciously. He doesn't look like he's lying.

"But . . . the plans," I say. "We've got plans!"

"Old." He raises his eyebrows. "Someone didn't do their research properly." He glances down at Robin. "Him, by any chance?"

Oh God. That actually has the ring of truth.

I can't quite take this in. They're not planning to build a shopping center here after all. We're all here, shouting and yelling . . . for no reason.

"So." Luke folds his arms. "Despite your extremely convincing publicity campaign, the Arcodas Group are not in fact villains. They have done nothing wrong."

"Oh, right." I shift awkwardly and glance past Luke at the three scowling Arcodas Group men. "So . . . I don't suppose they're very pleased, are they?"

"Not exactly," agrees Luke.

"Er . . . sorry about that." I sweep my eyes over the restive crowd. "So I suppose you want me to tell them. Is that it?"

Luke tugs his earlobe, the way he always does when he's got a plan.

"Well," he says. "As it happens, I have a better idea. Since you have helpfully gathered all this media together . . ."

He takes hold of the microphone, swivels to face the crowd, and taps it for attention. There's an answering roar of boos and hisses. Even Suze is shaking her banner at him.

"Ladies and gentlemen," Luke says in his deep, confident voice. "Members of the press. I have an announcement to make on behalf of the Arcodas Group."

He waits patiently until the jeers have died down, then looks around the crowd.

"We at the Arcodas Group are passionate about people. We are passionate about listening. We are the company that takes notice. I have spoken to your representative"—he indicates me—"and I have taken in all her arguments."

There's an expectant hush. Everyone is gazing up at him, agog.

"As a result of this . . . I can announce that the Arcodas Group has reconsidered the use of this site." Luke smiles. "There will be no shopping center here."

There's a moment of stunned silence—then overjoyed pandemonium breaks out. Everyone's cheering and hugging each other, whistles are blowing, and drums are being beaten to death.

"We did it!" I hear Jim yelling above the clamor.

"We showed them!" shrieks Kelly.

Jess is cheering along with everyone else, although

she keeps darting looks of suspicion toward me and Luke. I'll have to fill her in later on.

"I would also like to draw your attention to the huge number of environmental initiatives which the Arcodas Group sponsors," Luke says smoothly into the microphone. "Leaflets are currently being handed out. And press packs. Enjoy."

Hang on a minute. He's totally turning this into a positive PR event. He's hijacked it!

"You snake!" I say furiously, putting my hand over the microphone. "You completely misled them!"

"The field is saved." He shrugs. "The rest is details, surely."

"No! That's not the—"

"If your crew had done their research in the first place, we wouldn't be here and I wouldn't have to be saving the situation." He leans down and calls to Gary, who's been handing out literature to the crowd. "Gary, see the Arcodas folk into their car, will you? Tell them I'm staying on for some further negotiating work."

Gary nods, and gives me a cheery wave, which I choose to ignore. I'm still outraged with them both.

"So . . . where *is* the shopping center being built?" I demand as I watch the rejoicing crowd. Kelly and Jess are hugging each other, Jim is clapping Robin on the back, and Edie and Lorna are waving their pink wigs in the air.

"Why?"

"Maybe I'll go and protest outside it. Maybe I should start following the Arcodas Group around and making trouble! Keep you on your toes."

"Maybe you should," says Luke with a wry smile. "Becky, look, I'm sorry. But I have to do my job."

"I know, I suppose. But . . . I thought I was making a

difference. I really thought I'd achieved something." I heave a morose sigh. "And it was all for nothing."

"For *nothing*?" says Luke, incredulous. "Becky . . . just take a look at what you've done." He gestures at the throng. "Look at all these people. I've heard how you transformed the campaign. Not to mention the village . . . and this party you're throwing . . . You should be proud of yourself. Hurricane Becky, they're calling you."

"What, I leave a trail of devastation everywhere?"

Luke looks at me, suddenly serious, his eyes warm and dark. "You blow people away. Everyone you meet." He picks up my hand and looks at it for a moment. "Don't be like Jess. Be like you."

"But you said . . ." I begin, then stop myself.

"What?"

Oh God. I was going to be all grown-up and dignified and not mention this. But I just can't help it.

"I overheard you talking to Jess," I mumble. "When she was staying with us. I heard you say . . . it was difficult to live with me."

"It *is* difficult to live with you," says Luke matter-of-factly.

I blink at him, my throat a little tight.

"It's also enriching. It's exciting. It's fun. It's the only thing I want to do. If it were easy . . . it would be boring." He touches my cheek. "Life with you is an adventure, Becky."

"Becky!" calls Suze from below. "The party's starting! Hi, Luke!"

"Come on," Luke says, and kisses me. Over his shoulder I see Edie nudging Lorna and pointing to us, agog. God, I'm going to have to put them all straight. Otherwise they'll think I've been unfaithful to my husband with the evil Arcodas man.

"Let's get you off this ladder." Luke's strong fingers weave round mine, and I squeeze them back.

"By the way, what did you mean just now when you said you were frugal?" he asks as he helps me edge down the steps. "Was it a joke?"

"No! I'm frugal! Jess taught me. Like Yoda."

"What exactly did she teach you?" says Luke, looking a bit wary.

"How to make a water sprinkler out of a milk carton," I say proudly. "And gift wrap out of old plastic bags. Also, you should always write a birthday card in pencil so the person can rub out your message and use it again. It saves ninety pence!"

Luke looks at me wordlessly for a few moments.

"I think I need to get you back to London," he says at last, then helps me down the stepladder, holding my crutch under his arm. "Danny called, by the way."

"Danny called?" In my excitement I miss the last step of the ladder. As I land on the grass, everything goes a little swirly.

"Ooh!" I clutch on to Luke. "I'm all dizzy."

"Are you OK?" says Luke in alarm. "Is it the concussion? You shouldn't have been climbing ladders. . . ."

"It's all right," I say, a little breathless. "I'll sit down."

"God, I always used to get like that!" says Suze, passing by. "When I was pregnant."

Everything seems to empty from my mind.

I dart a startled glance at Luke. He looks equally jolted.

No. I mean . . . I couldn't . . .

I couldn't be—

All of a sudden my brain is doing frantic sums. I haven't even *thought* about . . . But the last time I . . . it must have been . . . It's been at least . . .

Oh my God.
"Becky?" says Luke in a strange voice.
"Um . . . Luke . . ."
I take a deep breath, trying to keep cool.
OK. Don't panic. Do *not* panic. . . .

WEST CUMBRIA BANK
45 Sterndale Street
Coggenthwaite
Cumbria

Ms Jessica Bertram
12 Hill Rise
Scully
Cumbria CA19 1BD

12 June 2003

Dear Ms Bertram,

I was surprised to see today that a sum of one
thousand pounds has been taken from your account.

This is most unusual activity for your account and for
this reason I am contacting you to ensure that a
mistake has not been made.

Yours sincerely,

Howard Shawcross
Customer Account Manager

WEST CUMBRIA BANK
45 Sterndale Street
Coggenthwaite
Cumbria

Ms Jessica Bertram
12 Hill Rise
Scully
Cumbria CA19 1 BD

22 June 2003

Dear Ms Bertram,

I was shocked and grieved by the tone of your last letter.

I do "have a life" as you put it.

Yours sincerely,

Howard Shawcross
Customer Account Manager

Rebecca Brandon
37 Maida Vale Mansions
Maida Vale
London NW6 0YF

Manager
Harvey Nichols
109–125 Knightsbridge
London SW1X 7RJ

25 June 2003

Dear Sir,

I am doing a piece of hypothetical research. I was
wondering whether it is true that if you give birth
in Harvey Nichols (accidentally, of course!) you are
entitled to free clothes for life.

I would be very grateful if you could let me know.

Obviously, as I have mentioned, this is a completely
hypothetical inquiry.

Yours sincerely,

Rebecca Brandon (née Bloomwood)

Acknowledgments

Hugest gratitude to the endlessly wise and supportive Susan Kamil, to Irwyn Applebaum, Nita Taublib, Barb Burg, Sharon Propson, Susan Corcoran, Cathy Paine, and Margo Lipschultz.

Thanks as ever to the fabulous Araminta Whitley, Celia Hayley, Kim Witherspoon, and David Forrer. A special thank-you to Joy Terekiev and Chiara Scaglioni for a wonderful welcome in Milan and some essential Italian!

Thanks to the members of the Board. To Henry, for everything. To Freddy and Hugo for suggesting I write about pirates instead (maybe next time).

And a big thank-you to my parents for taking me in off the streets so I could finish writing this. . . .

Sophie Kinsella's world . . .

an international bestselling phenomenon

SHOPAHOLIC TIES THE KNOT

The lovable shopaholic returns in a deliciously funny
tale of one blushing bride and . . . *two* weddings??

**With the same charm and humor that made
her Shopaholic novels beloved bestsellers,
Sophie Kinsella delivers two more
unforgettable novels
with two irresistible new heroines . . .**

CAN YOU KEEP A SECRET?

Meet Emma Corrigan, a young marketing
assistant with a huge heart, an irrepressible
spirit, and just a few little secrets . . .

THE UNDOMESTIC GODDESS

Meet Samantha Sweeting, a workaholic attorney
who finds herself in real hot water—doing the
job of a housekeeper on a country estate!

Available in Dial Press Trade Paperback Editions

SHOPAHOLIC & BABY

Wow. Venetia Carter looks like a movie star! She's far younger than I expected, and slighter. She's wearing a fitted Armani trouser suit and a crisp white shirt and her hair is drawn off her face with a chic tortoiseshell band.

"I'm so glad to meet you, Becky." Her voice is all silvery and melodious, like the Good Witch of the North. "Sit down, and we can have a nice talk."

She's wearing vintage Chanel pumps, I notice as I sit down. And look at that gorgeous yellow topaz strung round her neck on a silver wire.

"I want to thank you for fitting me in at such a late stage," I say in a rush as I hand over my medical file. "I really appreciate it. And I love your shoes!"

"Thank you!" She smiles. "So let's have a look. You're twenty-three weeks pregnant . . . first baby . . ." Her manicured finger is running down Dr. Braine's notes. "Any problems with your pregnancy? Is there a reason you've left your previous medical care?"

"I just wanted a more holistic approach," I say, leaning forward earnestly. "I've been reading your brochure and I think all your treatments sound amazing."

"Treatments?" Her pale brow wrinkles.

"Births, I mean," I amend quickly.

"Well now." Venetia Carter takes a cream file from a drawer, picks up a silver fountain pen and writes "Rebecca Brandon" on the front in a flowing italic script. "There's plenty of time to decide which approach to the birth you want. But first, let me find out more about you. You're married, I understand?"

"Yes." I nod.

"And is your husband coming today? Mr. Brandon, would it be?"

"He should be here." I click my tongue apologetically. "He's just having a quick business meeting outside in the car. But he'll be here soon."

"That's fine." She lifts her head and smiles, her teeth all perfect and shiny white. "I'm sure your husband's very excited about having a baby."

"Oh, he is!" I'm just about to tell her all about having our first scan, when the door opens.

"Mr. Brandon is here," says the receptionist, and Luke strides in, saying "Sorry, sorry, I know I'm late . . ."

"*There* you are, Luke!" I say. "Come and meet Dr. Carter."

"Please!" She laughs again. "Call me Venetia, everyone does—"

"Venetia?" Luke has stopped dead and is staring at Venetia Carter as though he can't believe his eyes. "*Venetia?* Is that you?"

Venetia Carter's mouth drops open.

"Luke?" she says. "Luke Brandon?"

"Do you two *know* each other?" I say in astonishment.

For an instant, neither speaks.

"We were at Cambridge," Luke says at last. "Years ago. But . . ." He rubs his forehead. "Venetia *Carter*. Did you get married or something?"

"I changed my surname by deed poll," Venetia says with a rueful smile. "Wouldn't you?"

"What was your name before you changed it?" I ask politely, but neither of them seems to hear me.

"How many years is it?" Luke still looks thunderstruck.

"Too long. *Far* too long." She runs a hand through her hair and it falls in a perfect red waterfall back into place. "Do you still see any of the old Browns gang? Like Jonathan? Or Matthew?"

"Lost touch." Luke shrugs. "You?"

"I kept up with few of them while I was in the States. Now I'm back in London a few of us meet up whenever we can—" She's interrupted by a bleeping sound from her pocket. She reaches for a pager and switches it off. "Excuse me, I just need to make a call. I'll pop next door."

As she disappears I look at Luke. His face is all lit up as though it's Christmas Day.

"You know Venetia?" I say. "That's amazing!"

"Isn't it?" He shakes his head incredulously. "She was part of a crowd I used to know at Cambridge. Of course, she was Venetia Grime, back then."

"Grime?" I can't help a giggle.

"Hardly the best name for a doctor." He grins back. "I'm not surprised she changed it."

"And did you know her well?"

"We were at the same college." Luke nods. "She was always incredibly bright, Venetia. Incredibly talented. I always knew she'd do well in life—" He breaks off as the door opens and Venetia returns.

"I'm so sorry about that!" She comes round and sits on the front of her desk, one long Armani-clad leg crossed casually over the other. "Where were we?"

"I was just saying to Luke what a coincidence it was!" I say. "You and him already knowing each other."

"Isn't it extraordinary?" She gives her silvery laugh. "Out of all the hundreds of patients I've had, I've never before had one married to an ex-boyfriend!"

My smile freezes slightly on my face.

Ex-boyfriend?

CONFESSIONS OF A SHOPAHOLIC

I swallow, take a couple of steps forward, then push open the door of the tiny shop. The door pings, and the nice blond girl who works there looks up. I don't know her name but I've always liked her. Unlike some snotty cows in clothes shops, she doesn't mind if you stand for ages staring at clothes you really can't afford to buy. Usually what happens is, I spend half an hour lusting after scarves in Denny and George, then go off to Accessorize and buy something to cheer myself up. I've got a whole drawerful of Denny and George substitutes.

"Hi," I say, trying to stay calm. "You're . . . you're having a sale."

"Yes." The blond girl smiles. "Bit unusual for us."

My eyes sweep the room. I can see rows of scarves, neatly folded, with dark green "50 percent off" signs above them. Printed velvet, beaded silk, embroidered cashmere, all with the distinctive "Denny and George" signature. They're everywhere. I don't know where to start. I think I'm having a panic attack.

"You always liked this one, I think," says the nice blond girl, taking out a shimmering gray-blue scarf from the pile in front of her.

Oh God, yes. I remember this one. It's made of silky velvet, overprinted in a paler blue and dotted with iridescent beads. As I stare at it, I can feel little invisible strings, silently tugging me toward it. I have to touch it. I have to wear it. It's the most beautiful thing I've ever seen. The girl looks at the label. "Reduced from £340 to £120." She comes and drapes the scarf around my neck and I gape at my reflection.

There is no question. I have to have this scarf. I *have* to have it. It makes my eyes look bigger, it makes my haircut look more expensive, it makes me look like a different person. I'll be able to wear it with everything. People will refer to me as the Girl in the Denny and George Scarf.

"I'd snap it up if I were you." The girl smiles at me. "There's only one of these left."

Involuntarily, I clutch at it.

"I'll have it," I gasp. "I'll have it."

As she's laying it out on tissue paper, I take out my purse, open it up, and reach for my VISA card in one seamless, automatic action—but my fingers hit bare leather. I stop in surprise and start to rummage through all the pockets of my purse, wondering if I stuffed my card back in somewhere with a receipt or if it's hidden underneath a business card . . . And then, with a sickening thud, I remember. It's on my desk.

How could I have been so stupid? How could I have left my VISA card on my desk? What was I *thinking*?

The nice blond girl is putting the wrapped scarf into a dark green Denny and George box. My mouth is dry with panic. What am I going to do?

"How would you like to pay?" she says pleasantly.

My face flames red and I swallow hard.

"I've just realized I've left my credit card at the office," I stutter.

"Oh," says the girl, and her hands pause.

"Can you hold it for me?" The girl looks dubious.

"For how long?"

"Until tomorrow?" I say desperately. Oh God. She's pulling a face. Doesn't she understand?

"I'm afraid not," she says. "We're not supposed to reserve sale stock."

"Just until later this afternoon, then," I say quickly. "What time do you close?"

"Six."

Six! I feel a combination of relief and adrenaline sweeping through me. Challenge, Rebecca. I'll go to the press conference, leave as soon as I can, then take a taxi back to the office. I'll grab my VISA card, tell Philip I left my notebook behind, come here, and buy the scarf.

"Can you hold it until then?" I say beseechingly. "Please? *Please?*" The girl relents.

"OK. I'll put it behind the counter."

"Thanks," I gasp. I hurry out of the shop and down the road toward Brandon Communications. Please let the press conference be short, I pray. Please don't let the questions go on too long. Please God, *please* let me have that scarf.

SHOPAHOLIC TAKES MANHATTAN

The tour guide leads the way out of the hotel, onto Fifty-seventh Street. It's a wide and busy street, with canopied entrances and trees planted at intervals and limousines pulling up in front of expensive-looking shops. As everyone else follows Christoph briskly along the pavement, I find myself walking slowly, staring upward. It's an amazingly clear, fresh day—with almost blinding sunlight bouncing off the pavements and buildings—and as I look around I'm completely filled with awe. God, this city is an incredible place. I mean, obviously I knew that New York would be full of tall skyscrapers. But it's only when you're actually standing in the street, staring up at them, that you realize how . . . well, how *huge* they are. I gaze up at the tops of the buildings against the sky, until my neck is aching and I'm starting to feel dizzy. Then slowly my eyes wander down, floor by floor to shop-window level. And I find myself staring at two words. *Prada* and *Shoes*.

Ooh.

Prada Shoes. Right in front of me.

I'll just have a really quick look.

As the others all march on, I hurry up to the window and stare at a pair of deep brown pumps with cream stitching. God, those are divine. I wonder how much they are? You know, Prada is probably really cheap over here. Maybe I should just pop in and—

"Rebecca?"

With a start I come to and look round to see the tour group twenty yards down the street, all staring at me.

"Sorry," I say, and reluctantly pull myself away from the window. "I'm coming."

"There'll be time for shopping later," says Christoph cheerfully.

"I know," I say, and give a relaxed laugh. "Sorry about that."

"Don't worry about it!"

Of course, he's quite right. There'll be plenty of time to go shopping. Plenty of time.

Right. I'm really going to concentrate on the tour.

"So, Rebecca," says Christoph brightly, as I rejoin the group. "I was just telling the others that we're heading down East Fifty-seventh Street to Fifth Avenue, the most famous avenue of New York City."

"Great!" I say. "That sounds really good!"

"Fifth Avenue serves as a dividing line between the 'East Side' and the 'West Side,'" continues Christoph. "Anyone interested in history will like to know that . . ."

I'm nodding intelligently as he speaks, and trying to look interested. But as we walk down the street, my head keeps swiveling from left to right, like someone watching a tennis game. Christian Dior, Hermès, Chanel . . . This street is just incredible. If only we could just slow down a bit, and have a proper look—but Christoph is marching on ahead like a hike leader, and everybody else in the group is following him happily, not even glancing at the amazing sights around them. Do they not have eyes in their heads?

". . . where we're going to take in two well-known landmarks: Rockefeller Center, which many of you will associate with ice-skating . . ."

We swing round a corner—and my heart gives a swoop of excitement. Tiffany's. It's Tiffany's, right in front of me! I *must* just have a quick peek. I mean, this is what New York is all about. Little blue boxes, and white ribbon, and those gorgeous silver beans . . . I sidle up to the window and stare longingly at the beautiful display inside. Wow. That necklace is absolutely stunning. Oh God, and look at that watch, with all those little diamonds round the edge. I wonder how much something like that would—

"Hey, everybody, wait up!" rings out Christoph's voice. I look up—and they're all bloody miles ahead again. How come they walk so fast, anyway? "Are you OK there, Rebecca?" he calls, with a slightly forced cheeriness. "You're going to have to try to keep up! We have a lot of ground to cover!"

"Sorry," I say, and scuttle toward the group. "Just having a quick little look at Tiffany's." I grin at a woman next to me, expecting her to smile back. But she looks at me blankly and pulls the hood of her baggy gray sweatshirt more tightly over her head.

"As I was saying," Christoph says as we stride off again, "above Fourteenth Street, Manhattan was designed as a grid, so that . . ."

And for a while I really try to concentrate. But it's no good. I can't listen. I mean, come on. This is Fifth Avenue!

SHOPAHOLIC TIES THE KNOT

As I make my way home, I can suddenly see everything clearly. My whole approach to the wedding has changed. I feel full of a fresh, clean determination. This is *my* wedding. It's *my* day. And if I want to get married in New York, then that's where I'll get married. If I want to wear a Vera Wang dress, then that's what I'll wear. It's ridiculous to feel guilty about it.

I've been putting off talking to Mum for far too long. I mean, what am I expecting her to do, burst into tears? We're both adults. We'll have a sensible, mature conversation and I'll put forward my point of view calmly, and the whole thing will be sorted out, once and for all. God, I feel liberated. I'm going to call her straight away.

I march into the bedroom, dump my bag on the bed, and dial the number.

"Hi, Dad," I say as he answers. "Is Mum there? There's something I need to talk to her about. It's rather important."

As I glance at my face in the mirror, I feel like a newsreader on NBC, all crisp and cool and in charge.

"Becky?" says Dad puzzledly. "Are you all right?"

"I'm very well," I say. "I just have to discuss a . . . a couple of issues with Mum."

As Dad disappears off the line I take a deep breath and push my hair back, feeling suddenly very grown-up. Here I am, about to have an adult-to-adult, straight-down-the-line conversation with my mother, for probably the first time in my life.

You know, maybe this is the beginning of a whole new relationship with my parents. A new mutual respect. A shared understanding of life.

"Hello, darling?"

"Hi, Mum." I take a deep breath. Here goes. Calm and mature. "Mum—"

"Oh, Becky, I was going to give you a ring. You'll never guess who we saw up in the Lake District!"

"Who?"

"Auntie Zannie! You used to dress up in all her old necklaces, do you remember? And her shoes. We were laughing about it, the sight you made, tottering around . . ."

"Mum. There's something important I need to discuss with you."

"And they've still got the same grocer in the village. The one who used to sell you strawberry ice-cream cones. Do you remember the time you ate too many and weren't very well? We laughed about that too!"

"Mum—"

"And the Tivertons still live in the same house . . . but . . ."

"What?"

"I'm afraid, love . . . Carrot the donkey has . . ." Mum lowers her voice. "Gone to donkey heaven. But he was very old, darling, and he'll be very happy up there . . ."

This is impossible. I don't feel like a grown-up. I feel about six years old.

"They all send you their love," Mum says, eventually coming to the end of her reminiscences, "and of course they'll all be at the wedding! So, Dad said you wanted to talk about something?"

"I . . ." I clear my throat, suddenly aware of the echoey silence on the line; of the distance between us. "Well, I wanted to . . . um . . ."

Oh God. My mouth is trembling and my newsreader voice has turned into a nervous squeak.

"What is it, Becky?" Mum's voice rises in concern. "Is something wrong?"

"No! It's just that . . . that . . ."

It's no good.

I know what Christina said is right. I know there's no need to feel guilty. It's my wedding, and I'm a grown-up, and I should have it wherever I like. I'm not asking Mum and Dad to pay. I'm not asking them to make any effort.

But even so.

I can't tell Mum I want to get married in the Plaza over the phone. I just can't do it.

"I thought I'd come home and see you," I hear myself saying in a rush. "That's all I wanted to say. I'm coming home."

CAN YOU KEEP A SECRET?

Of course I have secrets.

Of course I do. Everyone has a few secrets. It's completely normal.

I'm not talking about big, earth-shattering secrets. Not the-president-is-planning-to-bomb-Japan-and-only-Will-Smith-can-save-the-world type secrets. Just normal, everyday little secrets.

Like, for example, here are a few random secrets of mine, off the top of my head:

1. My Kate Spade bag is a fake.
2. I love sweet sherry, the least cool drink in the universe.

3. I have no idea what NATO stands for. Or even exactly what it is.
4. I weigh 128 pounds. Not 118, like my boyfriend, Connor, thinks. (Although, in my defense, I was planning to go on a diet when I told him that. And to be fair, it is only one number different.)
5. I've always thought Connor looks a bit like Ken. As in Barbie and Ken.
6. Sometimes, when we're right in the middle of passionate sex, I suddenly want to laugh.
7. I lost my virginity in the spare bedroom with Danny Nussbaum while Mum and Dad were downstairs watching *Ben-Hur*.
8. I've already drunk the wine that Dad told me to save for twenty years.
9. Sammy the goldfish at home isn't the same goldfish that Mum and Dad gave me to look after when they went to Egypt.
10. When my colleague Artemis really annoys me, I feed her plant orange juice. (Which is pretty much every day.)
11. I once had this weird lesbian dream about my flatmate Lissy.
12. My G-string is hurting me.
13. I've always had this deep-down conviction that I'm not like everybody else, and there's an amazingly exciting new life waiting for me just around the corner.
14. I have no idea what this guy in the gray suit is going on about.
15. Plus, I've already forgotten his name.

And I only met him ten minutes ago.

"We believe in multi-logistical formative alliances," he's saying in a nasal, droning voice, "both above and below the line."

"Absolutely!" I reply brightly, as though to say "Doesn't everybody?"

Multi-logistical. What does that mean, again?

Oh, God. What if they ask me?

Don't be stupid, Emma. They won't suddenly demand, What does "multi-logistical" mean? I'm a fellow marketing professional, aren't I? Obviously I know these things.

And anyway, if they mention it again, I'll change the subject. Or I'll say I'm post-logistical or something.

The important thing is to keep confident and businesslike. I can do this. This is my big chance, and I'm not going to screw it up.

I'm sitting in the offices of Glen Oil's headquarters in Glasgow, and as I glance at my reflection in the window, I look just like a top businesswoman. My shoulder-length hair is straightened, after half an hour with the hair dryer and a bottle of serum this morning. I'm wearing discreet gold swirl earrings like they tell you to in how-to-win-that-job articles. And I've got on my smart new Jigsaw suit. (At least, it's practically new. I got it from the Cancer Research shop and sewed on a button to replace the missing one, and you can hardly tell.)

I'm here representing the Panther Corporation, which is where I work. The meeting is to finalize a promotional arrangement between the new cranberry-flavored Panther Prime sports drink and Glen Oil, and I flew up this morning from London, especially.

When I arrived, the two Glen Oil marketing guys started on this long, show-offy "who's traveled the most?" conversation about air miles and the red-eye to Washington—and I think I bluffed pretty convincingly. But the truth is, this is the first time I've ever had to travel for work.

OK. The real truth is this is the first business meeting I've attended on my own. And my secret hope is that if I do well today, I'll get promoted. Career advancement! At the thought, I feel a familiar stab of longing. It would just show Dad I'm not a complete loser. And Mum. And Kerry. If I could just go home and say, "By the way, I've been promoted to marketing executive."

Emma Corrigan, marketing executive.

Emma Corrigan, senior vice-president (marketing.)

THE UNDOMESTIC GODDESS

SOPHIE
KINSELLA
The
Undomestic
Goddess

It takes me two trips to bring down all the washing to the laundry room, just off the kitchen. I dump the overflowing baskets on the tiled floor and look at the hi-tech washing machine. This should be simple enough. Experimentally, I open the door of the machine and at once an electronic display starts flashing at me. *WASH? WASH?*

Immediately I feel flustered. *Obviously* I want you to wash, I feel like snapping back. Just give me a chance to get the bloody clothes in.

Stay calm. One thing at a time. First step: sort the clothes. Feeling pleased with myself for having thought of this, I start sorting out the dirty clothes into piles on the floor, consulting the labels as I go. As I'm peering at one marked *Wash with GREAT CARE,* I hear Trish, my boss, coming into the kitchen, clearly on the phone.

"You're right," she's saying, her voice trembling. "You're right! But *he* doesn't see it like that! And let me tell you, I've tried!"

I freeze in embarrassment. Does Trish know I'm in here? Should I cough?

"I don't *want* to play golf! Is there nothing *else* we can do together?" I glance out of the laundry door into the kitchen and to my horror see Trish at the table, dabbing at her eyes with a pink tissue. "It's all right for him! He has no idea what it's like for me!"

Hastily I duck back into the laundry and start busily shoving clothes into the drum at random. If Trish comes in, she'll see me dutifully at work, impervious to her conversation. I shake some washing powder into the little tray at the top and close the door firmly. Now what?

WASH? the machine is still flashing at me. *WASH?*

"Er . . . yes!" I mutter. "Wash them." I jab randomly at a button.

ENTER PROGRAM? it flashes back.

My eyes dart about for clues, and I spot a manual tucked behind a spray bottle. I grab it and start leafing through.

The half-load option for small washes is only available for pre-wash programs A3-E2 and superrinse programs G2-L7 not including H4.

. . . What?

OK, let's forget the manual. Let's just use common sense. I briskly press at the keypad in my best housekeeper manner.

PROGRAM K3? the machine flashes at me. *PROGRAM K3?*

I don't like the sound of program K3. It sounds sinister. Like a cliff face or secret government plot.

"No," I say aloud, jabbing at the machine. "I want something else."

YOU HAVE CHOSEN K3, it flashes back. *HEAVY-DUTY UP-HOLSTERY PROGRAM.*

Heavy duty? *Upholstery?*

"Stop it," I say under my breath, and start banging all the buttons. "Stop!" I kick the machine in desperation. "*Stop!*"

"Everything all right, Samantha?" Trish appears at the laundry door. All signs of tears are gone and she's applied fresh lipstick. I wonder what she was so upset about. But it's hardly my place to ask.

"Er . . . fine! Just . . . getting some washing on."

"Well done." She holds out a stripy shirt to me. "Now, Mr. Geiger needs a button sewn on this shirt, if you would be so kind."

"Absolutely!" I take it from her, praying my trepidation doesn't show on my face.

"And here's your list of duties!" She hands me a sheet of paper. "It's by no means complete, but it should get you *started.*"

As I run my eyes down the endless list, I feel a bit faint.

Make beds . . . sweep and clean front steps . . . arrange flowers . . . polish all mirrors . . . store cupboards tidy . . . laundry . . . clean bathrooms daily . . .

"Now, there's nothing here that should present you with a *problem,* is there?" adds Trish.

"Er . . . no!" My voice is a little strangled. "No, it should all be fine!"

"But make a stab at the ironing *first*," she continues firmly. "There is quite a lot, I'm afraid, as you'll have seen. It does tend to mount *up* rather . . ." For some reason, Trish is looking upward. With a slight foreboding, I follow her gaze. There, above us, is a mountain of crumpled shirts hanging on a wooden drying rack. At least thirty.

As I stare up at them, I feel wobbly. I can't iron a shirt. I've never used an iron in my life. What am I going to do?

"I expect you'll whip through these in no time!" she says gaily. "The ironing board's just there," she adds with a nod.

"Um, thanks!" I manage.

I reach for the ironing board, trying to look matter-of-fact, as if I do this all the time. I tug briskly at one of the metal legs, but it won't move. I try another one with no luck. I'm pulling harder and harder, till I'm hot with the effort, but the bloody thing won't budge. How am I supposed to open it up?

"It's got a catch," Trish says, watching me in surprise. "Underneath." She takes the board from me, and in two movements has opened it up to exactly the right height. "I expect you're used to a different model," she adds wisely as she clicks it shut. "They all have their own little tricks."

"Absolutely!" I say, seizing on this excuse in relief. "Of course! I'm far more used to working with a . . . a . . . a Nimbus 2000."

Trish peers at me in surprise. "Isn't that the broomstick out of *Harry Potter*?"